The
Little
Paris
Patisserie

Julie Caplin is addicted to travel and good food. She's on a constant hunt for the perfect gin and is obsessively picky about glasses, tonic and garnishes. Between regular gin tastings, she'd been writing her debut novel which is set in just one of the many cities she's explored over the years.

Formerly a PR director, for many years she swanned around Europe taking top food and drink writers on press trips (junkets) sampling the gastronomic delights of various cities in Italy, France, Belgium, Spain, Copenhagen and Switzerland. It was a tough job but someone had to do it. These trips have provided the inspiration and settings for the trilogy, *The Little Café in Copenhagen*, *The Little Brooklyn Bakery* and *The Little Paris Patisserie*.

🐦 @JulieCaplin
f www.facebook.com/JulieCaplinAuthor

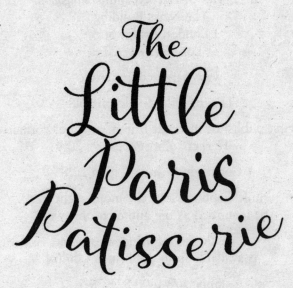

The Little Paris Patisserie

Julie Caplin

A division of HarperCollins Publishers
www.harpercollins.co.uk

Harper*Impulse*
an imprint of HarperCollins*Publishers*
The News Building
1 London Bridge Street
London SE1 9GF

www.harpercollins.co.uk

This paperback edition 2018

First published in Great Britain in ebook format
by HarperCollins*Publishers* 2018

A catalogue record for this book
is available from the British Library

ISBN: 978-0-00-825978-5

Typeset in Birka by Palimpsest Book Production Ltd,
Falkirk, Stirlingshire

Printed and bound in Great Britain by
CPI Group (UK) Ltd, Croydon CR0 4YY

For Alison, office bestie, unofficial cheerleader and all round wonderful egg.

Chapter 1

Stamping her sore and tired feet on the gravelled surface to get some warmth into them, Nina looked at her phone for the ninety-fifth time in ten minutes, almost dropping it. Where the heck was Nick? Fifteen minutes late already and her fingers were about to snap off, adding to her general sense of misery. Standing here at the back entrance to the kitchens in the staff carpark, there was little protection from the biting wind whistling around the sandstone manor house and certainly none from the bleak thoughts in her head.

'Hey Nina, are you sure you don't want a lift?' asked Marcela, one of the other waitresses, in her heavily accented voice, winding her car window down as she backed with some speed out of one of the spaces.

'No.' She shook her head. 'It's alright thanks. My brother's on his way.' At least he had better be. Nina wished she was in the little steamed up car with Marcela and the other two staff members, and almost laughed at the rather annoying irony. Mum had insisted Nick pick her up so that she'd know Nina was safe and here she was standing in a car park in the pitch black about to be completely on her own.

'OK then. See you in eight weeks' time.'

'Ha!' piped up a gloomy East European voice from the back seat – Tomas the sommelier, a perennial pessimist. 'You think the builders finish on schedule.'

A good-natured chorus shouted him down.

'See you soon, Nina.' They all waved and shouted their goodbyes, Marcela winding the window back up as the ancient Polo roared away, as if she couldn't wait to escape the end of her shift and put up her feet. Which was exactly what Nina was hoping to do, if her brother ever got here.

At last she spotted the headlights speeding down the drive towards her. This had to be Nick. Nearly everyone else had gone. With a speedy gravel-crunching turn, the car pulled to a halt in front of Nina.

She yanked the door open.

'Hi Sis. You been waiting long? Sorry, sheep emergency.'

'Yes,' snapped Nina, scrambling in grateful for the heat of the car. 'It's bloody freezing out there. I'll be so glad when my car's fixed.'

'Tell me about it. It took me all the way here to thaw out. Bloody sheep. There was a ewe stuck in the wire fencing up on the moor road. I had to stop and help the stupid creature.'

Was it really churlish to think that at least the sheep had a nice woolly coat while she was in a skirt and tights on a cold February evening?

'So how was it? The last night,' asked Nick, leaning down and turning the radio off, which had been blaring football commentary at full blast. 'And did your mate get a good send off?'

'Fine. Bit sad as we all won't see each other for a while due to the renovations. And Sukie will be in New York.'

'New York. That's a bit of a change.'

'She's a brilliant chef. Going places.'

'Clearly. To New York. And what's everyone else doing?'

'The regular staff are being redeployed and having lots of training.'

'Seems a bit unfair. Why not you?'

'Because I'm on a casual contract, I guess.'

'Well, I'm sure we can find you a few extra hours at the farm shop as well as in the café. And Dan can give you a bit of work at the brewery. Gail's sister might pay you for some babysitting and George can ask in the petrol station, they're always needing extra staff. Although that's late hours, so possibly not.'

Nina closed her eyes. She was absolutely certain that everyone in the family would pitch in to find something for 'poor Nina' to do while Bodenbroke Manor Restaurant was closed for refurbishment, whether she liked it or not. It wasn't that she was ungrateful, they all meant well, but she was a grown up, she was quite capable of finding work without the vast tentacles of her family network spreading their reach on her behalf. She loved her family to bits, she really did but...

'What's with the huffing and puffing?' asked Nick, turning his head to look her way.

'Nothing,' said Nina, closing her eyes. 'Holy moly, I'm tired. My feet feel like they've been stomped on by a dozen elephants.'

'Wuss,' teased Nick.

'I've been on the go since nine o'clock this morning,' said

Nina. 'And the restaurant was rammed. I didn't even get lunch.'

'That's not on. You should say something.'

'It's not that easy. Everyone's busy. There wasn't time for a proper break.'

'Don't tell me you haven't eaten anything today?'

Nina shrugged. She'd rushed out without breakfast, much to her mother's consternation. 'A little.' Her stomach rumbled rather inconveniently at the very moment as if to dispute her answer. Clearly it didn't think that a bread roll and a slice of cheese constituted enough.

Nick frowned heavily. 'Even so. Do you want me to say something to the manager, when they re-open?'

'No, it's fine. We'll be having dinner when we get home.'

'Well, it isn't—'

'You don't work there, you don't understand.' Nina's voice rose in heat. Typical Nick, assuming that he knew best.

'I don't need to understand. There are labour laws. You're entitled to breaks. It's—'

Whatever he was about to say was interrupted by the timely horn fanfare ringtone of his phone booming out through the radio on his handsfree set up.

'Nick Hadley,' he said pressing the 'accept call' button on the dashboard.

Nina slumped back in her chair, relieved at the interruption; it gave her the perfect opportunity to close her eyes, tune out and pretend to doze for the rest of the way home.

'Hey Shep, how're the socks?' Nina tensed, every sinew locking into place at the sound of a familiar mocking voice.

Her brother was often referred to as Shep, short for shepherd, by his friends who seemed obsessed with their childhood version of the carol, 'While shepherds washed their socks by night'.

'All good. How are you, Knifeman? Still supporting that shite excuse for a rugby team?' And apparently Knifeman was the not-so clever nickname for a chef. An arrogant, supercilious, one at that.

'No words, mate. They were a bloody useless against France. And I paid good money for tickets.'

'What, you went to Stade de France? You jammy git.'

'Not so jammy when the buggers lost.'

'Fancy coming over for the Calcutta Cup? You don't want to be too long in France. You might pick up some bad habits.'

'Slight problem there.'

'What?' asked Nick.

'I'm laid up. That's why I'm ringing you.'

Nina pressed her lips together in what some might call a snarky smile. Sebastian clearly had no idea she was there, and she didn't want him to either. Listening to this ridiculous conversation, no one would ever know they were grown men rather than a pair of adolescents, which would be the obvious inference. She definitely did not want to remember Sebastian as a teenager or how she'd made a complete dick of herself over him. Unfortunately having a teenage crush on your brother's best friend was possibly the worst thing you could do because ten years on, even now, someone in the family would still occasionally bring it up.

'What's happened?'

'I've only gone and broken my leg.'

'Shit, man, when?'

'A couple of days ago. Taken out by one of those bloody cabin bag pull-along fuckers. Twisted as I fell.'

'Ouch. You OK?'

'No,' Sebastian growled. 'Everything's gone tits up. Turns out one of the new places I bought in Paris has a metaphorical sitting tenant. The previous owner ran pastry courses and forgot to tell me that there's a seven-week course coming up that's all booked and paid for.'

'Can't you cancel?' asked Nick, flicking the indicator and turning the car off the main road towards the village.

'Unfortunately, I committed to it. I thought I might as well because I can get my French contractors to start work on the other two places first and they'll take a couple of months, so I might as well keep this going. Which would have been fine if I hadn't broken my sodding leg.'

In the darkness, Nina pressed her lips together. She wouldn't normally wish misfortune on anyone but somehow Sebastian just irked her. It wasn't his success she begrudged, Lord knew he'd worked hard enough to become a top chef with a small restaurant chain of his own. Too hard, if you asked her. No, it was his superior, dismissive attitude. Over the last ten years, whenever she'd seen him, she'd always managed to appear at a disadvantage. And the last time had been truly mortifying.

'Can't you get someone else to do it?'

'I'm not sure I'm going to find anyone at such short notice. The course starts next week. Besides, all I need is a spare pair of legs for the next few weeks. Until I get this cast off.'

'Nina could help. She's just been laid off at the restaurant she works at.'

Nina shot up in her seat, narrowing her eyes at her impossibly stupid brother. Had he had a brain fart or something? Seeing the movement in the car, Nick turned and she saw the flash of his teeth in the dark as he gave her a great big grin.

'With respect Nick, your sister is the last person in the world I'd want helping me.'

Nick's grin faded. There was a lengthening silence in the car.

Then Sebastian muttered, 'Oh shit, she's there, isn't she?'

With an icy smile, Nina drew herself up. 'Oh shit, indeed. But don't worry, with respect Sebastian, castrating the lambs on the farm with my own teeth would be preferable to helping *you* out.'

With that, she leaned forward and disconnected the call.

Chapter 2

The family kitchen was a hive of activity and her mother was bustling about with hands in floral oven gloves, the big kitchen table laid for eight and several pans steaming and bubbling on the big range oven.

'Nina, Nick. Just in time.'

'Something smells good,' said Nick chucking his car keys on the dresser to join the assorted detritus that seemed to collect there on a daily basis, no matter how often their mother tidied up. Despite all four of her grown up sons having left home in varying degrees they continued to treat the kitchen as their own, which Nina's mother just adored. None of her offspring had strayed very far. Nick, older than her by two years, lived in the farm cottage across the courtyard and helped Dad with the farm and the sheep. Still single, he seemed in no hurry to find a wife and was taking his time checking out potential candidates.

'Sit down. You must be starving. Where are Dan and Gail? They'd said they'd be here five minutes ago.'

'Mum, it's Dan. It's guaranteed he'll be late for his own funeral,' said Nick, giving her a quick peck on the cheek as he unwound his scarf.

'Don't talk about things like that,' she shuddered. 'They were very busy in the brewery and the farm shop today. Had a coachload in from North Wales. Poor Cath.' Nina's mother, Lynda, shot a sympathetic look at Nina's sister-in-law sitting down at the table slumped over an empty cup of coffee. Cath, who was married to her second oldest brother Jonathon, one of twins, lifted her blonde head and gave Nina a pathetic little wave.

'It was mental. We ran out of scones and coffee and walnut cake. Honestly those OAPs are like locusts. You'd think they hadn't had a square meal for days. The cupboards are bare.'

Her mother gave Nina a worried half-smile.

Nina groaned as she slipped off her coat. 'Don't worry, as soon as I've had dinner I can knock up a batch of scones and make a quick cake. I can do the buttercream in the morning.'

'Oh darling, you've just got in from work. You must be shattered. I'm sure Cath can manage for a day.'

Nina caught Cath's quick eye-roll. 'Mum, it won't take long.'

'If you're sure, dear.'

Thankfully, her eldest, by five minutes, brother Dan came barrelling into the kitchen pulling his wife Gail along by her hand, the door swinging wildly on its hinges as the two of them came in giggling.

'Hi guys, the favourite child is here,' boomed Dan. His wife gave him a quick poke in the ribs.

Suddenly the noise in the kitchen increased tenfold as Jonathon and her father appeared from the hallway. Chairs scraped on the flagstone floor, beer bottles chinked as a handful were retrieved from the fridge, the crown caps dispatched quickly with a firm flip to rattle on the side, while Dad set to work with a corkscrew and there was the satisfying pop of a bottle of red wine being uncorked. Seamlessly, everyone took their seats, a variety of conversations erupting around the table. Nina slipped into her place, next to her mum at the head of the table.

'Are you sure you're alright to make the cakes? I could get up early and make a batch of scones to tide Cath over.'

'Mum, its fine honestly.' She'd caught the quick look exchanged by her sisters-in-law and then Gail had winked at her. 'Once I've had dinner, I'll get my second wind.' It was only a couple of cakes for goodness' sake – and it would give her an excellent excuse to escape the usual bedlam here and have some peace and quiet in her own little flat over the old stable block, without anyone worrying about her being on her own.

Her mum firmed her lips and turned her attention to the casserole dishes on the table.

'Jonathon, you're dripping that spoon everywhere.'

'Oh Jonathon!' chorused Dan, immediately taking the opportunity to tease his twin. The rest of the male contingent joined in.

'Dan, don't you want more than that?'

'See, favourite child.' Jonathon pointed his spoon at his brother, quickly remonstrated by his wife.

As always, it was like feeding time at the zoo but Nina was relieved that the attention had moved away from her. She managed to stay under the radar until the very last scrapings of the large casserole dish on the table while Dan and

Jonathon bickered over who was going to get the last piece of lamb.

'So what's happening with this car of yours, lovie?' her dad asked.

'It's still in the garage. They couldn't get the part but they're hoping it will be in tomorrow.'

'It's going to take more than a part to fix that thing.' Her mum shuddered. 'It's a death trap.'

Nina muttered under her breath, but no one heard her because they'd already pitched in with their own views on her car. There was absolutely nothing wrong with her little Fiat.

'Mum, you don't need to worry about Nina in that thing, she can't pedal fast enough to get into any trouble,' teased Nick.

'A sewing machine's got more power,' chipped in Dan.

'I do wish you'd get something a bit more sturdy. I worry about you getting squished by a bigger car.'

'Ma, you don't need to worry, Nick's truck would go straight over the top of it.' Dan, having won the battle over the lamb, dropped his knife and fork with a clatter on the plate.

Mum shuddered again. 'That's even worse.'

'I love my car, leave it alone,' said Nina. She missed it desperately at the moment because she was so reliant on lifts from everyone else.

'Tom in the pub's wife is selling her car. I could take a look at it for you, if you wanted,' said Dad. 'It's a Ford. They're good reliable cars. Don't cost much to run.'

And as boring as hell, thought Nina.

'Oh, that's a good idea, darling,' her mum added.

Nina was about to say something calm and sensible like,

'As I'm about to pay for the repairs, it's probably not the best time to think about buying another car', but she'd had about enough of them all thinking they knew what was best for her. Honestly, they still thought of her as the baby of the family. So instead, she jumped up, glared around the table and yelled, 'I like my car as it is, thank you very much!' before grabbing her coat and storming off out through the back door to her flat.

As she slammed the door behind her it was rather satisfying to hear the shocked silence reverberating around the table.

When the soft knock came at her door, as four sponges were cooling on the rack, she knew it would be Nick. Despite the fact he nagged her the least, he was the most protective of all her brothers. Part of her wanted to ignore him and pretend to be in bed but she knew that her uncharacteristic outburst would have already caused a stir, and if she didn't answer the door, he would keep knocking.

'Yes?' She opened the door a couple of inches making it clear she didn't want company.

'Just checking you're alright.' His cheery grin held a touch of strain.

Feeling guilty, she opened the door wider. 'I'm fine.'

'Just fine?' He took a step into the open plan studio flat, shutting the door behind him.

'Yes, just fine.' She sighed. 'Do you want a cup of tea or something?'

He raised a teasing eyebrow. 'Something? You got a hidden stash of brandy or whisky I didn't know about?'

'Oh, for goodness' sake, would it matter if I did?' She was way past being teased and didn't care if she let her impatience show. 'In case you hadn't noticed I'm a grown woman. It was a figure of speech. You'll be relieved to know that all that's lurking in my sad cupboards are a couple of boxes of PG Tips.'

'Ooh, someone put her grumpy pants on this morning – or was it a certain phone call earlier?' Nick folded his arms and leaned against the wall.

'It has absolutely nothing to do with flaming Sebastian Finlay. I'm fed up with the whole family treating me like a baby. I'm nearly thirty, for fu...' She hesitated, as he frowned. If she actually swore, he really would go into a tailspin. 'For flip's sake. Mum and Dad fuss so and then bloody Jonathon and Dan join in. Cath and Gail both think it's ridiculous how you all worry over absolutely flipping nothing. And you're the absolute worst, coming over doing the big brother act. I don't need it.' She stood her ground, glaring up at him, her hands clenched by her side. Although it was tempting to flounce across the room and throw herself onto the sofa, it would look like a childish tantrum and she needed him to know that they were all driving her crazy. Maybe she was a bit hormonal today, perhaps a bit tired, but this had been brewing for a few months.

'It's only because we care,' explained Nick.

'I get that. I really do.'

'But?'

'I ... I feel...' The problem was she didn't really know what she felt. Frustrated. Irritated. Weak. Going nowhere. Treading water. Sukie, her friend from work, the pastry chef, was off to New York. Her career was taking off. Nina didn't even have a career let alone the opportunity to take off. Unfortunately, she didn't have the experience, let alone the cooking credentials or qualifications, to apply for Sukie's job. Nick wouldn't understand and neither would the rest of the family. They were all content and happy, although she suspected sometimes Nick would have liked to leave the farm and widen his horizons a bit. Only Toby, four years Nina's senior, had moved any distance away when he'd gone to Bristol to study to be a vet, and now he'd come back he was only fifty miles away, although that was at least out of range of daily scrutiny.

'I know it's hard being the youngest and the only girl and Mum and Dad do worry because you had a pretty rough start—'

'Don't you dare say it!' Nina held up a hand.

'What? That you nearly died when you were born? But it's true.'

Nina buried her head in her hands. 'Yes, and it's history. You'd think I'd been at death's door for most of my life. Apart from appendicitis and the usual coughs, colds, chicken pox, I've never been properly ill.'

Nick didn't say anything.

'Have I?' she prompted.

'No,' he admitted with a grudging smile. 'So I'm not going to get a tea or something?'

'Oh, for heaven's sake.' Nina did flounce this time, crossing to the kitchen area to flip on the kettle. It wasn't as if she could go to bed yet, she was still waiting for the sponges to cool down before she could sandwich them together with the coffee cream and walnuts. 'Oy.' She rapped his knuckles with a teaspoon as he snaffled one of her freshly made scones and took a bite quickly.

'Mmm, these are good.'

She ignored him as she made a quick pot of tea. There was something soothing about making it properly and it was a definite delaying tactic.

She brought the pot and, bowing to Nick's bigger frame, a mug as well as one of her favourite vintage cup and saucers, over to the small round dining table to the left of the kitchen area. The open plan living area was perfect for one and she deliberately kept the number of seats around the table to a minimum. This was her bolthole and she'd made sure it was her space. She'd used pastel colours on the walls and bought pretty, delicate floral fabric to make curtains and cushions to stamp her feminine identity on the place. Being surrounded by four boys all her life had definitely influenced her décor choices. Growing up at the farmhouse, most things had been practical and robust. Colour had not been a significant feature. Jonathon and Dan's idea of interior design had been to paint their bedroom walls in alternate black and white stripes to emulate their beloved Newcastle United.

'Here you go.' She pushed the mug of tea towards her brother.

'So what's brought all this on?' asked Nick, his face softening in sympathy.

'It's been coming on for a while. I feel a bit stuck. Like I'm going nowhere and I'm never going to do anything.'

15

'What do you want to do?'

Nina toyed with the edge of her saucer. It was a stupid idea. After all, she'd been there once and messed it up.

Of all her brothers, she was closest to Nick. Perhaps because they were both in the same boat.

'Don't you sometimes want to get away from here? Be on your own.'

Nick's mouth twisted. 'Very occasionally, I wonder if I've missed out. It's not exactly easy to meet people round here. But I love farming and it's not like I can up sticks and take the farm with me. And then I stand at the top of the fell and look down the valley, follow the curve of the drystone walls that have been there for centuries and I feel like I belong. It's continuity.'

Nina looked up at him and gave him a gentle smile. He'd always been her hero, not that she'd dream of saying that to him. His head was plenty big enough already. For all his childish banter and teasing, he was a good soul who knew his place in the world.

She sighed, not wanting to sound ungrateful. 'At least you're useful. You have a proper purpose and a proper job.'

'What do you want to do?'

Pulling a face, she traced the edge of the saucer again. 'Get away for a while. Be me. Find out who me really is.'

Nick frowned looking confused.

'Just now, I didn't use the 'F' word because I knew you'd disapprove.'

Now he looked even more confused.

'I feel like I'm treading water. I want ... I want to cook properly. Not just make cakes and things.'

'You want to be a chef? But you tried that before.' He pointed to her. 'You know, the raw meat thing. The, er, having a meltdown, panic attack thing. Didn't you throw up as well?'

'Thanks for reminding me, but what I didn't realise then was that there are other specialisms that wouldn't involve handling raw meat. I could be a pastry chef. Sukie, who's off to New York is, was, absolutely amazing. She's inspired me. You should see the things she makes. I ... I...' Nina stopped. She'd been trying a few things out at home, with varying degrees of success. It had been difficult at work to spend much time observing her former colleague, when she was supposed to be waiting tables, although Sukie had always been willing to let her hang around. She needed to be trained. Go on a patisserie course.

Ever since Sebastian's call in the car, her mind had kept circling back to his announcement that he was running a pastry course. He needed legs. She had seven weeks free, well, almost. And surely Mum and Cath could find someone else to make cakes for a few weeks.

This was the most serendipitous thing that had ever, ever, ever happened to her. She'd be mad not to pursue it. Surely it was meant to be, even if Sebastian was involved. This was the perfect opportunity for her to show everyone how passionate she was about patisserie. Prove to everyone that she'd finally found her 'thing'.

'Would you talk to him for me?'

'Talk to who?' asked Nick, puzzled.

'Sebastian.'

Chapter 3

As she stepped off the train at the Gare du Nord, finding it rather wonderful and amazing that she was now in *another* country and that she'd whizzed underneath the channel, she was tempted to pinch herself. Just two hours ago she'd been at St Pancras and now she was in Paris. Gay Paris. On her own. Away from the family. It felt as if she'd shaken off a very heavy feather duvet that was in danger of suffocating her. Even as she'd climbed into the car with Dad to go to the station, Mum had slipped a handful of Euro notes into her hand and muttered, 'For a taxi when you get there. So you don't have to worry about the Metro with all your bags.'

And then her dad had done exactly the same thing when he dropped her at the station. Bless them both. She wasn't ungrateful, but really! She was perfectly capable of getting the Metro on her own.

Despite listening to a French language app throughout her Eurostar trip, Nina was slightly disappointed to realise that she still couldn't understand a single sentence of the thousand-words-per-second, rapid delivery of the man at the information desk. Unfortunately, he was determined not to speak any

English and the only word they could agree on was taxi. So much for her first independent foray! At least Mum and Dad would be pleased.

The taxi brought her into a wide boulevard, lined with trees shading small cafes and their bistro tables and chairs. On either side of the street were buildings of five or six storeys running the full length of the road, where all of the windows had those cute wrought iron balconies and there were imposing looking wooden front doors interspersed at regular intervals.

Despite the old stone walls and the heavy wooden trim, the door to the building opened with an electronic buzz and she found herself in a stark entrance hall with a narrow, tiled staircase curling upwards. Sebastian had taken up residence in a hotel as there was no lift here at his apartment block. With a sigh, Nina looked upwards at the broad staircase. How on earth was she going to lug a big suitcase as well as the heavy tote bag and her handbag up to the top floor? *This is independence. Remember — what you wanted.* Even so she glanced around, almost hopeful that someone might materialise to help. But unlike in the movies, no handsome knight appeared offering to carry her cases for her. With a dispirited groan, she put her messenger bag across her chest, hefted her tote bag higher on her shoulder and picked up the suitcase and got on with it.

As per Sebastian's texted instructions, Nina rang the doorbell on flat 44b and almost before she'd taken her finger from the bell, the door opened, making her jump.

A slender woman looked out. Her dead straight blonde hair was arranged in a sleek ponytail framing her face accentuating high cheekbones and a firm chin. She might have written the book on classy chic and haughty sang-froid, as defined by her indifferent expression, glossy pointy shoes, the wide-legged cream trousers and a high-necked silk blouse in pale blue, all of which made Nina feel doubly hot and sticky.

'*Bonjour, je suis Nina. Je suis ici pour les clés de Sebastian.*' The words burbled out in desperation and from the quickly concealed smile on the face of the elegant woman, she'd not made a terribly good fist of it.

'Bonjour, Nina. I heard you coming all the way up the stairs.' Nina felt her disapproval. 'I'm Valerie du...' She didn't quite catch her surname, as Valerie sounded as if she'd swallowed every syllable. 'Here are the keys.' She held them out at arm's length with a rather regal, keep-the-peasants-at-a-distance touch. 'When you see Sebastian, please give him my very best wishes.' Her flawless English and very sexy accent highlighted Nina's sense of being under-dressed and travel-soiled. 'I shall miss him, he's such excellent company.' Valerie added with a knowing, naughty look.

Nina swallowed. 'I will. Erm, thank you.' Valerie looked at least fifteen years older than Sebastian. Without any more ado, Valerie shut the door.

'Welcome to Paris,' muttered Nina under her breath. 'I hope you had a good journey. If there's anything you need, please don't hesitate to ask, as you're in a strange apartment, in a foreign city and you don't know a soul around here.'

* * *

As she battled her way through the door, dragging her suit-cases, her phone pinged.

I'm assuming you've made it. I need you to bring some of my stuff over to the hotel from my apartment. Ring me and I'll talk you through what I need. If you come over here, we can have a meeting about what will be required from you. I suggest about 3 p.m. Sebastian.

She wilted slightly at the strictly business text. Couldn't he give her a break? She'd been in the city for less than an hour and had no idea where the hotel was in relation to here. At the moment, her priority was locating a kettle and coffee and ransacking a cupboard to find something to eat. He could at least have given her chance to settle in?

Sebastian was just being bloody pedantic, Nina decided as she hauled down a wheelie suitcase from the top of the cupboard in the hallway. Surely it would be easier to transport everything in this instead of the canvas holdall he'd asked for. The wheelie case, which looked like an oversized silver beetle with latched sides, would be much easier to pull along rather than having to carry the other bag.

After a brief conversation, in which he'd given her the address of his hotel, she'd scribbled down the list of what he wanted. First up, his laptop and papers, which she gathered up from the table in the lounge. Then she moved to the bedroom. Five shirts, as requested, folded and packed, the toiletry bag filled from the bathroom and dressing table, including the Tom Ford aftershave he'd specifically asked for – and no, she didn't do that girly thing of sniffing it, even

21

though she did wonder what it smelled like. Next, underwear. Hesitantly she opened his top drawer. Yup, underwear drawer. Somehow she might have guessed he'd be a jersey boxer man. And Calvin Klein rather than M&S. It wasn't as if she hadn't seen plenty of men's underwear in her time but ... this felt too personal. Thinking about Sebastian in this. No, she was not going there. He was just a bloke. Nick's friend. A silly boy once. She'd known him forever. Telling herself to get on with it and quit being so stupid, she grabbed a handful, and as she did, she nudged a cardboard box. Shit. That was different ball game. Wincing at the double entendre, she looked at the box. Condoms. A pack of twelve. Featherlite. Open.

Don't look inside. Don't.

With a bump she sat down on the bed.

Four missing. Sebastian. Had sex. Has sex. Is having sex.

And it was absolutely, definitely, no way of interest to her. Nothing to do with her. She was not going to look at the use by date on them. And there was no earthly reason for her heart to have that silly, stupid, ridiculous pinching feeling.

Sebastian was a good-looking guy. No state secret. Of course he had women. The last time she'd seen him, he'd had a girl-friend. And the time before that. Different ones. He had girlfriends. She knew that. This was hardly a surprise and meant nothing to her.

Oh heck. So what was she supposed to do with them? Ignore them? Pretend she hadn't seen them? But then he knew they were here. Would know that she'd see them. Or maybe he had forgotten. If she packed them, it would show that she was completely blasé about them being there. Show that she was grown up and worldly about such things. Although if he needed them, quite how he was going to manoeuvre with a broken leg would be interesting. And where had that thought come from? Hurriedly she stuffed them in. That was the responsible thing to do, wasn't it?

Unfortunately, there was a hold up on the Metro which made her late and then, when she emerged onto the street, it had started to drizzle. Of course it bloody well had, so her perfect bob which was supposed to represent her new, more grown up image, had gone slightly curly, her pointy high heels, showing Parisienne sophistication, were killing her and the horribly expensive sheer tights were splashed with dirty water. It also turned out that the five-minute walk to the hotel was technically correct, providing you were a certain Mr Usain Bolt.

By the time she staggered to the top of the flight of steps of the hotel, tottering in her heels with all the élan of Tony Curtis in *Some Like it Hot*, it was nearer five o'clock. The concierge opened the door for her and she managed to raise a very small smile, which was quickly wiped from her face when her wet shoes slipped on one of the tiles. Saving herself before she fell, she sacrificed the wheelie case which promptly popped open exploding clothes in a rainbow of colour and fabric. And of course, the damn box of condoms had to go skittering across the floor before it came to rest beside the highly polished chestnut shoes of a tall, dark Gregory Fitoussi lookalike.

Sod's law, he had to bend down, pick them up and hand them to her as she blushed like a sunburned tomato.

'Merci,' she stuttered trying to give him an insouciant smile, taking them calmly from him as if this sort of thing happened to her all the time and it really was nothing and she wasn't the least bit fazed by it or dying slowly inside.

With a charming smile, he nodded, said something in rapid indistinguishable French and walked away, stepping around a pair of boxers.

Aware that she'd become a bit of a spectacle in the busy lobby, not that anyone was rushing forward to help, she hurriedly snatched the scattered clothes and rammed them back into the case any old how, closed it and, smoothing her hair, she crossed to the front desk. Sebastian had told her to ask for him at the front desk so that they could give her a key for his room.

Goodness only knows what everyone thought she was doing with a suitcase of condoms and men's clothing. The receptionist gave her a decidedly glacial look. Everyone probably thought she was a call girl, which was almost correct as for the next few weeks she was going to be Sebastian's beck-and-call girl.

Chapter 4

Sebastian was on the ninth floor and his room, rather practically, was right next door to the lift. She knocked loudly with several firm raps before inserting the key card into the slot. Three attempts later the little light finally turned green and she pushed open the door, her heart thumping so hard that she could almost feel her ribs rattling. Which was ridiculous.

'Nina?' His voice called from beyond another door in the short gloomy corridor.

'Yes, its me.' Her voice sounded thin and reedy. She took a deep breath. It was ten years ago. They were both older and wiser.

'You're late.'

Sighing, Nina nibbled at her lip and pushed open the internal door.

She didn't see him at first and took a minute to stare around at the rather grand surroundings. It was cowardly, she knew, but her legs had gone all wobbly, not unlike one of the newborn calves on the farm. A wave of homesickness grabbed at her and a longing to turn the clock back to a time when Sebastian was her brother's best friend.

'Yes, it's a suite,' Sebastian's dry voice came from the sofa in front of her, where his head poked above the back.

This wasn't at all how she'd imagined their first conversation would go, but then she'd had trouble imagining how it would go at all.

'It certainly is,' she said, taking refuge in the grandeur of the room rather than meeting Sebastian's narrow-eyed gaze.

It was palatial, double the size of her little flat at home, with two sofas opposite each other, a series of French windows opening onto three balconies and a monster TV screen. Antique-y looking furniture lined the walls on either side with two double doors opening onto what she guessed were bedrooms. 'All this just for you.'

'I have handy friends,' said Sebastian, his voice scratchy and cross. 'And it was the closest to the lift.' She finally looked down at where he lay on the sofa, propped up against the arm with a pile of pillows, the offensively, bright-blue cast clashing horribly with the pale lemon of the silk damask cushions.

'You loo...' She stopped herself in time. Telling him he looked terrible probably wasn't going to go down well. Inside, some less than charitable little minx shouted, Yay! Sebastian Finlay looks horrible. Skanky. Yukky. Totally unfancyable. His skin had a grey pallor and his hair was greasy and yes, yuk, slicked to his scalp. Purple shadows underscored his eyes and his chin was dotted with several days of stubble. The white T-shirt he wore looked grimy and he was in his pants. Sebastian in his pants. Her mouth twitched. She wanted to do one of those victory dances footballers do when they run around the pitch with their shirts over their heads.

26

'Thanks,' he said, dryly second guessing the rest of her sentence. 'Excuse me if I don't get up.'

'Looks ... uncomfortable,' she said suddenly realising that she wasn't behaving normally at all and trying not to look at the top of the cast where it met his pants. What was wrong with her, for goodness' sake.

His mouth thinned but he didn't acknowledge her comment. 'I, erm ... your stuff. I brought it. Where do you want me to put your case?'

Sebastian closed his eyes as if summoning up some patience and then glanced down at his leg.

'Sorry, you need me to unpack it for you,' said Nina

'It would help,' he said with a hint of sarcasm in his voice. 'Did you bring my laptop? Phone charger? Can I have those first?'

Nina brought the case over to the second sofa and opened it up.

'Jeez, Nina.' Sebastian scowled. 'Why did you stuff everything in there? Those shirts were freshly ironed. They look like they've been used to wipe the floor.'

He had a point, and they sort of had but before she could apologise or explain, he carried on, 'If you're going to throw a temper tantrum every time I ask you to do something you don't want to do, this isn't going to work. I need someone to help me, not a spoilt prima donna who throws her toys out of the pram when things don't go her way. I knew this was a mistake.' He threw his arm over his face.

Nina whirled round, feeling her nose flaring. Possibly her most unattractive trait, but it only ever happened when she was really cross. And now she was really, really cross.

'I appreciate you don't have a particularly high opinion of me, Mr She's-the-last-person-I'd-want-to-help but I'm not that petty. I didn't do it on purpose. The stupid case just popped open by itself.'

'One, you weren't supposed to hear that comment and I'm sorry, it wasn't terribly tactful. And two, yes that case does that,' he bit out, 'which is why I specifically told you to bring the holdall.'

'So because I wasn't supposed to hear that comment, it makes it alright?' said Nina through pinched lips. 'And two, I'm not sure you were that specific.'

'How much more specific do you need than, make sure you bring the leather holdall on top of the wardrobe? The one with—' His face tightened and his eyes narrowed. 'Nina. This is never going to work. You might as well pack your bags and go back home.'

For a minute she stood, clenching her hands into fists feeling wrong-footed and foolish. This wasn't how it was supposed to be. This was supposed to be her showing everyone that she could stand on her own two feet.

'Look, I'm sorry. It's my first day here. I was rushing. I can take your shirts back and wash them. It's not the end of the world.'

'No, it's not,' he agreed with a wince. 'It's inconvenient. It means I have to get housekeeping to do them for me and I'm already pushing it on the favours front with my mate Alex, who's the general manager here.'

'He must be a really good friend. This looks expensive.'

'Like I said, he's doing me a favour. He keeps an eye on

me, otherwise I'd still be in hospital, so I don't like to take advantage. He's a busy guy, with this place to run. I told him the cavalry was on its way, which is why I was keen for you to get here.' He looked pointedly at his watch.

'I'm sorry. Have you been on your own all day?' Now she felt bad. 'When was the last time you had anything to eat or drink?'

'Last night,' he said curtly. 'But it's fine, it's a hassle to pee.'

Ah, so that explained his surliness. That, Nina, could cope with. She knew what hangry men were like.

'Information I could do without,' said Nina crisply. 'However, you probably need to eat something to keep up your strength.'

She picked up the room service menu. 'What do you fancy?'

'Surprise me. I don't really care. I'm bored with hotel food.' His listless sigh made her stop and study him more carefully. He didn't look great at all.

She sat down on the sofa opposite with the menu in her hand and even at that distance there was a distinct whiff of unwashed male. A part of her could have revelled in seeing Sebastian at such a disadvantage for once in her life, but the good part overruled all the petty, stored-up grudge-y stuff.

'You need to eat,' she said, softening her voice. 'I know you probably don't feel like it and I'm hardly medically trained, but I do think it will help. How about an onion soup? That's quite light.'

'I don't need a nursemaid,' he snapped, the listless droop vanishing in seconds. 'I need some practical help. I'm not that hungry but you can order some food although it would be more helpful if you could unpack my stuff for me.'

* * *

29

'Wow, these look great,' said Nina studying the mood boards propped up on two flip chart stands, relieved to find an impersonal opening topic. She'd unpacked Sebastian's clothing as quickly as she could, hanging up the crumpled shirts and hoping the creases might drop a little.

She looked closer at the various designs for restaurant interiors.

'The first two are coming along.' Sebastian scowled. 'Although, we still haven't quite got it right for the bistro I'm putting into the patisserie site.'

'It all looks very chic and trendy.' Not quite her cup of tea but judging from the success of his restaurants in England, Sebastian knew what he was doing.

'That's the plan.'

Nina nodded and was relieved to hear the knock at the door announcing room service.

Taking the tray from the waiter, she awkwardly realised she needed to tip him when he loitered for a second. Dumping the tray on the coffee table she got out her bag and fished out a couple of euros handing them to him. When she turned around Sebastian was wriggling like a worm on a hook, trying to reach the tray but unfortunately he had slid too far down the cushions to get enough purchase to push himself up again.

'Here, let me,' she said unable to bear watching him struggling any longer.

'I told you, I don't need any help,' he said, swiping at the sheen of sweat on his forehead.

She ignored him and went around the sofa and hooked her arms underneath his and around his chest to help him sit upright again. As soon as she touched him, her heart bounced uncomfortably in her chest as a flood of memories collided in her head, leaving her with a familiar sense of inevitability. It seemed as if Sebastian still had the physical power to affect her. She gritted her teeth. In future she'd be sure to keep her distance.

Despite his protestations that he wasn't hungry, the soup disappeared pretty quickly. No sooner had he put the soup bowl aside, he picked up his laptop and the papers she'd brought.

'Right. We might as well get started. Do you have pen and paper?' he barked.

'No, I arrived today. You said the job would be two days a week. The course doesn't start until Wednesday. I thought you just wanted me to bring stuff over today.'

His mouth snapped shut as if he'd thought better of what he was about to say.

'Count this as the clock starting from now. Take one of those.' He nodded at a foolscap pad. 'There's a lot to do before the course starts and unfortunately, I've been busy with the plans for the first two restaurants, so I hadn't done anything before...' He indicated the cast, his face signalling disgust. 'You're going to have start from scratch. It's a seven-week course, which will be a full day every Wednesday but I'm going to need you to work the day before to get everything set up. Over the seven weeks we'll look at different pastries and the techniques – except, I'm still thinking about the final day. I might do something a bit different then.'

Nina scribbled notes frantically for the next half hour, her heart sinking. This wasn't quite what she'd imagined. In her head she was the theatre nurse to a clever consultant, handing him his scalpel and suction at exactly the right moment, demonstrating how efficient and supportive she was while soaking up his brilliant skills. None of her daydreams involved the equivalent of prepping the patient, making beds, disinfecting the theatre or swabbing down the wards.

'Hello, Nina. Are you listening?'

Nodding fervently, she sat up straighter. *Concentrate, Nina.*

'I'll get my usual suppliers to deliver the fresh ingredients, eggs, butter and cream but there should be plenty of the basics – flour, icing sugar, caster sugar – in the kitchen already. You'll need to get the more specialist items from a wholesaler I know. We won't need them on the first day as we'll be covering the basics. I'll give you the account details. We'll need things like rose petals, pure vanilla extract, crystalized violets, pistachio paste, freeze dried strawberry pieces and mango powder later on.'

She perked up. This was more like it. The fun stuff. Baking for the farm shop wasn't exactly challenging, she could rustle up a Victoria sponge or a coffee and walnut cake in her sleep. You could make some amazing things with the ingredients Sebastian had just listed.

'Er, hello. You still with me?' Sebastian's irritated voice cut through her daydreams.

'Sorry, it's—' she nibbled at her lip again '—patisserie dirty talk. I can't wait to see what you do with all those ingredients.' She'd watched the pastry chef at the restaurant for months, intrigued and delighted by her creations but too shy to ask too much about how they were made.

'It's like all these secret spells you have to master, you have to be a sorcerer with sugar, a wizard with chocolate and a magician with flavours and fillings.'

'It's just science,' said Sebastian, his eyebrows drawing together in puzzlement.

'No, it's not,' retorted Nina, at first thinking he was teasing for a minute, but his face was deadly serious. 'It's magic. Making wonderful special sweet potions of sugar and all things nice. Like baking alchemy, spinning sugar into edible loveliness.'

'Still fanciful then, Nina,' said Sebastian turning back to his laptop. 'To be perfectly accurate, like with most cooking, patisserie is more about chemical reactions, where precise combinations of one or two substances react together to become another substance.'

She stopped and stared at him. 'But...' At eighteen she'd been inspired by his passion, his descriptions of the food he wanted to cook and his pilgrimages to visit new suppliers in the search for those special and unique ingredients.

'So what's with the sudden interest in patisserie?' he asked, his gaze sharpening.

'I ... want to learn how to make proper patisserie. I've been watching the pastry chef at work for a while and ... well, she's amazing and I love baking, so I thought—'

'Nina.' He shook his head with a rueful mocking laugh. 'You're living in cloud cuckoo land. Seven weeks here assisting me isn't going to train you. It takes years to become a pastry chef. You have to train properly.'

Nina felt the flush race along her cheekbones. 'I realise

that,' she snapped back in a bid to hide the rush of mortification. 'I'm not stupid. But I want to learn … and this is … a start.'

'What? And you're thinking about training? Or is that another…'

Nina wanted to ask, *another what*, but she had a pretty good idea what he might say. It was alright for him, he'd always known what he wanted to do. He'd been driven from day one and had had to fight against parental disapproval to pursue his goal, whereas her parents were always supportive, no matter what she did – and she had to face it, she'd done quite a lot of things. She'd worked in a garden centre when she thought she might be a landscape gardener, applied to the bank when she thought she might try a serious career, helped out at the children's nursery when she thought about being a teacher. It wasn't that she wasn't a hard worker or prepared to put in the effort, it was just that none of them ever quite turned out to be what she thought they would. But she really wanted to learn how to cook the amazing confections she'd seen Sukie making over the last year.

'Right, we'd better get started. There's a lot to do. I'll give you a set of keys, although Marcel, the manager, will be there. He's a miserable sod, so ignore him.'

'I guess that's because he's about to lose his job.'

'Once the new bistro is opened, there'll be work for him. I'll need waiters. Right, if there's anything missing or where there are particularly low supplies, you'll have to go out and buy them. You can use the company credit card.' He strained forward to reach a battered leather wallet on the table. 'I'm still working on the set up lists and recipes, I'll email them through to you. Check that the kitchen has all the right equipment and enough of everything for the three people on the course.' He looked down at the notebook on his lap. 'Anything missing, you'll need to go out and buy it. Thank God, it's only three of them. With any luck a couple will drop out and then I might be able to cancel the course. Here's the basic shopping list.'

She blinked at him. 'You want me to go shopping?'

'Is that going to be a problem?'

'No, but there's a lot more involved than I thought there would be.' She bit her lip.

'Say now if you think you're not up to the job.'

'Of course I am. I just didn't realise there'd be so much to do.'

'I'm not paying you to twiddle your thumbs. You wanted to come, it's not going to be a picnic. I'll expect you to work. And work hard.'

She straightened and ignoring the flash of fury inside, she said calmly, 'I'm not afraid of hard work.'

'Excellent.' He wriggled again, poking a finger down the top of his cast before he checked his notes. 'I think that's everything, then. Although I will pay you an extra day this week as there is more to do than I'd originally anticipated to get started. It's Thursday today. You've got four days to get yourself organised and set up. I'll see you on Tuesday, we'll go over to the patisserie and run through things ready for the course starting on Wednesday.'

He pushed the empty soup bowl over to her side of the

table and put down his notes. 'You can put the plates back on the tray and leave them outside the door when you leave.'

'Do you want me to ... well, do you want any help?' She nodded to the top of the cast which was dangerously close to his crotch. Realising what it might look like she blushed furiously. 'You look like you're itching. But I meant, like, help with washing your hair or anything.'

His ferocious glare could have frozen her at sixty paces. 'I employed an assistant, not a carer.' There was a lengthy pause. 'And what's wrong with my hair?'

She widened her eyes with innocence. 'Nothing.'

He pulled his laptop onto his knees and started tapping at the keys.

'I take it I'm dismissed then,' said Nina, unable to keep the snarkiness at bay any longer.

He pursed his lips. If he'd worn glasses, he would be giving her one of those over the top of his specs sort of looks.

'I'm gone.' She picked up her bag, gave him a jaunty wave and headed towards the door. 'Bye.'

'Bye Nina. See you on Tuesday.'

As she strode down the corridor, relieved to escape, she shook her head. She was so over the crush she'd once had on him.

Chapter 5

She almost walked past Patisserie C. That was it? She stamped down her disappointment, trying to find something positive to say about the outside of the double-fronted façade. It was difficult given the rather sad state of a too-virulent shade of turquoise paint which was curling and cracking, shedding its layers around the woodwork frames, making the shopfront look like an old lady that had been tarted up using too much make-up, while the door frame had an ominous stoop to it and the cataract-cloudy glass in the windows could have done with a good clean.

Peering through them, she could make out a rather functional looking café which bore no relation to the traditional, old-style, gilt-trimmed interior of her imaginings. Bentwood chairs, which had seen happier days, surrounded bistro tables arranged in stark, uniform rows, making it look like a prison holding bay rather than somewhere to go and enjoy a cake and coffee. In fact, it didn't look as if enjoyment was on the menu at all in this place.

She hadn't intended on actually going inside the patisserie as today was about getting her bearings, but as the weather was so miserable, she decided she'd warm up with a quick cup of coffee before heading back to the apartment.

Hesitantly she pushed her way through the doors into the gloomy interior. There was one customer, an older lady, seated at one of the tables and a man behind a run of glass counters which had a small selection of chocolate éclairs, fruit tarts and macarons, all housed in one central cabinet as if they'd congregated there for company. The cabinet hummed rather loudly as if it were struggling to keep up. The man didn't deign to look up, he just kept polishing a glass in his hands.

'Bonjour.' Nina gave him a tentative smile, already feeling from the intense frown of concentration on his face that he wasn't the sort to appreciate a friendly overture. He had a 'repel the boarders at all costs' sort of hunch as if he were trying to hide his face from the world.

'Ow can I 'elp you?' He lifted his head with the slowness of an octogenarian tortoise.

'You speak English?' That was a relief. 'How did you know I was English?'

The look he gave her spoke the sort of volumes a megaphone would be hard pressed to beat and then to add further insult, he included a you-are-completely-stupid-but-I-will-bear-with-you-because-I-have-to roll of the eyes.

Seriously? All from one *Bonjour*?

'I'm Nina. I'm … going to be working for Sebastian,' she said, trying to sound confident, which wasn't that easy in the face of his utter disinterest. If she thought Sebastian was intimidating, Marcel's cool indifference made her question whether she should be here at all.

Yesterday's meeting with Sebastian had rocked her more than a little, rather destroying her rosy vision of suddenly becoming a shit hot pastry chef. In the brief few days before coming out here she'd imagined observing him at work, absorbing everything like a sponge, while chopping things up, practising her skills under his tutelage as well as being his not so glamorous assistant. It certainly hadn't occurred to her that she'd be so involved in the donkey work, doing the setting up, buying things or being left to her own devices so much.

'Sebastian?' Was it possible for his mouth to curl up any more?

'Sebastian Finlay, he bought the patisserie.'

'Ah.' Or was it a pah? 'The new bossman.'

'That's right. He sent me to check on the ingredients for next week and look at the kitchen.'

'Feel free.' With a sweep of his hand the man waved towards the back of the shop. 'You won't be bothering anyone. Perhaps a few ghosts of chefs past who will be rotating very fast in their final resting places. Bistro!' He shook his head, a strand of hair slicked back to one side becoming dislodged, which he swiped away impatiently, his eyes flashing with indignation.

'Your English is very good.'

'I lived in London. I was maître d' at the Savoy for some years.' As he said it, he pulled himself up with a regal sneer. Nina imagined that behind the counter, his feet had clipped together.

'Wow.' Nina looked at him with renewed respect. The maître d' at Bodenbroke was a cross between a mother hen, a sergeant-major and a sheepdog, soothing, cajoling and ordering everything into place while juggling the needs of guests and staff in the restaurant with calm unflappable authority.

'I'm Marcel. For the time being...' He paused. 'The general manager here at Patisserie C.'

Making a quick decision, Nina held out her hand. 'Nina – and I'm very pleased to meet you, Marcel.' What was that phrase? Keep your friends close and your enemies closer. Making friends with Marcel seemed like a smart move.

Marcel ignored her outstretched hand and carried on polishing the glass in his hand.

Undeterred, Nina glued a pleasant smile onto her face. 'Perhaps you could show me around, when you have a moment, but in the meantime, I'd love a coffee and one of those delicious looking éclairs. Is it OK if I sit over there?' She pointed to one of the tables beside the window. She lied, the éclairs looked rather sad and forlorn. Worse still, Marcel's lip curled as if to say, *if you think that, then you're an even lower life form than I'd originally thought*.

'If you must.'

Nina winced inwardly. This was going to be so much fun. Not.

She headed to the little table and as she passed, the sole occupier of the other table reached out and tapped her on the arm, giving her a quick conspiratorial smile before saying very loudly, 'Don't worry, he'll soon cheer up.'

Marcel shot them both a dirty look which suggested that soon was a relative concept.

'I'm Marguerite. It's very nice to have you here.'

'Hi ... erm, I mean hello.' Marguerite did not look like a 'hi' sort of person, although she gave her a big smile. 'How do you do? Are you the owner? I mean old owner. I mean not old, previous.' Nina tripped over her words conscious of the grace of the older woman, who was immaculately groomed.

The woman let out a delightful peal of laughter, as she lifted her chin and trained periwinkle blue eyes on Nina. '*Alors*, no, my dear. I'm accustomed to being the only customer here. I suppose I do think of it as part of my little world. And what brings you here?'

'I'm going to be working for the new owner. Just for the next few weeks. Helping him with the patisserie course that he's running.'

'Ah, you are a patissier. Now that is a wonderful talent.'

Nina glanced round and lowered her voice; there was something about the woman's enquiring gaze that encouraged the truth. 'Actually, I'm assisting but don't tell Marcel, I'm not sure he would approve. I'm not even a proper chef. It's an opportunity to learn a bit more. I shall only be here for seven weeks.' Sebastian's caustic point that it took years to become a pastry chef still rankled. She knew that, of course she did.

'I would love to be able to make patisserie.'

'So would I,' said Nina with a rueful smile before adding politely, 'You should do the course.'

The woman looked at her gravely for a moment.

'Actually, I think that's a very good suggestion.'

'Oh,' said Nina completely nonplussed, suddenly

remembering that Sebastian had been rather pleased that there were only three on the course.

'Unless you think I shouldn't.' Marguerite's face settled into stern lines.

'Absolutely not,' replied Nina. One more person wouldn't make that much difference to Sebastian. 'I think that's an excellent idea. You're never too old to learn new skills ... except of course, you're not old.'

'My dear, I'm not in my dotage, I have all my mental faculties and I also have a mirror in my apartment which, alas, is rather honest.' Her face softened and she smiled.

'Well, you look good on it,' said Nina.

'Oh, I think I'm going to like you a lot.'

Nina grinned at her. 'I can book you on the course, if you'd like.'

'Excellent. And you still haven't told me your name.'

'It's Nina.'

'And as I said earlier, I'm Marguerite. Marguerite du Fourge, I live very near to here. Would you like to join me?' She inclined her head at the spare chair.

Nina sat down, suddenly unsure what to do with her hands. Marguerite was one of those very elegant older ladies who had that same self-contained superior air that Valerie had exhibited. Was it a Parisian thing? Her silver hair was coiffured – there was no other word for it – in perfect silver waves and her make-up was discreet with a fine dusting of powder that softened the wrinkles around her eyes. In a rich russet-brown long skirt and a vibrant teal shirt, she made Nina, in her black jeans, black sweatshirt and ballet flats, feel like a dull sparrow next to a peacock.

Marcel brought over her coffee and the éclair and refilled Marguerite's cup without being asked.

'Merci, Marcel.' She gave him an approving nod and his whole demeanour changed as he said something in rapid French back to her.

'He's a good man,' said Marguerite to Nina as he bustled away like an important penguin. 'He hides it rather well.'

'Do you come here often?' asked Nina, intrigued once more. It didn't look like the sort of place that someone like Marguerite would frequent – surely there were much smarter places around?

'It is convenient,' said the other woman, almost reading her mind. 'And I suppose I have the memory of what it used to be like.' She gave a wistful smile, which softened her rather haughty face and made her seem suddenly a lot less intimidating. 'And you live in Paris?'

'Temporarily. I only arrived the day before yesterday. It's a long story.'

'I have plenty of time and I enjoy a good story.' Marguerite's eyes twinkled with mischief again, transforming the elderly matriarch into naughty Tinkerbell, and Nina found herself telling her the whole story, omitting of course the bit where Sebastian said she was the last person in the world he'd want help from. Not because she wanted to spare him and make the other woman think well of him but because it would lead to far too many questions.

In the end, she stayed chatting with the older woman for

a good hour. Every time she thought they'd finished their conversation, Marguerite would ask her another question or tell her something about a part of Paris she should visit. She almost wished she'd brought a notebook. By the time she finally stood up and said she must go and do some work, Marguerite knew all about her family and that she was staying in Sebastian's flat. In turn, Nina now knew where the best boulangerie was in relation to the flat, the nearest good restaurant and the only supermarché she should frequent, if she must.

Marguerite rose to her feet and Marcel rushed over to help her shrug on her coat, escorting to her to the door, opening it for her and ushering her out.

Nina finished her second cup of coffee and decided to be helpful and take it over to the counter, to save Marcel a job. Despite standing in front of the counter, he carried on noisily slotting dirty coffee cups in the tiny under counter dishwasher. She waited until he finally looked up and acknowledged her.

'You're still here.'

'I am,' she agreed with a smile, which was tough to keep up under his stern glare. 'And I'd like to see the kitchen.'

'Be my guest,' he said, going back to his coffee cups. The song from *Beauty and the Beast* took up a refrain in her head, despite the fact that Marcel was as far from welcoming as he was a singing candlestick.

For some reason she started humming the tune under her breath.

Marcel looked up, his face morphing into an expressionless

mask and pointed to the back of the shop and then once again turned back to what he was doing.

So it was going to be like that, then?

For a minute she felt like an intruder stepping into the Beast's castle as she entered the kitchen. Oh heck. It was spartan. And filthy. Nina shivered as she walked into the centre of the huge room. A layer of dust coated most of the surfaces and she was convinced that if she turned the taps on it would take a while for the water to groan and splutter its way out of the pipes. It was going to take her hours to clean this place up. Something that Sebastian had failed to mention.

The floor felt greasy beneath her feet as she walked on the slightly slippery surface to put her bag down on one of the industrial stainless-steel benches. From the size and scale of the place, it was clear that once upon a time, the kitchen would have produced all the baked goods sold in the shop. There were still all the ovens along the opposite wall as well as large scale fridges on another.

She opened one of the drawers under the benches, the stiff runners making a metallic groan, the jumble of utensils popping up and trying to burst free like an unruly Jack-in-the-box, as if they'd been crammed in hurriedly. There seemed to be no rhyme or reason as to the contents; whisks, wooden spoons, spatulas and rolling pins. Even rulers? None of which looked particularly clean. There were traces of ancient pastry and cream crusted on some items. A second drawer held more of the same, as well as a third.

Shelving under the benches held an assortment of bowls,

glass, earthenware and stainless steel in a mind-boggling number of sizes, all tucked haphazardly into each other. Sauté pans, heavy-bottomed pans and frying pans were stacked in leaning Tower of Pisa piles, handles pointing every which way like a distorted spider's legs.

How on earth was she ever going to get this lot sorted in time?

And there was no chance of appealing to Marcel's better nature, she wasn't sure he had one. He'd made it quite clear she was on the side of the enemy. She was on her own.

Really on her own. There was no one she could ask for help.

For a minute the panic threatened to swamp her.

No, she could do this. She needed to make lists, prioritise and get some labels to mark up all the shelves and drawers so that everything had a proper place to live.

When she returned to the café area, it was still deserted. Marcel didn't even look up at her. Mischief prompted her to say. 'Is Marguerite your only customer?'

'There are few ladies like Madame du Fourge around. She is old school Paris. Genteel. Elegant. She comes here every day.'

'She does?' Again, Nina frowned.

'It hasn't always been like this,' snapped Marcel.

'Sorry, I didn't mean...'

'Yes. You did.' Marcel's eyes shimmered with sudden emotion. 'Once, this was one of the best patisseries in Paris.' He waved a dismissive hand towards the pale-blue,-painted panels on the wall under a pink-painted dado rail. 'When I was a child, I grew up four streets away. We would come here for a Saturday morning treat. They made the best mille-feuilles. It was the speciality of the house.

'But the owner passed it onto his children. They were not pastry chefs. Things changed. We stopped making patisseries here in the kitchen. Everything is delivered now. It is not the same. And soon we will close and your Monsieur Finlay will open his bistro.' Marcel closed his eyes, as if in pain.

'I guess if the patisserie isn't making money...' Nina gave a tiny lift of her shoulders, trying to be sympathetic.

Marcel glared at her. 'If it was run properly, it could. No one has cared for fifteen years.' With a sudden petulant pout, he added, 'So why should I?' With that, he flounced away to wipe one of the tables which didn't even look as if it had been used.

Nina frowned after him. Why was he working here then? Clearly, he'd been at the top of his game once.

With a sigh she looked at her watch and decided that she would come back tomorrow. She had a few days to get prepared and hopefully Marcel would be in a better mood, although she wasn't counting on it.

Chapter 6

'So what's Sebastian's apartment like?' asked Nina's mother on her fourth day in Paris.

'Nice,' replied Nina, lifting her eyes from the screen where she was Facetiming with her mother, to take a quick look around the flat.

'Nice. That doesn't tell me anything,' complained her mother, with a good-natured frown.

'OK, very nice. Will that do?' Nina looked over to the tall French windows with the voile curtains billowing in the slight breeze. Beyond them was a tiny balcony which overlooked the wide boulevard below. Up on the top floor, the corner apartment offered two different panoramas, both with great views including one of the Eiffel Tower. A view she was rather too well acquainted with. Being here on her own was a lot more daunting in reality. It was just as well that she'd needed to spend so much time in the patisserie kitchen getting everything ready. Marcel had flatly refused to help. Every day she told herself she had seven whole weeks to explore the city, and that there was no hurry.

'I like to be able to imagine where you are, darling.' Her

mother's plaintive smile made Nina feel guilty. Of course it did. Honed by years of experience and five children, it was her not so-secret weapon. Flipping her phone around, Nina went straight out onto the balcony.

'What views! And what a lovely sunny day. What are you doing inside?'

'Talking to my mother,' said Nina, facing her again.

'You should be outdoors. It's a gorgeous day.'

'I was planning to go and explore a bit later.' Nina didn't want to admit that her exploration to date had consisted mainly of prowling around Sebastian's flat and a char-lady visit to the patisserie, where she'd ended up scrubbing and cleaning the kitchen, and methodically reorganising the utensils and drawers.

'Well, make sure you're careful. I've heard the pickpockets in Paris are terrible. You should put your bag over your head and across you. Although I have also heard that sometimes they use knives to cut the straps.'

'Mum, I'll be fine.' If this was her mum encouraging her to go out, she wasn't doing a great job.

'Well, make sure—'

'Here, this is the lounge.' She did a slow motion three-sixty turn.

'Oh darling, that's gorgeous. Nice! It's delicious. You are naughty.'

Nina gave her mum a mischievous smile as she returned the screen to face her. 'OK, it's rather sumptuous. I think this sofa is the nicest I've ever seen.' She stroked the pale grey velvet surface and patted the teal wool cushions. 'I think

Sebastian must have got some kind of interior designer in, it's all very calming, cool colours.'

'Very summer,' said her mother, who was a big fan of colour analysis and having your colours done.

'Kitchen?'

With a sigh, knowing there'd be no satisfaction now until she'd done a tour of every room, Nina walked over to the other side of the room and turned the sharp right angle into the kitchen-diner.

'Oh my word! Nina, that is lovely.'

Nina had to admit the open plan room, with its view of the Eiffel Tower which at night was all lit up, was rather wonderful. The modern kitchen had shiny glossy cupboards with no handles and had every gadget known to man.

'Show me that coffee machine. Oh, John, John! Come here and see this.'

Nina could hear her parents cooing over the stainless-steel built-in machine and wondering where they might put one and how much it might cost.

She walked on through, showing her mum the wide hallway with its recessed soft lighting and slate floor and the bathroom with its huge shower and lovely aqua tiles.

'It all looks so nice, darling. You're not going to want to come home.'

'Don't worry, Mum, Sebastian will want it back as soon as he's mobile again.'

'And how is the dear boy? You will send him my love, won't you? We do miss him. He practically lived here.' Nina closed her eyes knowing exactly what was about to come. 'And then

... well, I don't know why he stopped visiting so often. It's such a shame we don't see him more often.'

'Maybe because he went away to university and then onto catering college,' suggested Nina for what felt the thousandth time over the years.

'He could have come in the holidays.'

Her jaw tensed and Nina was grateful the phone camera was still trained on the bells-and-whistles, state-of-the-art shower.

'Well, that's the guided tour,' said Nina. 'So how's lambing going—'

'You haven't shown me the bedroom. Come on.'

'It's just a bedroom. It's got a bed in it—'

'But it's so interesting seeing what's available in other countries, don't you think?'

Nina paused outside the bedroom door. There was no earthly reason why she shouldn't show her mother, but even so...

She opened the door, seeing the room for the first time again and feeling that same unsettled sense of voyeurism, of being an intruder into someone else's life. She felt it more sharply in the bedroom than anywhere else, perhaps because there were so many more personal items in here.

'Ooh, I like the duvet cover, that's very nice. Masculine but tasteful. Sebastian always did have good taste. Lovely lamps. And what's he reading?'

Nina swallowed. The masculinity of the grey, pale blue and black cover was a constant reminder that she was sleeping in Sebastian's bed and the facedown open David Baldacci, reinforced the unsettling sensation that Sebastian had only popped out and could be back at any moment.

It was always her intention to spend as little time in this room as possible, at least while she was awake. Sebastian's presence was too much in here.

'Let's have a look at his photos,' said her mother. Wearily, Nina crossed to the wall opposite the bed to the multi-sectioned photo frame with its selection of pictures from over the years. She hadn't paid too much attention to it before, as there were quite a few that were duplicates of others she'd seen of Sebastian with Nick and her other brothers.

'Oh, look that's me!' exclaimed her mother. 'I remember that day. He won his first cooking competition. And he came straight over to tell me and show me the trophy. Your dad took that one.'

Nina remembered the lead up to the competition. They'd been his guinea pigs for weeks. Good job the whole family liked pork.

'Nice one of him and his parents,' said her mother, the hint of sympathy clear in her tone. Nina, still holding the phone, peered at the picture of Sebastian on graduation day, standing between his parents looking stiff and uncomfortable. He'd stuck out his degree to please his parents despite wanting to go in a different direction. A week after he graduated, he signed up for catering college.

'Ah, that's a lovely one of you.'

'Me!' Nina's voice squeaked and bent to take a closer look at the picture in the corner that she'd completely missed. It wasn't lovely at all. It was a hideous picture. She was grinning like a loon, her teeth and shining eyes white amongst the splashes of mud across her face, as she held up the medal she'd won in the cross-country championship. With a jolt, she stared at the happiness glowing on her face and felt her heart do one of those flutters, almost an echo of the past. Tears shimmered in her eyes for a second. She'd been so happy. Almost bursting with it. Not because she'd come first. Not because she'd beaten her personal best. Not because she'd qualified for the Nationals. She'd been so happy because Sebastian was waiting for her at the finishing line. Because he threw his arms around her. Because he hugged her so tight. Because she thought his lips might have grazed the top of her head. Because his eyes were shining with pride and happiness when he looked at her. Studying it again, juxtaposed among all the other important events in his life, she frowned. She couldn't believe he'd kept a photo of her, let alone this one. She couldn't help but wonder why he had kept it.

A bold pigeon pecked around her feet as her croissant shed a flurry of crumbs with her last bite. She felt rather proud of herself that she'd ventured out and ordered a coffee and a croissant in a local bakery, which was exactly what she'd told her mum she would do when she finished their call. Tipping back her cup, she downed the rest of her coffee and stood up from one of green park benches that lined the path leading up to the Eiffel Tower. The sunshine warming her skin had tempted her out. It really was far too nice to be inside and talking to her mother had reminded her why she was here, pickpockets or no pickpockets. And today she was taking the day off. She was done with cleaning and organising, although she was rather pleased with all her neatly labelled shelves and the smooth sliding drawers where, as far as she was concerned, everything was now in the right place.

With a definite bounce in her step, tightening her hold on the strap of her messenger bag, she set off to walk towards the huge iconic tower, stopping to take and send pictures to the family Whatsapp group, Hadley Massive. Honestly, so much for escaping. She shook her head. Mum's phone call this morning was the tip of the iceberg. The rest of the family were equally voracious for news, demanding regular updates. If it wasn't Nick texting her to ask how she was getting on, then it was Dan emailing or Toby direct messaging her on Twitter. She was seriously considering losing her phone.

Playing it safe and wanting to get a sense of the geography of the city, she spent the morning walking at a slow amble, crossing the bridge from the Eiffel Tower to the Trocadero, mindful of the rather daunting traffic. As far as drivers were concerned, pedestrians were an annoying irritant and, if they put so much as one foot in the road, fair game. No one seemed to pay any attention to the designated crossings or red traffic lights as motorists and moped riders constantly nudged forward and nipped into free space like lions pouncing on prey.

Following the map she'd borrowed from Sebastian's apartment, she walked along the Left Bank, or rather, *Rive Gauche*, which was still a perfume in her head, and followed the wide open span of the Seine before she bore left towards the Champs-Élysées to take a look at the Arc de Triomphe which was so much bigger than she'd expected and the traffic surrounding it even more terrifying. It hadn't gained its reputation for being the craziest roundabout in Europe for nothing.

Enjoying the sense of freedom and not having to consult anyone else, she decided to stop for lunch at one of the restaurants off the Champs-Élysées because she could. Her brother Nick would have balked and immediately suggested they avoid the main tourist drag as it would be too expensive, Dan and Gail would have looked up the TripAdvisor recommendations for the area and her Mum would have spent ages perusing the menu outside before allowing any of her chicks to set foot over the threshold.

Feeling spontaneous and independent, she chose a restaurant she liked the look of and went in.

The moules she'd selected were delicious and she relished every drop of the rather decadent glass of wine she'd decided to treat herself to when she'd seen that most of the French diners ordered wine with their lunch. Although she was thoroughly enjoying her meal, she did feel a little self-conscious about eating on her own in the busy restaurant. She'd been stuck on a table in the corner by the loos. To stop her feeling completely Billy no mates, she kept scrolling through her phone and almost dropped it when it suddenly began to ring.

'Sebastian, hi.'

'Nina, we have a problem. I needed my suppliers to do me a rush job for the other restaurant. The new chef wanted to do some recipe testing. It means they can't deliver the fresh ingredients to the patisserie today. You'll have to go and do the shopping.'

'Today?' she looked at her watch. 'Can't they deliver tomorrow?'

'Today would be better. I don't like leaving things until the last minute. Unless, of course, it's too much trouble for you.'

Nina gritted her teeth. Oh, the man did withering sarcasm so bloody well.

'I realise that, but ...' She had absolutely no idea where to go shopping. Paris wasn't exactly teeming with Tescos. Was there anywhere near the patisserie? There was no way she was going to ask him.

'Is there a problem?'

'No,' said Nina. 'Absolutely not.'

'Excellent, I shall see you tomorrow. You do remember that you're coming to the hotel to pick me up. I've asked the concierge to book a cab for eight-thirty. Paris traffic is horrendous, so make sure you get there on time.'

Chapter 7

Nina asked for a key card for Sebastian's room and the same receptionist as last time gave her a look as if to say, 'What, you again?'

She knocked so that she didn't give Sebastian a nasty surprise but before she could swipe the key card in and out of the slot, the door opened, making her jump.

'You're not Sebastian,' she said, stepping back and looking into dark brown eyes. 'Oh, it's you!' It was the rather handsome French-actor lookalike she'd seen down in the foyer when she'd been on her knees.

'Ah, the lady with the misbehaving suitcase and the ...'

'They weren't mine,' she said, 'That was Sebastian's stuff. I was bringing it over for him.'

A rather cute dimple appeared in his cheek as he tried to suppress his amusement. 'I'm sure they'll come in useful in his current incapacitated state.' His unexpected Scottish burr with rolling 'r's thankfully diverted her.

'Oh, you're Scottish,' she said. He looked thoroughly French to her.

'And I left the kilt at home today,' he teased, a warm friendly smile breaking through, making him look a lot more approachable and less film-starry.

It was impossible not to smile back at him. 'Sorry, I assumed you were French. You must be Sebastian's friend, the manager.' Despite his formal three-piece suit, now that he was smiling at her, Alex didn't look particularly managerial. With that impish smile and readiness to laugh, he looked more like an overgrown naughty schoolboy.

'That would be me. Yes. And don't tell my mother you thought I'd be French. She'd be outraged. It's bad enough I'm working over here, rather than in a good, fine city like Edinburgh, which is only five minutes down the road from her.'

'Ah, she's on the same page as my mother. I'm Nina. Sebastian's new ... right-hand-woman.'

'Ah, the little sister,' he said, his eyes dancing with sudden amusement. 'I've heard a lot about you.'

'None of it good, I'm sure,' said Nina, her mouth twisting with a rueful smile.

'Don't worry,' said Alex with a quick reassuring grin and she was warmed by the flash of concern in his eyes. 'I take everything he says with a pinch of salt.'

'That hasn't made me feel any better.'

Alex's smile slipped. 'Hey, he's grumpy with everyone at the moment. I've known him for a while, I count myself as one of his best friends and he's being a complete pain in the arse. But it's always stressful getting a new venture up and running. Although—' his eyes lit up with mischief '—if the awkward bugger isn't careful he'll find himself down into the wine cellar with the rats.' Nina bit back a laugh. She liked Alex's cheery down to earth delivery, he reminded her of her brothers.

'It would be stupid to ask if the awkward bugger is in.'

Alex laughed. 'He's in and exceptionally grumpy. You might want danger money to enter. He got it into his head that he had to wash his hair this morning and insisted that I help him at silly o'clock. Trying to keep him upright in the bathroom over the sink was like helping Bambi on ice. Then the stupid bugger decides he wants a shower. I think we must have used an entire industrial roll of clingfilm.'

Nina smiled at Alex's comical face pulling.

'Sounds like quite a performance.'

'Put it this way, he's been resting ever since. I popped in to check he was still alive.' Alex's face sobered and he lowered his voice, glancing over his shoulder as if Sebastian might appear at any moment. 'Between you and me, I think—'

A walkie talkie at his hip crackled into life.

'Alex, we have a problem.'

'That's going to my epitaph.' With a quick frown, he snatched it up. 'Be there in five. Right, well, I must be away. I have a hotel to run. Nice meeting you, Nina. I'm sure I'll see you again.' He turned and yelled, 'I'm off Bas, I'll check in on the invalid tomorrow but Florrie Nightingale's turned up to relieve me.'

With a cheery wave, he walked past her to the door.

Sebastian was hauling himself to his feet as she walked in. 'You're late.'

'Sorry, I got …'

'Save it, we need to get a move on.' Sebastian's dry words made it clear he wasn't impressed.

She plastered her pleasantest smile on her face, the one where her grin stretched into her cheeks and made them ache just a little. She was not going to let him get to her. She was going to be sweetness and light. Learn all she could from him and suck it up.

'Would you mind bringing my laptop and paperwork?' He gestured with the crutches, indicating he couldn't manage both.

Before she could say anything, he was off like a racehorse at the starter gate. Once out of the lift, he made surprisingly brisk progress, swinging on his crutches, planting them quickly and ploughing through the lobby like a man on a mission before taking the ramp out of the hotel onto the pavement.

The concierge had a cab waiting for them and opened the back door for Nina and she was about to slide in when Sebastian tutted loudly.

'You'll have to go in the front seat.' He hopped awkwardly in a circle so that he got in bottom first.

'Oh, sorry. Yes, of course. Let me help.' She hurriedly dumped his laptop bag on the front seat so that she could take his crutches from him.

Sebastian slid back onto the seat so that both his legs were propped up lengthways.

The taxi driver turned around and let loose a torrent of French with urgent gesticulations.

'Yeah, yeah. I'll put the seat belt on,' said Sebastian, twisting around to try and pull the buckle around him.

After a couple of attempts, it was clear that he was at too much of an awkward angle to pull it out and round him.

The taxi driver folded his arms. They weren't going anywhere until that belt was secured.

As Sebastian let out a loud exasperated huff, Nina dumped the crutches on the floor next to him and leaned in to try and help. Unfortunately, it wasn't that easy and there was nothing for it but to plant a knee on the seat between his legs, which would have been fine if she hadn't then overbalanced slightly, her hand grabbing his crotch to steady herself.

'Oh, sorry,' she squeaked. Avoiding looking at him, trying to be practical and matter of fact, she reached around his shoulders to grab the belt behind him, which was an even bigger mistake as it meant she came nose to chest. His hands closed around her forearms to steady her and, startled, she looked up into his face, which was the biggest mistake of all. There were tiny russet flecks in the dark brown eyes which were now studying her warily. Her breath felt unexpectedly tight in her chest. She could see the nearly opaque S-shaped scar on the top of his cheekbone and the impossibly thick eyelashes. Her pulse thundered in her ears and then for some bizarre reason she blurted out, 'You smell a lot better.'

He raised one of those ridiculously elegant, for a man, eyebrows and stared at her.

She swallowed and shrugged, unable to look away. 'I meant...' Her voice trailed into silence. For a few seconds she met his steady gaze, her heart bumping uncomfortably.

It was impossible to read anything in his expression, the dark eyes watchful and unblinking, although she noted his jaw was tense and he still looked a little pale, with that tightness around his mouth. Mind you, that had been there for a long time. He always looked serious when she was around, probably terrified she might get the wrong idea again.

Ducking her head at the memory, which still had the power to make her blush, she gave the seatbelt another tug and managed to pull it round him but still not quite close enough to slide the buckle into place.

'Thanks. I can take it from here.' Sebastian's caustic voice cut through her thoughts as he took the buckle out of her hands. Her brief quick blink was the only sign she gave of the current of awareness that went sizzling through her, setting her nerve endings dancing with sudden glee. She snatched her hands away horrified that the barely-there impersonal touch could still have such an impact.

Chapter 8

Working for Sebastian, Nina decided, was not going to be much fun. With his growls and snarling bad humour he was the original bear with a sore head. No wonder Marcel was keeping a low profile, taking advantage of the inaccessibility of the shopfront. The taxi had brought them round to the back door of the kitchen, which had no steps, and Sebastian had no desire, it seemed, to venture any further and attempt the small flight of steps up into the corridor to the shop.

'Not there Nina,' corrected Sebastian, as she moved one of the benches. 'Over here, I want a "U" shape. And then you can put all the scales out.'

She pressed her lips together firmly, keeping her back turned as she lifted the corner of the heavy table and manoeuvred it with a series of horrible screeches into place.

'Christ, do you have to do that?'

She did it again just to bug him. The table was bloody heavy. What did he expect? She hadn't signed up for full scale furniture removal. Eventually, she'd arranged everything to his satisfaction.

'Right, I'd like you to prepare a work station for each of the participants. We've got four now. One extra booking I could have done without.'

Nina looked down at her feet, thinking of Marguerite.

'We'll set up with all the utensils they're going to need. First up tomorrow is choux pastry, so we'll need...' He reeled off a quick-fire list. He had her racing around the kitchen grabbing whisks, saucepans, measuring jugs, sieves, bowls and wooden spoons, while he perched on a stool, his blue cast propped on the rung of another stool, and peered at his phone, making regular exclamations, muttering to himself and scowling at her.

Feeling rather proud of herself that she'd managed to remember everything he'd said and laid it all out neatly, she stepped back to survey the kitchen.

Sebastian stood up and hobbled over to one of the set ups. 'Don't forget you need one for us, or rather you. I'll be directing you for the basic things and then I'll demonstrate when it comes to solid technique.'

That bit Nina didn't mind, she was hoping to learn a lot from him.

They were almost done when he tapped one of the flat glass weighing scales and frowned. 'You did check the batteries in all of them.'

'Uh...' Nina's eyes widened in panic. 'Erm...'

'Oh, for crying out loud, surely you checked they all worked.'

Nina flapped her hands. 'Well ... I – I...'

Sebastian had already flipped over one of the set of scales and pulled out the little lithium circular battery from the back. 'Go see if Marcel knows where we can get these quickly.'

'Sorry, I didn't...'

'Think, Nina? How were you expecting everyone to measure their ingredients out? And where are the eggs? I can't find them anywhere. And did you check the stocks in the pantry?'

Her mouth dropped open in a horrified 'O'. She'd completely forgotten both. She'd been so overloaded with butter and cream yesterday when she went to the shops for supplies, she didn't dare risk carrying eggs too. Plus, she couldn't find them in the supermarket and the French word 'oeufs' had completely slipped her mind. And then when she'd got back, she'd loaded everything in the fridge and completely forgotten to check the pantry.

'I – I...' Why was it, when he was around, she was reduced to an inarticulate wreck? 'Where is the pantry? I'll look now.'

He didn't quite roll his eyes but he might as well have. 'It's at the top of the steps halfway along the corridor. Bloody stupid place to have it, which is why this building needs completely remodelling. And once you've done that, find out from Marcel if there's anywhere nearby to get the batteries. Go buy some eggs and get back here pronto.' Sebastian's mouth tightened and with it came the familiar expression of dissatisfaction.

Nina came face to face with Marcel, whose mouth appeared to have permanently pursed like a prune – funnily enough, much like Sebastian's – lurking in the corridor beyond the door at the top of the steps.

'I need to take a look at the pantry.'

'I wouldn't bother,' said Marcel. 'It's empty.'

'Empty?'

'Yes. The previous owner sold everything.'

'Everything?' She was starting to sound like a gormless parrot.

'To a woman who was opening a patisserie school in Lille. She came with her campervan. Took everything.'

With a heart sinking faster than a lead balloon, she crossed to the pantry doors and flipped on the light switch. Shelves dusted with flour lay bare and forlorn, outlines of what was once there imprinted into the floury surfaces. Turning, she opened the double-doored fridge. Empty shelves mocked her.

'Shit!' She'd hoped that the basics would be there as Sebastian had assumed. Sebastian was going to have a cow. The shopping list was going to be huge and she didn't have a clue how she was going to carry it all. She could hardly ask him for any help and Marcel, even if he'd been the least bit willing, needed to be at the shop. And there was no one to ask for help. Nibbling at her lip, Nina suddenly wished that her helpful family wasn't quite so far away.

Her shoulders drooped and she closed the doors slowly.

'Perhaps this might be of some use.' Marcel pulled one of those old lady, brightly-coloured shopping trolleys from out of the corner of the pantry.

Nina took a minute to take a few deep even breaths, chasing away the threatening tears, before going back into the kitchen.

'I'm popping out to get some eggs and batteries,' she said, keeping her voice bright and cheerful.

'Can't Marcel go?' asked Sebastian, looking up from his laptop.

'He needs to be in the patisserie.'

'Why? Don't tell me there's actually a customer in there? I'm surprised the place hasn't closed down already.'

'Erm ... yes, there are a couple,' she lied.

'Well hurry up, I didn't intend to be here this long.' He looked at his watch. 'Good job I brought my laptop, I can work on the important stuff.' He was already pulling out his phone and tapping the screen. 'Yeah, Mike. Have the lights been delivered yet? The sparkies booked for tomorrow?'

He'd tuned her out, which was as well as it meant she didn't have to tell him the full extent of the bare shelves. It would be yet another black mark against her which was so unfair. He had no idea what a state the kitchen had been in and how hard she'd worked to get it ship-shape. He was a bastard. A complete and utter unfeeling git with absolutely no redeeming qualities whatsoever.

Did she really need to do this? Was it worth it? It was supposed to be a means to an end, but now she wasn't so sure. Especially not after his scathing observation that it took years to become a pastry chef. She wasn't completely naïve, she knew that, but she'd hoped being here would at least help her make a start. Suddenly Nina wasn't so sure that coming to Paris had been such a good idea after all.

Thank goodness for Doris, as Nina had named the granny trolley Marcel had given her, officially her best friend, saviour and heroine, despite one slightly wonky wheel. Given that the pantry was Mother Hubbard bare, she'd decided to double up on Sebastian's quantities on his list. She felt rather pleased with this efficiency, even if it did mean that poor Doris was positively creaking under the weight of what felt like several tons of flour, caster sugar, icing sugar, butter and eggs. (Thankfully, in a rare moment of solidarity, Marcel had sorted out the batteries for her.)

Bugger Sebastian. He had his laptop and his phone, he could carry on working in the kitchen, so she allowed herself to enjoy the sunshine and being away from the stress of the kitchen as she ambled down the street heading back towards the patisserie, taking her time staring in the windows of the nearby shops, a pet shop, a haberdasher with a striking display of three beautiful cable knitted jumpers, a bicycle shop and a florist.

The colourful display of flowers made her stop in her tracks and smile. Pink and yellow roses had been arranged in pretty posies, there were little silver pots of grape hyacinths decorated with lilac bows and a bucket packed with her favourite alstroemeria in pale pink, deep red and purple. A few steps past the florist and she stopped and turned back. A couple of bunches of flowers would brighten up the kitchen and the patisserie no end but there was no way she could handle them and the trolley. The little silver pots, however, she could manage and they would look cute on the tables and they would please her if no one else. Limited as he was to the kitchen, Sebastian would never know. With six bought and just about balanced in the top of the trolley, Nina set off again.

It was when the wonky wheel decided to veer one way, as

she was hauling the trolley the other, that she realised she'd overloaded herself a pot of flowers too far. Wrestling with it pushed her slightly off balance and, with horrible inevitability, one of the silver pots started to take a nose-dive out of the trolley, darn it, when she was at the junction literally across the road from the patisserie. As she made a lunge forward grabbing it with cricket-fielding accuracy that would have ensured a shout of triumph from any one of her brothers, she let go of the trolley, which started to tip forward, unbalanced by the extra weight at the front.

'Whoa!' A girl appeared from nowhere and snatched the trolley's handle as it was about to land and with a triumphant flourish pulled it upright, with a big grin. 'Blimey, what have you got in here? Half a quarry?' she asked in a very loud Brummy accent.

'With rocks and everything, yes,' said Nina, with a laugh, struggling to get hold of the flowers. 'You're English.'

'Just a tad. Although I thought this beret made me blend in.' She patted the bright red hat perched on her dark curls.

Nina eyed her sturdy frame and the belted trench coat before looking down at her footwear.

'I think the Crocs might have given the game away,' she said gravely, pinching her lips together.

The other girl burst into laughter. 'They are so thoroughly English, aren't they? No self-respecting French woman would wear anything this practical.'

Nina thought they might be Australian or American but from what she'd seen so far of French women, she was inclined to agree. She couldn't imagine either Marguerite or Valerie de what's-her-name being seen dead in the plastic rubbery shoes.

'I stubbed my toe, think I might have broken the bugger. These are the only things I can wear. I was hoping that rocking the Audrey Hepburn look up top might stop people looking down below.'

Nina struggled to keep her face straight.

'I'm not rocking the Audrey Hepburn look either, am I?'

Nina shook her head very slowly as if they might lessen the offence. 'Sorry. No. But thanks for your help. You've no idea what a disaster that could have been. I've got three dozen eggs in there.'

Together, they pulled matching horrified *eek* faces. 'Can you imagine?'

'Uh! Scrambled eggs.' The other girl shook her head with the dark curls bouncing up and down like enthusiastic puppies, as they grinned at each other.

'Which along with the flour, sugar and icing sugar would have been a recipe for disaster.'

'Instant cake,' she teased, amusement dancing in her eyes. 'Who doesn't love cake though?'

'Mm, and instant unemployment for me. Thank you, you've saved my bacon.'

'No problem, I'm Maddie by the way.'

'Nina.'

'Have you got far to go?'

Nina shook her head. 'Over there.' She pointed to the patisserie on the other side of the street.

'Oh, I've been meaning to go in there. Is it any good?'

'To be honest, I'm not sure it is, but don't tell anyone I said that.'

'Let me give you a hand. I'll carry the flowers and leave the eggs to you. So you work there?'

'Sort of.' Nina explained the whole story and told Maddie all about the patisserie course as they walked along in tandem.

'How exciting. I'm a terrible cook. I'm more of a hearty stews and nursery puddings sort of girl.'

'You should do the course,' said Nina, hauling the trolley along, thinking about how long it was going to take her to unload this lot.

'What a brilliant idea.'

'Oh no, I didn't mean it.' She must stop saying that. It had been an off the cuff remark. She was recruiting new candidates quicker than people ate hot dinners. Sebastian was not going to be happy. 'It starts tomorrow, so probably a bit—'

'Perfect, I don't have lectures tomorrow. And do you know what? It will impress the hell out of Mum. I could make her half-yearly birthday cake.'

Nina raised both eyebrows at the interesting statement.

Maddie laughed. 'We celebrate half-yearly birthdays. We like cake in our house. Although they normally come from Tesco. I once attempted apple pie. Let's say all of the words *burnt*, *irrevocably moulded* and *knackered* applied to the saucepan at the end. It had to go in the bin.'

By the time Nina was lifting the trolley up the step into the patisserie with Maddie's assistance, the other girl was already musing out loud what sort of cake she'd make when she went home.

'It might be a bit late to book for the course,' said Nina.

'Oh, no worries,' said Maddie.

Nina heaved a tiny sigh of relief. God knows what Sebastian would have said about an extra student, especially if he heard she'd suggested it.

'I'll just turn up tomorrow morning, if there's no space, no probs.'

Chapter 9

'We'll leave in five minutes, are you all done?' asked Sebastian barely looking up from his hunched position over his laptop as she walked back in still trying to manage the wayward trolley, which definitely had ideas of its own. With one leg hooked over a chair and working sideways onto the bench, he looked extremely uncomfortable.

'Actually,' said Nina, busying herself unloading the eggs, grateful that he seemed absorbed in his work, 'I need to ... erm, perhaps set up another work station, you know ... in case anyone else turns up.' There was a loaded silence and she thought for a moment that she might have got away with it. No chance. He looked up from his laptop with a suspicious frown. 'Run that by me again.'

'Well, you know...'

'No.'

Nina risked peeking up to find his eyes boring into her. Feeling self-conscious, she rubbed the back of her calf with her foot, doing her best not to look shifty.

'Oh, for Pete's sake, Nina!'

Nina winced. 'I didn't do it on purpose, I ... well, I mentioned it to an English girl I met and she was really keen and...'

'And you didn't think to tell her the course was full or anything,' he snarled with such feeling, Nina couldn't think what to say. Surely it wasn't that big a deal.

'For fuck's sake,' he snapped and snatched up his crutches. 'I've had enough of this. Call a cab. I'll be outside.'

As soon as he'd gone, she blinked hard. No, not going to cry. He was not worth it, he was a pig but he was not going to make her cry. She hated him. How had she ever imagined herself in love with such an arrogant, rude, bad-tempered, surly, rude, opinionated, rude, pig?

The taxi journey back to the hotel was completed in absolute silence, with Sebastian in the back seat again. Nina spent the forty-five-minute ride with a fixed gaze out of the window, mentally packing her bags. She didn't need this. As soon as she'd helped Sebastian up to his room, she'd be hightailing it to his apartment and getting the hell out of Dodge. He could find someone else to help him.

Her shoulder ached where the stop start of the hideous traffic threw her against the seatbelt. It was official, Parisian traffic was horrendous. The time in the car, which seemed to be going more slowly than regular time, seemed to have propagated the tense silence between her and Sebastian still further and was worsened by the driver's kamikaze tendencies as he lurched forward to take advantage of every space that opened up before ramming on his brakes inches from the bumper in front. It was a relief when he slammed to a halt outside the hotel, having crossed three lanes of traffic in one quick, last-minute swerve.

Sebastian handed over a fifty-euro note and manoeuvred himself painfully slowly out of the back as Nina waited with his crutches. The driver let out a torrent of French as Sebastian began hopping into the hotel.

'Don't you want the change?' asked Nina, realising that the taxi driver was claiming he didn't have enough change.

'No,' growled Sebastian not even turning around.

She shrugged at the driver, picked up Sebastian's laptop bag and followed him, glaring at his back and muttering under her breath. She was so out of here. Rude bastard, not even waiting for her. He was already halfway to the lift.

He dropped a crutch as he fumbled for the lift button and cursed vehemently. Nina sighed under her breath, amazed that it was possible for him to be even more bad-tempered.

When she picked it up and handed it to him, he almost snatched it from her hand. Biting her tongue, she kept her face impassive. Only ten more minutes. Ten more minutes before she walked out of here and never had to see him again. All she had to do was accompany him in the lift, open the door for him, give him his laptop – and the jury was out as to whether she might wrap the bloody thing round his head – say goodbye and leave. She'd had it with him. He was on his own from now on.

As soon as the lift doors opened, he was off, his crutches rattling as he ploughed his way straight to the room with his head ducked down as he waited for her to catch up and put the key card in the slot.

'Thanks,' he growled. 'See you tomorrow.' And he was off without a backward look.

For a moment Nina stood, clenching her hands into fists. How dare he treat her like this? Ungrateful git. Yes, she'd made a couple of mistakes today, but no one had died and everything was ready for tomorrow. She might not be perfect but she deserved better and she shouldn't let him get away with this. Simmering fury began to bubble up. It took a lot to make her mad. She didn't like confrontation but ... this time she had nothing to lose. Sod it.

She marched three full strides down the hallway of the suite into the lounge. There was no sign of Sebastian but anger propelled her towards his bedroom where she heard one of the crutches clatter to the ground.

Pushing open the door with an angry shove, she was about to call his name when the sight of him stopped her dead in the doorway.

He'd collapsed onto the bed, laying diagonally across it, one arm flung over his face. She paused as he let out a low moan. All the bubbling anger, threatening to explode, leeched away in an instant. Stupid, stupid, stupid man. Now she could see the pallor of his face, the tight jaw where his teeth were gritted, the reluctant movement of his lower half.

'Sebastian?'

He stilled.

'Are you...?'

'Go away.' His voice was gruff and he kept his face hidden behind his arm.

Yeah right, as if she was going to leave him in this state.

She crossed to the bedside table where she could see a couple of boxes of tablets.

Nina narrowed her eyes and took a more careful study of him. He was holding himself very still and he'd definitely turned even greyer. The stupid sod was trying to be brave. It hadn't occurred to her that he'd still be in pain but then she'd never broken anything.

'How much pain are you in?'

The answering silence told her enough.

'Sebastian?' her voice was gentle.

'Yes?' He lifted his arm and looked up at her, as wary as a small boy caught out in a lie. There was a suspicious watery glint in his eyes.

For a moment, she felt racked with guilt, he looked so beaten and vulnerable. It was horribly disquieting when he'd never seemed anything but invincible.

'When was the last time you had any painkillers?' Occasionally having brothers paid off. All four of them had played rugby and shunned painkillers. It was a man thing. Jonathon had broken his leg once and had moaned continuously about how itchy the cast was until her mum gave him a knitting needle.

Sebastian lifted his chin looking mutinous. 'A while ago.' Now she could see the chalky whiteness around his mouth and the tension in his body.

'Are these them?'

He nodded, wincing as he did so.

'When was the last time you took one?' she asked again.

'Breakfast.'

'Oh, for goodness' sake.' She hid her worry in the chiding tone as she snatched up the pack of tablets. 'How many are you allowed to have?'

'Two every four to six hours but they're very strong. They make me feel like hell.'

'And being in pain is preferable?' snapped Nina, cross with him now. No wonder he'd been so bad-tempered all day.

Sebastian didn't say anything but shook his head weakly, his eyes closed, and suddenly she realised how completely helpless he was and how much pain he must be in. Popping a couple of pills from the blister pack, she bustled into the bathroom to get him some water, giving herself a wry look in the mirror. Subdued Sebastian was a lot easier to deal with, but it wasn't nice seeing him like this and she knew he wouldn't want her pity either.

'What did the hospital say about after care?' she asked, as she put the glass of water and tablets down. She needed to get him sitting upright to give him the pills.

'Rest. Keep it elevated.' His flat tone suggested that he knew he'd been an idiot and he didn't need her to reinforce it.

'Right. Can I help you to get more comfortable? If you sit up, I can arrange the pillows and then put some under your leg to raise it a bit. Then painkillers.'

Sebastian gave her a bleak look and the grim line of his mouth wavered. When he blinked with a weak nod as if he was too exhausted to speak, she moved forward and started shifting pillows.

'Do you think you can lift yourself up?' she asked.

'Give me a minute. Sorry, that car journey…'

She didn't say the obvious – *and being on your feet all afternoon and not taking any medication.*

Once he was nestled into the pillows and had taken the painkillers, she spoke again. She'd been trying to keep things strictly impersonal but she wanted to make him comfortable.

'Do you want me to take your shoe off?'

He gave her a baleful glare.

Now she rolled her eyes. 'Look Sebastian, accept that you need help.' Moving to the other side of the bed, she unlaced his black brogue and eased it off. 'See, that wasn't so hard was it? I'm here. Able and willing. I haven't got any other plans for the rest of the evening. Why don't you have a sleep? And then I can order room service later.'

He nodded and closed his eyes, which she took as a small triumph. At least he was listening to sense, although she suspected that was more because he'd given up trying to fight the pain. For a moment, she stood over him fighting the urge to smooth his hair from his forehead and a strangely insistent impulse to press a quick kiss there.

With a start, she felt his hand slip into hers but he didn't open his eyes. With a gentle squeeze of her fingers, he whispered, 'Thanks Nina.'

Pulling the door to, she went into the suite. There was no way she could leave him in the lurch now. She could have kicked herself for not realising how much discomfort he was in. No wonder he was so damned irritable. Despite saying he didn't need a carer, he clearly did need someone around to look after him.

Pursing her lips, she pulled out the notes he'd prepared in readiness for the next day. According to the recipes they were going to be making choux pastry, crème pâtissière, chocolate profiteroles and coffee éclairs. Her mouth watered, reminding her that she hadn't eaten for quite a while, but she decided to wait another hour before ordering anything, then when it arrived she'd wake him up.

The discreet knock at the door signalled the arrival of room service. Nina had played it safe for Sebastian and herself and ordered both of them burgers and chips. Peeping in on Sebastian as she went to open the door, she found him still sound asleep. For a moment she studied him. In sleep his face had softened, the dark hair flopped down over his forehead and his mouth relaxed. He looked much younger, more like the Sebastian she remembered and she was horrified at the unexpected ping of her heart. Quickly she turned and headed towards the door, almost wrenching it open.

'Someone's hungry,' teased a laughing Scot's brogue.

'Alex, hi. You do room service?'

He grinned at her. 'Normally no, but the staff are primed to let me know if Sebastian needs anything and if I'm around, I pop up. How is he?'

Nina grimaced as she backed up to let him in with the tray. 'Not great, to be honest. Silly idiot has overdone it today.

'Sounds like Bas. Complete workaholic.'

Nina raised an eyebrow. 'And you're a slacker?'

'I'm not like him. He's driven.' Alex shrugged. 'I work

hard—' his cheeks dimpled '—and play hard, but man, he's super motivated. Determined to prove his dad wrong.'

Nina frowned as she followed Alex into the suite where he deposited the tray on the dining table overlooking the window and pulled back the curtain to peer out at the lights of Paris shining in the dark.

'I don't remember his dad, I'm not sure I ever saw him but then that's not surprising. Sebastian seemed to spend all his time at our house. Mum gave him free reign in the kitchen when she realised he could cook better than she could. It was always a bit of trial for her, she found cooking for four palate-indifferent, human dustbins a bit monotonous. At that age my brothers weren't terribly fussy and quantity over quality counted every time.'

'Sebastian's dad is…' Alex trailed to a halt. 'Bas! Brought your supper up for you, you lazy sod. Sleeping on the job, I hear.'

'You try getting around on crutches. Bloody knackering.' Nina turned. Sebastian stood in the doorway looking margin-ally better – but they were talking the slenderest of margins. 'What's on the menu?'

'Burger and chips.' Nina gave a self-deprecating shrug. 'I wasn't sure what you'd want.'

'Perfect. Thanks.'

She noticed he moved very slowly as he moved across the room as if he'd used up all his energy earlier in the day and still wasn't fully recharged. How would he feel if she suggested he ate and went back to bed? She caught Alex's eye who frowned as he watched Sebastian's laboured progress.

'Dear God, it's like watching the walking dead. Good job I upped your chip ration.'

Nina noticed that despite Alex's teasing words, he was casually helping Sebastian to sit down and taking charge of his crutches. She picked up the tray of food, took off her plate and handed it to Sebastian to eat on his lap.

'More bloody chips are the last thing I need. You'll be able to use me as the ball when I get back to playing five-a-side again.'

'It's alright, we'll stick you in goal,' said Alex, stealing a chip and throwing his lanky frame onto the opposite sofa. He looked as if he could eat chips all day without any problems.

Nina rolled her eyes as she sat down next to him, perching her plate on her lap.

'I saw that,' said Alex kicking off his shoes, pinching another chip and making himself comfortable.

'You two sound like my brothers. Mmm, these are good.' She munched on a chip, realising that she was starving.

'Ha! Except Nick can't kick a ball to save his life.' Sebastian gave her a rare grin. 'Nina's brothers are rugby men.'

'I seem to recall you played a mean fly half,' said Nina, responding without thinking, and she took a quick bite of burger hoping her slight blush wasn't obvious as she recalled all the matches supposedly watching her brothers, hanging around like a lovesick groupie. God, she really had made a fool of herself.

Sebastian sighed and a look of regret flashed across his face. 'That was a long time ago, but I miss it.'

'Why did you give it up then?' asked Nina, intrigued. Sebastian wasn't the sort of person to back off from a challenge or not do something he wanted. It was a shame, he'd been good. She had to wait a second as he swallowed down a mouthful of chips which, despite his protests earlier, he seemed to be enjoying with relish.

'Unfortunately, doing the Sunday lunch shift when you feel like you've been put through a blender got old quite quickly. And working seven days a week didn't help.'

'All work and no play makes Bas a dull boy,' said Alex, his hand snaking in for one of Nina's chips this time. 'Although that blonde ba... Katrin from the interiors company looks like she's enjoying mixing a bit of business and pleasure. What's going on with her?'

'Early days,' said Sebastian, suddenly very interested in a patch on his cast which he rubbed at with his palm, making his tray wobble precariously. 'She travels a lot. We'll see.' Lifting his head, he looked over at her. 'What about you, Nina? Boyfriend on the scene? What happened to that Joe guy you were seeing?' His clipped questions made it sound like an interrogation, a fact-finding mission without any real interest.

Nina dredged up a non-committal smile. 'You're well out of date. Joe and I stopped seeing each other about four years ago and he's just got married. I was bridesmaid.'

'Ouch,' said Alex, pulling a face and shifting on the sofa towards her as if in reflexive support. 'I bet that was uncomfortable.' Despite his blunt words, sympathy shimmered in his eyes and she was able to look at him rather than Sebastian as she responded.

'No, I introduced him and Ali, she's a good friend.' The words came out blasé and unconcerned. She'd been genuinely delighted for them but she wasn't about to admit that their relationship assuaged her guilt that she could never love Joe the way he wanted her to. Someone else had first dibs on her heart. 'I couldn't have been happier, especially as Joe and I were always more friends than anything else.' Nina prayed that her face gave nothing away.

'So, no one on the scene at the moment?' pressed Sebastian.

Nina shook her head. 'Too busy,' she said crisply, irritated that he had to highlight that she was steadfastly single. He was clearly being bloody minded.

'Well, you must have some downtime while you're in Paris,' said Alex, with a sudden cheery stridency to his tone. 'Sebastian can be a slave driver. Don't let him take advantage. You need to make sure you see some of the city. In fact, I know some great places.' He delved in his top pocket. 'Here, take my card, I can never remember my mobile.'

Sebastian glared at him. 'Nina is here to work! I'll need her to be flexible as things come up.'

Alex gave her a cheerful shrug and a discreet wink. 'Let me know if he's being a difficult boss. I can withdraw his food rations.'

Nina grinned back at Alex who promptly helped himself to another one of her chips. 'That sounds like a plan.'

Sebastian's mouth tightened. Nina only felt a tiny bit guilty ganging up on him but he'd been such a grumpy git all afternoon and it was nice to have the light relief of Alex's cheerful good humour.

When they'd finished eating, Sebastian yawned rather noisily. 'Right Nina, I'll see you tomorrow. Don't be late. You'll have to do the meet and greet in the shop.'

'Me?'

'I'm not risking those stairs and you're more than capable. You've got all their names and ... you've clearly met one of them already,' he added with a cross expression. 'All you need to do is wait for everyone to arrive and then bring them to the kitchen.'

'OK.' She nodded and gathered up her things. 'See you then. Night Alex.'

To her surprise Alex jumped up, and quickly rounded up the plates, relieving Sebastian of his tray with a speedy turn. 'I'll see you out and put these in the corridor.'

'Alex,' Sebastian said quickly. 'I need a word.'

'Be right back,' he replied, ignoring the implicit request that he stayed put. Sebastian's frown darkened. Nina wondered anew at how it was humanly possible for his expression to be any blacker.

Once at the door, having deposited the tray on the floor outside the room, Alex paused. 'Sorry about his nibs in there. Never known him quite so contrary. Don't let him get to you. Ignore him and if you want some light relief I was serious about the offer of a guide around Paris. You've got my card. Text me your number ... well.' He blushed. 'If you want to, that is.'

'Thanks, Alex. That would be really nice.' She gave him a cheerful smile, as her heart sank a little. He was lovely... friendly, kind, absolutely the perfect antidote to Sebastian and

85

– she felt ashamed to even think it – too reminiscent of Joe. Getting tangled up in a friendship where one party wanted more was something she wanted to avoid at all costs. And wasn't that a huge irony? No wonder Sebastian kept her arm's length.

'Alex,' came a bellow from the other room. 'I haven't got all day. And Nina has important things to do.'

'Something is really bugging him,' whispered Alex. 'Better go. See you soon.'

Chapter 10

'Hey, Nina.' Maddie bounced through the door first, shaking her head and dappling the floor with drops of second-hand rain, bringing in with her a tail wind of chilly spring air.

'Morning. You're the first one here.' At the sight of her, Nina immediately felt brighter especially as for the last half hour she'd been subjected to Marcel's rather apathetic help as she set up a coffee station at one of the tables in readiness for everyone's arrival. He was definitely on a go slow – in fact, any slower and he'd go backwards. As if that wasn't enough, there was no sign of Sebastian yet and he hadn't responded to her last text.

'I'm always early. Comes of having a big family. Trying to get everyone out of the house is always like herding cats.'

'I know that feeling. My dad used to threaten to get one of the sheepdogs to round us all up. Help yourself to coffee and take a seat. We'll wait for everyone to get here and then we'll go through to the kitchen. I'll be back in a minute.' She left Maddie helping herself to coffee and nipped downstairs, ignoring Marcel's impenetrable stare as she passed him.

The kitchen was all set, but where was Sebastian? She gave her watch an anxious look before returning to join Maddie as Marguerite arrived at that very moment with a middle-aged couple in tow. 'Bonjour Nina, look who I found on my way here. Monsieur and Madame Ashman.'

They both gave shy smiles. 'They're here on a prolonged honeymoon and got married three weeks ago.' Marguerite glided in ushering them in front of her like a serene swan.

'Hi, I'm Peter and this is Jane.' They were still holding hands as if they couldn't bear to be parted, which Nina thought was rather sweet. Peter took the umbrella from Jane and helped her remove her coat before taking off his own and observing, 'It's really not very nice out there.'

'No, it's horrid but come and grab some coffee. I'm Nina. We're waiting for one more and then we'll go through to the kitchen to meet Sebastian who is your course tutor today and then we introduce everyone properly.'

'Can I take your coats?'

Nina's head shot up at the sound of Marcel's voice. His face looked pained as if he really didn't want to join in but couldn't bear to see a customer not being looked after properly. She smiled at him and received a snooty nose-in-the-air look in return as he folded the coats over his arm and bore them to the old-fashioned bentwood hat stand in the corner.

'Am I in the right place?' boomed a loud voice with a definite northern twang.

'You must be Bill,' said Nina, nodding and quickly consulting yet another of the sheaf of notes from Sebastian as the tall, heavily-built man ambled forwards.

'That's right, Bill Sykes.' He gave an all-encompassing salute to everyone, two fingers to his forehead. 'And don't say a word, I've heard it all before.'

Marguerite looked blank as Maddie and Nina bit back smiles.

Once everyone had had their coffee, Nina herded them through to the kitchen. Surely Sebastian was here by now. He probably wouldn't have risked the small flight of stairs leading from the kitchen up to the hallway through to the patisserie.

Her heart slipped to her boots. Darn it, still no sign of him.

Everyone crowded in, grouped together looking uncertain, and Nina felt the weight of responsibility.

'Right, everyone.' She mustered a cheerful smile and prayed that her jolly hockey sticks voice sounded authoritative and confident. 'Thank you all for coming today. As you know, I'm Nina and I'll er...' What exactly was her role? She and Sebastian hadn't discussed it. 'I'll be looking after you. Sebastian, the chef, is on his way.' At least she bloody hoped so. She looked at her watch for what felt the hundredth time, feeling aggrieved, as she recalled his words, 'don't be late'. 'I expect he's been caught up in traffic, coming here, but he'll be here very soon. I'm sure.'

She gave another smile as everyone looked at her. 'Yes, he'll be here any minute.'

But what if he wasn't? What else could she say to them to fill this growing silence as all of them looked to her as if she held all the answers. With a quick look at another set of Sebastian's lists on the bench in front of her, she ran over in her mind what he'd said yesterday and came up completely blank. The prickle of sweat on her back made her wriggle uncomfortably for a second.

'I tell you what.' She scrabbled for the words. 'It might be nice if ... you introduce yourselves. And perhaps tell us all a little bit about your cooking experience and why you want to learn about patisserie.'

Everyone looked sheepishly at each other for a second and Nina swallowed, praying someone would break the ice. The deathly silence remained. Even Maddie shuffled and looked at her fingernails.

'So I'm Nina. And er ... I'm assisting Sebastian today. I'm...' Maddie gave her an encouraging smile. 'I'm not trained. But I bake a lot and I'm fascinated by patisserie. So I volunteered to help ... erm perhaps I should have told you ... Sebastian's broken his leg, so I'm helping and hoping to learn at the same time.' Her voice started to trail away as she glanced around at everyone. They all looked a bit uncertain. The last thing she wanted was for any of them to be disappointed, especially not when she'd suggested the course to two of them.

'But,' she said firmly, 'weeks of preparation have gone into the course to ensure that you all learn the basic building blocks of patisserie. Sebastian is an excellent teacher and a very fine chef. He's trained at several Michelin-starred restaurants including Le Manoir in Oxfordshire and has worked in the kitchens of some of the top chefs. He runs his own chain of restaurants and is about to open two new restaurants here in Paris.' She decided against mentioning his plans to turn the patisserie into a bistro. 'I can assure you, you're in an excellent pair of hands.'

'Just the legs that are the problem,' quipped Maddie with a laugh. And with that the ice was broken, as they all exchanged wry smiles.

'I'm Maddie Ashcroft, a student on my year abroad in Paris. I thought I'd give it a go…' She paused with a self-deprecating laugh. 'I can't cook to save my life, so it will be quite good if I can go home and impress my family with something incredible. I'm hoping Sebastian is a miracle worker.' Everyone laughed again and Nina was heartily glad that she'd bumped into Maddie in the street.

With a shrug, she added, 'And to be honest it seemed as good a way as any other to spend a dull Wednesday morning.'

'I will concur with that. When you're as old as I am, the days can be monotonous.' Marguerite glanced around the room. 'My name is Marguerite and I can cook—' she shot a sympathetic smile at Maddie '—but I don't have anyone to cook for. My grandchildren are coming in the summer and I – I…' Her voice shook and the regal matriarch suddenly looked a touch frail as she blinked hard. 'I haven't seen them for some years. I want this visit to be really special.' Her voice gained strength and the confident hauteur was back. 'They live in England, so I want to show them how patisserie is in France. Give them a taste of what it is to be French and show them some of the traditional recipes.'

'That sounds wonderful,' said Nina, with a warm smile, realising the grand old lady was a lot more fragile and uncertain than she appeared. 'I'm sure your grandchildren are in for a real treat.'

'I'm Bill Sykes … and despite the name, I'm a good bloke.

Well, at least I like to think I am. No one's ever told me I'm not.' He dived in, speaking quickly as if to get it over with. 'I've been a chef in the army for ten years, but...' He broke off to grin at everyone in the room, having got into his stride. 'As you can imagine, there isn't much call for fancy stuff. I'm a frustrated pastry chef and after leaving the army last year, I really wanted to learn a new skill. I'm staying with a friend to help him renovate a house in Paris. These days I'm a builder, electrician and general handyman, so I'm not sure I'm going to have the delicacy of touch.' He waved large sausage fingers in exaggerated jazz hands.

Nina shook her head. 'I'm sure you'll be fine,' she said, trying not to compare them with Sebastian's long elegant fingers.

She turned to the couple with a nod inviting them to speak.

'I'm Peter Ashman and this is Jane, my lovely wife. We've recently married and we love cooking, so we're spending three months in an Airbnb in Paris, so that we can shop Paris markets. And get away from our disapproving families for a while. We heard about the course and fancied having a go.'

Jane nudged him with a naughty twinkle in her eye. 'And ... tell them.'

With a self-deprecating smile he explained, 'And on one of our first dates, I tried to make profiteroles for Jane but they were a disaster. I made three attempts and they all came out as flat as pancakes. I wrote in the recipe book in capital letters, DO NOT EVER ATTEMPT AGAIN!!!'

Everyone burst out laughing before a dry voice cut in. 'Choux pastry requires absolute precision. It's easy when you know how and one of the building blocks of patisserie. By the end of today, I'll guarantee you'll be making profiteroles in your sleep.'

Nina whirled round as Sebastian clinked forwards on his crutches to move to the front of the semi-circle, immediately capturing everyone's attention. Wow, he looked better. A lot better, Nina could scarcely believe the difference. It was more than the way he looked though, even Nina couldn't deny he carried off the handsome pirate look a bit too well, but there was that charisma, an indefinable something that made everyone look his way and seek his attention.

'Good morning. I'm Sebastian Finlay and I'm going to be teaching you how to make French patisserie. You'll have to excuse a certain immobility. I had a run in with a cabin bag and as you can see the cabin bag won.' He hobbled his way to the stool that Nina had arranged for him, carefully stowing his crutches to one side.

Everyone laughed politely but Nina could see they were all immediately charmed.

'However, luckily for me, I have my very efficient assistant, Nina, who has kindly, forgive the pun, stepped in for the next few weeks.'

At the unexpected warmth of the smile he sent her way, she blushed. She realised he was playing to the crowd but it was the first time he'd smiled properly at her for a very long time. Studying him through fresh eyes, she realised that yesterday's weary, worn down and tired looking man had been replaced. Today, in a chest-hugging black T-shirt that enhanced a pair of broad shoulders she'd forgotten about, his slightly olive skin glowed and his eyes were bright, lighting up as he gave his appreciative audience a welcoming smile. He actually looked pretty tasty as long as you didn't look down. She smirked, those baggy black joggers, at least a size or three too big, didn't do him any favours.

She quickly re-introduced everyone.

'Today we will start with choux, which as I said is the basis for so many of the greats, the Paris-Brest, gâteaux Saint-Honoré, éclairs, religieuse and of course profiteroles.' He shot a quick grin at Peter. 'I shall be watching you carefully and hopefully we can sort you out.'

'Hallelujah,' cheered Peter. 'I'll give it my best shot.'

Nina couldn't help but stare at the light-hearted, charming man that had suddenly materialised. Authoritative and calm, Sebastian gave off an aura that everyone was in safe hands. This was a man who knew exactly what he was doing.

'Right, well let's get cracking. Find yourselves a space at one of the benches. You'll find a recipe sheet next to your utensils. Ingredients are all over here with the scales.'

There was a delicious rustle, a sense of anticipation, as they all took their places at the benches arranged in a U-shape facing the worktable in front of Sebastian. Marguerite and Bill immediately picking up the recipe sheet to read it.

Sebastian turned out to be a far better teacher than Nina expected and she saw vestiges of the kind, patient boy he'd been as a teenager. He was good-humoured and informative with quiet, understated sympathy when anyone struggled. Marguerite took her time to combine the eggs and Nina caught

Sebastian laying his crutches to one side to beat the mix to the right consistency, constantly encouraging her throughout and batting away her asides that she was rubbish. Once her piping bag was loaded up she did a more than a fair job of piping even shaped éclairs.

Nina glanced over to the other side. Poor Maddie, still with her tongue protruding, was having a tough time. Her éclairs ranged from fat misshapen lumps to thin, strung out worms with nothing in between. Opposite her, Peter's were all on the plump side, while Jane's thin streaks were the polar opposite, which amused Nina. Together, their efforts would have been perfect. It seemed a rather apt analogy for their partnership.

'Dear God, this one looks like a wayward sea cucumber,' laughed Maddie. 'Why is this so much harder than you made it look?' She'd squeezed so hard that she had undulating waves in her next éclair. 'I'm rubbish at this,' she sighed, rolling her eyes.

'Oh dear,' sympathised Marguerite, who'd clearly used a piping bag a time or two before. The five éclairs she'd completed so far were arranged with uniform precision.

'Why do yours look so perfect?' Maddie laid down her own piping bag and went over to Marguerite's station. 'My excuse is I've never done anything like this before in my life. Have you? And look how many Bill's done.'

'That's being in the army,' said Bill, grappling with his bag, his large fingers dwarfing it. His tray was already full and while not in Sebastian's league, they showed a workmanlike uniformity. 'Get in, get the job done.'

Sebastian gave Bill's tray an approving nod. 'If you slowed

down, they'd be even better. But a very good first attempt.' He moved on down the row and then paused, shaking his head. 'Maddie—' his eyes twinkled with a sudden naughtiness '—has anyone told you not to squeeze quite so hard? You need a gentle constant pressure.'

Maddie let out a roar of laughter. 'Are we talking éclairs?'

Sebastian had already moved on with a murmured, 'Well done Marguerite.

'Don't worry everyone, it just takes a bit of practice and don't forget this morning is just the start. We've got seven weeks to perfect your technique. I realise some of you may not have used a piping bag before and today it's about getting the consistency of the pastry right.'

Once everyone's éclairs were piped and Nina had written their names on the greaseproof paper before sliding the trays into the oven, they stopped for a coffee. She couldn't believe that it was already half past eleven. While everyone trooped out, Nina picked up Sebastian's discarded icing bag and refilled it, taking the opportunity to have a go herself. Sebastian was absorbed in the laptop he'd switched on the minute the others turned to leave.

A big fat blob exploded from the tip with a splat. 'Oops,' said Nina, stepping back but increasing her hold on the bag at the same time, which made things worse; the mixture oozed out of the tip in a big fat trail over the edge of the baking tray like an escapee worm. This was harder than it looked and now she couldn't let go of the bag without making more mess. She stood there for a second feeling totally incompetent as she heard Sebastian clumping towards here.

'Here.' Sebastian stood behind her and rather than take the bulging bag from her hand, he put his hand over hers and slid it under the weight of the bag. 'Use your left hand to gently cup the bag, don't squeeze with it.' That gentle, encouraging tone with a hint of chocolate brought back memories. She'd always loved his voice. Sometimes when he spoke quietly it held a certain timbre that ran over her skin like an electric current.

His shoulder brushed hers as he leaned forward to take her right hand, making her conscious of his nearness. A sudden flush of heat raced over her body, aware now of his height beside her, of his strong arms as the silky hairs on his forearm tickled the skin on her wrist, and the sense of warmth emanating from his body.

She realised she was holding herself still and tried to ease out a breath as she looked down at his hand. His fingers gently tugged hers higher up the bag, their barely-there touch sending flutters to places that had no place fluttering.

'Here, you hold it up here, to push down the mixture rather than squeeze it.' He put his hand over hers, and a tingle shot up her arm as he gently squeezed her hand to demonstrate the movement. Maybe it would have been fine if she'd kept her head down and she could have ignored it all and pretended it was just ... something and nothing, but no, she had to look up at him. He was studying her intently, his eyes solemn and for a moment, they both looked at each other that fraction too long. Nina felt her lips part and could have kicked herself at the unconscious movement. His eyes strayed to her mouth widening for a the briefest of seconds. He opened his mouth.

'Keep...' His voice was hoarse and he paused as if the words had got stuck. Nina could feel her heart thudding away at a million beats per second.

'You need to keep up—' he swallowed, she saw the dip of his throat '—a gentle consistent hold.' He pressed her hand and she glanced back down. She heard him exhale sharply.

'Now you try.' The words tumbled out quickly as he took a step back.

Nina focused on the bag in her hands, hunching her shoulders as she bent over the tray, her back to Sebastian. Carefully she squeezed out one perfect éclair.

'Excellent,' said Sebastian's voice, overly loud and enthusiastic for one puny éclair. He was already hobbling back to his laptop. She could hear the *clump, step, clump, step, clump, step*, as he went.

Pretending that nothing had happened, she carefully iced another six lines of choux pastry until the mixture in the bag ran out. By then her pulse had just about returned to normal and Sebastian was busy tapping away at his laptop. For a second, she studied him. Surely he couldn't have missed the electric charge that had sizzled between them ... or was he just determined to ignore it?

Chapter 11

As Nina joined the small group gathered around one table in the patisserie, her heart lifted as she listened to the conversations around her. Everyone seemed to be gelling rather nicely. Maddie and Bill were chatting happily as it turned out they'd both lived in the same area just outside Salisbury at some time. Moving past them, she heard Marguerite deep in conversation with Peter and Jane asking all about their wedding and their grown-up children as both had been previously married. Marcel, who was serving coffees and offering the limited selection of pastries to the guests, hadn't quite got a smile on his face but did seem to be genuinely happy to serve everyone.

It was a shame that Sebastian hadn't made the effort to come into the shop area, at the very least it might have mended a fence with Marcel. She wondered if he would take a job here once the new bistro opened; it would be a pity if he didn't, he was great with customers.

'You never said Sebastian was a bit of alright,' said Maddie, with an unsubtle nudge.

To her absolute mortification, Nina blushed.

'Oh,' said Maddie putting two and two together and coming up with the jackpot.

'No,' protested Nina. 'It's nothing like that. I've known him forever. He's my older brother's best friend.'

'And?' Maddie's arch question made her blush again.

'And nothing.'

Maddie raised a teasing eyebrow.

'We're not even friends. Most of the time we can't stand each other. He only agreed to have me because he was desperate and I only came because I really want to learn more about patisserie.'

Nina busied herself making coffee so that her face was hidden. Maddie was far too perceptive and persistent.

'I ought to take him a drink.' With that she fled back to the kitchen with one of the strawberry tarts and a cup of coffee.

Her soft-soled trainers, chosen deliberately to weather whatever today threw at her, concealed her return when she descended the small flight of steps into the kitchen. Sebastian had his head thrown back, his eyes closed and his lips pinched tightly.

'I brought you coffee,' said Nina quietly, not wanting to startle him. 'Would you like a glass of water as well?'

He nodded, pain etched into the lines around his mouth and then gave her a wry smile. 'Yes, Nurse Nina.'

She looked at her watch. 'By my reckoning, you could probably do with another pain killer right about now.'

'There are still nine minutes and thirty-six seconds,' said Sebastian looking at his watch.

'I'm sure the pain relief fairies will give you a bit of leeway,' said Nina.

Sebastian's mouth crinkled as if he might just smile. 'Pain relief fairies?'

'Not heard of them?' Something made her give him a cheeky wink as she handed over his coffee. 'I'm not sure if you still take sugar or not. I put one in. And yes, there are guardian angels of people with nasty breaks in their legs.'

'Guardian angels as well? Who knew? And who said it was a nasty break?' He took a hesitant sip of coffee. 'And yes, I've never managed to kick the sugar habit. On a really bad day I take two.'

'Alex mentioned you'd had surgery.' She ignored the sugar comment, wishing she'd not brought it up. It brought back memories of her rushing to make him and Nick coffee when they were round at the house in her desperate attempts to get him to notice her. God, she'd been so obvious back then, it was embarrassing.

'Telling you everything, is he? Yeah, who knew that one innocent cabin bag could do so much damage? They put a plate and a few screws in.'

Nina winced. She wasn't normally that squeamish; with four rugby-playing brothers she'd seen her fair share of dislocated thumbs, black eyes, split lips and broken ribs but nothing that involved internal metal work. It seemed horribly unnatural and very painful. Worse still was the thought of being in hospital all by yourself with no family support.

'How long were you in hospital for?'

'Five days. They didn't want to let me out until I said I could stay with Alex.'

'Stay with Alex? That's a rather elastic use of the term *stay with*.'

'I hate hospitals. I was desperate to get out.'

'Even though it probably would have been better for you?'

Sebastian's face darkened. 'You know how much time my mum spent in them. Visiting her was ... you know. Not the best. I ... I have a real...' He checked himself as if he'd given too much away.

'I don't blame you,' said Nina quickly, patting his arm. His mother's chronic illness and father's business interests had meant that Sebastian virtually lived at her house from the age of fourteen until he went away to university. Hospitals and the constant threat of death hanging over him couldn't have been good companions for a teenage boy.

'How is your mother?'

'As well as she's ever going to be. She has to carry an oxygen cylinder with her everywhere, but she doesn't complain.'

'And your dad?'

He shrugged and took a long slug of coffee and closed his eyes again. 'Just what the doctor ordered. Thanks, Nina.' With a nod, he gave her a rueful, genuine smile that hit the jackpot. Like an arrow zeroing in right on bullseye, it made her feel ... well, just wonderful. It was as if he'd been himself without worrying about encouraging her or trying to keep her at a distance. For the first time in forever, she felt like his equal, a work colleague, a friend. No sides or hidden nuances to worry about.

'No problem.' She turned. 'I'll just clean this lot up.'

'Thanks. Sorry. I didn't really think this through. I should have got more help. I forgot about the washing up and that side of things. I was so focused on preparing, I overlooked the practicalities.'

'I'm sure I can manage. Besides—' she looked over her shoulder at him '—we could always rope Marcel in.'

Sebastian snorted. 'You think?'

'No,' she said, trying to keep a straight face.

Together they burst out laughing.

With a heavy sigh, Sebastian shook his head. 'I don't know what I'm going to do with him. Once the bistro is up and running, I'm not sure what he can do. He's far too superior to be a waiter.'

'Couldn't he be maître d'?'

'Marcel? I don't think being a glorified manager of a patisserie quite qualifies him.'

Nina frowned. 'You do know he worked at the Savoy?'

'What, Marcel?'

'Yes. He was maître d' there.'

'You're kidding.' Now it was Sebastian's turn to frown. 'Why didn't I know that?'

Nina refrained from rolling her eyes, instead she shrugged.

'So what's he doing here then?'

'I've no idea, but he certainly knows how to look after customers.'

Sebastian's lips clamped together, scepticism written large on his face.

'I'm serious. You should see him out there, buzzing

around like a mother hen. He absolutely dotes on Marguerite.'

Sebastian lapsed into thought and Nina carried on with the washing up. It was easy work and she flashed through the dirty bowls, whisks and pans as the others began to troop back in.

Chapter 12

Nina caught the muttered groan as Sebastian sat down on his stool. The second part of the day had been much busier as Sebastian taught everyone how to make crème pâtissière with varying degrees of success. Only Marguerite had managed to get a truly smooth, creamy finish. Bill's wasn't bad and Jane's had a few stray lumps in, but Maddie and Peter were in competition to see whose most resembled scrambled egg.

'Don't worry,' Sebastian had said as the day came to a close, 'Patisserie is all about timing and chemistry. Today is only the first day. And as they say, patisserie wasn't built in a day.'

Nina's lips quirked at the image of Maddie, Peter and Bill all groaning in unison while Marguerite had exchanged a wry smile with Jane when she gave a gentle tut. Sebastian had been very good with all of them but he must be exhausted. He'd been on his feet for too long.

'Why don't you order the taxi now?' she asked gently, conscious that he was probably about ready for another painkiller.

'Because there's still a lot to do,' said Sebastian, eying the untidy room, his lips clamped in a pinched line.

'It's just a bit of washing up. And I can always come back tomorrow and give the place a thorough clean.' She shot him a quick look trying to gauge his mood. 'And I thought if you didn't mind I could practise making choux pastry again and improve my piping skills.'

He shrugged. 'Fine by me, if that's what you want to do.' He looked utterly disinterested and rose to scoop up one of the dirty mixing bowls, wincing as he tried to manage with one crutch.

'Oh, for goodness' sake. Leave it, I'll tidy up.' Was the man trying to prove he was superhuman or something? 'You need to get some more painkillers down you and put that leg up.'

He dropped the bowl with a clatter and glared at her but then at the sight of her face, nodded. 'Yes, nurse.'

As he'd capitulated just a tad too easily, she refrained from adding, 'Glad to hear it.' Clearly he was in more pain than he was prepared to let on.

Only once Sebastian had limped out to his taxi, his laptop bag swinging from his neck, (his choice, it was easier, he said) looking like a St Bernard with an overlarge brandy barrel, did Nina stop and slump onto one of the stools. Bloody Sebastian. Why couldn't he bloody follow doctor's orders?

Holy moly, the kitchen looked like an icing sugar tornado had swept through. Despite her sensible trainers, her feet throbbed and the mountain of washing up facing her made her feel distinctly like Cinderella. Wearily she rose to her feet, deciding that if she could just get all the benches wiped down and clean and make a start on the washing up, she could come back tomorrow morning and finish up and wash the sticky patches from the floor.

'There you are, Nina.' Maddie popped her head through the door. 'Come and sit down for a minute. Have a coffee. You bloody deserve one. And you can judge who made the best éclairs.'

'I can't do that,' said Nina, with pretend horror on her face.

'Course you can,' said Maddie. 'Come on.'

Casting a brief look at the washing up, Nina peeled off her apron, a nasty plastic thing that Sebastian had handed out to everyone at the beginning of the class, and dumped it in the nearest bin before following Maddie.

As she appeared there was a rousing cheer.

'Well done today, Nina,' yelled Bill above the noise. 'You worked like stink. You're a proper little trooper. I'd have you in my unit any day.'

She turned pink with pleasure.

They were all sitting around two tables which had been pulled together. Maddie and Bill around one, Peter, Jane and Marguerite around the other.

'You've been wonderful,' said Marguerite, patting the empty chair next to her. 'Come sit down. You deserve a coffee and a rest.'

'She certainly does, although she could probably use a proper drink, I'm not sure coffee fits the bill,' said Peter, draining his cup.

'Not much fits me,' said Bill, laughing across the table at Peter, patting the belly overhanging his trousers.

'That's an excellent idea, Peter,' said Marguerite. 'Marcel. Champagne, please.'

'Champagne?' Maddie looked worried. 'Not on my student grant.'

'Don't worry, dear. This is on me. Marcel always keeps a couple of bottles for me.'

In a flash Marcel had rustled up a tray of flutes and was carrying them over to the table, along with a gold-foil-topped bottle.

'This is very kind of you, Marguerite, I adore champagne,' said Jane with her quiet smile.

'She certainly does,' said Peter, giving her a quick hug. 'Would bathe in the stuff, given half a chance.'

Jane laughed. 'That would be expensive.'

'And you'd be worth every penny.' He winked at her.

'Oh, you.' She squeezed his knee.

Marguerite smiled at them. 'And I think the first toast should go to our newlyweds. It's a joy to see.'

Marcel undid the wire, popped the cork and poured the champagne, without spilling a drop or any of the liquid fizzing over the top of the glasses. With effortless efficiency, he'd poured seven glasses and served them up as Nina took her place at the table.

'To Peter and Jane,' said Marguerite. 'May you have as long and happy a marriage as I did to my husband, Henri.' Everyone raised their glasses. 'And to Nina for being such a wonderful hostess today and working so hard.'

'Hear, hear,' said Bill.

'It really has been a lovely day,' said Jane, leaning into her husband. 'And Peter can now make me profiteroles every day for the rest of my life.'

Maddie looked a little disconsolate and let out a big, gusty sigh.

'Don't worry, pet,' Bill patted her on the arm. 'Sebastian said that we'll be making choux pastry plenty of times over the next few weeks.'

'But it was ... horrible.' She peered inside her box. 'These are...' She shrugged her shoulders, a chagrined expressed on her face. '... Like zombie éclairs. I think my new motto might be "cooking into the apocalypse, food for those beyond all hope."'

'You'll improve,' said Nina. 'Just think, in seven weeks' time, how much better you'll be.'

'Hmm, is that a herd of rainbow unicorns I see prancing along the horizon?' asked Maddie with one last despairing look at her éclairs.

Eventually everyone started to drift off. Jane volunteered to escort Marguerite down the street as it was on their way and Peter and Bill, who rather bizarrely had discovered a mutual love of ice hockey, decided to go for a beer together and watch an international game between Canada and Russia.

'Right then,' said Maddie rolling up her sleeves. 'Better get cracking on with the washing up then.'

Nina looked at her horrified. 'You can't do that. You're a paying customer.

'Don't be daft. I can't leave you here with that lot.'

'I'm being paid.'

Maddie shrugged. 'And?'

The light was starting to fade with appropriate timing as Nina dried the very last bowl. With Maddie's help, they'd laughed and joked their way through washing up sticky bowls, cream-covered whisks and chocolate-smeared knives.

'I can't believe how much fun today was,' said Maddie, reaching for the last bowl.

'It was rather lovely.' Nina couldn't believe how well the disparate group had gelled. They were already on their way to being firm friends after only one day.

'I loved how Marguerite took Jane under her wing. They're both so kind.'

'I loved how you and Bill were so competitive!' laughed Nina. 'And how Marguerite was so refined ... even when she swore. Haven't you got a home to go to?' she asked with a smile as Maddie picked up the broom and started sweeping the floor. She was already looking forward to putting her feet up and vegging out on Sebastian's large sofa, although it would have been nice to know that tomorrow she had something to do. She still hadn't plucked up the courage to go exploring the city on her own.

'Not really.' Maddie sighed and began brushing the floor with energetic sweeps of the broom.

'Oh,' said Nina, a bit nonplussed.

'Well I have but ... I applied late, so I'm in a studio apartment on my own.' The broom clanked noisily against the steel leg of one of the benches. 'Turns out I'm not built for solitude.'

She glanced up and gave Nina an unhappy look. 'Listen to me. I should be grateful. It's just that everyone else in the block is in a flat of six. You'd have thought after sharing a room with my sister for ever and tripping over my brothers' crap all the time, I'd enjoy the novelty.' She pulled a face.

'Who'd have thought I'd miss... putting the kettle on and knowing someone will join me for a cuppa, those signs of habitation, a coat on the post in the hall, falling over Brendan's shoes, Mum's shopping bag hanging up and Theresa's make-up scattered in every room in the house. When no one's home, I know one them could walk through the door at any minute. I miss that.' She screwed up her face and took in a funny breathy sob.

'Now, when I shut the studio door, I know that's it, until I go out again the next day. It gives me an achey feeling. You know kind of unsettled, a waiting for nothing sensation.' She perched her chin on top of the broom, blinking furiously. 'Pathetic eh? Today's been one of the best days since I came to Paris.'

'Oh, Maddie.' Nina dropped her tea towel and crossed the room to give the other girl a hug.

'Bloody stupid, eh,' muttered Maddie against the top of her head.

Nina gave her a squeeze and looked up – Maddie topped her by a good few inches. 'No, not at all. Being lonely is horrible. You don't need to apologise for it.'

'Yeah, but you came here on your own. You're managing.'

'Ha! That's what you think.' Nina knew she could confess to the other girl and not be laughed at. 'I've been watching far too much Netflix.'

'You can never watch too much Netflix,' said Maddie staunchly.

'You can if you've binge watched the first three seasons of *Once Upon a Time*.'

'Yikes ... aren't there like twenty-two gazillion episodes a season?'

'Not far short.'

'Girl, you so need to get out.' Maddie hopped up and sat on the clean bench, which less than half an hour ago had been covered in flour.

Nina covered her cheeks with her hands and pulled a rueful face. 'Yeah, I do, don't I? Can I blame it on the weather?'

'No, although it has been crap. Paris in the springtime my arse. But I don't blame you. You miss your family?'

'Ha! You have to be joking.' Nina rolled her eyes. 'They never leave me alone. If I don't check in on the hour every hour, they start threatening to alert Interpol. They're a flipping nightmare.'

Maddie gave a snuffly half-laugh as she swung her legs backwards and forwards. 'Families, eh? Can't live with them, can't live without them.'

'I could live without mine, believe me,' said Nina grimly. 'They love to interfere. I thought coming to Paris might give me a bit of space.'

'Whereas my lot are probably high-fiving each other on a daily basis, glad I'm not around giving them grief about not doing their homework, not helping Mum enough and not leaving their flipping shoes where everyone can trip over them.'

'I take it the shoe thing is a problem,' teased Nina in response to Maddie's exaggerated exasperation.

Maddie rolled her eyes. 'I swear, Brendan is flaming Imelda Marcos mark two. That boy is definitely in touch with his feminine side. He's got more pairs of trainers than JD Sports.'

'Oh, God,' said Nina with feeling, thinking of her brothers and sweaty sports kit. 'I hope they don't smell as bad as the twins' trainers. You needed a face mask to go in their room.'

Together, they smiled. 'Thanks, Nina. You've cheered me up.'

'Tell you what. Why don't we meet up one day in the week, if you've not got lectures? I've barely seen anything of Paris.'

'All that *Once Upon a Time*, how will you tear yourself away?'

'I'll survive.'

'OK. But it'll have to be next week. I've got an essay to hand in and I haven't even started yet. Where do you fancy going? Mona Lisa at the Louvre? Which is totally mad. Train spotting at Gare du Nord? Impressionist hunting at the Musée d'Orsay? Huge. Serious perfume shopping at Galeries Lafayette? Awesome roof by the way. Notre Dame? Nice. Les Invalides? Interesting. Or just drinking red wine in a bar all afternoon?' Maddie's eagerness had Nina laughing again.

'You tell me. There's so much. I've been a bit ... you know ... fazed by where to go first and I don't know much about art and stuff but I want to see it all.'

'That's a bit of a tall order, but let's see what the weather's like. Give us your phone number and I'll text you.'

Chapter 13

Midway through trying to hand over her euros for a bag of apples, Nina's phone rang. Busy trying to juggle her purse and purchase, and assuming it would be Sebastian, she answered it quickly. She hadn't heard from him since the first day of the course, a few days ago, and was fully expecting him to ring her any day now before the next class this week.

'Hello.'

'Hey Nina. It's Alex.'

'Oh hi,' she straightened, surprised and a little flattered. 'How are you?' She'd liked his sense of humour immediately when she'd met him and he was a good antidote to Sebastian who seemed so horribly serious these days.

'I'm good. I was…' There was a pause, which was just as well as the market vendor suddenly yelled a loud greeting at a couple passing the stall. 'Where are you? Sounds noisy.'

'I'm at Saxe-Breteuil.' She rolled her tongue around the French words, feeling rather wonderfully authentic. 'I'm at the market and I've just bought the most gorgeous looking apples, some fabulous cheese and the most divine bread.' And the smell of it was reminding her she hadn't eaten since breakfast.

She'd already decided to double back to a stall selling flat-breads with tabbouleh, thyme and sesame seeds.

For the last few days she'd finally been exploring the local area and enjoying the spring sunshine sitting at pavement cafés watching the world go by. People-watching in Paris was fascinating, there was always a drama to see, a character to watch and imagine a life history for and a little dog to observe. The French seemed to love their pint-sized pooches.

'Ah, you've gone native, have you?' She could hear the amusement in his voice and could picture his smiling, handsome face.

'Well, it was something of a necessity. The fridge promised possible starvation if I didn't toute suite a la marché. I'm beginning to wonder if Sebastian has turned into a vampire, there's absolutely no food in his place.' She'd planned to stock up but had got a bit carried away by the sheer temptation surrounding her; cuts of meat she had no idea what to do with, even if she could have brought herself to touch them, a selection of charcuterie that made it impossible to narrow her choice, fresh fish and seafood that made her itch to cook. She'd also been charmed by the wicker basket she'd found in Sebastian's kitchen, which made her feel liked she belonged and was now filled with an eclectic mix of items.

'Your French is execrable,' laughed Alex, reminding her of her brother Dan who never missed a chance to tease her.

'Thank you, I've been working on it.'

'Excellent job then.'

'I think so. Although I'm not sure the market traders here are terribly appreciative. Most of them pretend they can't understand a word I say. Deux pommes de terre is quite straightforward isn't?'

'Hmm it is, but didn't you just say you'd bought apples?'

'Yes. Pommes de terre,' said Nina, still irritated by the snotty attitude of the Frenchman who'd rolled his eyes and snatched the apples out of her hand to put them in a paper bag.

Alex sniggered, she could hear him. 'You do know that the direct translation is apples of the earth.'

'And?'

'Potatoes. Pommes de terre are potatoes.'

'Oh, bollocks ... of course they are. No wonder he looked at me as if I was a complete idiot. Oh God, I'd better watch out for him next time. Thank goodness there are plenty of stalls here, hopefully I won't make a complete prat of myself and run out before I go home.

'There's always Bastille market. It's on a Sunday and it's very good. Huge.'

'This one is pretty awesome,' said Nina. Even now her eye was caught by the gorgeous contrast of a display of green beans fanned out in a wooden box, bordered by scarlet tomatoes and the delicious touch of oranges and lemons still adorned with leaves. 'We just don't have this at home. It makes you want to cook.'

She'd just walked past a stall selling a huge variety of lettuce leaves, all laid out in individual boxes, bright green lamb's lettuce and frisée, alongside the deep ruby red of romaine, lolla rosa and the darker green of baby spinach. In jewel-bright contrast was a box of loose cherry plum tomatoes in red, yellow and purple. It looked like an uber healthy pick'n'mix and made her mouth water.

'If you say so. I'll let you into a secret, I'm more of a beans on toast man.'

'You're not a cook?' asked Nina horrified, her eye caught by the selection of bread on the opposite side. How could you not want to cook, when all this was available? *Fougasse olive et lardons, flute tradition, grand campagne, cramique*. They all sounded so thoroughly French she wanted to wrap her tongue around the words as well as try all of the rustic looking loaves.

'Professional aversion. One, I don't really get the time ... and two, there isn't really the necessity to be honest. Working in a hotel, there's always food on tap. And it's always fancy, so every now and then—' he let out a ridiculously heavy sigh '—I long for beans on toast and a wee bit of haggis.'

Nina burst out laughing at his mournful tone. 'Haggis? Really? I think you're pulling my leg.'

'Both of them.' She could hear the sunshine and amusement in his voice. 'But I miss home-cooked every day stuff.'

'I can understand that.' Perhaps that explained why Sebastian's cupboards were quite so bare. It had been preying on her mind since she'd seen the market today, all the amazing cheese, the fresh vegetables some with the mud still clinging to their roots, huge bundles of rosemary and parsley. Of course, he had no need to cook at home. And she'd been worrying that he'd lost his cooking mojo. One of her favourite memories was him standing in front of the fridge at home being challenged by her despairing mother, who was sick of cooking the same stuff every day, to come up with something different to cook.

'Hello, Nina?'

Oops, she realised she hadn't been paying attention.

'Sorry, I missed that, the signal went ...' She trailed off to allow the sentence to lie for itself.

'I ... well I said, I'd still like to go out ... to dinner. Especially if I can persuade a gorgeous woman to go with me.'

'Oh,' said Nina, flattered and unused to this sort of blatant charm. 'So who were you thinking of?'

'Ideally Kylie Minogue, but as she's out of the country at the moment, perhaps you'd like to take her place.'

She smiled; he would get on so well with her brothers.

'Let me check my diary, it's a bit chocka at the moment. You'll have to wait in line behind Chris Hemsworth who's been on at me for a date for weeks. You know what it's like being in such big demand.'

'What if I told you I come paparazzi free?'

'Ah, you should have said. That's definitely pushed you to the top of the pile.'

'How about lunch?'

'I...' She was about to turn him down, habit more than anything else, but she was fed up with comparing everyone to Sebastian. Why not enjoy some pleasant, cheerful company for a change? 'That would be lovely.' And it would be, she was fed up with grumpy, ill-tempered companions.

Finishing the call, she wandered back through the market towards a stall she'd spotted earlier. With a big smile she caught sight of the florist's stall down the aisle. Feeling a lot brighter, she decided to spoil herself with a bunch of flowers.

'Oh, don't they look gorgeous?' said Marguerite, as Nina walked into the patisserie, feeling rather authentically French and romantic with her wicker basket and an armful of long stemmed alstroemeria, considerably more than the one bunch she'd intended.

'You look like Little Red Riding Hood after an allotment raid,' said Maddie.

'Aw, darn it,' said Nina, delighted to see the pair of them sitting in Marguerite's favourite corner by the window as she laid down the bunches of deep red, pale pink and creamy hued flowers. 'And here I was hoping for Audrey does the French market with verve and style.'

'You'll have to borrow my beret,' said Maddie with a quick grin. 'But the flowers are a good look.'

Nina laughed. 'I'd only planned to buy one bunch but the market was closing and some of these were a little damaged, so he gave me the whole lot. Far too many for me, so I thought I'd bring them here.'

'And they are a very welcome addition, they look so bright and cheerful,' said Marguerite. 'What a lovely idea. When I used to come here as a girl, they would have fresh flowers every week. The most superb displays in a rather wonderful marble planter. It used to stand just over there.' She pointed to a mirrored alcove on the opposite wall. 'I wonder whatever happened to it.'

Nina studied the spot but before she could say anything,

Maddie piped up, 'Oh gosh, that's exactly where the flowers should go. It will make the place look much nicer. It's a bit ... oops.' Her eyes danced with distinct lack of remorse. 'My tongue runs away with itself sometimes.'

Nina laughed. 'You're right. It does look a bit...'

Marguerite smiled serenely. 'It has seen better days, hasn't it, Marcel?'

He grunted as he deposited a fresh coffee on the table in front of Maddie.

'Oh, just what the doc ordered,' she said. 'Are you going to have one with me, Nina? Only my second of the day and that first one woke me up. Powered on caffeine and cheese, that's me.'

Marguerite's eyes danced with amusement. 'Well, one morning coffee is plenty for me. I have a hair appointment.' With a discreet wave of her hand, she signalled to Marcel that she'd like her bill. 'I've enjoyed your company Maddie, and lovely to see you Nina. I will see you here perhaps for morning coffee another day or at the next class.' With that she turned to Marcel and spoke in rapid French. He escorted her to the door and she gave a regal wave before she strolled away down the street.

Maddie was so easy to chat to and they whiled away a very pleasant half hour before Nina remembered that she really ought to get the flowers into water.

'Marcel, do you have anything we might put these flowers in?'

He eyed the bouquet with his usual sullen expression.

'I thought they might cheer the place up a bit.'

'It will take more than flowers.' His mouth did its familiar prune impression again. 'There might be something suitable up in the storerooms upstairs.' With a bony finger, he pointed to a door that she hadn't noticed before. Decorated with the same pink dado rail and blue paint, it blended in rather well. Now as she looked up, she could see where a staircase bit into the room behind the counter. The space had been cleverly used with a mirrored back wall and glass shelves to create a display area, although the only things displayed were a couple of bluebottle corpses.

'Ooh. A secret passage. Very Enid Blyton,' said Maddie. 'Shall we? Or do we need to stock up on lashings of ginger beer before we set out?'

'I'm far too nosy to wait for provisions,' said Nina, already itching to explore. Probably as a result of reading too much *Famous Five* as a child. It had been a good escape from a boisterous and noisy household.

'Wow, a treasure trove,' Nina said at exactly the same time as Maddie said in a disappointed voice, 'Wow what a mess.'

They both laughed as they stared around the first room they'd come across at the top of the stairs.

Maddie pointed to the assortment of furniture dotted here and there. 'Most of that looks like its seen better days.'

'It just needs a bit of TLC.' Nina ran a hand over one of the tables, sending up a puff of dust which danced in the shaft of sunlight coming in through the open window. 'Look at the detail on the feet. It's lovely.'

Next to the table was a stack of yellowing newspapers and

brittle paged magazines. Curious, Nina picked up a copy of *Paris Match*, dislodging a puff of dust, and looked at the date: 1986.

'Before I was born,' she said, letting it slip back through her fingers staring around the room in amazement. 'Do you think all this stuff has been up here all this time?'

'I guess it must have been,' said Maddie crouching down by a picture propped up against the wall, blowing on it to try and dislodge the dust.

As the other girl studied the painting, Nina crossed to one of the boxes. Kneeling down, heedless of the dirty floor, she unlaced the flaps which were interweaved to secure them, her fingers leaving marks in the dusty tops. Feeling a flutter of excitement, she lifted the newspaper-wrapped parcel out of the box.

'It's like Christmas, when you start unwrapping the decorations to put on the tree and you can't remember what's inside,' said Nina as she began to unwrap the oddly shaped parcels, shedding loosely crumpled newspaper sheets like cabbage leaves.

'Oh, isn't that gorgeous?' she exclaimed holding up a beautifully painted bone china teapot, before rummaging some more in the box. 'And these are pretty too,' she added, finding delicate pale pink china cups rimmed with gilt.

By the time both of them had rummaged through several boxes, periodically holding up the latest find with the enthusiasm of archaeologists hunting down Egyptian antiquities, they'd unearthed dozens of cups and matching saucers, china tea plates, bundles of silver forks – or at least Nina thought they were silver – jugs, sugar bowls, a box of tiny clawed silver sugar tongs and some rather gorgeous cake stands, the pretty floral-patterned china punched out with a lace pattern and topped with an ornate gilt loop.

'Wow, I love all this vintage stuff,' said Nina, her eyes shining as she stood up to brush the dust from her knees. 'I guess it all belongs to Sebastian now.'

Maddie frowned. 'Do you think he'll want to use any of it?'

'Ha! Unlikely. He's going to turn this place into a bistro restaurant, it's going to be super trendy. It will be all slate serving boards and plain white china.'

'You can't blame him. It's not exactly buzzing and the patisserie selection isn't up to much compared to other places. And this stuff is hopelessly impractical. They'd last approximately five minutes in my house,' said Maddie.

'Mine too. I've got four older brothers. In fact,' Nina said wistfully thinking of her strapping brothers and ignored the slight pang, 'I don't think they'd even make it into the house. They'd be vetoed.'

'Four brothers. Oh no! I've got two and that's bad enough. At least I've got two sisters to balance it out. No wonder you don't miss your family.'

'And where do you sit?'

Maddie pulled a rueful face. 'I'm the eldest. Which is why I'm so bossy.'

'Ha! I should have guessed,' teased Nina. 'I'm the youngest. They all think they know what I should do and try to boss me about all the time.'

'Which is why you can be direct when you need to be,' said Maddie with a quick grin. 'You know it's because they care. They've been there, got the T-shirt.'

Nina rolled her eyes with good humour. 'Yes, but I don't want to wear the same T-shirt as my brothers.'

'Fair point,' said Maddie.

Nina perused the pile of goodies. 'Still no vases, although I think I'll take a few bits and pieces downstairs,' she said, lifting up one of the pretty cake stands. 'Marcel might like one for the shop and it would be nice to a have a couple in the kitchen so everyone can display their finished wares on them. You never know, Sebastian might be impressed with the quality of the china and decide to keep some of it.'

They put the cake stands to one side and Nina carried on digging through the last of the boxes.

'Hurrah! Look.' Nina held up a heavy wide necked crystal cut glass vase with a shaky hand. It weighed a ton. 'This is perfect and...' She had to put it down hurriedly but then she pointed to a piece of furniture nestling in the corner. 'That looks exactly like the thing Marguerite was talking about. The vase will look perfect on top. Which reminds me, I really need to get those flowers into water.'

'And I really I ought to crack on with my essay,' said Maddie. 'Although I'd love to know what's in the rest of the rooms.'

'Another day,' said Nina rising to her feet.

'You have to wait for me. No sneak previews. I want to know what else is up here.'

'Er, hello, Miss This-is-a-dumping-ground. It's all junk.'

'A girl can change her mind,' said Maddie. 'Now do you want hand lugging that plant stand thing downstairs or not?'

In the end they made a couple of trips down the stairs, as Nina couldn't bear to leave the cups, plates and teapots upstairs. They had to abandon the marble plant stand in the narrow hallway behind the door to collect on another day. On their final run, when they emerged back through the door carrying one last box each, Marcel gave Nina a distinct don't-even-think-about-leaving-those-in-here look, so they went straight through to the kitchen and dumped their prizes still in their boxes under the sink.

'Ungrateful so and so,' muttered Nina. 'I'm not sure he deserves any flowers in the shop. He won't appreciate them.'

But she was happy to be proved wrong when she took them through and Marcel's mouth twitched in what might have been a near miss of a smile. 'You can put them there,' he decreed, pointing to the alcove where, magically, the marble plant stand had been placed while they were in the kitchen.

Chapter 14

'Sebastian, what a surprise. How lovely to hear from you.' Could he tell she was scowling down the phone at him? 'At last.'

'I sent you an email.'

A comment in the subject line, an attachment with a lengthy list and nothing in the body of the email, did not count. Apart from that she hadn't heard from him since he'd got in the taxi nearly a week ago.

'Is that what you call it?' Using sarcasm was the best way to disguise her disappointment at his silence, and to try and get her body to back off with its usual overexcited response at the sound of his voice. When was her heart or whatever part was in charge of the silliness – it certainly wasn't her brain – finally going to tune into sense and get the message that that boat had sailed, long ago?

'Very funny. I've been busy. Where are you?'

'In your apartment.' She rose from the table where she was having a late and rather leisurely breakfast and wandered to the window to admire the view of the Eiffel Tower. Every day when she came into the kitchen it was a welcome reminder that she'd chosen to come here, a symbol of her independence, which went a long way to appeasing the solitude of her quiet, unhurried breakfast. No one in their right mind would miss the chaos of the Hadley family orchestrated bundle in the mornings with hurried cups of builders' strength tea, bodies dodging each other as toast was grabbed and arms were thrust into coats, packed lunches swiped from the side against the sounds of Radio Two, sizzling bacon in the pan and shouts of 'anyone seen my car keys/phone/phone charger!'

Nina realised that Sebastian had gone quiet too. Was he picturing his kitchen and missing the rather wonderful view?

'Did you want something?' she asked. Of course he did, he wasn't just ringing up for a friendly chat. She was his employee if you wanted to be precise about it. That was the sum total of their relationship.

'Actually, I do. Can you bring over my chef whites when you come to the patisserie tomorrow? I should have worn them last week. Icing sugar on black doesn't look good.' Nina allowed herself a small smile. Not from where she'd been standing. That black T-shirt hugged his chest and shoulders rather nicely. No doubt about it, he had muscles in all the right places. Surprisingly well-contoured biceps. And the ugly joggers, which should have kept any illicit thoughts at bay, kept slipping down to reveal a taut stomach and a trail of dark hair. Seriously, couldn't he have kicked the stereotypical handsomeness and have the decency to be a bit pudgy around the belly after a couple of weeks of inactivity?

'OK. Where will I find them?'

'Er ... do you know what? I'm not a hundred per cent sure. They might be in the bottom of one of the chest of drawers or they might be in the top of the wardrobe or failing that in one of the boxes in the utility room. I must have brought them to France when I moved here but I can't remember where I put them.'

'Don't you wear them anymore?' Nina was astounded.

'Too busy to get in the kitchen that often. Now, is everything ready for tomorrow?'

'No,' said Nina, rolling her eyes even though he couldn't see her.

'What do you mean, no?' Sebastian's voice pitched up a level and Nina bit back a naughty smile and let the silence speak for itself for a minute.

'Of course it is.' Honestly, did he really think she would deliberately let him down? 'I can read,' she pointed out with a bite to her words, letting him know that the solitary email she'd received the day before yesterday had irked her more than the fact that she hadn't heard a single word from him since the first day of the course.

'Honestly Nina, some of us are busy. Email is the most effective way of communicating sometimes. I'm running a business. If you recall I'm trying to set up two new restaurants as well as the bistro and run the ones back in the UK. As far as I'm concerned, I've employed you to run the patisserie side of things, so that I don't have to think about it. The only input I need to make is turning up on the day and teaching. Everything else is down to you.'

Nina straightened, surprised that he was willing to let go of that much. 'I'll remember that.'

'So everything ready?'

'Yes, I've done all the shopping. I've set up all the work stations.'

'You found the wholesalers OK?'

'Mmm,' said Nina guiltily, thinking of her visit to the next best thing to a patisserie heaven.

'And you used the account there OK?'

'Ah, yes.' The wholesalers had been absolutely mind-boggling. She'd never seen such a variety of specialist ingredients in her life.

'I gave you a list.'

'You did.'

'Please tell me you stuck to it, I know how easy it is to get carried away in there.'

'I might have bought a couple of extra things, but I didn't spend as much as I could have done.'

'And I'm supposed to be thankful for that.'

'Very,' said Nina with a smug laugh. He'd got off lightly. The gold leaf had looked so intriguing, and so had the chocolate couverture and of course the praline sauce. She hadn't been able to resist any of them and had crossed her fingers when she'd signed for the account, hoping that perhaps Sebastian wouldn't check the bill too closely. Who was she kidding? At least she'd been too bamboozled by the incredible selection of highly specialised equipment to buy any of the sugar paste tools, silicon cases in a multitude of shapes and sizes or any of the array of different shaped cutters and cake tins.

'I'm relieved to hear it.' For a moment, she could have sworn she heard dry amusement in his voice.

The next morning, she walked briskly to the patisserie carrying Sebastian's chef whites, grateful that the promised rain was still holding off. At this time of day, the wide tree-lined street was calm and pedestrian free, the quiet broken by the occasional scooter. It had taken her ages to find the white jacket with Sebastian's name embroidered on the chest in red italics. A fair amount of cursing him had gone on until she'd finally found the darned things, buried at the bottom of a box in the utility room, along with a hot water bottle and an unopened pack of sensible black socks, the sort of thing your mother might pack you off with.

She was looking forward to seeing everyone again. Everyone. Not just Sebastian. They were such a lovely bunch of people and she'd really enjoyed seeing Maddie this last week. Even Marcel seemed a tiny bit more approachable, although that was relative.

Who was she kidding? As usual there was the same old stupid part of her that was a little bit tingly, the same old anticipation that danced and sang in her veins despite the stern lectures she regularly gave herself. If only when she heard his voice, she felt the same as she did when Alex, for example, had phoned up. On short acquaintance he seemed a lovely guy and there was no denying he was good looking and charming. Why didn't she get a tingle around him?

'Morning Nina.'

Jane's gentle pat on her shoulder made her realise that Peter and Jane had said it before.

'Oh, sorry.' She stopped in the street. 'Good morning. I was miles away. You're both very early. How are you? Have you had a good week?'

Peter took Jane's hand. 'We've had a wonderful week. None of the family bothering us. Just the two of us wandering around Paris. Shopping. Cooking.'

'And eating far too much,' said Jane, running a hand across her tiny waist. 'It's been bliss.' She and Peter exchanged a wry smile. 'And definitely worth coming to Paris.'

Nina sensed there was more behind their words but didn't want to be nosy. 'And are you looking forward to lesson number two?'

The three of them fell into step, bunching together as they skirted the trees that lined the wide street.

'Yes, I can't wait to get cracking. After Sebastian said it was all about science, it suddenly makes a lot more sense to me.'

Jane let out a tiny teasing sigh. 'There's just no romance in his soul. An engineer through and through. You can see what I have to put up with.'

'Romance, my darling, is my middle name.' He tucked her hand in the crook of his arm and patted it.

Once they reached the patisserie, it seemed everyone was an early bird or perhaps, Nina guessed as she watched them all greet each other like old friends, they were keen to meet up again. Maddie and Marguerite hugged each other while Jane and Marguerite exchanged quick kisses on the cheek and Bill and Peter shook hands with hearty enthusiasm. Even

Marcel raised a smile and gave Peter an approving nod as they all congregated around the counter ordering coffees.

With plenty of time before the course, they sat down and began chatting with enviable ease. Nina, sitting between Maddie and Jane, was laughing so hard at Maddie's terrible Welsh accent as she attempted to imitate a character from *Gavin and Stacey,* that she didn't hear her phone ringing until it was too late. Whoops, it was five past ten and Sebastian had texted her five minutes ago, with an impatient: *Where are you?*

It took her another few minutes to round everyone up and chivvy them along down the hall. By the time she descended the short flight of stairs into the kitchen she felt like an incompetent sheepdog. They were still chatting as they fanned out around Sebastian to their stations, in exactly the same spots as the previous lesson. Standing isolated at the bottom of the steps, the tight expression on Sebastian's face reminded Nina of a forlorn child excluded by his disability and unable to be with his peers.

Before she could frame an apology, he leaned towards her and hissed, 'I wanted my whites before we started.'

'Sorry, I bumped into Jane and Peter and then everyone was here and there was—'

'Spare me the excuses,' sighed Sebastian and with a lightening change of expression, turned to the others. 'Good morning everyone. I hope you had a good start to the day. So today we're going to making one of my favourites. Millefeuilles.'

And he was off, explaining the history of the pastries and the different ways of filling and presenting them. Today's lesson was going to be more about technique and practical skills, which put Nina on a much better footing. Pastry, she could do. Nothing fancy but she knew what she was doing. Cold hands, cold fat, minimal contact – she knew the rules.

Over the course of the morning, as Sebastian taught them how to make puff pastry, Nina darted here and there, collecting bowls, wiping up flour and rounding up utensils but she also helped guide Jane's hands on the rolling pin when her pastry threatened to go AWOL over the edge of the worktop, showed Peter how to be more gentle with rubbing his butter into his flour and demonstrated to Maddie how to liberally coat her rolling pin with plenty of flour to stop it sticking to the pastry. A couple of times Sebastian's eye caught hers as she was helping one of them and he would give her a quick nod as if to say, 'good job'. Despite his best efforts he was still slow, his progress cumbersome around the kitchen and he couldn't quite get to people to help before their pastry went pear shaped. Leaving Nina to it, he focused on Bill and Marguerite, who both seemed to have a pretty good idea of what they were doing. Both had some previous experience.

'Good job, Nina,' said Sebastian, when the others headed for their lunch break.

'Thanks,' she said, still miffed that he'd been so short with her earlier. Turning away from him, she began filling the sink full of hot soapy water.

'I owe you an apology. And I should have said thanks for looking after me the other night when you came back to the hotel with me'

She shrugged but didn't turn around.

'Nina, please look at me.'

With a disgruntled sigh and a pursed mouth, she turned around slowly and folded her arms.

'I'm sorry, I've been difficult this morning.'

'Do you know what, sometimes sorry doesn't cut it.' Was that really her speaking? But hell yes, she was fed up with him taking out his bad moods on her. 'And difficult doesn't even cover it. I get that you're frustrated, that your leg bothers you, fine. But you manage to be civil to everyone else.'

Sebastian had the grace to wince. 'Before you get into another snit with me, I was about to say, you've been great this morning. Anticipating things and really saving me moving about too much. I'd forgotten how many things can go wrong with pastry and amateurs.'

'I think there's a compliment in there somewhere,' said Nina, trying to sift through what he meant. She had to admit he was a very good teacher, explaining things with great patience and never making anyone feel stupid when they asked a question, even her.

'I wasn't being funny. It's so long since I've made puff pastry, but it's still second nature to me. So when someone over rubs the fat or adds too much water, I have to take a second to catch up whereas you were straight on it.'

'Years of incompetence,' said Nina completely blank-faced.

'You manage to misread what I say so often, I wonder if you do it on purpose.'

'Maybe because you underestimate me so often,' said Nina with a snap, immediately regretting it when she realised she'd let some of her resentment towards him show.

'I've never underestimated you,' said Sebastian, looking a little nonplussed.

Nina stared back at him. 'You mean you don't still think of me as Nick's little sister.'

Sebastian looked pained for a brief second before muttering. 'I try hard not to.'

Sebastian and Nina were standing to one side of the kitchen while the others had gathered around one of the benches, where the last of the mille-feuilles to be completed had been arranged on the stands for the official tasting session at the end of the day. Marcel had just brought coffee through and was invited to take the first bite.

'Very good,' he said, with his usual dignified air, having studied them carefully before selecting one from the middle tier. 'Excellent. Who made this one?'

Everyone laughed, before Maddie said, 'Of course, that's one of Sebastian's.' She rolled her eyes.

Marcel's mouth twitched, it might almost have been a smile. Sebastian stepped forward and took a small bow while flashing everyone a charming smile before stepping back.

'I meant to ask you, where did the cake stands come from? They're a nice touch.'

'I found them up in one of the rooms upstairs. There's a ton of stuff up there. China, cutlery, furniture. It's all—'

'Going in a skip. I'd forgotten there was all that junk up there.'

'But some of it's lovely.'

'And of no use to me.'

'But you like the cake stands.'

'Only in so far as they're useful today.'

'But you can't just throw all that stuff away.'

'I can if it's never going to be used. It's just not a good use of time to go through it all. I've got a business to run, if I was going into the salvage business, that's what I'd have done.'

Ignoring Nina's horrified face, Sebastian hobbled over to the group and helped himself to a coffee.

The man was a business automaton. How could he even think of throwing away all that beautiful china? Nina shook her head and picked up a broom to start sweeping up the near sand dune piles of flour on the floor. As she passed the back door, she saw it open and a very svelte blonde woman step inside.

'Bonjour,' she said before rattling along in a stream of very fast French. The only word that Nina could distinguish was 'Sebastian' but of course pronounced very sexily as if there were about ten 'n's on the end of his name.

'He's over there.' She indicated with her head in case this woman didn't speak English.

'Ah bon. Merci.' The woman flashed her a thousand-watt smile and tapped across the floor in extremely elegant high heeled shoes which did fantastic things to her already amazing legs.

'Sebastian, cherie,' she called, as without any hint of self-consciousness she waded through the crowd of people around him and planted her plump plum painted lips on his.

'Katrin.' He glanced at his watch. 'You're early.'

She shrugged, the languorous movement somehow chic and effortless, like a gentle wave rolling up her body.

'Everyone, this is, Katrin. Sorry, I'll be just a minute.'

'Hello everyone, lovely to meet you.' Suddenly her English was impeccable as she fluttered her eyelashes at Bill and Peter who both looked slightly dazed.

Sebastian finished up, making his goodbyes to the others and Katrin came to stand by the back door, a bit like a bouncer, clearly keen to get him out of there.

Nina had never felt more at a disadvantage in her life. Limp-haired, sugar-stained and sweaty, she took in the other woman's pristine fuchsia pink linen shift dress, the itty bitty black Chanel leather handbag dangling from her wrist and the discreet, expensive-looking jewellery adorning her wrist and ears.

'You must be Nina, Nick's little sister,' Katrin suddenly volunteered as she intercepted Nina's curious gaze. 'I've heard a lot about you.' Her smile was wide and winsome, showing off perfect teeth framed by fuschia pink glossy lips.

'Oh,' Nina shot a glance towards Sebastian, surprised.

Katrin tittered, Nina's lest favourite word ever, but at that moment oh-so-appropriate.

Well, I've heard very little about you. Unfortunately, as the cattiness gene had bypassed her, Nina couldn't bring herself to say it out loud.

'Yes, I was there when your brother, how do you say it, begged Sebastian to give you this job.' She shook her head as if very amused. 'He really didn't want to. I don't think he likes you very much.' Her broad smile, with eyes holding just that touch too much twinkle, didn't take the sting out of her words, not that Nina suspected for a second they were supposed to.

'Sebastian is my brother's friend, not mine,' said Nina, clutching the broom in her hand, feeling horribly like Cinderella as Sebastian hobbled towards them on his crutches.

'But of course. Ah Sebastian cherie, shall we go. I am taking you out to dinner at the most divine little restaurant. You will love it. Very exclusive.'

She missed the slow weary blink of Sebastian's eyes as she brushed down her dress but Nina spotted it. The man was exhausted. The last thing he needed was to go out for dinner. And he was moving more slowly, a sure sign his leg was hurting. She stepped forward, unable to help herself.

'You OK?' she asked before adding in a jokey way, 'Been taking your painkillers?'

Sebastian gave her a half-hearted smile. 'Busted, Nurse Nina.'

'Painkillers?' pouted Katrin. 'Oh darling, why didn't you say?' She gnawed at her lip. 'I don't know if I'll be able to get another reservation at this place.'

'Don't worry, I'll be fine.' He gave her a reassuring nod. 'I'll take one now and I'll be as right as rain.'

She patted him on the arm. 'Oui, ma cherie. A man like you doesn't like a fuss.' She shot Nina a dry look which Nina interpreted as, 'Ha! what do you know'.

Nina shrugged and watched as he pulled out the packet of tablets and punched two out of the blister pack onto his palm and then looked across at the sink on the other side of the room where the rest of the group were now rinsing out their coffee cups. Nina picked up her broom and began to sweep up again and as she passed by Sebastian she said, 'I'd offer to get you a glass of water, but I know you don't like a fuss.'

With a resigned look, his mouth flattening, he picked up his crutches and swung his way over towards the sink. Nina ignored the brief pang of guilt. If he needed help, Katrin could pitch in.

Chapter 15

'Bonjour.' Marcel rushed over to relieve Nina of her dripping umbrella.

'Bonjour. Yuk, that rain is awful. It's just like home. Whatever happened to Paris in the spring?'

'This is Paris in the spring, we're not so far from London. What did you expect? Leslie Caron dancing through the streets?'

Nina blinked warily. 'I don't know who Leslie Caron is.'

'Dancer. Film. *An American in Paris*,' said Marcel with a heavy sigh, his mournful mouth turning down even more. 'What can I do for you this morning?'

'I er ... erm. I thought I'd do some cooking.'

Thankfully Marcel didn't think there was anything odd in this and just nodded. 'Café?'

'Yes please, au lait.'

'I know how you take it.' He turned his back on her and she dithered a second. 'I'll bring it through.'

'Thank you.' Feeling dismissed, she hurried towards the kitchen. On the way there, she had decided that after the course a few days ago she would practise her choux pastry and make éclairs.

It was rather nice having the kitchen to herself and with Sebastian's training fresh in her mind as well as his criticism, she knocked up her first batch of choux rather quickly but paying careful attention as she watched anxiously for exactly the right boiling point before she tipped in her flour. Beating the eggs into the slippery mixture seemed a bit easier and this time the icing bag didn't feel quite like she was trying to take control of a wayward python, although she wasn't sure the two dozen éclairs she piped out were anywhere near professional standards but, she told herself, they were a start. Playing it safe, as they were baking in the oven she made up a batch of coffee cream to go into the middle and coffee icing for the top.

'More café?' Bearing a small cup and saucer and placing it on the kitchen work bench beside her, Nina decided that Marcel's question was definitely rhetorical and judging by his quivering nose, his sudden thoughtfulness had more to do with abject curiosity.

'What are you making?'

'I'm attempting éclairs, but don't get your hopes up.' She tilted her head towards the oven. 'It's my first time solo, so I'm not expecting much but I just wanted to practise.'

'At least the kitchen is being used.' Marcel did a slow three-sixty. 'Once upon a time, this kitchen would have been full of people. Working from midnight to make the day's pastries and the baguettes.'

'Did they make everything here?'

'Yes. And now it is delivered by a van from a factory unit on the outskirts of Paris.' Marcel's lip curled. 'I preferred the old ways. No wonder we have no customers.'

Nina thought it might also have something to do with the tatty exterior, which was hardly welcoming.

'And what's in the boxes?' he asked, poking a finger at the larger of the two boxes that Nina had pulled out from under the sink.

'Some old cutlery and china. Look.' She took out a plate and a tea cup and saucer. 'Aren't they pretty?'

Marcel's face brightened and he stroked the plate reverentially. 'These were used when my wife and I used to come here.'

'Well, if Sebastian decides to get rid of them, maybe your wife might like one as a souvenir?' she suggested.

His eyes went flat and dull, his mouth firming. 'She's dead.' He withdrew his hand from the plate as if it had burnt him and with an abrupt turn, almost clicking his heels together, left the kitchen.

OK, so they weren't about to win a star baker award but she was quite pleased with her éclairs and if she said so herself, the slightly bittersweet coffee cream centre combined with the sweet coffee flavoured icing was a pretty good combo.

Arranging the best of them on one of the pretty china cake stands, she took them through to the patisserie to show Marcel who, despite his disinterested demeanour, had popped back into the kitchen several times to see how she was getting on. She rather thought he had a bit of a sweet tooth and wanted to try one.

'Here you go, Marcel,' she called, walking up from the kitchen into the shop.

His eyes widened and his mournful mouth suddenly lifted in a broad proud beam lighting up his whole face.

'Hey Nina,' Maddie's cheerful voice came from the corner where she was sitting with Marguerite. 'How are you? And what are you doing here? Is scorching Sebastian with you?'

'Hi, Maddie,' said Nina with a laugh. 'No, he's probably tucked up with—' she lowered her voice to a breathy whisper '—Katrin.'

'Blimey, I thought she was going to knock herself out with those eyelashes. They had a life of their own.'

'Mm, but she was very gorgeous. Perfect for Sebastian. He likes the glam type.'

Marguerite let out a very elegant snort. 'I'm not sure Sebastian knows what he wants or more importantly what he needs. I don't see Katrin, attractive as she is, as perfect for Sebastian. He needs someone more supportive and interested in his needs.'

'Oh, I think she was all for servicing his needs,' said Maddie raising her eyebrows. 'The way she was stroking his chest! Although how she thought he'd manage to get his leg over with that cast, I don't know.'

Nina wrinkled her nose thinking of the half-used pack of condoms and then wished she hadn't.

'I though you had work to do,' she said suddenly to Maddie, changing the subject.

Maddie smiled. 'I do. This is procrastination of the highest order. I brought my laptop with me and I thought I'd do some work here, but Marguerite was here and now you are. Beats being in the studio on my own.'

'That's a good idea. And I'm here on my own. No Sebastian. I just thought I'd check a few things.' Her eyes met Maddie's. 'And I was a bit fed up with *Once Upon a Time*.' They both smiled, united by the realisation that this rather scruffy patisserie was the only place they could both think of coming to. Somehow it felt more like home than anywhere else at the moment and it was comforting to see Marguerite, Maddie and Marcel's friendly faces, not that until now Marcel had looked particularly friendly. She walked up to their table, passing Marcel who was hissing something at her from the corner of his mouth.

She looked uncertainly his way.

He hissed again. 'Wait.'

'Wow, they look delicious. I'm not sure even if I practise every day for the rest of my life, my éclairs are ever going to look like that.' With a teasing smirk, Maddie narrowed her eyes. 'Did you make them?'

'Yes!' Nina shook her head. 'Cheeky mare. What do you think, Marguerite?'

'They do look rather lovely,' said Marguerite with a regal tilt of her head.

'I wouldn't go quite that far. Would you like to try one?' asked Nina, suddenly rather proud of her slightly misshapen éclairs. 'Fresh from the kitchen.'

'Ooh yes, please,' said Maddie. 'They look yummy.'

'I'm not sure about that,' said Nina. 'But I'm hoping they'll taste OK.'

'*Excusez-moi.*' With several rapid steps, Marcel had zoomed out of from behind his counter with a speedy self-importance reminiscent of Manuel from *Fawlty Towers*. '*Un moment, si-vous-plait*.' Without further ado he whipped the plate from her hand and whisked it away and disappeared back into the kitchen.

The three women exchanged uncertain glances.

'Do you think I've offended him or something? I know they're not as good as Sebastian's,' said Nina.

'Yes, but they look a million times better than any of ours on the course the other day. And as they say, the proof of the pudding is in the eating.'

'Which we may never get to do if he doesn't bring them back. What is he doing?' From beyond her, there was a sudden shout.

With a frown she looked back to where Marcel had now reappeared, suddenly making a lot of noise.

'Voila!' And with a rattle of china and spoons, like magic, Marcel stood in front of them with a hastily assembled tray.

'Allow me,' he said, bearing it with pride to the table. Nina smiled at the sight of the china tea plates and silver forks she'd rescued from upstairs, which sat on the tray along with some neatly pressed damask napkins. With great finesse and careful attention to each place setting, he laid out the plates and forks in front of Marguerite and Maddie, before laying two more at the empty places. He pulled out one of the chairs for Nina to sit down.

'Excuse me.' With a precise little bow, he dipped at the waist, and then scuttled over to the doors, where he bolted them top and bottom and then with his nose in the air he minced back to the table and sat down. 'This should be done properly. These are the first patisseries to be baked and eaten here for over ten years. The occasion should be marked. It may never ever happen again.'

'It's a terrible shame this place is going to close,' said Maddie. 'I kinda like coming here. I mean it's nothing special but ... it feels sort of homey. Does he have to close it?'

Nina suddenly felt the need to defend Sebastian. 'I don't think it's making any money.'

Marguerite raised one refined eyebrow but didn't say anything. Nina swallowed, recognising her as the sort of person who often left silences to fill themselves, the pressure of which weighed so heavy, you often found yourself volunteering to do something or agreeing a donation to the cause.

After a pause, where Nina was sure Marguerite was working out her total game plan, there was a rustle as the older lady finally picked up her napkin. 'Well, this looks rather wonderful,' she said, as Marcel jumped to his feet.

'Allow me, Madame.' He took the damask cloth from her and shook it out before laying it on her lap with the serious drama of a matador with his cape. 'Nina, as pastry chef, would you like to do the honours?' He handed her a pair of forks.

As she served the éclairs he poured coffee from a slightly chipped glass cafetière.

'Bon appétit,' he said and picked up his fork as everyone followed suit.

Metal clinked against china and then there were a few seconds of silence.

'Mmm.'

'Excellent.'

'Très bien.' Marcel nodded and closed his eyes.

'Oh my goodness, Nina. This is divine,' exclaimed Maddie.

'It's very good, my dear,' said Marguerite. 'A fine balance of bitterness and sweetness. That coffee cream is excellent and the icing isn't too sweet. And the choux is lovely and light.'

Nina nodded. 'They've turned out well. Next time I need to make them look a bit prettier.'

'They look fine,' said Maddie loyally as Marguerite and Marcel smiled.

'I don't think you could sell them, looking like this,' said Nina.

'A question of practice, that's all,' said Marguerite. 'The taste is what's important.'

Two cups of coffee turned into three before the rattle of the door disturbed them as Maddie was midway through talking about a fascinating lecture she'd been to on the history of the guillotine and its use in Paris.

Marcel let out another one of his sighs. 'I suppose I must let them in.'

With ill-concealed bad grace, he marched over to the door, slid open the bolts and threw it open, and without saying a word went back to his usual position behind the counter.

'Do you think it's open?' asked a diffident voice in an American accent.

'Honey, the man opened the door, didn't he?'

'Yes but he didn't look very happy about it.'

'Don't worry about him,' called Marguerite with a royal wave. 'He's always like that.'

The middle-aged American couple in their sensible walking trousers and tennis shoes folded up the maps they both carried, as if neither trusted the other not to miss something, nodded and smiled at Marguerite with that not-sure-if-she's-joking restraint before sitting down at a table on the other side of the room.

Almost immediately another, slightly younger couple came in behind them and took another table.

'Blimey, it's the most people I've ever seen in here,' said Nina, 'Although it is still raining. They probably wanted to shelter from the rain.'

'Well, this place did have quite a reputation in its day. I quite often meet tourists who've been sent here by friends or relatives who came ten years ago.' Marguerite's eyes darkened. 'It's such a shame to see them disappointed. It used to be the most wonderful place.' With a blue veined handed she tapped the china cake stand. 'And I haven't seen these used properly for many years. I remember coming here when my son was little. My husband would give him some Francs, so that my son could bring me here for coffee and pastries. It was always a big occasion and we would spend a long time choosing.' She pointed to the long glass counter, which was empty apart from the front section, which held a limited selection of uninspiring gâteaux, fruit tartes and croissants. 'The entire length of the counter was filled with Paris-Brest, macarons, mille-feuilles, rum babas and so many more. It was so colourful and pretty.'

'Mattieu's favourite thing was the chandelier. There used to be a huge one suspended, just there.' She looked up at the plaster rose in the centre of the room. 'He thought it looked like diamonds. He was such a happy little boy.' Her lip quivered and Nina wanted to lay a hand on hers. 'And now he lives in England.'

'How often do you see him?' asked Nina.

'I haven't seen him for two years. He and his wife are getting divorced. They have two children, Emile and Agatha, but because they are still fighting over the divorce and custody rights, he is not allowed to bring the children out of the country and of course he wants to spend all the holidays with them.'

'Oh that's a shame. Will your ex-daughter-in-law not let you see them?'

Marguerite lifted her shoulders in elegant despair. 'I don't know. We always used to get on so well. I haven't spoken to her since Mattieu left her.' Her mouth firmed. 'He's an idiot. I don't care about seeing him.'

Maddie and Nina both looked startled.

'Just because he's my son doesn't mean I don't recognise an idiot when I see one. Oh no, the foolish boy has run off with his secretary. Fine but be discreet if you must do that sort of thing and not when there are children involved. He was always a greedy boy. What? You look as if I'm not being very maternal. It's the children I miss and Sara, his wife. She was a lovely girl.'

'Have you tried talking to her?' asked Maddie. 'If you told her that you thought your son was an idiot, she'd probably love you.'

Marguerite shook her head. 'I didn't like to at first, I didn't

want to interfere and now it has been so long. I don't know …
but I miss the children. I'm so looking forward to seeing them
in the summer but I'm worried they won't remember me.'

'You should Skype them,' said Nina, suddenly feeling guilty,
as she'd deliberately avoided doing that with her mum. 'My
brother used to do that when he was in Australia last year. I
think your daughter-in-law would probably be glad to hear
from you.' Then she realised that Marguerite was well into
her seventies and might not have the technological facilities.
'Do you have a computer or a tablet?'

'I have a laptop which my son bought me. He set it all up
for me so that I can play online bridge,' she said rather proudly
before adding, 'But then he's always complaining that I never
respond to his emails. I daren't admit I can't remember how
to find them.'

'Would you like some help?' asked Nina. 'Not that I'm a
computer whiz but I know the basics.'

'That would be very kind of you. It's rather heavy though,
would you mind coming to my apartment.'

'Not at all. If you don't mind.'

'Well, I can't promise you homemade patisserie, but perhaps
you'd like to come for lunch on Saturday. Both of you.'

'I'm a student,' said Maddie. 'I never turn down free food.
Yes please. And I need something to fortify me, I've got an
essay to hand in in three days' time and I haven't started yet.'

'That would be lovely, but…' Nina shot a quick glance at
Maddie, not wanting to deprive her of a free meal but not
wanting to take advantage of the older woman. 'You don't
need to do that. I wouldn't want you to go to any trouble.'

'Spoilsport,' said Maddie with a good-natured groan.

'It's no trouble and it will make a very lovely change to have the company of two young people.' Her eyes twinkled. 'Most of my neighbours are either almost dead or extremely dull.'

Suddenly as they were finalising arrangements for Operation Skype, Marcel appeared and whisked the cake stand away. Nina watched him take it over to the American couple's table, where he served them each an éclair.

'He can't do that,' she whispered in horror, putting her hands on her cheeks.

'He just did,' said Maddie with a chuckle.

'But they're not...'

'Not what? Fit for human consumption?' teased Maddie. 'They tasted jolly good to me.'

Nina bit her lip. 'But ... I'm not ... you know qualified or professional.'

Marguerite patted her hand. 'I wouldn't worry, *n'est ce pas*. Marcel's a stickler. If he didn't think they were good enough to eat, he wouldn't serve them.'

'But...' And now the waiter was taking the cake stand over to the other couple! What was he doing? Perhaps he was offering them on the house. Yes, that would be fine. He couldn't possibly charge for them.

It was only when she'd bade goodbye to Marguerite and Maddie and finished tidying up the kitchen, that she discovered that not only had Marcel been charging customers for the éclairs, but that he'd sold every last one and was insisting she came back the following day to make a fresh batch.

151

Chapter 16

Marguerite's voice greeted her through the intercom at the pair of handsome wooden doors that led off the street into a pretty courtyard full of potted trees and gravelled paths rather like a secret garden, the tidy landscaping a sharp contrast with the wide boulevard beyond.

Following her instructions Nina walked through to a second courtyard and to another set of wooden doors where the older woman waited for her.

'Morning, Nina. Do come in.'

'Thank you. This is lovely,' Nina pointed to the courtyard. 'You'd never know it was here. It's beautiful.'

'Thank you.' Marguerite inclined her head and led the way inside, walking briskly in her elegant low-heeled court shoes, her pale-blue-tinged grey hair perfectly styled.

'Watch the wheelchair. I had a hip replacement last year and haven't got rid of the horrible thing yet. I refused to use it.' If it was possible she tipped her head even higher in the air, her disdain quite clear as she skirted the offending item.

Despite being at home she was dressed immaculately in a blue silk dress with a wide collared cropped jacket, a classic vintage style that it looked as if it might be something Chanel had designed. Nina was glad she'd made a bit of effort and had changed into smart black trousers rather than her usual jeans as they passed through a wide hallway lightly perfumed by the roses in tall white china vases placed on little onyx tables in front of large gilt-edged mirrors. Marguerite pushed through another pair of tall doors into a high-ceilinged room. Magazines and books were scattered on the table, a piece of crochet abandoned on one of the sofas and there were lots of family photos in silver frames on a large, round, highly polished table in an alcove in the corner. Many were of Marguerite and a very handsome man and more of a good-looking boy in various stages of growth. The more recent photos at the front of the table were sparse. The boy had become a man, and was pictured with a bride. There were a couple of baby photos and then two gap-toothed children in what were clearly school photos, with the familiar cloudy blue background that seemed to be universally favoured.

'This is your family?' asked Nina, immediately drawn to the table, thinking of the huge collection of photos at home that her mum carefully curated to ensure that despite constant new additions, there was always a faithful representation of the decades of family life.

'That was my husband, Henri, and my son, Mattieu. Henri died six years ago.'

'I'm sorry. How long were you married?'

Marguerite's blue eyes misted. 'Over forty years.'

'You must miss him,' said Nina, unable to imagine what that must be like. Living on her own felt strange enough and quite liberating at the moment but, she realised with a sense of relief, it was finite. What must it be like if someone you loved was never coming back?

'I do,' said Marguerite. 'But I can't imagine sharing my life with anyone else.'

'Do you have any other family?' asked Nina.

'No, my sister died before my husband. She had two daughters, one of whom lives in Switzerland and the other in America.'

'So, you have no family in France?'

Marguerite gave her a brave smile. '*Non*, sad eh? You have family?'

Nina nodded. 'A big, noisy, interfering family. I love them but it's nice to be away from them. To be myself.'

Marguerite nodded, with a serene smile. 'Ah, we're never satisfied. I would very much like to have a family around me.'

Nina shook her head. 'And I want to get away from mine. But today we're going to try to connect you back up. Where's this laptop then?'

By the time Maddie arrived in a whirl of scarves and layers, apologising profusely, Nina had helped Marguerite to set up a Skype account, downloaded the application onto her laptop and get her into her email.

'Well, that deserves lunch,' said Marguerite.

'Can I help? asked Nina.

'Actually, I'd like you to do something for me.' A ghost of a smile hovered at the older woman's lips.

Nina gave her a quizzical look as Marguerite took a

notebook and fountain pen from the console table behind her and opened it. Writing in beautiful flowing script, she quickly drew up a list of five names. 'While I go and ring Sara, my daughter-in-law, on the telephone, you should see if you can find these places on the...' She waved a hand towards the computer.

'The web,' supplied Maddie helpfully.

Marguerite nodded and left the room.

'I can't decide whether to be intimidated by her or not.'

'Me neither,' said Nina, 'but I think she's lovely – just very old school. And she's been on her own for a long time and is probably used to speaking her mind. Things always sound more direct in another language, don't you think?"

Nina had to update Marguerite's web browser which was several versions out of date, and then she typed the first name in the search engine.

'Ladurée, I've heard of that,' said Maddie. 'It's on the Rue Royale just up from Place du Concord. There's usually a queue outside. It's very fancy.'

'And famous for its pastries. Oh my, look at that.' The screen was filled with images of amazing looking cakes. Suddenly Nina felt that her éclairs were horribly amateur.

'Oh God, I can't believe that Marcel was actually selling them yesterday. I haven't got a clue. Just look at these chocolate éclairs. They make mine look like a Reliant Robin next to a Ferrari.'

'Don't be silly,' said Maddie 'They tasted delicious.'

'And my dear, you had the balance of flavours.' Marguerite reappeared at the door. 'Patisserie is just as much about the marriage of flavours, that delicate balance. It takes real skill to get it right.'

Nina felt a quick heat suffuse her face. She'd done a lot of tasting of the cream filling and pleased as she was with the results, it was nice to hear someone else praise the 'delicate balance' although she still thought that the cream could perhaps have had a bit more coffee flavour.

Nina was glad that Maddie was with her, otherwise she might not have felt quite as at ease. Even though they were eating in the kitchen, the table looked like a 'Summer in Provence' styled *World of Interiors* photoshoot. It had been laid with a checked table cloth, coordinating table mats, matching napkins in pretty china napkin rings and large chunky pottery bowls. The rustic style place settings looked bright and colourful, as if a sunbeam was playing on the table and the rural feel was enhanced by the earthenware bowl of fat olives and basket of sliced baguette in in the centre of the table.

'This looks wonderful, Marguerite,' said Maddie. 'Can we do anything to help?'

'No,' said Marguerite, firmly. 'You are my guests. Now I do hope neither of you are vegetarian or anything. I never thought to ask.'

'I eat anything,' said Maddie. 'Comes of being from a large family.'

'Me too,' giggled Nina. 'My brothers all have healthy appetites. You have to get in quick. A minute's hesitation and you've had it.'

'Say that again. I've known my brother to steal a Yorkshire pud from my plate.'

'Or the last meatball you've been saving.'

'And the special bit of crackling.'

'Soo annoying!'

They both laughed in shared understanding. Then Nina had a sudden flashback: Sebastian practising one of his dishes on them and keeping the boys from stealing the last mouthfuls of sausage from her.

'You both make me very glad I only had one child,' said Marguerite, bringing over a large blue Le Creuset casserole dish, her hands wrapped in a pair of oven gloves.

'Ooh, that smells amaaazing,' said Maddie as Marguerite took off the lid. 'What is it?'

'It's a traditional cassoulet. Would you mind serving while I get the wine?'

As Nina spooned the piping hot bean and duck casserole into bowls, the older woman crossed the kitchen to retrieve the bottle of red wine sitting on the side.

As she opened it, wielding a corkscrew with consummate expertise, Maddie commented, 'Ah, that's why I love being in France. Lunchtime drinking without the guilt. At home it always feels horribly decadent. Here it's perfectly normal.'

'I find it is better to have a glass at lunchtime and if I do have a drink in the evening, I stick to having a small glass of champagne,' said Marguerite as she took her seat. 'And today I have something to celebrate.'

Marguerite had said nothing about the outcome of her phone call and Nina hadn't liked to ask in case it was bad news. Luckily Maddie had no such qualms and with a squeal dived right in there. 'You spoke to your daughter-in-law?'

'I did.' Marguerite gave a cool nod, dipping into her bowl of the delicious smelling stew.

Maddie rolled her eyes. 'And?' Her impatient delivery made Marguerite's serene, and if Nina was honest, rather snooty face, relax into a broad smile and there might even have been a hint of moisture in her sharp blue eyes.

Without taking a mouthful she dropped her spoon back into the bowl. 'It was ... très ... wonderful. Sara was very pleased to hear from me. She's going to set up a Skype account today. When the children are home from school after their bath tonight, we're going to speak.'

'That's fantastic.' Nina could tell from Marguerite's unusually rapid sentences, how excited and pleased she was.

'Bon appétit.'

'This looks wonderful, thank you. It's very kind of you to go to so much trouble.'

'It's no trouble. I like to cook.' Marguerite looked uncharacteristically wistful for a second. 'But it is nice to have an appreciative audience for a change. Wasn't it nice yesterday?' Her direct gaze made Nina feel uncomfortably under the microscope.

'What?'

'Those people eating your éclairs. Marcel offering them to customers.'

'Yes but, I wish he hadn't. They're not...'

'Yes, they are,' said Maddie shaking her head impatiently. 'What are you like?'

'I still need to improve. I ... started to train as a chef once.'

'Did you?' asked Maddie. 'You kept that quiet.'

'Actually, Sebastian inspired me. He was so passionate about food and cooking, then. He's my youngest brother's best friend. They're two years older than me and were at nursery school together. I can't remember a time when he wasn't hanging around our place. And my mother loved him, especially when he got older and got into cooking. He used our kitchen and us as guinea pigs, and the boys, well they would eat anything, but he was always very good.'

'You didn't complete the course?' asked Marguerite, with that quick insight she seemed to have.

'No,' said Nina. 'I didn't even last a month. I ... I couldn't bear to touch raw meat. I had a bit of phobia about it.'

Maddie sniggered. 'Seriously?'

Nina nodded. 'Seriously.'

'Oh God, I'm so sorry.' Maddie pressed her hands into her cheeks in sudden horror. 'You really have.'

She nodded, conscious of Marguerite's sympathetic gaze. 'Caused no end of hilarity at home too. They all didn't stop taking the p... mickey for ages. They still bring it up now.'

'That must have been disappointing.'

Nina shrugged. 'Just one of those things.' At the time the main disappointment came from not being able to have that in common with Sebastian anymore. She'd gaily imagined them holding sensible conversations, without the stupid interruptions from her brothers, where he'd listen to her opinion as they shared advice and tips.

'I guess that's why I'm interested in patisserie, no chance

of having to come into contact with raw flesh. Much safer.'

'So, are you going to train as patisserie chef?' asked Marguerite, those piercing blue eyes seeming to see more than they should.

Nina shrugged. 'Oh no. I'm never going to be good enough. I just ... well, I wanted to ... have a go. I cook a lot of cakes for the family farm shop. I wanted to try something different, but not as a career or anything. I mean look at my wonky éclairs yesterday. I still can't believe Marcel sold them. After seeing that website, I'm never going to be good enough.'

'I believe there's an English phrase. Practice makes perfect.'

Nina hastily scooped up a spoonful of cassoulet, mumbling, 'I'm just helping out until Sebastian gets back on his feet,' as she took a large mouthful, deciding not to confess that she planned to do a bit of practising in the kitchen over the next few weeks. She wanted to experiment in private and not let Marcel or anyone else near the results.

Having the kitchen to herself was an unexpected bonus. She could play with ingredients and bake to her heart's content without any critical eyes. This is what she'd come to Paris for, to immerse herself in patisserie, improve her technique and ... she had to admit, perhaps she could one day impress Sebastian just a little.

Chapter 17

Suddenly, on Tuesday, after another week of radio silence, Nina received a flurry of texts from Sebastian asking her to check on the ingredients for tomorrow.

What he didn't realise was that she'd spent the last few days in the kitchen practising her éclairs. Yesterday and Sunday, she'd made up several batches of choux and with painstaking care piped them out onto greaseproof paper in neat parallel lines, practising to get a perfect finish. She'd stored the cooked choux fingers in airtight boxes ready to fill today.

By the second batch they looked a lot more professional, and the third and fourth, almost worthy of being sold, except she had no intention of doing that. Instead she texted Maddie and suggested she gave them away in the halls of residence, as a way of breaking the ice and getting to know a few people there.

Today she'd been experimenting with a few flavoured creams and icings and had come up with a mocha éclair that she was rather pleased with, as well as a slightly more ambitious hazelnut and chocolate éclair which brought back memories of Nutella. She'd also improved her presentation skills. She'd been trawling the internet looking for ideas and after a quick trip to the wholesalers on Monday, she'd come back with some eye-wateringly expensive gold leaf and some nibbed hazelnuts for decoration.

'Café?' Marcel appeared at the door with a steaming cup, just as she was texting back a lengthy reassurance to Sebastian that everything was ready for the following morning.

Following her nose, she headed for the delicious scent with a sigh. She'd been filling the éclairs and icing the tops for the last three hours and was more than ready for a break. She'd arranged a selection on one of the cake stands, more for her own pleasure than anything else, to see how they looked. They were still a bit wonky and misshapen but she was definitely getting better.

'Thank you very much, Marcel.' Whatever else his faults, he made fantastic coffee and was very good at bringing regular caffeine injections. She'd hoped to bar his path but the minute she'd relieved him of the cup, he darted around her like a monkey hellbent on mischief.

'No, Marcel.'

'But these look even better than the last ones.'

'They're not really, well, maybe a little.'

'Excellent.' He picked up a cake stand.

'No! You can't sell them. I've promised them to Maddie. For the other students.'

'Why not? You make them. People want them. They pay money for them.'

'They're really not that good.'

Marcel took a quick bite and closed his eyes with a blissful expression.

'Délicieux. Oh, this is very, very good.' He gave her an appraising stare. 'These are very good indeed. Chocolate and coffee. And they look perfect. You have done very well.' Coming from him this was actually very high praise.

Inside, a little squirl of happiness warmed a spot in her chest. 'You think?'

'I know.' He took another bite and this time closed his eyes. 'Yes, very good flavours. The bitterness of coffee and dark chocolate with an underlying *sweetness*. You have the touch.'

'You still shouldn't be selling them,' she said half-heartedly. 'I was going to give them to Maddie for the students in her halls.'

'Pfft, they're far too good. Why not sell them?'

She gave him a quick conspiratorial sidelong glance. 'Because Sebastian doesn't know.'

'Pfft,' said Marcel with a decided sneer. 'He doesn't care.'

'But I'm just practising, they're not for sale.'

'But the customers want to buy them.'

'What customers?'

'The American couple came back especially and they sent people from their hotel around the corner. Word is spreading.'

'Rather slowly. I don't think four people constitutes a stampede.'

With one of his gallic shrugs, Marcel marched past her and loaded up her latest batch onto another of the china cake stands and when he came back for a second cake stand, she watched him go with resignation. And now she had to tackle the aftermath of all that cooking.

Mid clean up, her phone rang.

'I need you to check we have sugar thermometers and that they all work.'

'Sorry? Good morning Sebastian, how are you? How's the leg?'

He huffed down the phone. 'Sugar thermometers. Can you look for them? Ideally, we want digital ones, they're easier to use.'

'I don't remember seeing any.' Not that she had the first clue what she was looking for.

'We're making macarons and it's essential that the sugar syrup is exactly the right temperature. If you can't find any, you're going to have to go and buy some.'

'Right. Because I've got time to do that. The course is tomorrow.'

'You've got all afternoon or did you have other plans? Funny I thought you were working for me.'

'It's going to take me ages to clean up the kitchen before I even start preparing for tomorrow,' she said, looking at the state of the benches covered in flour and cream after all her experimenting.

'Why?'

She bit her lip. Oops. Of course, he had no idea that the sink was piled with pans and bowls or that there were a dozen empty egg shells strewn across the top. Making choux was a messy business, especially when you didn't have a personal tidy upper to swan around after you.

'Y – you know. I thought I'd pop in and give it a good spring clean.'

'Well, now you don't have to, you can go sugar thermometer shopping. I'll see you in the morning.'

Before she had a chance to say anything, he'd snapped off the call.

'Miserable pig,' she muttered to herself.

Chapter 18

The door opened with a crash and then a bang and then the rattle of falling crutches. Nina hurried over to find Sebastian hanging onto the doorframe, his laptop bag slung across his chest and his crutches at his feet.

'Bastard things,' he growled, hopping through the door and immediately leaning against the nearest bench. 'Can you pick up my crutches for me?'

'Good morning, Sebastian,' she trilled, deliberately chirpy – and received a scowl for her trouble. Urgh, it was going to be one of those days, was it? She scooped up the crutches and handed them to him.

'Nina,' he grunted back, settling his arms into them and swinging forward to the front of the kitchen. 'Have you got everything ready? The eggs separated. The ingredients weighed out. Sugar and water in the pan.'

'Yes,' she ground out, tempted to add, *I can read, you know.* Instead she said, 'I've done everything that was on the list.' She glanced around the kitchen. He was earlier than she'd expected but Nina was confident that she'd hidden all trace of her endeavours over the last few days. Somehow, she just felt that it would be another thing for him to disapprove of and she wasn't sure her various éclairs would pass muster by his professional standards.

Without another word he hauled his laptop over his head and dumped it before inspecting the benches, which Nina had laid out in readiness.

'You got some, then,' he said inclining his head towards the newly purchased sugar thermometers. 'Digital. Well done.'

Not a word of thanks, of course. Instead, he stumped around the kitchen like a territorial dog, checking that each preparation area had been laid out to his liking. It was impossible for him not to tweak the angle of a wooden spoon or to line up a knife in parallel with a whisk. Talk about anal.

'It's nearly nine-thirty. Don't you think you ought to go and check on today's guests? Make sure they're all here. I don't want any complaints about anyone not getting their money's worth.'

'They're all lovely, I can't imagine any of them would do that.' Nina's quick defence brought a sudden frown to his face. She wheeled around and left the cold kitchen.

Immediately she was struck by the warmth and chatter of the patisserie as she walked towards the front of the shop.

Everyone was talking away to each other, like old friends, most of the conversation focussing on the dramatic difference that Marcel had wrought with the move around of the fittings.

'It looks so much better,' enthused Maddie.

'Yes,' said Marcel, without any trace of false modesty. 'And it will look even better when I have moved the coffee machine as well.'

'Big job,' said Bill.

'*Exactement*.' A smile hovered around Marcel's mouth as he gave Peter and Bill a rather direct look.

'And you'd like us to help,' said Peter.

Marcel nodded.

'At lunchtime, if you can, or the end of the day.'

'What made you move things around?' asked Maddie.

Marcel shot Nina a look and she gave him a tiny shake of her head. She didn't want this getting back to Sebastian. What he didn't know wouldn't harm him and it was only going to be for a couple of weeks.

She was actually rather proud of the fact that when Marcel had put her éclairs in the window they had sold out.

Conscious of the clock ticking and Sebastian's uncertain temper, Nina decided to round everyone up and herd them towards the kitchen.

Everyone moved straight to what had now become their places in the U-shaped arrangement facing Sebastian who was seated at the front with his laptop open and a notebook at one side.

'Good morning, everyone. Good to see you all again. This week we are going to learn to make a French classic.' He paused for a moment as if any moment now a drum roll would follow. 'Macarons. They've been a French classic since they were made popular by the famous patisserie Ladurée in the mid-nineteenth century. You will often see pyramids of them in the windows of luxury patisseries in Paris. They are not too difficult to make—'

'Easy for you to say that,' interrupted Maddie with a flirtatious smile.

'—as long as you follow the golden rules of patisserie, that exact science.' Sebastian continued his spiel without so much as a bump in the road but he flashed Maddie a broad, playful grin. Nina felt her pulse do a little hiccough. The Sebastian she remembered. It was followed by a painful pang of regret. It was a long time since she'd seen that open, easy expression on his face when she was around. These days the smiles she got were miserly, pinched jobs as if he were holding on to them in case one got away and she took it the wrong way.

It hurt, she realised. This treading on eggshells around each other. For God's sake, when was he going to realise that it was nearly ten years ago? She wasn't that teenager anymore. Had she made a terrible mistake coming out here? Had she been less than honest with herself? In that second, she knew she had. She wanted to redeem herself with Sebastian, show him that she didn't have feelings for him and that they could be friends. And now she wasn't sure if they could even do that.

'And with science, a gadget always helps.' Sebastian held up one of the new sugar thermometers. 'Anyone know what this is?'

'I'm not sure I want to know, mate,' piped up Bill, with a dramatic wince.

Everyone laughed, including Sebastian. 'Well, if I get less than perfection from you today, you could find out! Being serious, it's a digital thermometer and for this recipe today, it's very important. Making macarons relies on making a sugar syrup by boiling sugar and water together. It needs to reach exactly 114 degrees.'

Again, Nina wondered who had discovered that. Had there been a laboratory of scientists beavering away to discover the alchemical mysteries of sugar? She envisioned them making endless batches of macarons, checking and measuring the temperature. What sort of barrage of scientific tests would have been done or would they have relied on a simple tas—

'Nina!'

She realised everyone in the class was looking at her.

'Sorry. Miles away.'

Sebastian pursed his lips in disapproval. Just what was his problem! She felt her nails dig into her palms. No one else ever made her feel quite so cross inside.

'Would you mind weighing the egg whites? While Nina's doing that, can you all start weighing out your other ingredients. And for this recipe we're very precise about the measurements so we do weigh everything.'

Once everyone had done that, he invited them all back to watch as Nina started whisking the egg whites. 'They need to be whipped enough so that you can pull them into soft peaks. If you whisk too much, the egg whites start to collapse. One way of knowing if the egg whites are ready is if they stay put when you tip the bowl. While Nina is doing that I'm going to put the water and the sugar onto boil.'

Nina carried on with the handheld beater until Sebastian raised a hand to halt her to show everyone what the mix should look like. He got her to drift a fork in to raise a soft peak.

Sebastian gave her the thermometer. 'You need to be very careful you don't splash yourself as this can give you a very nasty burn. Now for this next bit, unless you have a fixed mixer like a Kenwood or a KitchenAid, you're going to need a bit of teamwork. You need to beat the mixture as you pour in the hot syrup, pouring it down the side of the bowl and not directly onto the beaters.'

Nina switched the beaters down a notch and held her hand steady as he poured the hot mix in.

'Now you'll see the mixture start to become a little glossy and a bit stiffer.'

'Gosh, you made that look so easy,' said Jane.

'It is easy if you know what you're doing,' said Sebastian, flashing another easy smile at her wide-eyed admiration. 'Now it's your turn.'

'Mmm, that's what I was worried about,' she laughed. 'Peter, you can be in charge of the mixing.'

'Chicken,' he teased.

Their banter seemed to ripple out through the room. Bill and Maddie were already taking the piss out of each other and Marguerite had teamed up with Jane and Peter. They all seemed to be getting on beautifully. That just left her and Sebastian, who was still treating her with stiff formality, which was ironic given they'd known each other at least five times longer than anyone else in the room.

As soon as they broke for lunch, Marcel commandeered Peter and Bill to move the coffee machine, so that it was now back behind the counter which had been moved so that the end cabinet was in the window. The change made the patisserie feel a little cosier and left one long wall exposed.

'What's this? asked Peter, pointing to a patch of wall where the panelling didn't quite meet.

Marcel gave one of his shrugs. 'The old décor, I believe. Once, the walls were all hand-painted,' he said with a twist to his mouth.

'I remember,' said Marguerite. 'Wasn't it *Neptune's World*, where the sea and the sky met. Very detailed and pretty. But that was a long time ago.'

'They probably put the panels over the top to hide the wear and tear,' said Peter knowledgeably. 'A quick decorating fix rather than get someone in to repaint it.'

'It's a shame,' said Jane.

'It is, as it was once rather beautiful in here,' agreed Marguerite.

'Personally, I think the outside could do with a good lick of paint,' said Bill. 'It wouldn't take much. A day or two's hard work at the most.'

'I don't know what Sebastian's plans are,' said Nina, 'but—'

'Well, he's going to have to do something with the outside,' said Maddie. 'And you've still got paying customers at the moment.'

'More customers,' said Marcel. 'The Americans come back every day and they brought friends. Word is spreading about Nina's éclairs.'

'Maybe we could paint the outside one weekend,' said Bill. 'I've got some mates coming to stay soon. It would give the lads something to do.'

'They're coming to Paris and you want them to do DIY.' Nina laughed. 'Seriously.'

'Nina, love. They're not the museum and art gallery type. They're coming for the craic and cheap booze and a free floor to sleep on.'

'Well, it's very kind of you but I don't think—

'That's a great idea,' said Maddie. 'I'm free most weekends. I'd love to help. Any of them single?'

Bill gave her a grin. 'Don't tell me a gorgeous girl like you doesn't have a fella?'

Maddie grinned back and indicated her curvy body. 'I know, shocking isn't it, when I'm a goddess.'

'Don't do yourself down, love. You look grand just as you are.'

'That would be excellent,' said Marcel, quickly turning the subject back to the painting, snatching at the opportunity before it was completely side-tracked. 'The place needs some love.'

'But we can't,' said Nina, feeling that things were spiralling out of control before her very eyes. 'Not without Sebastian's permission – besides he's planning a refurbishment in a few months, so it will be a complete waste of time.' Given the mood boards she'd seen for his projects, she was guessing that the interior would be undergoing a complete revamp to create the kind of sophisticated décor that Sebastian was aiming for but she hadn't seen any plans for the exterior.

'So he won't mind,' said Maddie. 'If he's planning to change it anyway, he's not going to worry.'

'But ... but who will pay for the paint? I can't ask Sebastian.'

'The éclair money,' said Marcel, triumphantly waving a jar of Euros.

'What?'

'I've been keeping the money separately. We can use it for the materials.'

'Great!' chorused Bill and Maddie, fist bumping each other.

'No. We. Can't,' said Nina with a touch of desperation. 'It's still Sebastian's money, he paid for the ingredients.'

'So take that out,' suggested Peter. 'Although what about your labour? Is he paying you for that?'

'Sort of.'

'He's paying you full time?'

'Ah…' Nina stuttered to a halt. Sebastian was paying her for two days a week. She'd definitely done more than that, although she was benefiting by practising her skills. And maybe the patisserie deserved to go out in a blaze of glory.

'Exactly!'

By the end of lunch there was an air of suppressed excitement. Operation Éclair had been agreed with Bill as self-appointed foreman.

'Me-an-the-lads can get here early. Me-an-the-lads can strip the paint. Me-an-the-lads can sand. Then we'll need to prime the wood.' He opened his mouth to draw breath again and everyone joined in. 'Me-and-the-lads.' He stopped and grinned. 'They're grand lads. From my old unit. Salt of the earth and good workers. And when we've done all the hard work, you lot can set to with paintbrushes.'

Even Marguerite was planning to come along as provisions supplier. Jane and Peter had plans for the Sunday but would help on Saturday.

'And I can help direct everyone,' said Maddie. 'I've got the bossy credentials.'

Bill and Peter folded their arms in united scepticism.

'Some men like to be told what to do,' said Jane, with a teasing glint in her eye.

'And some don't,' Peter mock growled back.

When Nina nipped back to the kitchen ahead of the others to warn Sebastian of their imminent return, he was on his mobile, his laptop set up in front of him. 'I don't care, Patrice, it has to be done this Friday. The cookers are arriving on Monday and the electricians need to have got all the wiring done.'

He looked up and checked his watch, his mouth firming in a line of frustration. 'I gotta go. I'm teaching this bloody course. I'll speak to you later but make sure those electricians realise they're not getting paid if the work isn't done in time for the cooker's arrival.'

He snapped off his phone and put it down, his gaze coming to rest on Nina.

'Bloody course,' echoed Nina.

He didn't answer.

'Really?'

Sebastian sighed. 'What do you want me to say? It's not as if I object to any of them but I'm only running it to fulfil the terms of the sale. I really don't have time for it, I could be doing a hundred other things.'

'They all have a reason to be here. You should respect that.'

'I do respect it.'

'So you should be making a bit more of an attempt to teach them.'

'What are you talking about?'

'Macarons. There are hundreds of flavours and colours. What are you doing?'

For a second, Sebastian looked hunted and she knew she'd got him. Since she'd been to Marguerite's, she'd been busy researching patisserie online. Macarons were big news in Paris.

His body language told her everything she needed to know although to be honest she'd know him long enough to know that he already knew he was taking a shortcut.

'I'm teaching them the basics. Patisserie takes years of training. No one is ever going to be an expert after seven weeks.'

'Yes, but you're not making any effort to show off or show them what could be achieved, are you?'

Sebastian looked mulish.

'Are you?' It made a change for her to feel that she was the one in the right and she pressed her advantage. 'You didn't ask me to buy any special colourings or flavourings.'

'I don't need to. I'm teaching them how to make macarons. What more do you want?'

'I want you to put some effort in. They're good people. You're short changing them. Plain macarons with vanilla buttercream isn't that adventurous.'

'If they wanted adventure they'd be kayaking down the Amazon or hiking up to Machu Picchu,' retorted Sebastian.

'Or you could show them how to include raspberry coulis to make rich pink-coloured macarons – or yuzu-flavoured cream. The possibilities are endless.'

'That's not why they're here.'

Nina looked up sharply at him, surprised. She knew that, but did he? Everyone in the group was looking for something.

'So why are they?' she challenged him.

'To learn to cook the basics.'

He hadn't seen beneath the surface, that nearly all of them were looking to reconnect with their lives in some way.

'But you could inspire them, inspire them to achieve so much more.'

'You think Peter and Jane want to create *medal d'honneur* pastries while they're here? Or that Bill wants to become a pastry chef?'

'Blimey. When did you turn into such a raging food snob who looks down on people who want to learn but haven't had the opportunity yet?'

'I'm not a food snob. I'm just a perfectionist. I want to educate people.'

'So why won't you educate these people? Give them your best shot, show them everything you've got?'

Sebastian gave her a sharp look. 'When did you become so evangelical about it all?'

'I'm not but you used to be ... so much more.'

'More?' he asked with a quizzical frown.

'*You* used to be evangelical. Passionate about cooking and ingredients. Experimental. I don't know, this seems a bit...' She lifted her shoulders trying to choose her words carefully.

'I'm teaching people the basics. The building blocks. You have to learn to walk before you run.' Despite his words, for a moment he looked lost in thought. Did he remember how he'd once talked to her about his hopes and dreams of being a top chef? How he wanted people to appreciate good food, locally sourced ingredients and encourage them to try new things. After a moment, his eyes met hers, a wistful expression crossing his face, and he looked as if he were about to say something, but just then the others started trooping in and Sebastian pasted on his customer-friendly smile and she slipped to the back of the room.

She'd learned after the first lesson that washing as you went was far more efficient. So by the time everyone had said their goodbyes at three-thirty, she was just about all done. Despite her sensible waitressing shoes, her feet were still complaining, so goodness only knew how Sebastian felt. Although she did much of the running, he still needed to get up and down to supervise and advise people.

'Well done, Nina,' said Sebastian as he thumped back on his stool. 'We've survived another day.'

'How are you feeling?'

'Bloody terrible. Achy, tired and starving. That's the problem with being surrounded by food all day and not touching anything.'

'Didn't you eat anything?'

'No. If I tried one, I'd have to try all five. I wouldn't want to be accused of favouritism. And I thought you might like to take the demonstration ones home.'

'What? All of them? I'll go back to the UK the size of a blimp.'

Sebastian gave her figure a quick appraising stare, frowning as he did as if he'd never noticed it before. 'There's nothing of you. I think you can afford a few extra pounds.'

Nina gave an inward sigh, drooping slightly. Not that she expected Sebastian to be particularly complimentary but the impersonal observation stung just a little.

'Sorry.' For once Sebastian looked genuine. 'I didn't mean that you look ... bad or anything.'

Nina shrugged and quickly moved to pick up the last of the mixing bowls and stow them in the labelled cubby hole. With a satisfied nod, she gave the kitchen a last onceover glance as if that were her primary concern.

'I meant to say—' Sebastian cleared his throat, for once looking a little awkward '—you've done a really great job today. Even if I'd been mobile I couldn't have coped without you running these classes. I'd forgotten how super-organised and methodical you can be.'

'No problem,' Nina said, draping the last of the wet tea towels over the radiator, trying to keep herself busy.

'I'm serious Nina. You always work so hard.'

She shrugged.

'You must be hungry too. You've worked nonstop today.' When everyone else had stopped for lunch, she'd carried on as there was a ton of washing up to do and the prep for the afternoon session. It had paid off, and the afternoon had gone very smoothly. So Sebastian Finlay, Mr Perfectionist, couldn't find fault.

'And don't shrug again.' Sebastian pushed himself to his feet. 'You've done a great job and I'm trying to say thank you.'

She shot him a quick look. He seemed quite sincere as he carried on. 'Like I said I am starving and quite honestly, I can't face that bloody room service menu again. I've had enough of those posh burgers and thrice cooked fat chips and I really don't fancy saffron chicken or a club sandwich. Do you know what?' He paused with a rueful almost guilty smile on his face. 'I fancy a McDonalds.'

'McDonalds! Sebastian Finlay, I don't believe you.'

'Shh, don't tell anyone,' said Sebastian, putting a finger to his lips. 'We can ask the taxi driver to drop us at the nearest one and then get a cab back to the hotel.'

'I'm not sure I have any choice,' Nina replied, her eyes dancing. 'Although I might take photographic evidence.'

'You wouldn't do that to an injured man, surely?' asked Sebastian, his lips twitching.

'To most, no, but you're a different matter,' she responded repressively. 'Besides you seem a lot more mobile and less in pain these days.'

Chapter 19

Bizarrely, a wave of homesickness rolled over her at the sight of the brightly lit restaurant, familiar graphics and pictures. McDonalds Paris felt rather too similar to the one on the dual carriageway five miles from home, a regular post-night-out stopping off point. As a teenager, she'd often bribed her brothers with the promise of a Big Mac to chauffeur her there before she could drive. With a smile, she acknowledged, they'd rarely said no.

Sebastian hobbled in after her and arranged himself in two plastic seats, his legs propped up on one as she headed to the counter to order. After a bit of a language tussle, she came back with a tray of burgers, chips, onion rings (Sebastian's choice) and two large cokes.

'Here you go.'

'You OK?'

'Yeah,' said Nina, trying hard not to think about what her family would be doing right now.

'Sure?'

'Just wondering what everyone is up to at home.'

'Why don't you give them a ring?'

Nina shook her head vehemently. 'No.'

Sebastian unwrapped his burger without looking at her, his forehead furrowing. 'That sounded very determined.'

Nina vacillated for a second, wondering whether to open up to him or not. They weren't exactly friends. Perhaps being honest with him might make him see her in a different light.

'I'm trying to ... distance myself sounds too harsh, but I just want a bit of space. Mum, Dad, Nick they all ... I know they do it because they care but sometimes it's just too much. Telling me what I should be doing. Or doing things for me, whether I want them to or not. And I know that sounds ungrateful but I want to have a chance to stand on my own two feet for a change.'

'So coming to Paris wasn't a whim then?' asked Sebastian.

She shot a glance at him and he held up his hands. 'Honest question, I didn't mean that's what I thought.'

'But you did,' suggested Nina feeling defensive.

'OK, at first I did. But Nick...'

'Oh, great. You see, still interfering. What did he say? "Nina's at a bit of a loose end at the moment. Can you do us a favour? Nina's having a midlife crisis twenty years too early."'

Sebastian winced. 'Something like that but then when you actually arrived, I thought that perhaps it wasn't a whim and when I saw you ... you look so different to ... how you looked last time I saw you.'

'What, done up like an overripe orange in a peach dress, throwing red wine everywhere?'

He let out a sharp bark of laughter. 'Oh God, I'd forgotten all about that. What a disaster. That shirt never did get clean again. I meant compared to when you were younger. You look...' He paused, as if choosing his words carefully, which she realised he did a lot with her, as if terrified he might give the wrong impression. 'Your hair suits you like that.'

Nina patted her neat bob a touch self-consciously, suddenly relaxing that his abiding memory of her wasn't one of her most embarrassing moments in life. He didn't even remember the peach number or the Tango tan. Then she couldn't decide if that was a good or a bad thing.

The radical change of hairstyle a few weeks ago had paid off then. As she sat here now she realised that trip to the hairdresser had been her first step of rebellion and wanting to make a change, although at the time she hadn't recognised it.

As she took a welcome bite, her stomach grumbling at her, she realised Sebastian was still watching her with an odd expression on his face.

'I thought you were desperate for your Big Mac,' she said.

'Yes,' he said, still looking thoughtful. 'Starving.'

There was an odd silence as he busied himself unwrapping his burger, unfolding the paper with careful fingers and smoothing it out. He picked it up and sank his teeth into it, a look of relish on his face.

'Oh, that's good.'

Unable to resist, Nina picked up her phone and took a picture. 'Evidence.'

'No one will believe you,' he smirked confidently. 'Besides I could be eating a gourmet burger,' he teased.

'Not with a big Maccy D's poster behind your head, you couldn't,' she replied, with a cocky shake of her shoulders.

He whipped his head round and laughed. 'Busted. And how do you plan on using it?'

'I haven't decided yet,' Nina teased back, relieved that they'd moved on so quickly and pleased to see him in a jokey mode. He always seemed so serious these days, it could be quite intimidating. This was the most light-hearted she'd seen him for a long time. He always seemed coiled tightly like a spring wound down into submission.

'At this moment, I don't care. It's a relief to be out of the hotel room. The thought of going back to the same four walls is rather depressing. I've been going stir crazy. I think you probably cop a bit of my frustration.'

'A bit?' Nina raised exaggerated eyebrows.

'OK. I've been a bad-tempered sod and I'm sorry. You should have told me where to go.'

'On that first day—' she pinched her mouth wondering whether to admit it or not '—I was this close—' she held up her forefinger and thumb '—to telling you to shove it and walk out.'

'I'm very grateful you didn't. Today went well, I think. I don't think any of them are going to be winning any prizes anytime soon.'

'No, but they're an interesting bunch.'

'Mmm.' Sebastian's non-committal answer had her asking, 'Don't you think so? There are definitely some stories there, and I think some of them are rather sad.'

Sebastian didn't quite roll his eyes but he might as well have done. 'I thought they seemed a jolly enough bunch, especially the newlyweds. I'm not used to working with complete amateurs. As far as I'm concerned, they want to learn to cook, they've paid their money. It's my job to teach them.' He didn't say it but the sentence might as well have been punctuated with the words. *'End of story.'*

Nina smiled. 'I don't think I've ever seen a pair more in love with each other than Jane and Peter, but don't you think that strength of feeling is because they've come out the other side. Theirs is the kind of happiness that comes from experiencing a depth of sadness.'

Sebastian frowned. 'If you say so.'

'I do, it's the feeling I got when I looked at them.'

'OK, so they have a story but what about the others?' Sebastian folded his arms as if humouring her.

'Bill, I'm still figuring out and Marcel, well, there's a mystery there.'

'If what you say is correct.'

'Why would he lie about working at the Savoy?'

'He may well have done and there could be a thousand reasons why he gave it up. Burnt out. It's hard work in the hospitality business. Unsociable hours. If you want to stay on top of your game, you've got to be a hundred per cent committed. Or he could have been caught with his fingers in the till and was sacked.'

At Nina's frowning face, he said, 'It happens.'

She shook her head. 'I think there's more to it than that. Did you know he was married? He's a widower.'

'No, I don't know anything about him. He came with the furniture.'

Nina rolled her eyes.

'OK, Miss Know-it-all,' responded Sebastian. 'What about Maddie and Marguerite? They both seemed OK to me.'

'Ah, you're definitely wrong there. Marguerite is very sad. She's been missing her grandchildren and family desperately, but she's learning to use Skype, to keep in touch with them. So she's a little less sad but I think she's a bit lonely. And Maddie is very lonely.'

'You're telling me there's no chance of cancelling the course then?'

Nina wasn't sure if he was serious or not. 'No! You can't do that. I thought you were committed to running it.'

'I am but with this bloody leg, it's not that easy. You were a great help today but I still spent a lot longer on my feet than I planned. And the contractors working on my other restaurants are nearly done. If they finish in the next five weeks, they'll move on to another job and I'll miss the slot for this place.'

'And will that be really bad?'

'Yes, because it delays opening up the bistro and starting to bring in some income.'

'Couldn't you just keep the patisserie open a bit longer?'

'I don't need to be able to access the shopfront at the moment to know that customers are thin on the ground.'

'True.' She thought of the dingy paintwork outside and the sad selection of pastries on offer. It was hardly surprising.

'Which reminds me. Can you check the ingredients list for next week? We're going to be concentrating on fillings – ganache and Chantilly cream – and using different flavourings.

I think everyone managed quite well today apart from Peter. He is clueless.'

'I don't think he's ever held a whisk in his life before this course.' Nina shook her head. 'But it is rather romantic. He's doing it so he can cook for Jane.'

Sebastian winced. 'I can think of more romantic gestures.'

'Like what?' challenged Nina. 'For you, cooking a meal or making patisserie is an easy thing. But for Peter, who's an engineer, this is a real endeavour and something he's determined to master to show her how much he loves her. What would you do? For your current girlfriend. What would please or impress her?' Nina immediately wished she hadn't said that. It sounded as if she was fishing for information.

Sebastian looked a tad hunted. 'A piece of jewellery.'

Nina raised a sceptical eyebrow.

'That's what I bought her for her birthday and she liked it.'

'OK, so she likes jewellery. So wouldn't you commission a special piece for her or find one with a special meaning? You know, like a memory of somewhere you've been together.'

'We've been out to dinner a lot. Before I broke my leg.'

'Not to McDonalds, then?'

Sebastian laughed. 'Katrin wouldn't be seen dead in here. She designs restaurant interiors and writes a restaurant critic column.'

'Ah, hence dinners out. Is she the one you were with at the wedding where you don't remember me chucking a whole glass of wine over you?'

'I didn't say I didn't remember, just that it wasn't my last recollection of you. And no, that was Yvette, she was a restaurant critic.'

'So you're a serial critic dater? I hope you get great reviews.' Nina slapped her hand over her mouth. 'And I so didn't mean that to come out the way it sounded.'

Sebastian's mouth quirked, a dimple appearing in his cheek that Nina remembered of old. Once upon a time she'd obsessed over that dimple and trying to make him smile.

'No one's ever rated me on my performance that I know of.'

'I'm sure you'd score full marks.' She closed her eyes. *And what had made her say that*! 'I m – mean from a restaurant point of view. You're a perfectionist. And a brilliant chef.'

'I seem to spend more time with spreadsheets these days than in a kitchen.'

'That's a shame. I can't imagine anything worse. I'm rubbish at that sort of thing, thankfully my sister-in-law does all the finance stuff for the farm shop café.'

'You have to learn these things, whether you want to or not. It's the price you pay for success,' said Sebastian, suddenly grave. 'Not all of us have the luxury of being able to...' He pulled up short and studied the empty packaging in front of him as if it were the most fascinating thing known to man.

'The luxury of what?' asked Nina, in a quiet, dead tone, her heart sinking with a sense of dread. Did she really want to know what Sebastian thought of her?

He glanced at her, quick and furtive. She clenched her jaw tightly and met his second glance full on, her chin lifted.

'Well ... you know. You always have your family to fall back on. They're always there to pick up the pieces when things go wrong. I mean you were able to drop everything at the farm shop to come here, weren't you? Knowing your mum and sister-in-law would pick up the slack. You don't do spread-sheets because someone else will. You didn't finish catering college.'

'I had a phobia,' she said hotly.

Sebastian raised an eyebrow. 'Or you just weren't hungry enough for it. There's no shame, it's not for everyone. It's hard work.'

'I'm not afraid of hard work.'

'I didn't say you were, just that you didn't want it enough and not finishing the course didn't matter because you had the fall back of your family to take care of you.

'The point I was trying to make is that not all of us have that luxury. I had to learn to master spreadsheets, whether I wanted to or not. Talking of which, I ought to get back. Today was a distraction I really don't need. I'm trying to get two new restaurants open, before I even tackle the bistro. I shouldn't be running patisserie courses, which is why I *have* to be able to rely on you.'

Nina bristled, too shocked and hurt by his comments to say anything other than, 'You *can* rely on me.' Was that what he really thought of her? A spoiled princess who relied on her family. She fought hard against the sudden tears threat-ening. There was no way she was giving him the satisfaction of seeing that he'd made her cry.

'Excellent.' He looked at his watch. 'We can spend the next ten minutes running through what I need you to do to prep for next week and then I need to get back.'

Chapter 20

The week had raced by and Nina had spent nearly every day perfecting her éclairs. She was still brooding about what Sebastian had said about her never needing to stick at anything. As fast as she made them, Marcel sold them, which was just as well as they'd be overrun with the things otherwise. What had Marguerite said? Practice made perfect.

They'd just completed the fourth lesson, which had focused on fillings and how to add and use different flavourings. It was a lovely sunny day and no one was particularly upset when Sebastian had asked if anyone minded if they wrapped up early. He needed to meet with his architect. Apparently, there was a problem with a wayward chimney flue.

'I'm quite glad,' said Marguerite, taking a seat and trying to squish herself backwards into the only bit of shade outside the front of the patisserie. 'It was a little hot in the kitchen this afternoon.'

'I'm very glad,' said Maddie, 'I can't get the hang of whipping the cream, I'm always scared I'll miss the point of no return.'

Nina was glad because each time Sebastian came to the

patisserie was another chance for him to discover that she was selling her éclairs and that they were starting to get customers. She wasn't sure he'd be too pleased about that.

Marcel came out to take their orders, although he now knew everyone's preferences.

'I don't suppose you have a parasol for the table, do you?' asked Nina conscious that Marguerite was looking a little uncomfortable.

Marcel glanced at the older lady with a quick frown. 'There used to be some.'

Maddie jumped to her feet, her eyes gleaming. 'We haven't checked out those other storerooms.'

Nina drooped. 'Really, it's such a hot day.'

'Come on.'

'Mind if I come?' asked Bill. 'I wouldn't mind a look around. Renovating the house I'm working on, makes you realise how different French buildings are to ours. I'd like to see if there are any original features or fittings.'

Upstairs, the three of them split up, each taking a different room. Nina took the second door off the corridor and ground to an immediate halt as soon as she'd stepped over the threshold. The floor space was filled with black plastic-wrapped piles. Intrigued, she unwrapped one of them to find a pristine white damask table cloth along with a set of matching stiff – as if they'd been starched – napkins. As she reached out to check the next pile, she heard Maddie yelling her name.

'Nina! Nina! You've got to come and see this.'

Hurrying next door, she found Maddie and Bill grinning and pointing to the floor.

'Look what we found.'

'Oh my goodness.' Nina clapped her hand over her mouth as the three of them gazed down at the glass and crystal monster sprawled in front of them like a limp octopus. 'That's amazing. It must be the chandelier Marguerite's been talking about.'

'We've got to put it up,' said Maddie, as usual cresting the wave of enthusiasm.

'Needs a bit of a clean first,' said Bill, rubbing his fingers over a large piece of crystal.

Nina stared down at the chandelier and, even dirty, it glittered in the sunshine coming through the windows. 'It's...' She crouched down next to it, her fingers drawn to trace the edges of the crystals. Even like this, stranded on the floor, dusty and grimy, it was magnificent.

'I'm not even sure if we could get it up. Or how.' But it was so beautiful she knew that they had to try.

'What do you think, Bill?' asked Maddie.

'Well, it puts me in mind of that *Only Fools and Horses* scene. As long as we don't drop it we'll be fine. See there on the floor. Looks like it might be the original fixing. I reckon this room is right above where it would have been. Why don't we get Peter up here?'

There was a fair amount of head scratching and muttering and eventually Bill and Peter both agreed that getting the chandelier back up would take some doing but it wasn't herculean. They decided that they needed to ponder the matter further and to do that they had to head to the nearest bar to discuss it over a litre or two of lager.

Marguerite, who'd stayed downstairs with Jane, was very excited to hear about the discovery of the chandelier and Marcel was wandering around with a decided cat that had got the cream expression.

'It's going to need cleaning,' said Nina repeating Bill's comment, as she and Maddie sat back down at the table. Luckily the sun had moved and Marguerite had her own patch of shade, as in the excitement of discovering the chandelier, all thought of looking for a parasol had been forgotten.

'I should love to see it back in place,' said Marguerite. 'And so would Marcel. It will bring back so many memories. I must tell my son ... when I Skype him.'

'You're skyping your son as well as your grandchildren now?' asked Jane.

'Yes,' said Marguerite. 'The children told him they'd been speaking to me, so he called me.' Her face flushed with pleasure. 'I still think he's an idiot ... but he's my son.'

'So the Skyping is going well,' asked Nina, delighted to see the happiness in the older woman's face.

'Oh yes, I talk to Emile and Agatha twice a week. I can't thank you enough for putting me back in touch with my family. Even my son.'

'That's lovely,' said Jane, a little wistfully. 'We've deliberately taken Skype off our laptop. That's why we came out here. To escape for a while.'

'Why?' asked Maddie, blunt as ever. 'I can't believe you two would ever upset anyone.'

Jane's gentle smile faded. 'We never intended to.' She gazed away towards the buildings on the other side of the street. 'My husband died very suddenly ... just over a year ago.'

Marguerite lay a hand on Jane's in a silent show of understanding.

'Oh, that's tough. You're so young to be a widow,' said Maddie.

'It is but I was lucky. I met Peter, very soon after.' She chewed her lip, her pretty eyes filling with tears. 'We didn't mean to hurt anyone ... but well, it happened. We fell in love. Neither of our families are terribly happy about it. They think it's too soon. Peter's wife died a year before. They've all been so ... difficult, that we decided to run away and get married and stay away for a while. Which is how we come to be in Paris.' Her face brightened.

'And only you know how you should feel,' said Marguerite. 'I had forty wonderful years with Henri and I still miss him. If I met someone who I would be as happy with, then I certainly would marry again.'

'How do you explain to other people, when you know it is so completely right? That being with that person is like the last piece of the jigsaw slotting into place. It makes things feel finished. Complete. Whole.' Jane broke off looking a little embarrassed. 'And listen to me.'

'We are,' said Maddie. 'And we're dead jealous. I'm still waiting for my jigsaw piece.'

Nina stared down at her feet. Was Sebastian really her jigsaw piece? And if he was, she was some kind of crazy masochist because he was always so grumpy. What was it inside her that was so convinced that he was the right person for her? Had she longed for him for so damned long that it had become a habit? Had it stopped her looking at other people?

Fading out of the conversation, leaving the other two consoling Jane about her 'difficult' family, about which Maddie had bluntly said, 'if you call them difficult, Jane, they must be a nightmare', Nina pulled out her phone and sent a quick text to Alex. He'd invited her out twice in the last few days and each time she'd said she'd been busy. Maybe it was time. Maybe she need to give herself a chance to get over Sebastian once and for all.

Chapter 21

There was a queue outside but Nina didn't mind, the sun was shining and a palpable sense of excitement and anticipation fizzed among the waiting people as if they were queueing for the theatre or a concert rather than for a very exclusive cake and cup of tea.

'You know, I've never been here all the time I've been in Paris,' observed Alex as they joined the queue.

'I guess it's more of a tourist thing,' said Nina, gazing up at the sign above them. 'And thanks for bringing me here. Marguerite, one of the ladies on the course, suggested it. She's rather elegant, I can imagine her having afternoon tea here. I've been dying to come since she told me about it so thank you.'

'No problem, it's ... not quite dinner or lunch. And I'm sorry it took so long to fix up. It's been madder than usual at the hotel.'

When Alex had asked Nina where she wanted to go, Ladurée was the first place she thought of.

And she was glad she'd suggested it; with its delicate sage green and gold décor it was clearly the doyenne of the patisserie world and, judging by the queue, well worth a visit.

'Do you mind if I pop next door and take some pictures?'

'No, although I'm tempted to give into my Scottish stereo-typical roots and suggest it would be cheaper to buy a couple of the cakes and take them away.'

'And where would the fun in that be?' asked Nina, with a laugh, skipping along to the shop next door, where a long glass cabinet displayed a rainbow selection of cakes and the distinctive puffs of macaron in pastel colours. By the time she'd taken her fill of pictures, Alex was at the front of the queue.

When it was their turn to be seated they were led up a flight of stairs to a sedate salon full of quiet chatter and the delicate chink of china. At over six foot and dressed in jeans and a *Star Wars* T-shirt, Alex looked decidedly out of place, especially when perched on the seat behind the small rather delicate table.

'Very grand,' he said, looking around him before whis-pering, 'and a bit girly.'

Nina laughed. 'Perfect for me then.' What wasn't there to like about the pale wood panelling that graced the walls and probably had done for at least a hundred years? And how could you resist thinking about all the faces that had caught sight of themselves over time in the speckled mirrors? Had grand ladies of old drunk tea and chatted over macarons, in silks and lace?'

'Earth to Nina? Still with me?' asked Alex.

'Sorry, this is just lovely. Everything.' She looked up at the ceiling painted with a mural of a cloud puffed sky. As she admired the gorgeous décor she remembered what Marguerite had said about Patisserie C. It would be interesting to know if the hideous MDF panels hid former glories.

'And you haven't even had a pastry yet?' teased Alex.

Nina picked up the menu the waiter had just delivered. 'Ooh! Where do I start? I think I might drool. Do you think they might throw me out?'

'Not if you can afford these prices. Ten euros for a cake? Even we don't charge that in the hotel.'

'Yes but are they as good as this? And it's a one-time-only treat.'

Alex put his menu down laughing at her. 'It's good to go out with a girl who likes her food and isn't afraid to show it. I went out with a girl a few months back and when I took her out to dinner, she insisted on asking the waiter how many calories were in each dish before she would choose anything.'

'Oh, I'm a complete pig, don't you worry. But seriously, how am I going to choose? I want everything.'

There were the Claire Heitzler's Creations – Fleur Noire and blackcurrant blueberry cheesecake – which sounded divine, or one of the Ladurée Classics – pistachio religieuse, Saint-Honoré, plaisir sucré or vanilla mille-feuille – which were bound to be exquisite.

'Go and take a look.' Alex pointed to a marble slab over to her right where she realised all the divine cakes listed on the menu were displayed.

Unfortunately, when she went to take a closer look, it didn't help.

'I want to try all of them,' she complained to Alex who was standing at her elbow.

Each one of them looked like a mini work of art.

'How many do you reckon you could eat, before you were sick?' he asked, tilting his head as if seriously considering the question.

Shaking her head, Nina sniggered and nudged him with her elbow. 'You are just like my brother, Toby. He would ask that sort of thing.'

When the waiter arrived to take their order, Alex replied quickly and she was amused to see he picked the biggest cake on display. She still hadn't made up her mind. 'What would you recommend?'

'Everything.' The waiter's stern professional face relaxed into a quick smile. 'It is all good.'

'That's no help,' she said, with a disgruntled smile up at him. She took another look at the menu and this time homed in on something that had intrigued her. What was an ordinary cheesecake doing on a menu like this?

With her choice made, she sat back and relaxed.

'So how are you finding Paris?' asked Alex.

'I ... I love it, although...' She looked around, and lowered her voice. 'Don't tell anyone, but I've not seen that much of it.' She'd spent all her time in the kitchen now that the éclairs were selling so well.

'Sebastian being a slave driver, is he? Want me to sort him out?'

'No, I hardly hear from him. I just ... you know, it's easier to keep putting things off, rather than doing stuff on your own.

Although I've met a couple of people from the course and I'm going to do a couple of museums and things with Maddie.'

'You should have said, I'd have...' He pulled a face.

Nina let out a laugh. 'No, you wouldn't. You don't strike me as a museums and gallery type of guy.'

'True. I'd prefer to be outside. Doing stuff. Paris is good to walk around. It's quite compact. You can see a lot in a short space of time.'

They were interrupted by the return of the waiter who, with a slightly officious air, unloaded his tray on the table, handing out each item with solemn precision as if his life depended on the exact placing of the silver teapot and milk jug in the centre of the table. It all looked absolutely gorgeous, especially Alex's choice with its matt chocolate topping and the Ladurée logo in gold and cream placed with symmetrical precision on top but when the waiter presented her, almost reverentially, with the tiny delicate cheesecake, she'd knew she'd made the best choice.

She reached out to touch the gold gilt trim around the china plate. Lovely as it was, with the pastel blue stripe and the coordinating cup and saucer, this time with a pastel pink stripe, she couldn't help thinking that the china at home – she smiled, she meant in the patisserie – was prettier.

Across the table from her, Alex had picked up his fork and was holding it in the air as if waiting for starter's orders. No reverential appreciation from him, he was clearly itching to tuck in but had the good manners to wait for her.

'Are you going to eat that? Or just keep staring at it?' asked Alex after a couple of seconds.

Nina tilted her head. 'It looks too good to eat.' She took a sip of the delicately scented jasmine and orange tea, she'd selected, hiding a smile.

Looking pained, Alex put down his fork.

Nina laughed.

'Gotcha!'

'That's just mean.'

'Sorry, I couldn't resist. I'm the youngest of four, I learned to take every advantage to mess with my brothers.'

She tucked in and let out a groan of ecstasy. With its beehive of piped creamy cheese atop a deliciously rich buttery biscuit crumb base and the secret pocket of blackcurrant and blue-berry, which just had to be one of the yummiest combinations ever, the cheesecake was a culinary triumph.

'Want to try some of mine?' asked Alex.

She looked greedily at the chocolate confection and manners went out the window – she was dying to try it.

'Are you sure?' she asked but he was already offering her a forkful.

'My, that's lovely.' She licked her lips as she savoured the richness of the chocolate ganache, the delicate nutty texture of the hazelnut meringue base and the smooth Chantilly cream, marvelling at the flavours and the perfect shape. How on earth did they do that? Someone had a very sharp knife.

'Would you like to try mine?' she asked, giving the tiny cheesecake a plaintive look.

He laughed. 'I don't think I dare. And this is pretty good, although, I could eat another three.' He'd polished his off pretty quickly and was now staring down at his empty plate rather glumly.

'Me too. Well, not three, but I'd love to try another. Do you think that's terribly greedy?'

'No,' said Alex with a grin. 'Terribly normal.'

'This place is lovely, it makes Patisserie C look a bit sad.'

'That the place Sebastian has bought?'

'Yes. Apparently in its heyday it was quite something.'

'You know Sebastian didn't want the site in the first place. If he could offload it, he would.'

Nina frowned. 'I thought he wanted to turn it into a restaurant.'

'Only because he got landed with it. When he secured the other two sites, this one came as part of the deal. He's been desperate for the units at Canal Saint-Martin and the Marais – that's where the first two restaurants will open – so he couldn't turn it down. The plans are looking great. Have you seen them yet?'

'Very briefly.' Nina nodded, distracted by the news that Sebastian had obtained the patisserie by default. She gave the sumptuous décor around her a second thoughtful study.

The waiter came back and asked if they'd like anything else. Nina caught Alex's eye.

'We'd like to see the menu again,' said Alex and, as soon as the waiter scurried off, he added, 'I'm still peckish.'

Nina laughed. 'And I'm dying to try something else. I'm so glad you are here, I probably wouldn't have dared on my own.'

'I have my uses. Now, instead of these sophisticated Parisians thinking you're a greedy wee piglet, they'll just think you've been led astray by the strapping Scottish lad.'

'I'll need to go for a long walk after this to burn off the gazillion calories.'

'I don't think you need to worry but I'll happily walk you home. We could walk down through Place de la Concorde, cross the river over the Pont de la Concorde and down past the Palais Bourbon into the 7th arrondissement?'

'That sounds perfect.'

On second perusal of the menu, she was torn between the pistachio religieuse or the rose Saint-Honoré.

'I can't decide.' She pulled a mournful face which made Alex laugh. 'I need to go to the loo. And as you think it's so funny, I'll leave the decision with you. Both will be delicious but you can choose for me.'

When she returned Alex had an I'm-about-to-burst-with-a-secret expression on his face.

'What?' asked Nina, narrowing her eyes. He looked like he was up to no good.

'Nothing.' The saucer-like eyes didn't make him look any more innocent.

'So, what did you order me?' she asked and then with a sudden afterthought added, 'Please tell me you didn't order both.'

'Wait and see,' said Alex, with a mischievous, infectious grin.

She laughed, realising that he probably had.

'The responsibility was too much for me.'

A few minutes later a waiter appeared carrying a small table and behind him, two waiters with a tray each. There was a polite to-and-fro dance as the new table was set up and the waiters proceeded to unload ten plates from the trays.

'Alex! You didn't.' Nina started to laugh at the sight of so many of the colourful pastries, the pale green of the pistachio icing of the two-tiered religieuse, the vivid pink of the glorious Ispahan, a raspberry macaron filled with rose cream and topped with deep red rose petals and the glistening caramel glaze of a rum baba. Extravagant swirls of cream rubbed shoulders with delicate peaks of meringue. 'You've ordered one of everything!'

Alex beamed, delighted with himself. 'I figured what we can't eat we can always take away with us.'

'You ... idiot!' She giggled. It was ridiculously indulgent but totally glorious and spontaneous. 'But I love it. It all looks heavenly ... and almost too good to eat.'

They took their time, and it felt terribly decadent, taking a forkful of this and a taste of that but luckily the pastries weren't huge. She was just savouring her second bite of the vanilla mille-feuille, almost sighing with pleasure, when her phone rang, loud and shrill in the quiet, demure atmosphere.

Alex laughed at her as she scrabbled with the mute button.

'Embarrassing,' said Nina glancing at the screen. 'Oh, it's Sebastian, I wonder what he wants. I'll call him later.'

'Well, I hope he's in a better mood. He was foul this morning when I popped in.'

'Maybe he's still in pain.' Although now he was taking his

painkillers properly, because she'd nagged him, he seemed a lot better if still grumpy.

'No, he's bored. Wanted me to take him out somewhere today. Was well pissed off when I said I couldn't because I was taking you out. Poor bugger is bored rigid.'

Nina glanced up sharply.

'I suppose I should have been a bit more sympathetic, he's been cooped up in there for days. I'd be going bonkers. Maybe I'll take the poor sod down to the bar later. A change of scene might cheer him up.'

Five minutes later, Alex's phone rang.

'Oh balls, do you mind if I take this. Downside of being GM, you're pretty much always on call.'

It was funny; almost before her eyes, Alex straightened up and turned back into general manager mode. Again, it reminded of her brothers Nick and Toby who both joked about perpetually at home but in a work situation were totally responsible and sensible.

'Bollocks. If he's really kicking up that much of a stink, try offering him the presidential suite. Otherwise he'll have to wait a couple of hours to check in and we'll have to move Sebastian and get housekeeping to clean the room pronto. That's what I thought. I'll be there soon.'

'Damn.' He removed his phone from his ear glaring at it with a thorough look of dislike. 'I'm sure life was better without these things.' His mouth twisted. 'Duty calls, I'm afraid. An irate customer who booked the suite Sebastian is in for his anniversary. I need to go back to calm him down and see if an upgrade will placate him, otherwise I'll have to move Seb. It's one thing to put your friend up but another thing to ask the staff to start packing for him.'

As they left the patisserie – having had quite a battle over the bill, which to Nina's dismay Alex had won saying she could pay next time – he gave her a kiss on the cheek, hopeful eyes meeting hers. 'It's been great, Nina, and I'm really sorry to cut and run. I'd like to—'

Much to her relief, his phone beeped again.

'I've got to go, I'll call you.' With a last quick kiss, he grazed her lips before raising a hand in salute and dashing off.

Nina took her time ambling down to the Pont de la Concorde tipping her face up to the sunshine and trying not to think what she was going to say next time Alex called. What was wrong with her? He was lovely, how could a man who bought an entire shelf of cakes just for her not be right? But he didn't give her goose bumps or that stomach-in-freefall-after-a-dip-in-the-road feeling. Was that important? Shouldn't being with a nice guy, who made you laugh and looked after you, be enough? Cross with herself, she wandered over the bridge where people lined the low balustrade taking photos and she stopped to look at the broad expanse of river, gazing down at the houseboats and the barges below as they slid slowly and languorously along the surface of the water. Their paths looked serene and uncomplicated. Why wasn't life that simple? Amused by one of the boats sliding beneath the bridge, which bizarrely had a small car on the back upper deck, she took a quick picture, knowing it would appeal to Jonathon's sense of the ridiculous and unusual. As she sent him the picture on WhatsApp, her phone buzzed into life and she very nearly dropped it into the river.

Typical. It was Sebastian. Feeling out of sorts, she answered with ill grace.

'Hi.'

'Hi, Nina.' There was a pause. What did he want now?

'I'm ... erm, just checking that you ... haven't got any queries for our next session.'

Nina frowned. What? She held the phone away from her, giving it a quizzical look.

'Nina? Are you still there?'

'Yes.'

'Where are you? Sounds noisy.' There were a group of loud teenagers to her right, shouting and messing about, and a tour guide talking in a loud American accent to a group of middle aged tourists.

'I'm on a bridge looking down at the Seine,' she answered, watching the barge with the car chug away disappearing under the next bridge straddling the river.

'Romantic,' he said, with a definite edge to his voice.

'Not particularly. I'm surrounded by tourists and I'm on the phone to my boss.'

'I'm sure Alex is looking after you.'

'He's hot footing it back to the hotel to stop you being evicted from your suite by a rather irate customer.'

'He is?' Sebastian sounded pleased.

'Feeling lonely?' asked Nina.

'No.'

Nina quirked an eyebrow even though he couldn't see it. Someone sounded a touch defensive.

'So, what are you up to?'

'I'm just headed back to your apartment. Walking. I love walking through Paris. I really feel I've got my bearings now.'

'And is everything alright? Finding everything in the apartment?'

'Do you not think it's a bit late to be asking that? I've been here for several weeks,' said Nina, slightly bemused by his uncharacteristic woolliness.

'And you're alright for next week's course?'

'Yes. Sebastian. This is the fifth one, I think I've got the hang of it now.'

'And we're doing sugar craft, remember.'

Nina frowned, completely puzzled by the conversation. 'Nothing wrong with my memory or your lists Sebastian.'

'I'm just checking.'

'Right.' She leaned against the parapet, now amused. 'I'm really looking forward to that. You can do amazing things with spun sugar. That will be fun,' she said with genuine enthusiasm. 'Everyone's really enjoying the course. Have you ever thought about keeping the patisserie open?'

'No.'

'Apparently back in the day, it was quite famous. Both Marguerite and Marcel remember when it was something really quite special.'

'Back in the day so was George Best, but times move on. It's old news. Sad and tired. Nothing short of a miracle is going to make that place look any better.'

'But if you could make it look better ...'

Sebastian snorted. 'With respect Nina, I've been working in the business for the last fifteen years, I think I probably have considerably more expertise in these matters than you.' He didn't say it but she could almost hear the words ... *and you didn't even manage a full term at catering college.*

'So have you seen any of the sights?' he asked suddenly.

'Pardon?' The complete about-turn of the conversation made her stop dead on the pavement, eliciting a series of tuts from the people behind her.

Nina frowned again and started walking. Now this was odd. Sebastian making small talk. What was wrong with him? 'No, but I've arranged to go to the Musée d'Orsay with Maddie tomorrow.'

'Tomorrow?' he echoed. 'Oh. That sounds nice. I've not been there.' Did he sound envious?

'Right then. I'll see you next week.'

'Erm, Nina,' he started again. 'Actually I ... need some stuff from my flat. I wonder if you would mind bringing it over.'

'Yeah sure, but it will have to be the day after tomorrow.'

'That would be OK. And maybe we could go out for lunch or something.'

'What do you need?'

'Erm... er ... a book. Yes, my book. The one I was reading. It might be on the ... er ... coffee table.'

'That's it?' *That was all he wanted?*

'Yes.'

'There's a book by ... the bed.' Thank goodness he couldn't see her turning bright red, as she very nearly said *our* bed.

'Yes, that one,' said Sebastian just a shade too quickly. Nina frowned. Did he even know the title of the book or what it was about? If it had been her or her bookworm mother, she'd have asked for the book on the very first day.

Suddenly the penny dropped. Was Sebastian feeling bored? She could bet her last penny that he had no idea what the book was called or what it was about.

'The thriller?'

'Yes.'

'Enjoying it, were you?' asked Nina, amused to have the upper hand for once with Sebastian.

'Yes, it's very good.'

'What's it about?'

'Nina, I don't have time for this. If you could bring it over, that would be great.'

'Anything else?'

'Just the book. About lunchtime?'

'I'll see if I can squeeze it in,' said Nina, enjoying herself now.

'So I'll see you at twelve?'

Was that a hint of desperation in his voice?

'I'll see you then.'

'Thanks. Bye.'

And suddenly he was gone, leaving Nina totally bemused. Presumably during the day his girlfriend and other friends would all be working, if they weren't in the hospitality trade. Clearly, he was so bored even her company would do.

Chapter 22

S he eyed the thriller on the bedside table, still pondering Sebastian's odd phone call from the day before. Stretching, she got out of bed quickly. She was meeting Maddie later that morning to go to the museum but ever since she'd been to Ladurée yesterday, something aside from Sebastian's call had been nagging at her. Before she left the apartment, she hunted down a few tools she'd spotted in one of the cupboards and set off to the patisserie.

'Bonjour Marcel,' she called as she walked through the door. The patisserie was empty this morning but it was still early. She looked at her watch. It was only a few minutes after ten. It suddenly struck her that she had no idea what time Marcel started or finished. He just seemed to always be here.

'Bonjour Nina.' He gave her one of his nods, which was as close to him being friendly as she was going to get. 'Café?'

'Yes, please.' She put down the plastic bag of tools with a clatter on one of the tables. Marcel looked up with a brief frown, exhibiting the closest thing to curiosity she guessed he could muster.

She crouched down by the panelling which ran the whole

length of one wall beneath the pink dado rail. Above the rail the walls were painted pale blue and sported two large gilt mirrors, which were rather lovely and looked quite old with tiny spots where the silver had worn from the back. They reminded her of the mirrors in Ladurée and firmed her resolve.

'Have these always been here?' she asked.

'Not there, no. They used to be at the back. When the chandelier was here—' he pointed to the blank plaster rose above, now heavily painted, and gave a little smirk before continuing '—they were placed at opposite sides of the salon to reflect the crystals and light.'

'Well, if Bill and Peter have their way, the chandelier will be put back up any day now,' said Nina with a grimace.

'Yes,' said Marcel, again with the little smirk.

'What do you know?' she asked suddenly suspicious.

'I believe that Bill is looking for a suitable ladder. I might have made a few enquiries on his behalf.'

Given what she was about to do, she could hardly complain.

'Would you mind if I take a look behind this panel?' she asked.

Marcel's eyes widened for a moment before his face settled into its usual impassive indifference. 'It's not my patisserie.'

With the large screwdriver she pulled out of the plastic bag, she jimmied the bevelled edge into the top of the loose panel and used the handle to lever against the dado rail. With a creaking groan that set her teeth on edge, she pried the panel away from the wall. Despite being a little loose at the top, it was much harder work than she'd expected and it took a good five minutes battling with the MDF material before she'd prised enough away from the wall to see inside. Grabbing her phone, she switched on the torch and shone the beam down into the gap between the panel and the wall. She was loathe to remove the whole panel if there was nothing there but it was difficult to see much; she was going to have to go for broke and take the whole panel off. With a sigh, she sank onto her haunches.

Marcel brought her coffee over and put it on the nearest table.

'How certain are you that the original décor might be behind this panel?' she asked.

He lifted his shoulders in his usual Gallic shrug. 'I'm not sure but I remember the decorators were very lazy. They painted around the mirrors.'

'They did?' She stood up and went over to the nearest mirror, pushing at the frame moving it slightly to one side. Beneath the mirror the wall was painted a paler, more delicate blue, with tiny puffs of cloud scattering across the top. Once upon a time this place must have been beautiful.

She turned around and inserted the screwdriver down the side of the panel pulling at the edge, until with another unworldly groan the panel gave way, the whole thing popping out.

'Oof.' Surprised, she fell backwards onto her bottom, both hands clutching it like a shield, feeling like an upside down tortoise.

Marcel rushed forward and helped her to her feet and together they stared down at the wall.

'Can I have your cloth?' she asked and when Marcel handed her the cloth that was always tucked in the front of his apron, she gently rubbed away a layer of slightly greasy dust. 'Oh my word.' The tiny clear patch revealed an azure blue eye tipped with golden eyelashes and circled with creamy skin. It was a tantalising promise of more.

Marcel actually smiled. Well, it was almost a smile.

'That's beautiful.' She leaned forward and touched the painted surface, her finger removing another layer of dust and beneath the patch the colour intensified.

'Why would anyone cover this up?' asked Nina, her eyes shining with sudden unshed tears.

Once again Marcel shrugged, although she hadn't expected an answer.

She sat on her haunches considering the grimy paint. Despite her efforts it needed a really good clean but already she could see the potential.

She bit her lip and looked at the rest of the MDF panels lining the wall. And then she looked at Marcel.

'What do you think?'

He gave another crooked half-smile but didn't say anything and disappeared back to his spot behind the counter.

Considering the task, she sat there for another few minutes. What if she peeled all the panels back and the painting was damaged in any way? What then?

A drip of water hit her back and she turned to find Marcel bearing a large bowl of soapy water.

'Do you think we should? Will it damage the painting?'

Marcel shook his head. 'No, I remember seeing the waiters cleaning it. I've only put a little soap in.'

Gingerly, Nina dipped a cloth in the water and squeezed

it out so it was damp rather than wringing wet, and very carefully started to clean the paint. Within seconds, the colours emerging from the grimy layer of dust sharpened and she could see the tiny brush strokes.

Sea greens and blues swirled across the surface, while half of a mermaid with silver flowing hair smiled shyly holding out pearly conch shells. Tiny fish dotted the scene dancing in and out of a triton held by a hand, the rest of which was hidden behind the next panel.

She wished she knew something about art...

'Maddie!' she said, and turned to Marcel. 'She knows about art.' With that she pulled out her phone, swiping the screen quickly.

'Hi, it's me. Would you mind meeting me at the patisserie instead of the museum. I've got something to show you?'

'Oh goodie. I'm starving,' replied Maddie. Nina smiled – she couldn't wait to see Maddie's face. The other girl was going to get so much more than she expected.

Now that the layer of greasy dust had been removed and she could see the jewel-bright colours, she could see some parts where the paint had faded or been scraped away but despite that it was absolutely beautiful. She felt Marcel crouch down next to her.

'Shall we?' he asked, holding up a small crowbar.

They worked side by side, the only sound the groans of the panels creaking away from their bearings. As Marcel removed them, she moved in and carefully cleaned the surface.

'Can I ask you a question?' asked Nina suddenly. Silence didn't suit her.

'You can ask.'

'You were once at the Savoy. How did you end up here? I mean surely you could work anywhere?' Now she'd voiced the question, she felt horribly intrusive.

'Sorry, its none of my business.'

'I worked at the Grosvenor. The Dorchester. Chewton Glen. Gleneagles.' Marcel let out a sour laugh. 'I earned well but there was a price to pay. I lost my wife. We were going on holiday but I had to work, so we agreed I'd meet her in Brittany. But I was late leaving work. I was always late leaving work. It was a continual complaint from my wife. I missed the ferry. My wife was killed in a car accident while I was on the ferry. If I'd have been there, she wouldn't have been driving.'

'I'm sorry,' said Nina, feeling totally inadequate at the sound of listless acceptance in his voice and unable to voice the platitude that it hadn't been his fault. He clearly believed it was.

'It was a long time ago.' He shrugged. 'I live with my sister. She's on her own. A single mum and she works shifts. It's ironic.' He curled his lip. 'I help with her children. It means she doesn't have to worry about being late.'

Even though he was one of the stiffest, least tactile people she'd ever met, Nina couldn't help but reach out and touch his shoulder.

'That must be nice for her. Having family to support her.'

For the first time since she'd met him, a full smile lifted Marcel's sad, basset hound face, reaching his eyes which shone with pride. 'They are wonderful children.'

For the next few minutes Marcel spoke of his two nephews, and it was clear that he adored them.

'You should take them some éclairs,' said Nina.

'Thank you. If I may, I will but...' Marcel's mouth pursed but there was a rebuking twinkle in his eye. 'I think it's time you spread your wings. You have mastered the éclairs. We need something new for the customers.' He nodded at the wall. 'Something worthy of this fine art.'

By the time Maddie arrived they'd stripped the panelling from the whole of one wall.

'Oh my God.' Maddie barrelled to a halt as she came into the patisserie. 'Oh my God.' She came to stand next to Nina. 'That's just stunning.' She stood gazing at the first section of the mural before slowly walking along the whole length. 'It reminds me of John Williams Waterhouse, but more impressionistic. It's ... it's...' She lifted her hands palms upwards.

'Who's he?' asked Nina feeling rather ignorant.

'You'd recognise his work. He did the famous *The Lady of Shallot* and quite a few of Ophelia. Pre-Raphaelite. English but Italian inspired.' Maddie couldn't take her eyes off the painting and reached out to trace the silky skein of red gold hair of one of the mermaids. 'Mermaid or nymph. This is just gorgeous. Why would anyone hide it away?'

'I guess it went out of fashion,' said Nina. 'And there are some parts, look—' she pointed to a very faded patch '—that need some work. Maybe they couldn't afford to restore it ... or didn't love it enough.'

'Hmph,' said Marcel and muttered something under his breath as he stomped back to his usual spot behind the counter. The brief fragile accord between them seemed to have shattered but Nina had a handle on him. Underneath the scowly, grumbly maître d' was a man with a heart. Not a soft heart but a heart. And that would do for starters.

'What if you had someone who could restore it and love it enough to do the most fabulous job?' Maddie cocked her head to one side. 'Not being modest or anything but I'm a ruddy good painter.'

'Really?'

'Yes ... well, good enough. Why do you think I'm studying History of Art? I love paintings.'

'You're an artist?'

'Ha! No. I'm not bad with a paintbrush, dab hand with charcoal but ... seriously? People like me don't become artists.' She laughed good-naturedly. 'We need to earn money. History of Art is bad enough ... who knows if I'll ever get a job?'

'Do you think you could...' Nina nodded towards the mermaid.

Maddie pursed her lips together for a moment and then took a step forward, bending down to study the faded section of the picture, her finger tracing an outline on the wall, before saying thoughtfully, 'Yes, I think I could. It looks like oil-based paint. The only problem is going to be matching the paint and pigments. It would be helpful to know when this was painted.'

'Do you think it's really old? Could it be valuable? We washed it...' Nina put her hands to her cheeks. 'Maybe we shouldn't have.'

Looking down at the bowl of water, Maddie patted her on the hand. 'Don't fret. A little bit of soap and water won't have done any harm and I'm sorry love, it's not that old. Not buried treasure. Definitely post-war. I've got a reasonable idea but...' She bent again to look at the mermaid.

'Marcel!' Nina called to him, hoping he might know. 'Do you know when this was painted?'

She could see him muttering to himself and any moment now she expected him to start counting on his fingers. He came over to join them, still frowning in concentration.

'I believe it must have been sometime after the Fifties. That's when the patisserie opened. I remember my mother telling me it used to be ... *un cordonnier* ... to mend shoes.'

Maddie high-fived Nina. 'Told you I was good and that's brilliant because it means they would have used reasonably modern paints and pigments, which I can pick up.' She pulled out her phone and began taking pictures. 'I need to get an idea of the paint colours I need.'

After half an hour of photo taking, scribbling notes and lengthy mutterings to herself, Maddie finally sat down to drink the coffee Marcel had brought over.

'Shame about the pink dado rail,' said Maddie, 'and the paint above. I wonder what it was like before. If we're going to restore Melody here, it would be nice to do it all properly.'

'I can show you.' Nina walked to the first of the gilt mirrors and beckoned Maddie over. 'Ta-dah!'

Within an hour Maddie was back, armed with paints, brushes, china palettes and other materials that she flatly refused to let Nina pay for. 'I tapped one of the other students on my floor for some of this stuff, so I didn't buy much. This is going to be the best fun ever, I should be paying you,' she said as she set up camp on the floor. 'With the exception of one really worn patch, it's really just going to be touching up.'

Nina suspected it was a lot more than that and that Maddie was being modest. She'd certainly brought enough tubes of paint.

Leaving Maddie lost in intense concentration, Nina retreated to the kitchen, smiling as she took the steps down into the big silent room. It was the quietest and most still she'd ever heard or seen the other girl.

'And how's the delectable Sebastian?' asked Maddie, with a sly look on her face as they settled down in the café with a glass of red wine each.

They'd both worked hard all day, forgoing the museum trip and only stopping for lunch when Marcel had insisted they come and eat the sandwiches he'd made for them. Nina felt a little despondent this evening. Her attempts today to branch out and make something different had not been a wild success. She'd tried to make religieuse, like she'd seen in Ladurée, and she'd got the icing and flavours right but ... her presentation skills had a long way to go. Individually each one looked alright but she hadn't been able to achieve the uniformity of size of the choux buns. Frankly they looked more like snowmen instead of the well-proportioned head and body of a nun which was the direct translation of the word. The idea was that the delicate white icing between the two choux buns resembled the old-fashioned collars the nuns had worn.

'Weird,' replied Nina still distracted by thoughts of her rubbish pastries.

'How so?'

Nina focused properly, realising Maddie was interested. 'He phoned me and then wittered on about absolutely nothing. And then asked me to take over a book to him, that I swear he's not that interested in.'

'Maybe he just wants to see you,' said Maddie with a teasing grin.

'I don't think so.' Nina shook her head vehemently. 'He's probably just bored and all the people he knows in Paris are probably working. Because I'm working for him, he assumes I'm available and will drop everything and come running.'

'Yeah but if he's stuck in a hotel room. He's probably going stir crazy.'

Being holed up, even if it was in a suite, must be a complete anathema to Sebastian, who was always on the go. Even during the cookery course, when he was supposed to be sitting down, he couldn't manage to stay seated for more than ten minutes.

'Oh God, I'm so dense. Of course, that explains it. He's not the least bit interested in seeing me. He's desperate and he knows I'm obliged to him, so I'll have to go over.'

Maddie laughed. 'Don't you feel the least bit sympathetic?'

'No,' said Nina. 'Not really. Well, a little bit. OK, yes I do.'

'You know whenever you talk about him, you get all tense and hunched in the shoulders.' Maddie gave her a very direct look. 'He seems pretty nice to me. A bit intense. But he's quite a hottie. So, what's the story between the two of you?'

'What do you mean?' Her rapid fire defensive response brought a superior look to Maddie's face.

'I thought as much.'

'There's nothing between us. Never has been. Never will be.'

'Sounds like you've given it thought.'

'He's my brother's best friend. Hanging around in my life for as long as I can remember. We don't get along. End of story. And stop!' Nina swiped at Maddie's hand on the table at the sight of the sly smile playing around her lips.

'So what happened?'

'Maddie!' Nina pursed her lips. 'God, you really are like a dog with a bone.'

'Yup, tenacious terrier, that's me. So something did happened between you and sexy Sebastian.'

'Oh, for God's sake. He's ... OK, yes there's something about him.'

'Even Marguerite thinks he's smoking.'

'Really? That was her description?' Nina raised a sceptical eyebrow unable to help herself smiling.

Maddie gurgled with laughter. 'No, more along the lines of he's very handsome and if she were forty years younger she would be dusting down her feminine wiles. And Jane said, out of earshot of Peter to be fair, that he had a certain *je ne sais quoi* about him.'

'I suppose,' said Nina with a huff, 'he's OK looking.' Maddie's mouth twitched as Nina rolled her eyes. 'He certainly seems to attract a legion of drop dead gorgeous, legs up to their armpits, skinny blondes who think he's God's gift in the kitchen.'

'Ah, but is he God's gift elsewhere? That's what we want to know.' Maddie raised her eyebrows in Groucho Marx style making Nina burst out laughing.

'That, I definitely don't know.'

'Ooh but you do know something.'

'God, they should employ you at MI6. I've never told anyone this.' Nina traced the metal rim of the café table with one finger, already feeling her face flushing. 'I kissed him. Once.'

'*You* kissed *him*.'

'Yup.' Nina winced. Even now, the memory was excruciating. That heart-pounding moment when she'd screwed up every last bit of courage, raised herself onto her tiptoes and kissed him right on the lips. She'd even convinced herself in the first few seconds of her amateur onslaught that his lips might have softened and even maybe moved and that he'd perhaps taken a step towards her. And for one delicious *yessss!* moment, all her dreams and fantasies came true. And then they came crashing down in crushing rejection when he firmly took her arms and pushed her away.

'Oh God.' Nina put her head in her hands. 'It wasn't reciprocated. I've never been so embarrassed in my life. I had this stupid teenage crush and convinced myself that he felt the same way. So I went for it.' She shook her head. 'Honestly, the look on his face. Sheer horror.'

Maddie's face crumpled in sympathy. 'Eek. What did you do?'

'The only thing I could do. I fled. Left the house. Hid in the barn until really late. Luckily I'd been supposed to be going to a schoolfriend's house after school, so no one missed me.'

'But what about the next time you saw him?'

'That was about my only saving grace. By pure chance,

desperation I guess on my part, he was going back to university the following day. Down to London. I didn't see him again for years. And it's never been spoken of since.'

'And you've never told anyone?'

'Nope, although I think my brother Nick suspected something as I was at such pains to avoid Sebastian whenever he came back from uni and I guess he was reluctant to visit the way he had before. Yeah, Nick definitely knew something wasn't right.'

'That does sound ... how many years ago was that?

'Nearly ten. And I know it's stupid, at some point I should have said something, like "oops what an idiot. Sorry I had a crush on you." But the next time I saw him was at a wedding and he had this super-duper, glamorous, gorgeous, grown up woman with him.' The sort of woman that was everything Nina wasn't and he was probably totally unaware that she felt her nose was well and truly being rubbed in it, almost as if he were saying, this is what I like, not you. 'And over the years I've just sort of over compensated and been very cool with him. Make sure he knows that I'm absolutely not interested.' She groaned. 'Except that I always seem to manage to make a complete prat of myself whenever he's around.'

'Oh dear.'

'Oh dear indeed. I was at my friend's wedding. I love her dearly but her idea of a bridesmaid's dress, well, think peach meringue and the kind of fabric that could fire up a small power station with the amount of static electricity it produces and you have it. Unfortunately, the dress was so highly charged that the fabric wrapped itself around my legs and I kind of stumbled, which would have been fine if I hadn't been carrying two glasses of red wine and Sebastian and another one of his uber cool girlfriends weren't right in my path.'

'Ouch. What did you do?'

'Well, I would have apologised and offered to take her to help get cleaned up and borrow some other clothes, if I'd got the chance, but she was incandescent and let rip.' The scene was permanently embedded in her mind on a loop of doom. Blondie screaming, 'You stupid girl! Why don't you look where you're going?!' 'Of course, all I could do after that was stutter random half apologies like a pathetic idiot.'

'That sounds awful.'

'It was because she made such a big scene that everyone knew about it. I wanted to die. It was bad enough that I looked my most hideous, did I mention I also had an eye infection so was already rocking the Quasimodo look, but then to stand there with everyone looking at me dripping in red wine. Quite the worst thing. So, there you have it. Reasons why me and Sebastian are not the best of friends.'

'So if it were anyone else but Sebastian holed up in that hotel room, what would you do?' The sly look was back on her face.

'Don't go feeling too sorry for him. He's in a suite.'

'Ninaaa.'

'How do you do that?'

'Do what? And stop changing the subject!'

'You're the same age as me but you're doing that voice of reason thing, that mums do.'

Maddie grinned. 'That's because I'm the oldest of four, remember?'

'And you have no idea how it is to be the youngest of four. And if it were anyone but Sebastian, I'd ask Marguerite if I could borrow her wheelchair and offer to take him out for a while.'

Maddie shot her a cheeky grin. 'Go on. Do it. You know you want to.'

Nina gave her a mock glare. 'I'm not sure I do. He probably won't even appreciate it.'

'You'll never find out if you don't try,' said Maddie, with an altogether too knowing expression on her face.

Chapter 23

It was only when she was loading the empty wheelchair into the lift, having walked through the lobby to a few bemused glances and feeling as if she were Nurse Numpty with no patient, that she began to worry about the wisdom of what she was about to suggest. The Sebastian of her youth, friend to her brother, would probably have found it a hoot to use a wheelchair, and she could imagine Nick charging along pushing him. Elder statesmen and full-blown fuddy-duddy Sebastian probably wasn't going to be that keen, in fact this was probably a complete waste of time. Added to which, she'd gone and left his blasted book behind. Not that she believed for one minute that he actually wanted it.

She left the wheelchair outside the door and knocked sharply to announce her arrival.

'Good Lord, you're on time.'

'Morning, how are you?'

'Fine,' he growled. 'Bored. Everyone is either working or away.'

The windows were all open and a light breeze played with

the voile curtains tossing them playfully into the room around Sebastian.

'It's gorgeous out there.' She hesitated a fraction of a second and then decided there was no point building up to it. 'Do you fancy going out?'

'Where do you suggest?' The flat tone wasn't much of a giveaway – not a sarky 'don't be ridiculous', nor a 'yay, where shall we go' but it also wasn't a flat-out no.

'Well, I figured you've been cooped up here long enough. So ... well ... the thing is...'

He turned and stared at her, that piercing gaze making her feel totally stupid and gauche as usual. 'The thing is I borrowed a wheelchair and I thought I could take you out for a spin. Get some fresh air.' Sebastian's mouth twitched as she stumbled on. 'A change of scenery. Get you out of here. It's lovely and sunny and you must have been indoors for ages and it's, yes, it's so nice out, that you might, you know...'

'You borrowed a wheelchair? For real?' His face ran through a gamut of expressions before finally fixing on one that she was rather pleased to see looked impressed. That was a first.

She nodded, brushing away at an imaginary piece of lint on her black jeans

He let out a reluctant laugh. 'That's ...'

Pinching her lips hard, she held her breath, waiting. Here came the downer.

'Brilliant.'

'Really?' Her head shot up.

'Yes. Although with a pitch like that, you'll never make a salesperson, Nina.' Sebastian's grin was broad. 'And I'm not sure you've got the muscles but providing we don't venture up Sacré-Cœur let's give it a whirl.'

'Really?'

'Don't look quite so surprised.' He smiled at her. 'I'm not a complete ogre. If it were pissing down with rain and I was completely immobile I might be having second thoughts, but I can get up and walk if I need to. And where did you magic up a wheelchair?'

With an insouciant smile, she shrugged her shoulders. 'Let's leave it at magic and let me bask in this unusual approval from you.'

'Am I really that bad?' His eyes crinkled as he teased her.

She gave him a level stare. 'Yes, you are.'

He sobered for a second. 'I'm sorry. I'm not very good at switching out of work mode sometimes and I know you so well, that I kind of forget to reign it in. You know familiarity...'

'Breeds contempt? Not that you do know me anymore.' She gave him a determined look. 'I've changed a lot in ten years. I'm not a silly teenager with a stupid crush anymore.' There, she'd said it, got it out in the open.

'Not contempt, definitely not, but it makes people take things for granted. I'm sorry. I've been a bit snappy.'

'A bit snappy!' Her voice peaked in squeak. *How could he completely have missed her attempt at clearing the air.* 'You make Jaws look like a tame goldfish.'

Sebastian grinned. 'I said I was sorry. Now are you going to take me out in this fine chariot or keep reminding me that I've been a churlish bastard?'

'Hmm, don't get your hopes up too much. I think on a

scale of wheelchairs, this is about as bog standard as it gets. More Fiat than Ferrari.'

'If it gets me out of here, I don't care. As far as I'm concerned it's my chariot for the day.'

'Mavis,' said Nina suddenly. 'It's name is Mavis.'

Sebastian groaned and ignored her.

'Right, where are you taking me in my chariot?' he asked after he'd settled into the chair, arranging the pair of crutches down by his side and with his leg propped out in front of him. For once, he looked rather relaxed. Nina felt a sudden boost at his confidence in her. If the boot was on the other foot, she wasn't sure she'd feel that relaxed.

They'd only walked a few paces down the street and she'd already realised that pushing a wheelchair was a real eye-opener, especially for someone who'd never had to worry about dropped kerbs before or people who meandered slowly off course. Stopping or turning the wheelchair at short notice was rather like driving an ocean liner, or so she imagined. It wasn't easy. Thankfully, Sebastian hadn't got into the wheelchair until they were outside the front of the lobby of the hotel as the wheelchair almost ran away with her down the ramp which really wasn't a good start but he didn't seem to notice.

'This is my maiden voyage with this thing, don't get too excited. I'm not sure it's built for speed or manoeuvrability.'

'Don't you worry about that, today I'm embracing my inner Ben Hur. It's my chariot. It's freedom. And a day off. I can't remember the last time I got away from spreadsheets, contractors' calls and rotas.'

'Have you been taking extra pills?' asked Nina with a smile, grasping the handles of the chair, starting to push it down the street, unused to this light-hearted side of Sebastian.

'No, it's the dose of sunshine, it's beefed up my vitamin D and my cheer quota.' Over his shoulder he gave another dazzling grin. He was so close she could see the faint bristles breaking through on his chin and the tiny hazel flecks in his eyes, triggering a memory so sharp and incisive she almost gasped. Sebastian asking her to taste a chocolate mousse, feeding her a spoonful and grinning in a way that made her heart do somersaults when she told him it was orgasmic. Not that at sixteen she'd had the first clue what that might feel like.

With a perfunctory shake, as if trying to dislodge the memory, she lifted her chin and said crisply, 'You can be chief navigator,' even though she had a pretty good idea where they were going. 'I thought we'd motor up to the Place de la Concorde and walk through Le Jardin des Tuileries as it's such a lovely day. And then depending on how you feel we could stop for lunch somewhere or pick up *le sandwich* and eat al fresco.'

'Sounds good to me, push on and don't spare the horses.'

The Jardin des Tuileries was the perfect venue, although the pale gravel paths in the brilliant sunshine reflected the light a touch too brightly and Nina was grateful that she'd had the foresight to pack her sunglasses.

'Are you OK?' she asked, realising Sebastian was shading his eyes.

'Yeah, I'm just not used to daylight. I feel like a vampire

231

getting his first taste of sun. I'm worried I might shrivel up and disappear in a pile of ash.'

After walking through the gardens for about half an hour they came to a stop.

'You OK?' asked Sebastian.

'Mm,' she said. In fact she was a bit bored, it wasn't much fun talking to the back of Sebastian's head and he'd grown quieter in the last ten minutes. 'You?'

'Yeah ... it's nice to be outside.'

'But?'

'Now I'm going to sound like an ungrateful churlish bastard again. But it's a bit dull. And trying to talk to someone behind you, I've got neckache. Would you mind if I had a go at pushing myself? Then you could walk beside me.'

'Feel free.' She let go of the handles.

'Do you think you could give me a bit of a push to get a bit of momentum going? Easier than a standing start. In fact—' he turned and shot her a look full of mischief '—I'm tempted to find out how fast this thing will go. I dare you to push me as fast as you can.'

'You're mad.' She rolled her eyes.

'I'm serious. I dare you.' He gave a searching look.

'That's not fair.'

That tiny quirk of his eyebrow told her didn't give a damn.

'How old are you?'

'Thirty. Are you chicken?'

She stood pondering for a minute. In the Hadley family no one ever backed down from a dare, her least of all. With four brothers on your case all the time, it was one of the times where you couldn't be beaten. There were few occasions where she could be equal to their height and strengths. A dare was always winnable.

'I'm never chicken, Sebastian Finlay, and that's a dirty trick to play.' A smile hovered around her lips.

'You still running?'

'Not here, it's not my idea of fun running in a city.' She grinned at him. 'Not enough mud.'

'Still fell running then?'

'Yes, but not seriously.' As a child she'd run for county in the cross-country competitions. It was something her rugby playing brothers had never been able to understand the appeal of. For them sport meant being part of a team. They couldn't relate to the solitude and she'd never bothered to explain that running on her own gave her some space and privacy. The chance to be alone with her thoughts.

'It always seemed an anathema, you were so dainty and neat and yet you'd go charging off like a tiny determined dynamo and come back like some swamp fairy covered from head to toe in mud.'

'Swamp fairy.' Nina's laugh pealed out, a little too loudly. She'd just remembered the picture he had of her in his flat. And him waiting for her at the finish line. 'Which charm school did they throw you out of? Running gave me the chance to do my own thing. Get away from the boys telling me how I should be doing things. Under my own steam, out of sight, just me.' And him when he'd come to support her, how many times? Five? She was kidding herself, she knew it was exactly five times because each of them was branded into her memory.

And those five occasions had been the evidence for the jury when she'd decided to go for broke and kiss him.

'So go on then. Show us what you've got, Hadley.'

'You really want me to?'

'Yes, I need the buzz. I feel punchy and scratchy, after two weeks of inactivity and being confined to barracks. It's quiet around here. We're not going to crash into anyone. And there's a nice straight stretch.'

'Yes, but what if I tip you out?'

'I'll hang on tight. Or are you still chicken?'

'Take my bag.' She dumped it in his lap and made a big show of rolling up her sleeves.

'Last chance to back out Finlay.'

They must have made quite a sight careering down the wide path, Sebastian yelling, 'Faster, faster! Don't spare the horses!'

The gravel flying under the wheels spattered upwards as she charged along, clipping her ankles. It only took a short while to pick up the pace and she had to adjust her usual running stride so she didn't bang her knees on the back of the chair but quickly she mastered it and lost any sense of self-consciousness.

With the wind whipping her hair across her face and Sebastian's delighted whoops, exhilaration filled her and she got braver and picked up her speed.

'Yee-ha!' yelled Sebastian. And suddenly they were eighteen and twenty again and she could remember the good times they'd had together before she'd spoiled things. The memories rushed up with the wind in her face. Sebastian going out training with her one summer's day. Sebastian teaching her how to roll pastry. Sebastian helping her home after a party and putting her to bed so that her brothers and parents didn't know how horribly and disgracefully drunk she'd got. And never breathing a word. No wonder he'd been her absolute hero. Where had that Sebastian gone?

'Turn, turn!' yelled Sebastian, his voice ringing with glee as they neared the end of the path where a large fountain completed the vista. Taking as wide a circle as she could, she veered around the base, fearful that any second one wheel might lift, but Mavis was a sturdy contraption and held its centre of gravity as they hurtled around. It was hard going trying to steer and she hauled backwards bringing the chair to an eventual halt beside the fountain.

'Priceless, Nina, priceless.' Sebastian laughed, his head thrown back a wide beam on his face. 'That was so much fun.

'I'm glad you think so, I'm bloody knackered,' she wheezed, bent double, grateful for the fine mist of water from the fountain beside them. She sat down on the low stone edge with a thump next to him.

'Bit out of condition, are we Hadley?'

'When you've got that thing off your leg, I'll let you push me round Paris and see how you feel, you cheeky sod. You weigh a ton. Been eating a few too many pies.'

This was more like it, keeping things light and matey. The perfect way to show Sebastian that she was over her silly crush on him. Perhaps she should broach the subject with him.

'Tartes to you, young lady,' he retorted. 'And I wish. I've been begging Alex to change the room service menu. In fact.' His eyes lit up. 'What's next on the Nina Hadley tour of Paris?'

'Well, I thought maybe a boat ride. It'll save my poor arms. We can catch the Batobus at Quai des Tuileries, although we need to get tickets first from Rue des Pyramides which isn't far from here. It's like a shuttle bus, except it's a boat—'

'I think I got that.' He gave her a teasing smile.

She ignored him. 'And you can get off at different places. I thought it would let us cover more ground and be easier than trying to get you up and down in the Metro.'

Maybe on the boat ride, with this light-hearted atmosphere between them, she could make some joke about what an idiot she'd been when she was eighteen and get it all out in the open. Show him she'd moved on and that it had meant nothing.

'Great idea. I'm impressed. You have been doing your research.'

'Can't take the credit for that one, I'm afraid. Maddie's suggestions. She knows Paris pretty well.'

'Excellent. Which has given me an idea. I'm going to make a phone call. I know just the place we can go for a late lunch.' He'd pulled out his phone and made a quick call speaking in rapid, impressive French.

Catching the boat was a great way of seeing the city from a completely different angle and gave Nina the chance to rest her aching arms.

The boat revved up and reversed back into the wide river and she sat back, happy to watch the scenes as they rolled by. She was grateful for the spring sunshine because it did feel much colder out on the water. Behind her she could hear a group of German tourists talking with great enthusiasm, even though she couldn't understand a word, and on the row in front an English family were teasing their Dad about his fear of heights and whether he'd go up to the top of the Eiffel Tower with them or not.

Sebastian was scrolling through the screen on his phone, his dark head bent. She studied him for a minute before crossing her fingers under her thighs. 'Sebastian ... remember...'

'Look.' Sebastian, held up his phone. 'If we get off at Saint-Germain-des-Prés, this restaurant is only a couple of streets over. And we get to see quite a bit on the way.' He held up the map on his phone. 'It's run by an old friend of mine and I've been meaning to visit since I came to Paris and there just hasn't been time.'

Nina relaxed her hands and felt the tension leave her shoulders. Maybe she'd bring it up over lunch, when it was just the two of them.

'So how do you know him?'

'When I left college, I worked in a couple of restaurants in England and met Roger. His father ran a Michelin-starred restaurant in Lyon. When he went back to work for his father, we kept in touch and I was lucky enough to get a placement at his father's restaurant in Lyon.'

Nina remembered Nick mentioning that Sebastian had gone to work in France. At the time, the news had been a curious heart-tripping mix of disappointment and relief.

'I worked there for six months and then I was offered a

job as a sous chef. It was the best possible apprenticeship for me. I learned so much. Not just about the cooking but Marc was a brilliant businessman. So many restaurants fail because they're not profitable. He taught me how to watch the pennies without sacrificing quality as well as managing a menu and maximising the number of covers. When I opened my first restaurant, I called it Marc's as a tribute to him for everything I learned.'

'What a lovely thing to do, I bet he was touched.'

'I think so. Roger cried, that's for sure. Marc was good to me, a father figure, even though he probably bawled me out a thousand times more than my dad.' Nina didn't need to see his face to see that his mood had changed. There was a sudden stillness to his shoulders. 'He died not long after that but Roger and I have stayed in touch. I should have gone to Roger's restaurant before now, but you know what it's like and then this bloody leg. I hope you'll like it. Sorry I didn't ask if you had any other lunch plans.'

She was grateful that the decision had been taken out of her hands. Left to her own devices, she probably would have opted for one of the cafés in the park.

The boat passed around the fascinating Île Saint-Louis and Île de la Cité with Notre Dame. It seemed incredible that the river in the centre of the city was wide enough to accommodate not one but two islands. 'Gosh, it's weird to see it in real life,' she said as the boat passed the familiar twin towers of Notre Dame.

'I know what you mean. You almost think you know it because you've seen it in countless films and books.'

'A bit like spotting a celebrity in the street and saying hello,' said Nina.

Sebastian laughed. 'A good analogy, although it helps if you know the local celebrities. When I was working in the restaurant in Lyon, a very famous French actress came in and of course I had no clue who she was and couldn't catch her name when she said she had a reservation. She was not amused when I asked her to spell it three times.'

Nina winced. She couldn't imagine Sebastian ever being nonplussed or at a loss. In her head he always seemed so in control and confident. It had almost slipped her mind that once upon a time he hadn't been so worldly and experienced.

Nina would remember Roger's appalled face for quite some time and it took Sebastian a bit of explaining to persuade him that the wheelchair wasn't permanent. She'd also remember this red wine for the rest of her life. She took another sip, leaning back in the spacious leather chair, listening to the two of them as they indulged in chef's shop talk, speaking at a thousand miles an hour and switching easily between French and English. The menu was discussed and debated at great length and Nina found it fascinating to hear Sebastian so animated for a change. Despite the menu, there was no way that they would be allowed to choose anything from it – instead Roger kept bringing tasters of this and that for Sebastian's approval.

A sliver of beef with an amazing salad of peppery greens with a bite of mustard, a slice of chicken in a pool of the most zingy lemon sauce, a piece of sole that melted in her mouth, a spoonful of tomato risotto that exploded with flavour and a tiny ramekin of mushroom and parmesan soufflé. She felt utterly spoiled and really rather privileged, especially when she saw the eyewatering prices on the menu.

Finally, Roger departed when a large party came into the restaurant and took up residence at one of the large round tables at the back of the room.

'Sorry about that,' said Sebastian, reaching for his glass and swirling around the rich dark wine which Roger had insisted on them having on the house. 'We tend to get a bit carried away when we're together.'

'If I get to drink wine like this,' she said, taking an appreciative sniff, 'I don't mind at all.'

Sebastian paused and put down his glass. 'That's what I've always liked about you, Nina. You've always been very patient and understanding. Too much sometimes. Your brothers took advantage on occasion, it used to wind me up.'

And there it was, another one of those memories creeping through the cracks. Sebastian being her hero. Giving her a lift home because Nick had forgotten. Telling Nick off when he'd made her wait for fifty minutes before he took her to her friend's while he finished a game on the Xbox. Living in the middle of nowhere had its downsides until you learned to drive. Now would have been the perfect time to make her confession but...

'Katrin would have been a bit put out at me ignoring her for—' he flicked his wrist to take a look at his watch '—ouch, sorry, twenty minutes.'

Nina tensed at the mention of the sophisticated French

woman. *Would have?* Was that past tense? Or just a figure of speech.

'You weren't ignoring me, you were just distracted and to be honest it was…' Nina paused, sliding her hands under her thighs again. 'It was good to see. You've always been so passionate about food. You inspired me. I've not seen that for a while.'

Sebastian gave a shrug, a touch defensively she thought.

'So how many restaurants do you own?'

With a rueful laugh, he shook his head. 'I don't own any outright, I have quite a few investors. In fact, Roger and Alex have invested in my two new ones in Paris, both of which are on track to open next month and then the bistro a month later, once I get the contractors in after the patisserie is closed. And then there are four in the UK, with British investors, in Oxford, Stratford, Towcester and Olney. They're all ticking along quite nicely which is why I decided to branch out.'

'Because you didn't have enough on your plate?'

Sebastian winced. 'There is that.'

'So what drives you?' Nina was amazed that she'd dared ask the question. But she was intrigued. He never seemed satisfied with what he'd achieved. Even Nick had been surprised that he'd moved to Paris.

Sebastian glanced back down at the menu, his mouth firming. 'I guess building a business. Being a chef isn't enough. You've got to strive for more.'

'But isn't being a chef what you wanted?'

'Of course I did, but… My dad was a banker in the city. Being a chef was a luxury, but it's not really enough. You should own your own restaurant. The business side of things is equally important.'

They were interrupted by the waiter bringing a dessert menu and asking if they wanted coffee.

'Thanks for this, Nina,' said Sebastian quietly at her side, catching her rubbing at her sore biceps at the end of the meal as the final coffee cups were cleared away. 'I do appreciate you bringing the wheelchair over, it was thoughtful and it's been great to get out. I really didn't expect you to give up a whole day for me.'

'It's fine, and ... don't repeat this, but it's much more fun seeing Paris with someone else.'

'Ah, got fed up with the wanting to be alone campaign.'

'No, not at all. It's not that I want to be alone. I want to be independent and not have someone worrying or chipping in with their opinion every five minutes. But even that's too much to ask.' She picked up her phone and showed him her WhatsApp feed.

'Ouch.' He bit back a smile. 'I used to envy your family. Everyone looking out for each other, but this ... I can see it might get a bit much sometimes. Hell, are these all today's?' He scrolled through the chat. 'That's mad.'

There were messages from every member of the family.

'Yup. And if I don't check in, like once an hour, I start getting texts as well.'

'I guess it shows they care.'

'It does but...' She sighed. 'But it feels like I can't ever escape.'

'You could not answer.'

'Tried that.'

'I know.'

She shot him a look so he elaborated on his admission. 'Last Tuesday. I started getting anxious texts from them.'

'Oh, for fu— Pete's sake.'

'Nina Hadley, you weren't about to swear then?'

'Yes, I bloody was. Honestly, you are as bad as my brothers. They have this view of me being a perfect doll that needs to be looked after.'

'I could have a word.'

'Yes, you could and then that would be someone else looking out for me.'

'Only trying to help. You do it then.'

She sighed. 'I can't, I don't want to hurt anyone's feelings.'

'Well, you can't have it both ways. At some point, if it bothers you that much you are going to have to do something about it.'

'Thank you, Einstein. What do you think coming out here was about?'

He grinned cheerfully. 'I thought you were rushing to my rescue. Couldn't resist my charms.'

She stiffened and clenched her fingers under her thighs. This was it. The chance to clear the air and finally move on from what happened ten years ago. 'Sebastian, at eighteen I imagined myself madly in love with you because you were nicer to me than my brothers. I realise now it was a crush. I hate to tell you this but you are definitely not my type. And I'm sorry I kissed you, it was a silly, rash thing to do and didn't mean anything. Teenage hormones going a bit doolally and I'm embarrassed by it now and I embarrassed you. So, I'm sorry but I don't … you know… and as soon as you'd gone, I fell in love with another boy. That's what girls that age do.' She forced out a self-deprecating laugh. 'God, it must have looked so stupid to you. This silly little girl trying to kiss you. You must have had quite a laugh about it later. Anyway, that's all water under the bridge. Rather apt after our boat trip, don't you think?' She could feel herself getting pinker and pinker, and her cheeks hurting with the forced smile on her face. It all just came out at once and she couldn't stop herself. She could read sympathetic concern in his face which was the last thing she wanted and in panic, she blurted out, 'I really don't fancy you anymore. I don't even find you very good looking or anything…' Her voice trailed away. His face changed.

'Good to know,' he said, dismissively. 'It's not every day I get told that.'

'Ouch, sorry that came out wrong but you know what I mean, you're not my type. I'm sure there are some women who would find you, you know, good – er – a – attractive … but not me. Not that you aren't but…' Why couldn't she just shut up? 'I just wanted to set the record straight, you know, so there's no awkwardness between us anymore.'

'Well. That's quite a speech.' He didn't look amused, which was what he was supposed to do. 'And for the record, I didn't laugh about it.'

He picked up his phone and started checking his emails.

That was it? She'd just laid herself bare with the most embarrassing moment of her life and he was reading his emails?

244

'Damn. Will you excuse me for a minute? I need to make a couple of calls. It looks like the flooring contractors have delivered the wrong tiles.'

Nina stared down at the pristine white tablecloth, grateful for his absorption in a conversation about grouting and square metres. The thudding pain in her chest felt as if it had been hollowed out by an ice cream scoop. Unrequited love was a stinker. It felt even worse now, to know that the moment, so indelibly printed on her mind, had meant nothing to him. If ever she knew that her misplaced love was of absolutely no interest to him, it was now. Disinterest was written across his face, and in the way he didn't even acknowledge what had happened and how casually he switched back to his work. What had she been thinking coming out here? She was as much in love with the stupid bastard as ever. So much for all her bravado. Nina had never felt so deflated.

Chapter 24

'Oh God, they look terrible.' Maddie poked at the sticky crumbling mess which was a disgusting shade of puce. 'Truly, truly awful.' Nina could see her biting her lip trying to hold back the laughter.

'Thanks,' said Nina, with a wobble in her voice, tempted to point out that Maddie wasn't looking brilliant, what with the big blue streak of paint down her face and the bright yellow dot on her nose, but as she was working on touching up the mermaid, it would have been a bit mean.

But it was hard to see the funny side of things when you'd just wasted nearly a dozen eggs and a ton of sugar and all you had in return were five cooling racks worth of sugary splodges. They looked nothing like Sebastian's perfectly risen circular macarons. Nina pursed her lips as Maddie nudged her, her eyes twinkling in amusement and then conceded, 'Yes, alright, they look terrible.' She smiled. 'How come they don't even look vaguely pink, I put enough food colouring in to sink a small fleet of ships.'

'They look puke-coloured,' said Maddie, with a twinkle, as she attempted to peel off a piece of macaron that was firmly welded to the baking paper. They were so sticky she had to spend a minute picking off bits of paper that stuck to her fingers before she was able to pop it into her mouth. 'Mmm, they taste good.'

'If you could get them off the paper.'

'Yeah, there is that. They have definite superglue properties.' She chewed manfully, picking at her back teeth with her fingers.

'I don't know what I did wrong. Maybe tripling the recipe wasn't such a good idea. But if we did the small batches we'd be here for ever.' She sighed. 'Sebastian made it look so easy. Same with the spun sugar lesson.'

'Which was a complete nightmare, I was still finding strands of caramel in my hair yesterday. I'm not sure I'm ever going to get the hang of this cooking malarkey,' said Maddie before adding with a huge grin, 'but I'm having so much fun.'

'I wish I was,' said Nina gloomily. 'What am I going to do? Marcel's relying on me today.'

'Better stick to éclairs,' said Maddie, practical as ever. 'You're ruddy brilliant at those.'

'I can't keep making nothing but éclairs forever.'

'Marcel won't mind, not really. He's just delighted that he has fresh goods to sell. I think he's mortally embarrassed by the bought in ones. He can barely look the delivery driver in the eye.'

'Well, he needs to get over that, besides it's not for that much longer,' said Nina, immediately regretting saying it. The poor man was about to lose his job. 'And making éclairs is not exactly expanding my repertoire.'

'Yes, but the customers love them. Especially the chocolate and hazelnut combo.'

'They were rather good, weren't they?'

'Good, they were pure heaven.' Maddie smacked her lips.

'That reminds me, what do you think about coffee and walnut flavoured ones? Like coffee and walnut cake at home.'

'Genius! What a brilliant idea. See, you can make éclairs forever.'

Nina rolled her eyes.

'No seriously, it's a British twist on a traditional French favourite. Anglo-French fusion. You could market that.'

'Anglo-French fusion,' Nina laughed. 'I think the French might be horrified at that concept and I don't need to market anything. I'm just practising my skills while I've got the opportunity and a commercial kitchen, and Marcel is taking shameless advantage. I can't believe he cancelled today's delivery.'

She turned to Maddie with sudden horror, realising that the cabinets in the patisserie were virtually empty. 'I need to come up with something else, quickly.'

Nina started gathering together the ingredients to make fillings for the éclair shells which were already made. She'd got it down to a fine art, making a big batch of choux pastry and baking enough that could be kept for a couple of days before filling. But she'd been doing it on an ad hoc basis to please Marcel rather than as a serious supplier – she was thrown now he'd cancelled the order. How on earth was she going to fill the gap? At home she'd knock up a quick batch of scones, some shortbread and a Victoria sponge, all of which she could do in her sleep. Traditionalist Marcel would have a fit if she tried to palm those off on him.

She stopped for a moment and turned to Maddie. 'Anglo-French fusion. I think I've got an idea. It's not proper patisserie but...' The more she thought about it the more she liked the idea, if she could pull it off.

'When I went to Ladurée, there was this amazing cheese-cake, but it was a modern twist. Really clever. Maybe I could do a patisserie twist on an old faithful that I do at home.'

Maddie looked very interested and hopped up on one of the benches, her eyes beady and head cocked like an impatient robin. 'Spill.'

Nina winced. The idea was a little too new to share yet. It could be a complete disaster but Maddie looked so bright eyed and enthusiastic it was difficult to resist.

'I was thinking of a twist on millionaire's shortbread. I'm copying the idea of the cheesecake base, where the base was biscuit crumbs but really lovely buttery ones. So I thought I'd make up a batch of very fine shortbread, I've got a brilliant recipe I use, then crumble it up and combine with more butter to make the base, then put a thin layer of salted caramel on top of the shortbread base and then a thick layer of chocolate mousse on top of that, topped with a very fine layer of crisp chocolate, dusted with a few flecks of gold leaf.'

'Oooh scrummy scrummy. I adore millionaire's shortbread and that sounds amazing.'

'Yes, but whether I can make it and it all stays together is another matter.'

'Let's bin these bad boys and get started,' said Maddie, jumping off the counter.

'What, now?' Nina looked around at the messy kitchen.

'I'll get started on the washing up and you can knock up the éclairs so Marcel's got something to start with, and then we make your multi-millionaire's shortbread. I can't wait to try it.' Maddie was already picking up the trays of deflated macarons and sliding the baking sheets into the bin.

'You don't have to help,' said Nina. 'Shouldn't you be studying or something?'

'Or something,' said Maddie with a mischievous grin. 'I've an essay to do but I'm a last-minute merchant. I've got a week to get it done. I'd far rather be doing this. Plus I get fed which is always a bonus.'

'You look like you know what you're doing,' observed Maddie from her spot at the sink, taking surreptitious licks of the caramel pan. 'This is delicious.'

'And you're going to make yourself sick,' said Nina with a laugh. 'God, I sound like my mother.'

'I don't care,' said Maddie with a grin taking another swipe at the pan with her finger. 'And I sound like my younger brother, when I used to nag him. I don't miss that. Being the responsible one all the time. Even though I miss them all like crazy. Thanks for letting me help.'

Nina couldn't help laughing. 'You mean I had a choice?'

'Not really, no,' said Maddie complacently. 'But you do look different.'

'How?' asked Nina, wrinkling her nose as she tried to

concentrate on spreading a layer of caramel on the short-bread biscuit base. She'd decided to make them in the small metal rounds she'd found in one of the drawers at the back of the room, so that they looked daintier and more like patisserie.

'You're more decisive and confident.'

'I guess it's because I know what I'm doing. What the consistency of each thing should look like. I make this kind of stuff all the time at home. It's almost second nature. And Sebastian's not here.'

'Ah,' said Maddie.

'He makes me nervous because he's the professional.'

'He makes me nervous because he's so damn good looking. My hormones get all a bit giddy looking at him.'

'They need to get a grip then,' said Nina with a sudden snigger at the memory of her conversation with him at lunch yesterday. After he'd finished his call, he'd promptly called a cab to take them back to the hotel, the wheelchair bundled in the boot, the laughter of their day together forgotten, and he'd spent most of the journey on his phone.

She began to giggle. 'I've just re – remembered...' She held back a snort, her hand over her face. 'I – I to – told him...' She tried to breathe in but laughed again.

Maddie looked at her impatiently, taking one last lick of the finger she'd been using to swipe around the pan.

'I t – told him...' It was no good, she held her stomach.

'Do you know how irritating you are?' asked Maddie, rolling her eyes as Nina carried on giggling and clutching her stomach.

'S – sorry,' gasped Nina. 'It's really not that f – funny.'

'I dread to think what you'd be like if it was funny,' said Maddie, laughing as she crossed to the sink to start running the water.

Nina took a breath and started rounding up the dirty utensils. 'I told Sebastian he wasn't very good looking.'

Maddie's mouth crumpled as she tried to keep a straight face. 'Seriously?'

Nina, clutching a chocolatey whisk and a handful of sugar-covered wooden spoons, nodded, her face almost aching as she tried to keep it perfectly straight.

They both burst out laughing.

'And what? This just came up in conversation? I mean, I'm sorry but how do you tell someone they're not good looking?' Maddie put on a silly high-pitched voice as she plunged her hands into the hot soapy water. 'Hey Sebastian, did you know you're not very good looking?'

Nina, dropping the whisk and spoons into the water, paused. 'Oh ... no, it wasn't like that but ... oh God, I can't believe I said it now.'

'How does something like that come up in conversation?' asked Maddie, getting cracking on the pile of washing up.

'It gets worse.' Nina grimaced at the memory. 'I also told him I didn't fancy him.'

'Oh God, that is double speak for I really really fancy you. Denial is the next best thing to admitting it.' Maddie dropped a handful of suds-covered forks on the draining board with a clatter.

Nina groaned as she grabbed a tea towel. 'No! It can't. I

was just trying to clear the air and explain that I'd moved on since I was a teenager.'

'So you told him he wasn't very good looking and you didn't fancy him,' said Maddie, turning to her, amusement dancing all over her face. 'Nice job. And what did he say to that?'

Nina looked shamefaced and paused as she rubbed dry a mixing bowl. 'He told me it was good to know and that it wasn't every day he got told that.'

Maddie started to snigger.

'It's not funny really,' said Nina

'Yes, it is. It's ab-so-lutely bloody hilarious.' The two of them dissolved into helpless giggles.

'Mercy me, I've died and gone to heaven,' drawled a strong American accent. The young woman had one of those loud look-at-me voices and had been commenting at full volume on her Instagram feed for the last five minutes, every now and then breaking off to take photos of the patisserie.

'This is banging,' she said, taking a selfie of her with a forkful of the caramel and chocolate mousse.

Maddie nudged Nina, who smiled despite her aching feet. Nothing beat the feeling of satisfaction when people enjoyed food you'd made. She drained her coffee cup catching Marcel's eye. My goodness, was he almost smiling?

'They're a hit,' whispered Maddie.

'I have to admit...' Nina bit back the grin threatening to engulf her face. 'I'm rather pleased with them.' The multi-millionaire shortbread as Maddie was insisting on calling it, had gone down rather well. 'But we still need to come up with a better name. It's a shame millionaire is the same in French.'

'How about millionaire gâteaux?' asked Maddie, sitting back and rolling her shoulders.

'Chocolat caramel suprême,' said Marcel, suddenly appearing behind Nina, his tone intimating they were both too stupid to live and the name was completely obvious. Darting between them with his usual neat efficiency, he scooped up their empty cups. 'And we've nearly sold out, so you need to make some more.'

Nina glared at him. 'Only if you promise me you haven't cancelled the delivery again tomorrow.'

'I can't make that promise,' he said, a shadow of a smile threatening to lighten his sombre face. A sound drew their attention and with a subtle tut, he straightened. 'What is that woman doing now?'

'I think she's having a Meg Ryan moment,' said Maddie with a naughty twinkle.

Marcel didn't deign to reply and instead, spotting another couple leaving, swooped in to remove the plates and cups.

'Honestly, he is super-efficient,' said Nina. 'It's such a shame, he's wasted here.'

'And a slave-driver. Shall we crack on? I think you'd better make another batch for tomorrow.'

'As it's the grand painting day for the outside of the shop, I'd better. I'm not sure how much time there'll be for baking.'

Chapter 25

The high-pitched whines of multiple sanders greeted Nina as well as a mile-long queue when she arrived at the patisserie the following morning.

'Morning,' she called to Bill who was out on the pavement next to a couple of trestle tables which had been set up with cans of paint, primer, filler, brushes and other bits of equipment she didn't recognise. He clearly didn't hear her as he carried on opening a can of paint. In brown work overalls with a baseball cap planted firmly on his head, he looked like he meant business and was holding a rather official-looking clipboard in one of his meaty hands on the back of which read the words Operation Éclair.

'Morning Nina,' he yelled above the noise as he spotted her.

'We're preparing to paint,' he said, nodding down at the cables and extension leads snaking in a rat's tail mess across trailing back into the patisserie. For a moment, Nina winced; this was a much bigger operation that she'd expected.

And more worryingly who were all the people waiting outside the café?

'I can see that,' she replied, waving weakly and blinking as the dust filling the air caught at her eyes. At the sight of the resurrection of Patisserie C in full swing she felt slightly sick and just a touch out of her depth. Suddenly the task looked so much bigger than slapping a bit of paint on to smarten the place up. This was a big job and not her decision to make. Even though Sebastian planned to completely revamp the place in a matter of months, she'd be lying if she thought he'd welcome what they were doing. She nibbled at her lip as the horrible realisation dawned on her. This was exactly the sort of impetuous, 'someone will rescue me later and pick up the pieces' sort of behaviour he'd accused her of. She'd gone ahead, deliberately not consulting with him, which was rude and arrogant in the first instance but worse still, she'd made excuses for her behaviour by trying to justify it with the assumption that it would be OK in the end because of the refurbishment work that was planned. Oh God, what had she done? And now it was too late to stop it, half the paint on the shop front had been sanded away to a pale ash wood colour.

'Let me introduce you to "an-the-lads",' said Bill, peeling back a dust mask from around his nose and mouth with a delighted grin. 'We've made good progress already.'

'Yes,' said Nina slightly dazed. 'What time did you start? I thought we said ten.'

'Well, we were up and raring to go ... and the lads fancy watching a footie match in a bar this afternoon. So we thought we'd get ahead of ourselves and started at eight. 'Now, this is Tone.' A tall lanky man who was scraping away at the old paint around the door turned and nodded. Bill yelled above the noise – 'Jizzer!' – and the man who was whizzing the sander over the panels on the right-hand side of the frontage, glanced over his shoulder and gave a sort of shoulder shrug and then switched off the sander. Next, Bill pointed to a scary looking bald bloke with a tattoo covering his thick neck, hard at work wiping down the panels on the other side which had already been sanded. 'And that's Mucker.' Mucker grinned and put down his cloth saying, 'Pleased to meet you,' in the most unexpectedly posh voice.

'AKA me-an-the-lads,' finished Bill.

'Hi everyone,' said Nina with a welcoming smile at the unlikely group of friends as they all downed tools and stepped close, crowding around her. She was itching to find out what the queue was in aid of but didn't want to be rude to Bill's friends, especially when they were doing her such a massive favour. 'Thank you so much for coming.'

'It's our pleasure,' said Mucker. 'Bill's told us what a power-house you were. And that you needed some help.'

'He also said you make a mean éclair,' said Tone in a low growl which was accompanied by an unexpectedly puckish grin.

'He's got such a sweet tooth on him,' said Jizzer, wiping his forehead by lifting his T-shirt hem. 'The things this man will do for cake.'

'And beer, don't forget beer,' said Tone.

'I haven't got any beer,' said Nina, suddenly wondering if she should go and get some. Although she was pretty sure that beer and power tools didn't mix.

'Don't you worry, love,' piped up Mucker. 'This'll keep us out of mischief. As long as we're in the bar by lunchtime, we'll be happy. Bill's buying the first six rounds.'

'Six?' protested Bill. 'I'm sure we agreed on five.' The four of them nudged and jostled each other with the easy familiarity of brothers.

With a quick nod their way, she scuttled inside the café.

'Bonjour Marcel,' she said, smiling at the sight of him. Even he had dressed for the occasion, although he clearly had no intention of joining in with the painting. He'd donned a plastic apron over his usual waistcoat and black trousers instead of the usual white one tied around his waist. 'What's going on?' she whispered, looking round at the full patisserie.

'Good morning, Nina. Coffee for Bill's compatriots?'

'Yes please, I'll take them out. And they're demanding éclairs.'

'They'll have to get in line,' said Marcel. 'I'm rather busy.'

'But? How?' Nina spread her arms wide.

'They were waiting outside the door when I arrived, demanding chocolat caramel suprême. I've nearly sold out. You'll need to make some more.'

As the others still hadn't arrived and Marcel seemed to be managing perfectly well despite the unexpected influx of customers, she nipped into the kitchen to take stock and decide whether she should abandon the others and keep baking.

'Right,' said Bill looking around at the motley group as Nina handed the coffees out twenty minutes later. Jane, Peter and

Maddie had arrived while she was in the kitchen and were wildly excited about something.

'Look,' said Maddie, pulling out her phone. There was a picture of the chocolat caramel suprême with the caption, 'Best cake in Paris'. 'I spotted this on Instagram.'

'That's amazing.'

'Yeah and look how many likes it's got.'

'Bloody hell. Four thousand. That's crazy.'

'Crazy but good publicity. Hence the queue outside this morning.'

'Eek, I'd better get cracking on making some more then. I've just checked and I haven't got enough ingredients,' said Nina. 'Do you mind if I duck out? I need to go shopping and then I'll be spending most of the day in the kitchen.' Nina nodded at Bill.

'Not at all. Me-an-the-lads have done most of the prep work. We're good to go on the right-hand side. We can start painting. Got the good stuff, so no priming needed. And is this what you wanted Nina?'

He showed her an open tin of paint.

'Wow, that looks a pretty good match,' she said, looking at the dark grey colour. The sudden vision of what the frontage would look like and the eager faces of everyone around her made her swallow her concerns. She'd have to find a good moment to tell Sebastian what she'd done. 'This old lady is going to look so smart, she won't know what's hit her.'

'Maybe if Sebastian sees it, he might decide to keep it open,' said Jane, softly, standing behind Bill, her hair tied back with a rainbow striped scarf. She was wearing the most enormous pair of jeans cinched in at the waist with another scarf. You could have got one of her in each leg. She kept hauling them up one-handed like a clown worried about being caught short, unaware that Peter was mischievously giving them a quick tug every now and then.

Nina smiled at her. She loved that Jane could only ever see the good in people. 'Sadly, that's not going to happen. Sebastian lets his head rule. It's never been an option.'

'Right then, let's get cracking, then I can get the lads down the bar. And don't you worry Nina, there are plenty of us here.'

Paintbrushes had been dished out and work allocated by Bill whose sergeant major tendencies had come to the fore this morning, but he was the happiest Nina had ever seen him. Peter's job was to tape up all the windows so that they wouldn't get paint on the glass, and then to paint the large panels underneath the windows. Jane was given the fiddly twiddly bits as she called the beading around the edges of the door as Bill and his team finished stripping the last of the paint. Maddie was carrying on her work on the painting of the mermaid, which she'd been working on in every spare minute and hoped to get on painting the upper walls pale blue in readiness to sponge on the white clouds later.

Feeling guilty that she'd left them with the dirty job, Nina headed off to the nearest supermarket to stock up on cream and butter.

By lunchtime when Marguerite arrived with a picnic, Nina had managed to knock up a quick batch of choux pastry and bake several dozen éclairs and make up her new variant on an éclair as well as make three dozen of the chocolat caramel suprême. Thankfully, Marguerite had arrived in time to offer a hand and when everyone trooped in for lunch, the kitchen was spotless.

'Come. There's plenty for everyone. *Fromage, jambon, du pain*.' Marguerite waved her hands above the mouth-watering spread as they congregated around the kitchen sink to clean their hands and recharge their batteries. Bill's friends, having completed the sanding and made mutterings about too many cooks, had departed in search of beer and frites leaving Bill to carry on supervising the work.

'Marguerite, I think you've bought up an entire market stall,' said Nina.

'Good that I had Doris,' the older woman smiled, referring to the shopping trolley that was now a permanent feature of the patisserie. 'And it's such a pleasure to peruse. It's been so long since I had a party. Henri and I used to throw parties all the time,' she said with a wistful smile.

'Well, you've done a wonderful job today,' said Jane. 'Doesn't it look lovely?'

'That was Marcel,' said Marguerite.

Nina smiled. Marcel, it seemed, couldn't help himself. For all his grumpiness, he loved looking after people. Just by spreading a white table cloth over the practical stainless-steel tables, arranging an array of different meats on two big platters and creating a delicious looking cheese board as well as putting out thick slices baguettes in little baskets, he'd made the simple lunch look like a feast. He'd even taken the time to wrap cutlery in coloured napkins, which were dotted across the cloth along with little pots of pate and tiny pottery bowls of olives and cornichon. In the centre he'd placed a vase of flowers which finished things off nicely and added to the rather festive air.

'I think I love you, Marguerite,' said Bill, sinking his teeth into a thickly cut slice of baguette smeared with pate. 'This is delicious.'

'Thank you, Marguerite,' said Nina wondering how much money the older woman had spent and how she could diplomatically repay her. Everyone was being so generous with their time.

As they all buzzed around one another loading up their plates, chatting away, Nina leaned against one of the stools listening to Maddie and Bill teasing each other with Jane and Peter joining in.

They made quick inroads into the food and Marcel disappeared to make coffee. When he returned with a big jug of coffee, Nina crossed to the fridge and pulled out a plate of her latest batch of éclairs to go with the coffee. She put them in the centre of the table as Marcel bustled out to get some tea plates and patisserie forks.

'They look very good,' said Marguerite.

'I think I've got them mastered now,' said Nina. 'These are chocolate and strawberry.'

'Chocolate and strawberry?' repeated Maddie. 'That sounds yum.'

Next to her, Jane nodded enthusiastically. 'How did you make them?'

'Puree of strawberry mixed with the cream and then a chocolate icing on the top.'

'I can't believe what good progress we've made,' said Jane.

'Yes.' Maddie waved her half-eaten éclair in the air. 'We could finish today.'

'If the weather holds,' said Peter, who had a tendency to err on the sensible side.

'It's a glorious day, darling. I think we're safe.'

'We may need to pop an extra coat on tomorrow,' said Bill. 'No point leaving a job half done. But it would be better if we could finish today then we don't have to faff about cleaning ... cleaning ...' Bill's voice suddenly went rather croaky. 'Cleaning up the kitchen for a second time.'

Nina frowned, she thought she'd done a pretty good job of cleaning up given the amount of baking she'd done. 'Don't worry about the kitchen, I'll get on top of that later. We should focus on the p—'

'Yes, we should, so that the kitchen is really clean,' said Maddie, who was pulling the most extraordinary cross-eyed expression.

'Well, I can't thank you all enough,' said Nina, wondering if she was missing something. Her heartbeat slowed to a crawl as she suddenly registered the frozen features on Maddie's face and a distinct widening of Jane's eyes. There was a furtive rustle as everyone went deadly silent.

Nina swallowed and turned.

'Sebastian, what a...'

'Surprise?'

'Yes, yes. A surprise.'

'Having a bit of a party, are we?' he asked, his voice as dry as dust and full of suspicion.

'Well, you know, we thought...' Nina's voice died as her brain completely blanked.

'Lunch,' said Maddie quickly, giving Sebastian a big smile. 'We decided to have lunch.'

'Here?' Sebastian kept his gaze on Nina.

'It's my birthday,' said Marguerite without batting an eyelid, which Nina thought was genius. No one would dare question her.

'So we decided to have lunch for Marguerite's birthday, didn't we?' said Maddie brightly.

'In the kitchen?'

'You know what they say. All the best parties are in the kitchen,' said Bill.

'I didn't think you'd mind,' said Nina, desperately.

'Mind? Why would I mind?' asked Sebastian, deceptively quietly. 'Although I do find it a bit strange, congregating here where there are any number of restaurants and bars throughout the whole of Paris.'

'You're more than welcome to join us,' said Marguerite. 'Now why don't you take a seat?'

Bill rushed forward with a stool.

'You should try one of these delicious éclairs that Nina has made.'

Nina winced.

Sebastian raised an eyebrow.

'I thought I'd practise.'

Marcel came in with the plates and forks and almost

swerved to a halt at the sight of Sebastian. He put the plates down and retreated in one fluid movement.

'Don't let me spoil the party,' said Sebastian.

'Would you like a coffee?' asked Nina, realising that her heart had picked up its pace and was galloping away, threatening to take her sanity with it. What on earth was he doing here? Why today of all days?

'That would be nice. Aren't you going to offer me one of these delicious looking éclairs?'

Aware that her hand was shaking a little, she scooped up one of the éclairs and handed it to him.

'So what brings you here, today?' asked Nina.

'Any reason why I shouldn't call in to my own premises?'

'No, no, but well … you know.'

'I don't as a matter of fact.'

Everyone had started talking busily asking questions that didn't need asking. It was all rather excruciating and Nina was almost on the verge of confessing to the makeover of 'his own premises', when Sebastian groaned.

'Wow!'

Everyone turned to look at him. He held out the éclair in front of him, a slightly blissed out expression on his face. 'These are delicious.'

Nina froze in delighted surprise.

'Who made these? Has Marcel got a new supplier?'

'Nina did,' said Maddie, coming to flank her, almost pushing her forward like a reluctant child being forced to the front of the class.

He gave her a slow appraising stare and took another bite,

chewing slowly, his eyes scrunched up. 'It's ... incredible. You really made this?'

She nodded.

He gave her a sudden brilliant and totally unexpected smile. 'Nina, these are seriously impressive. So that's why you're here? Practising.'

'Yes,' said Nina eagerly. 'And I invited the others to come and try them. I wanted their verdict.'

'And they brought lunch,' he observed.

'We were just leaving actually,' said Maddie, as she and Jane started packing up the food and stuffing it into Doris.

There was a flurry of activity and within ten minutes it was as if the picnic party had never happened save a few crumbs left here and there on the floor.

'I'll just see you out, shall I?' said Nina, her back to Sebastian, her eyes wide with the question: *What do we do now?*

She followed Bill out into the shop, the others lagging behind.

'What shall we do?' she hissed.

'Don't worry pet. You keep him occupied in the kitchen and we'll crack on.'

'But what if he comes out?' She glanced over her shoulder as Maddie and Marguerite emerged from the kitchen.

'Marcel can be lookout,' said Marguerite. 'And if he gets this far, I'm sure Marcel can halt him.'

'Yes.' She bit her lip. 'But then he'll see the walls. He'll see that we've taken off the panels. Oh God, you don't think he's heard something from someone, do you?'

Maddie's eyes widened. 'He'd have said something, wouldn't he?'

'It doesn't matter,' said Marguerite firmly. 'They deserve to be seen.'

'Don't worry pet. We'll move all the work gear away to the left, then it'll be out of sight of the window to one side, he might not even notice,' said Bill.

Nina thought that was somewhat wishful thinking. The masking tape all around the windows was somewhat of a giveaway.

'I can stay here with Marcel and keep him occupied if need be,' said Marguerite, patting Nina's hand.

'You do realise he's going to find out eventually,' said Peter, practical as ever.

Jane nudged him.

'I know but ... if it's at the end of the course, well, we won't be around and the work will be about to start and he might not notice.' Nina lifted her shoulders. Maddie snorted. Jane hid her smile behind her hand and Peter rolled his eyes.

'I'm being ridiculous, aren't I?'

'Yes, love,' said Bill patting her on the back. 'And he might be grateful, it's looking so much smarter already.'

'He might be,' said Nina in a small voice.

'Don't worry, he probably won't come out of the kitchen. He hasn't to date.'

But he was getting far more mobile on his crutches.

'In fact, he's more likely to follow you out now.'

'You're right. I'd better get back in there. I'll come and help as soon as I've got rid of him.'

* * *

'What are you doing here?' Nina tried to make her voice sound upbeat and casual so it didn't convey what she was really thinking, which was *what the hell are you doing here, today of all days!*

'Fed up with my own company and ... well, you got me thinking the other day when you complained my macarons were boring,'

She raised a teasing eyebrow, her heartrate starting to slow down.

'I realised that maybe I am a bit rusty. I haven't even started on the bistro menu, so I thought I could do some recipe development for the dessert menu.'

'I think I might be having an out of body experience. You're not admitting that I was right, are you?'

Sebastian laughed. 'You never give me an inch, do you?'

'No. Should I?'

He laughed again. 'No chance of me getting too big for my boots with you around.'

'Hmph. I'm not so sure about that.'

'Are you ever going to forgive me for being so grumpy when you arrived?'

'The jury is still out,' she said with a smirk. 'You need to be on your best behaviour for the next couple of weeks.'

'Have we really got so little time?' He shook his head. 'What are you going to do when you go back?'

Nina scrunched up her mouth and pulled a face. 'I haven't got the foggiest.'

'If you're serious about being a pastry chef, you could train.'

'I could.' She looked away, leaning forward and nudging one of the éclairs back into the centre of the plate.

'Or maybe you're not that serious.'

'Would you like a hand?' asked Nina, looking pointedly at his leg. 'You should probably still keep that elevated as much as possible.'

Sebastian gave her a sharp look but wearily conceded and sat down on the stool. 'I'm heartily sick of this bloody cast, so yes some help would be welcome. I'm also rather impressed with the filling of this éclair. What made you think of that? It's an inspired choice.' He put his elbow on the table and leaned forward picking up another of her éclairs and taking a bite.

'I was just thinking of favourite dessert combinations, like chocolate dipped strawberries and I...' She gave him a rueful grin. 'Do you want the truth?'

He nodded, the sudden warmth of his smile transforming his face as his dark eyes focused on her.

She felt her heart lurch sideways, a ping of sensation in her chest that set off alarm bells. She'd mistaken that intense way he had of looking at her in the past, but now he was doing it again and stupidly it seemed to have even more impact on her. It would be so easy to lean forward, stare into his eyes and kiss him ... *stop, stop, stop Nina*. What the hell was wrong with her? Been there, got the T-shirt and look how that ended.

You'd have thought she'd have learned by now. The whole reason for being here – for the first time since she'd arrived, she acknowledged the truth – was about proving that she was completely over him. Proving to him that she was a different person.

'To be perfectly honest...' She struggled to push away the thoughts but it was hard when he was still smiling at her. Smiling like he used to, smiling in that all encompassing way that made her feel like she was the only person in the room. 'My macarons ... they were a disaster. I thought I'd experiment with flavours and fillings. I had all these wonderful ideas but I fell at the first hurdle. Like you said, I didn't stick at it.'

'Or maybe you didn't have a very good teacher,' said Sebastian, still bloody smiling at her.

'You think?'

'Tell me what was wrong with them.'

'What was right with them? Despite copious quantities of food colouring, instead of being red, they were a puce colour.'

'Ah,' he nodded. 'Did you use liquid food colouring?'

She nodded.

'The amount you need to get that richness of colour can ruin the texture of the mixture.'

'Well, they didn't rise and they were so sticky we ... I couldn't get them off the baking sheet. Maddie came to help,' she finished with a rush. The half-truths were starting to stack up and suddenly she didn't feel quite so good about not being honest with him.

'They are tricky to get right,' he said sympathetically. 'And I'm not sure, if I'm completely honest, they're worth the effort. Not my favourite thing. Although I'm going to knock up a few up today for an idea I've got.'

'But they look so lovely. I wanted to sell ... celebrate, make them for a celebration, for celebrations. You know birthdays, presents, little gifts.' Oh heck, she was babbling as she hoped he hadn't noticed her slip up.

'Well, you've nailed the choux, if that's any consolation. This is good. Can I pinch the idea?'

'You want to pinch my idea?' Nina almost spluttered.

'Only if you don't mind.' He gave her another one of those teasing, warm smiles which did stupid things to the pit of her stomach.

'Of course not. I think I might be slightly flattered.' And ever so slightly shocked.

Sebastian had come armed with a list, of course, of ideas, flavour combinations that he wanted to try. And given what was going on outside, she was all for encouraging him. Luckily he was so intent on his work, setting to work by mixing up an initial batch of Italian-style buttercream, that he seemed to have put the odd shenanigans with the others in the kitchen completely out of his mind.

He chatted as he worked and after the first ten minutes, Nina felt her shoulders begin to settle back into their normal position. Providing Sebastian stayed put in the kitchen, they would be fine and given previous experience, he'd shown no interest in moving beyond the steps. All she had to do was keep him focused on the job in hand.

'I'm looking to create and combine some really subtle flavours. People are always amenable to having a tea or a coffee after dinner but less so these days to a dessert, so I'm thinking about offering a tea and macaron selection that people can choose instead of a dessert.' He paused and nodded his head as if reassuring himself. 'And there's a good profit margin. So I was thinking about some light floral and tea-flavoured fillings like jasmine, Earl Grey and green tea combined with lavender, hibiscus and rose.'

'Interesting,' said Nina doing her best to look impassive. They didn't sound like proper fillings to her. Patisserie, whether biscuits, cakes, meringues, éclairs whatever you wanted to call them should be enticing, interesting and make you want to wrap your lips around in a delicious mouth smacking kiss.

'What?'

'Nothing?'

'You have that look on your face.'

'No, I don't ... I worked hard so there wouldn't be a look.' She sighed and relented. 'You're asking the wrong person. I like my desserts with big full flavours...' She nodded at her éclairs. 'Your macaron combinations sound very subtle and sophisticated and all that bollocks.' She decided to go for broke. 'But to be honest they sound boring and ... well a bit dull ... sort of cowardly, apologetic sort of flavours. A bit grown up but clueless.'

'Thanks for your incisive comments,' said Sebastian with a scowl.

'I wasn't deliberately being rude ... just honest. As a potential customer.'

Sebastian frowned and looked at the éclairs again, a worried expression creeping into his eyes. 'Hmm.'

'But I'm probably not your target audience. I consider myself cheated if I've not had a dessert when I go out to dinner. I want chocolate. I want rich. The people in your restaurants are probably dead sophisticated and have a much posher palate than me.'

Sebastian was lost in thought for a minute or two. With a frustrated gesture, he pushed his hand through his hair. 'I'm still not sure I've got the concept for the bistro here right. And now the contractors won't be available for another two months. The designs still aren't right and I haven't got a handle on the food at all. It's frustrating especially as the ones in the Marais and Canal Saint-Martin came together so easily. The vision was there. The interior designer nailed it after my first brief. This one—' he shook the hair that had now flopped forward on to his face and Nina realised he needed a haircut '—has been a problem from day one.'

'Can't you use the same concepts and ideas?'

'No, the shape of the building is all wrong and the location isn't right. This place was never meant to be part of my plans.'

'Your plans for world domination?' quipped Nina. 'Isn't this where you do the evil he-he-he and rub your hands together in a villainous, evil genius sort of way?'

'You are so like your brother.' There was a flash of warmth in his eyes, despite the disparaging tone. 'Same stupid sense of humour.'

'Runs in the genes, I'm afraid.'

'At least you're much better looking.' Sebastian froze, looking as if he'd swallowed something he shouldn't and suddenly went puce.

There was a horribly pregnant pause where they just looked at each other, but it was impossible for Nina not to dive in and rescue him, knowing that he didn't mean it the way she would dearly love him to.

'Of course I am, I'm younger, a lot less hairy and I smell a darn sight more fragrant.'

'There is that,' said Sebastian. His gratitude was almost palpable. 'Now back to my plans for restaurant domination. I got stuck with this place because the only way I could get the leases on the two restaurants I wanted was to take this one on as part of the deal. Hence being saddled with Marcel and the patisserie course.'

Nina waited for a second or two, wondering whether she should say anything or not and finally grabbed courage with metaphysical hands and said, 'You do know that this was once a renowned patisserie. Both Marcel and Marguerite remember it in its heyday.'

'You told me that the other day.'

'Yes, because it really was special. It would be a shame to lose it. So maybe you could keep it as a patisserie.'

'No.' Sebastian turned his back on her and started arranging the bowls and reading his recipe sheets.

'No? You're not even prepared to consider it.'

'No.' He turned over a sheet of paper.

'Not at all?'

He didn't even look up and now looked completely absorbed, muttering under his breath. 'Earl Grey and Lavender. That would be one. Jasmine and ... perhaps rose, would that be too floral?'

'That's a no, then,' said Nina.

'What do you think about rose and lavender?'

'Not bad,' she said, it wouldn't entice her. He was absorbed in his recipe sheets again. She stared at the back of his head. Stubborn idiot.

Maybe she should take him to Ladurée, visit some of the iconic patisserie places in Paris. Not even considering a patisserie was cutting his nose off to spite his face. Perhaps if he could see that it was potentially a good business model, he might change his mind. What did she have to lose?

She kept pondering this as she helped him make up a batch of macarons, which of course came out looking like bite-sized fairy perfection. How did he do it? She could have sworn she'd followed exactly the same process and steps as him.

'Are you alright?'

'Yes.' She snapped the word at him, finding his proximity annoying or maybe she just objected to him breathing.

'You're pulling faces.'

'I'm just trying to figure out how I got it so horribly wrong and you've managed to produce the most perfect pink macarons.

'Oh. Practice. Remember I worked at that hotel in Wells, and they did afternoon teas. They were a feature of the menu. Now, please can you help me decide on the fillings?' The macarons he'd made were delicately rose-flavoured and he'd managed to get them a blush pink colour. They looked pretty and feminine and she knew as she looked at them that she couldn't achieve the same result in a million years ... and that she probably wouldn't want to.

No, she wouldn't want to. This wasn't what she wanted to cook.

It was a thunderbolt revelation. Cooking was about feeding people, delivering the punch of taste and flavour. Pleasing them. Appealing to that raw desire of hunger and pleasure. Bringing people together. The delicate flavour and insubstantial bite of a wispy, barely-there macaron wasn't her idea of a treat.

She spent the next hour helping make up batches of buttercream, but all the time her head was full of the cakes and patisseries she really wanted to make. Big, bold flavours, tried and tested combinations but upgraded with more innovative presentation. The millionaire's shortbread had been a huge hit. The more she thought about it, the more she wanted to get started making mini patisserie versions of British favourites. She could make posh jammy dodgers, fine shortbread biscuits sandwiched with Chantilly and fruit coulis, miniature Victoria sponges with a strawberry glaze top and fresh fruit filling, a jam tart version of a mille-feuille.

Her head whirled with ideas as she watched Sebastian dividing up the batches of buttercream into a series of bowls, which he lined up before he started adding the flavourings using everything from the steeped water from a couple of Earl Grey teabags, to rosewater and dried powdered jasmine flowers. Interesting as it was to see how he achieved those delicate flavours, the painstaking, almost scientific laboratorial approach didn't inspire or enthuse her.

'Nina?'

'Yes?' She started, realising Sebastian was looking at her.

'Are you alright? You're pulling faces again. Really weird ones this time.'

'Sorry, just thinking.' She smiled, unable to help some of her excitement leaking out, and grabbed a bowl, taking it over to the sink to wash up.

He glanced back at her with decided suspicion.

Balancing on one crutch, he mixed and tasted and added, completely focused on the job in hand. Despite her epiphany, she still found it fascinating to watch him. He'd always been like this, with a drive and focus that she'd never seen in anyone else before. She wondered if it made him lonely, set apart from his peers. When he was younger, she, along with Nick and the boys, had always managed to tease him out of that total absorption. Drag him away from the kitchen with light-hearted banter and challenge.

'Here.' He lifted a teaspoon and offered it, his other hand lifting to her face to cup it as if to steady her. Her mouth went dry at the unexpectedly intimate touch and, startled, she automatically opened her mouth as the teaspoon grazed her lip. She lifted her eyes to his and in that moment a frisson of awareness sizzled between them before she slowly scooped a bit of the sweet mixture with her top lip. Despite his intense gaze on her she couldn't help licking her lips, even though it felt horribly suggestive and ridiculous. Her pulse tripped as she saw his Adam's apple dip.

'What do you think?' Sebastian's low voice held a hint of huskiness.

She swallowed hard, feeling rather hot, quivery and unsettled. 'Nice, very ... delicate. Earl Grey?' Her words felt a bit babbled, as her thoughts were a million miles away from flavoured buttercream. He was still looking at her lips and her temperature control had gone haywire. She suddenly felt very, very hot but she couldn't stop looking back at him.

Then he touched her lip, scooping in a tiny bit of the cream that had escaped. The bottom of her stomach dropped through the floor as she held her breath. She watched as awareness sank over him, a frown starting to furrow his brow. He pulled back.

'And what about this one?' He dropped the spoon into the next bowl picked it up and offered it to her as if playing safe this time, except his eyes kept straying to her lips.

Darn it, she could feel one of her ever-ready blushes staining her cheeks already. Reaching for the spoon, she kept her eyes on the mixture and didn't look at him. He was already reaching for the third bowl.

'I'll ... er ... just sandwich up a few of the macarons with the different flavours.' He moved away quickly round to the other side of the work bench, as if he couldn't get away from her fast enough.

She watched his thin, elegant fingers as with a quick slick of a palate knife, he quickly spread the fillings into the macarons they'd made earlier. Never in a million years would she have that consummate skill. He'd worked so hard to get where he was and it showed, the macarons looked like little tiny fairy-kissed works of art. The pale Earl Grey filling contrasted beautifully with the rose blush halves, as did the pale jasmine cream and then the pale pink rosewater cream.

As she watched, Sebastian arranged them on one of the cake stands, the three mix-and-match colours all working beautifully. He'd obviously spent a long time thinking about not just the flavours but how they would all look together. It looked fabulous. Of course it did, this was Sebastian, the perfectionist bar none.

'Try one,' he said, holding out the cake stand in front of him, rather like a shield. She took one and nibbled at it. 'Nice.'

'Nice? Is that all you can say? Hmm, maybe we should ask Marcel's opinion, if he's as much of an expert as you think he is.' Sebastian lifted the cake stand and with one crutch started to hop his way to the steps.

'Wait, I'll take them ... you don't want to ... fall on the stairs or anything.'

'No, you take the cake stand.'

She rushed over to him and took the stand. 'I'll take them through, shall I?'

As she started to walk up the steps, she heard him swing into place behind her.

'What are you doing?' she asked from the top of the steps.

'I'd like to hear what he thinks.' He planted his crutches on the first step and hopped up. Nina froze.

'Be careful,' she said.

'It's fine,' he said swinging the crutches and preparing to take the next step up.

Nina looked anxiously through the doorway and down the corridor towards the patisserie before saying in a very loud voice, 'These really do look fantastic,'

Sebastian looked up at her, puzzlement on his face before he hauled himself up the second step.

Nina hesitated, feeling the sharp beat of her pulse in her throat as her earlobes turned bright pink. Should did she abandon him on the steps and run ahead to get Marcel to warn everyone? Or take it really slowly and hope that Marcel heard them?

'I'm sure Marcel would love to try your macarons,' she said, as loudly as she could.

'I'm sure he's not lurking in the corridor.'

'Ah, I just didn't want to startle him, you know appearing from nowhere.'

'I'm sure he's not gone deaf either.'

'Oh ... he's not got good hearing at all,' she said quickly. 'Very hard of hearing, he is.'

'I hadn't noticed,' said Sebastian, planting his crutches once again on the next step.

As she took a hesitant step towards the patisserie her foot caught on a loose piece of lino and she tripped and started to pitch forward. Just in the nick of time she righted herself, still hanging on to the cake stand. She took a minute to steady the cake stand swinging from her hand and tidy the nearest macaron which was threatening to take a nose dive from the far edge.

'Close call,' said Sebastian stopping and pulling his crutches back from the fourth step. 'That would have been disastrous, if you dropped the whole lot.'

'Phew. Although you need to be careful.'

'I'm fine Nina, just need to take my time. But I'm in no hurry. In fact, it's a nice day, we could sit and enjoy our macarons in the sunshine with a cup of coffee.'

Her eyes widened as she frantically tried to think of a way of diverting him.

'Something wrong, Nina?'

Standing on the penultimate step, he was now at eye level with her and so close she could see the fine lines around his lips. And why was she looking at them? For a lost daydreamy minute she imagined tipping ever so slightly forward and just grazing them. What would he say? What would he do? And what was she thinking? Er, hello. Been there got the T-shirt. And then she realised he was the one leaning forward ever so slightly, his eyes intent on her. Her heart fizzed with ridiculous excitement as he leaned closer still, she could feel his breath on her lips. Just as his mouth touched hers, the sensation of skin on skin sending a thousand electric pulses dancing through her system, he lurched to one side and wobbled dangerously. With a start she put out her free hand to steady him, grabbing his upper arm as she heard the clatter, clatter, bang, bang, bang as one of his crutches bumped its way down the stairs, the cake stand swaying dangerously in her other hand.

'Shit,' said Sebastian immediately, his eyes wide with alarm.

'It's OK, I've got you,' said Nina. She could feel a slight tremble beneath her fingers and wasn't sure if it was her or him. 'Why don't you sit down?' She put down the cake stand at the top of the stairs and helped him manoeuvre around slowly and oh so carefully, a painfully choreographed move of crutch, shuffle, crutch, shuffle, crutch shuffle until he was able to sink onto his bottom on the step.

'You alright?' She sat down next to him, worried that his face looked so pale, all the colour had leached out leaving his eyes wide and troubled.

'Close call, I thought I was going to fall backwards.' He shuddered, closing his eyes for a second as if reliving the moment and the what-might-have-happened. 'The crutch just slipped out from under me.' He lay the other crutch down on the steps and put his elbow on his bent knee propping his chin in his hand. 'Just give me a minute, my heart's pounding like a freight train. The thought of falling again ... really freaks me.'

She scooted closer to him and put her arm around his shoulder. He looked like a lost, lonely boy and with a sudden flashback as clear as if it were yesterday, it reminded her of taking stolen glances at him, at home around the dinner around the table when all the boys were bantering and he thought no one was looking at him.

'Hey,' she said softly. 'It's OK.'

'Sorry.' He swallowed. She could feel his back muscles tense under her arm. 'I'd forgotten ... the accident. It's just brought it all back.' She wasn't sure if he was aware he was doing it but he nestled closer to her. 'You know that awful falling sensation, the point of no return when you know there's nothing you can do about it and you're just bracing yourself for landing.' He winced 'And that crack. Shit.' He shook his head. 'And feeling so fucking helpless, useless and humanly frail. I must have looked a right berk, lying flat on my back with all those people looking at me. Bloody girl with the case, kind of whimpered apologies and said she had a train to catch.'

'No!'

'Probably just as well. There was nothing she could have done.'

'So I presume someone called an ambulance.'

'Yeah, only after I'd done that "I'm fine, I'm fine just give me a minute" thing. Of course I tried to move ... and I think I must have passed out. When I came to there were a couple of people trying to help. I feel bad now, there was a woman and a man, not together, but they stayed with me until the ambulance arrived. I never got their names. I would have liked to say thank you to them.'

'I take it the break was quite bad.'

'Bad enough that I had to stay in hospital and have an operation.' He clenched his fists. 'I'm dreading going back. Bloody hate hospitals.'

'I could come with you,' she offered.

He turned his head to look at her, a sudden greedy hopefulness on his face. 'Would you?'

'Yes, of course.'

'Thanks Nina.' The sweetness of his smile pierced her and as she looked at his familiar face, every line and feature ingrained in her memory, she knew she was as much in love with him as ever.

'Mm.' Marcel's perennially grumpy face relaxed. 'The Earl Grey is very subtle. Delicate and even, may I say, whimsical. The flavour with the rose macaron is particularly well balanced. I must congratulate you.'

'Thank you, Marcel.' Sebastian shot a wry smile at Nina when Marcel dipped his head to select a second one from the plate.

After the near miss with the stairs, Nina had invited Marcel into the kitchen and if Sebastian was surprised by his unusual amiable cooperation, he didn't say anything for which she was very grateful. Guilt was playing havoc with her conscience.

At first, Sebastian had been rather subdued as she'd helped him back down the stairs and into a chair. She'd left him to get Marcel and a second chair from the patisserie shop to prop up his leg. By the time Marcel arrived with coffee and they'd brought through one of the bistro tables and two other chairs, Sebastian had regained his colour and was much more his usual self.

'What flavour is this one?' Marcel asked holding up one of the rose and jasmine flavoured macarons.

'Perhaps you can tell me?'

As if he were tasting a fine wine, the Frenchman popped it into his mouth, closed his eyes and savoured the sweet bite. 'Hmm, rose and ... ah, an excellent subtle flavour. This I like. I like very much. After the other one, it's a delightful finish to the palate.'

Sebastian nodded and quickly grabbed his ever-present notebook. 'I like that, I might use that in my tasting notes for the menu. Would you mind?'

'I'd be honoured,' said Marcel with a grave, starchy nod. 'Rose and jasmine, I believe.'

'That's right.'

'A lovely companion to the Earl Grey, and what do we have to finish this rather triumphant trilogy?'

'Triumphant trilogy!' Sebastian shouted with laughter, his eyes shining with delight that Nina was relieved to see. The shock of the near miss and that unexpected vulnerability which had shaken her, had worn off.

'Marcel! You are a wordsmith. I might have to borrow that as well.' Sebastian tipped his head on one side. 'I might have to consider asking you to write the menu for me.'

There was the slightest raise of Marcel's eyebrows and Nina smiled to herself. Initially, she'd been sure that his effusive praise for the subtle flavours and the finely balanced combinations were born of a desire to keep Sebastian on side and in the kitchen.

Marcel shook his head as he tried the last of the macarons. 'No. There needs to be more of a triumphant finish. Something clever and challenging. Rose macaron with rose cream filling is too ... safe.'

Sebastian nodded. 'Damn, you're right.'

And suddenly they were discussing flavour combinations in great depth, sharing ideas and listening avidly to one another. Nina slipped away with a big smile on her face and went out through the patisserie to the workers at the front.

'How's it going?' she asked in a low voice.

'Nearly done,' said Jane standing up from where she'd been crouching and rubbing her back. There was just a tiny patch of the panel still left to paint.

'We'll be finished in the next half hour,' said Bill. 'But it would be good if we could get into the kitchen to clean up. Is the boss still here?'

'Yes, he's just talking to Marcel but he's finished cooking, so I'm hoping he'll leave soon.' She glanced at her watch; it was five-thirty already. 'I'd better get back before he wonders where I've gone.'

* * *

285

'Are you all done?' she asked Sebastian, starting to carry bowls over to the sink.

'Yes. You don't have to wash up. I appreciate the help, but ... I wasn't expecting you to work today.'

She gave a pointed look at his hands as his balanced on his crutches, raising one eyebrow. 'What? And you're going to wash up, how?'

The sheepish grin he flashed her made her smile. 'You can make it up to me another time.' Eek, that had come out more flirtatiously than she'd meant.

'I can, can I?' There was a ghost of smile haunting his lips as he looked back at her and then his face softened in the sort of way that made her stomach go all gooey and her hormones start misbehaving. 'Perhaps I could take you out to dinner?'

Stop, she told herself. This was him being grateful.

She filled the sink with hot, soapy water, keeping her back to him, so that he didn't see the expression on her face. 'You fed up with hotel food again?' she asked with cheery calm.

'No.'

'Oh, is there a restaurant you want to try? Check out the competition?'

'No, Nina.' She could hear a touch of irritation in his voice and risked turning around, to find him leaning against the work bench, the crutches hanging loose from his elbows and his eyes flashing as they bored into her.

'McDonalds?' she asked.

'Oh, for God's sake, Nina,' he said with an exasperated smile. 'Perhaps, I'd like to take you out to dinner to say thank you. For going above and beyond ... when you took me out in the wheelchair. That was really thoughtful.' His eyes met hers. 'You've always been good like that, thinking of m – others. It's ... well not everyone would have done that. I really enjoyed the day. Being with you. I'd like to ... you know, spend some time with you. I don't know, perhaps like a date.'

He looked slightly horrified as if the words had escaped from him unwittingly and stood there with a hunted expression on his face as if he were still trying to decide whether to flee or not, but Nina wasn't letting him off the hook that easily.

'A date?' she asked in a voice so quiet as if she couldn't believe she was saying the word.

He pulled a face. 'Sorry, that didn't come out properly.'

Of course, it hadn't. He hadn't meant a date at all.

'I meant, I'd like I take you out to dinner to say thank you for all your help.' His voice was firmer and slightly less cross than earlier. 'And that it would be a ... an event. You know planned. I want to take you somewhere nice to say thank you, so it wouldn't be a date, date but it would be like a date.' He finished with a no-nonsense nod.

Ah, that was more like the Sebastian she knew. Back on firmer ground. Seeing him so vulnerable earlier had been unsettling. Stern, gruff, arrogant Sebastian was much easier to deal with. It was easier to try and dislike him. After all, he had no idea how she felt.

'You don't have to do that,' she said crisply. Emotion had no place here. 'You do remember you're paying me.'

'Meet me at the hotel at seven, Nina.'

A quick thrill ran through her at his at his strict tone.

'OK.' Her voice came out in an embarrassing squeak. Why couldn't she just once manage to play it cool around him, she wished, as she caught his quick wry smile.

Chapter 26

'Hey Nina,' called Jane as she entered the patisserie, where the others were sitting around a table with tall glasses of citron pressé.

'Hi everyone. Are you all done?'

'Yes,' said Maddie, with a broad beam. 'We've done a brilliant job.'

'I could tell,' said Nina, 'from the amount of paint you've got on your face.'

Maddie lifted her hand and patted her face. 'Where?'

'It's OK, grey freckles are in,' said Peter to her right.

Jane nudged him with a laugh. 'Since when have you known anything about fashion?'

'I have hidden depths,' he replied with a twinkle at her before turning back to Nina. 'And well done on keeping his nibs at bay. That must have bit nerve-wracking, although it made us all feel a bit *Mission Impossible*. Bill had the music playing on his iPhone at one point.'

'I'm glad it gave you some excitement. I felt...' Well, she felt horribly guilty now, going ahead without telling him. 'There was one close call. When he wanted to come into the patisserie.' Her heart pinched at the memory of sitting on the step with Sebastian. She was cross with herself. How had she let herself fall in love with him all over again. What was wrong with her? And why couldn't she just tell him about the patisserie?

'What did you do?' asked Maddie. 'I'd have kissed him.'

Nina blushed.

'You didn't!'

'No, of course not.' She swallowed, feeling the rush of heat at the thought of that near kiss, something she hadn't had time to dwell on since the barely-there graze of his lips on hers.

'Shame. He's rather yummy.'

'And far too sophisticated for you,' said Bill, a little too bluntly, Nina thought, although Maddie didn't seem to mind as she patted his big hand. 'Not my type at all, but I like to look. I'm an Art History student, we're all about looking at beautiful things. Talking of which...' She drew herself up proudly. 'I. Have. Finished repainting the mural and I've only got a few clouds to sponge in on the walls.'

Everyone turned to looked at the sea painting, the mermaids smiling sunnily at them and the fishes so colourful it was easy to imagine that if you blinked they'd dart away.

'Oh my gosh, it's absolutely beautiful,' said Jane.

'It is wonderful to see it again,' said Marguerite. 'I'd forgotten how stunning it was. Seeing it again brings back lots of happy memories. It will be lovely when the chandelier is back in place,' she added with a wistful glance up at the plaster rose above them.

Nina felt she was in the path of a runaway train with about as much chance of stopping it. She held up a hand. 'Look this is all great and I really appreciate the work you've done today.'

'Aw pet, you haven't even seen it, yet. Come on, you need to see what we've done.'

They all nodded and as one they rose and, crowding round her, they led her out of the shop.

What do you think?' asked Bill as he stepped out into the sunshine.

'Oh my goodness! You've done an amazing job. It looks...' She let the brilliant smile on her face do the talking. They'd done a fantastic job and the front of the patisserie in its smart dark grey livery looked so different. A place that you would take a second look at, you might consider stepping into. The worn, battered old lady was gone and in its place was a smarter, more elegant woman. What Nina really loved was that the new paint wasn't some brash upstart replacement but a respectful, sympathetic updating that didn't scream 'look at me'.

The windows sparkled in the late afternoon sunshine and through them you could see the glass counter centre stage. What a transformation. Then she laughed as she caught sight of the small selection of Sebastian's recently made macarons on display.

'Thank you so much, all of you. Bill, you must say a big thank you to "an-the-lads". I...' Sudden tears filled her eyes. 'I can't believe what a difference there is, and I didn't even help. I feel bad now.'

'Don't you worry, pet.'

'We've had so much fun, haven't we, Peter darling?'

'What?' He pretended to rouse himself as if he'd been miles away. 'Yes dear,' he teased.

'Seriously Nina, we've had such a laugh but...' Jane's voice trailed away.

'Some of us have been thinking...' said Bill, looking at Peter.

Peter nodded, he had clearly been nominated spokesperson. 'The thing is Nina, we've really enjoyed working on the building today. It's been a rare privilege to see the transformation, especially with the painting on the walls being revealed and we've all become quite attached to the place. It would be lovely to see the patisserie be returned to its full glory. Seeing it as it should be. We'd like to carry on working on the fabric of the building tomorrow.'

'We thought the floor,' said Marguerite. 'All it needs is the old seal stripping off the tiles and giving them a really good clean and then resealing. With all of us working on it we could do it in a day and we could close the patisserie.'

'And Peter and me sorted a ladder, we'll get the chandelier up tomorrow,' Bill added.

'Whoa! Whoa!' Nina held up her hands to hold back the tide of enthusiasm. 'It's not my patisserie. It belongs to Sebastian. And remember he's planning to close it and refurbish it.' *Although he still didn't have clear plans for this site.*

'Yes, but if he saw its full potential, he might change his mind,' said Maddie. 'People are loving your Anglo-Fusion patisseries.'

'Yes, but I'd need to make a lot more on a daily basis.' Although if she got herself organised, that was possible.

'I can help you,' said Maddie. 'My lectures don't start until ten most days.'

'And so can I,' said Marguerite. 'I'm always up early.'

'We can have a little production line,' said Maddie.

'We can help too,' said Jane.

'The royal we,' said Peter with a resigned expression on his face which he then spoilt by winking at his wife.

'Yes but...' Nina frowned. 'You can't all do that. And I'm only here for...' She pulled a panicked face, where had the time gone. 'I'm only here for another a week and a half. After this week's class, there's only one more. And I'll be going home. But ... I've got so many ideas I want to try out.' She started telling them about her twists on traditional recipes.

'Well, that's it, then,' said Maddie. 'Posh Jammy Dodgers, I'm in.'

'And clotted cream and strawberry éclairs sound divine,' said Marguerite.

'But I can't ask you to do all the work, and not for free,' said Nina, feeling totally out of her depth.

'Of course we can,' said Marguerite firmly, with that regal tilt of head that indicated she'd take no nonsense.

'You do realise Sebastian's going to have his cast off and then...'

'So, we've got the rest of this week to bring this place back to life. If Sebastian sees it then, he might see the potential and change his mind.'

Nina wavered. Was it wrong to encourage them? What if she were to really work hard, creating her cake ideas? If the patisserie was full of her Anglo-French creations, Sebastian might be impressed.

'Well.' She shouldn't really be entertaining the idea, but she turned and saw Maddie's eyes shining with hope and enthusiasm. 'The thing is...' Should she tell them? Bill laced his fingers together over his belly. Her breath hissed out. 'Sebastian's contractors have been held up elsewhere and so work isn't going to start here for a while.'

'So, the patisserie could stay open for longer and then if you showed it was making money, he might change his mind,' said Marguerite clasping her hands together over her heart in a gesture that melted away any further doubts in Nina's mind.

In fact, the more she thought about it, the more she persuaded herself it was quite a good idea. Better that the shop was busy with customers and making some money than lying empty.

'So, shall we go for it?' asked Maddie.

'OK,' said Nina, 'but there are no guarantees.'

'Oh, you'll bring him round, I'm sure,' said Jane linking her arm through Peter's and giving Nina a warm smile.

'Jane. Jane. Jane. You're a bad woman,' Peter gave a reproving shake of his head as he winked at Bill. 'Encouraging Nina to use her feminine wiles.'

'Why not?' she asked, her eyes bright with mischief. 'It worked with you.'

Everyone laughed. 'Right troops. Dinner. I'm starving. Nina, you coming? We're all off to the brasserie around the corner for a quick bite.'

'I'd love to...' And she would have loved to but despite the draw of their happy post-job-well-done camaraderie, dinner with Sebastian was just too tempting. She had to know what was going on.

'Aw Nina, come on,' said Maddie leading a chorus of protest.

'OK, I can come with you for one drink.' It would help calm her nerves, she reasoned to herself, which were jangling for England at the thought of going to dinner with Sebastian.

Chapter 27

Not going on a date still didn't stop Nina doing that tripping over her own knickers thing as she tried to strip them off and walk at the same time.

She took out the silky orange shift dress from the wardrobe where it hid in the third of the space that she'd taken for herself. Looking at Sebastian's clothes hanging on the rest of the rail, she felt the familiar sense of intrusion. There was still the feeling that he might come back any day. An unconscious hand strayed to touch the sleeve of one of his shirts. She shouldn't be here. With a horrible feeling of embarrassment, she realised she was a bit like her clothes, even after all this time still trying to find a space in his life.

She was an idiot. A complete idiot. It was well past time that she stopped hoping that one day he might notice she wasn't that love-struck immature teenager.

With a shake of the hanger, she eyed the orange dress that she'd packed at the last minute and laid it on the bed. Eminently suitable for a dinner not-date, it had only been worn once, at her cousin's wedding. They were the posh side of the family. With a wince, she remembered the day, the dress elegant and expensive making her feel as if she fitted in but it had been tight across her chest, a touch scratchy on her back and constricting when she sat down.

Fresh from a very quick shower, she picked up her hair straighteners, and advanced on the mirror prepared to do battle with her hair which had a slight curl. At first when she'd whirled into the flat having been persuaded by the others to stop and have one drink with them, she'd planned to straighten it, to reinstate the perfect glossy bob that was there when she came out from the hairdressers but which she never managed to achieve again without straightening. With a decisive twist of her mouth, she put down the hair straighteners. Life was too short to be beholden to them and if a key part of this trip was to show Sebastian the new grown up her, she'd failed miserably. In the kitchen, she was invariably darting around, and a red shiny face wasn't exactly flattering. Over the years he'd seen her in just about every guise, so being glossy and perfect for one evening was hardly going to give him complete memory loss. With a sudden lowering of her spirits, she mused, he pretty much always saw her at a disadvantage.

So while this should have been an opportunity to dress up, put on her make-up, wrestle her hair into glossy perfection and show him that Nina ballerina had a sophisticated side, she put down the straighteners and pushed aside her make-up bag. What was the point of trying to show him someone that didn't exist? As a teenager, she'd been desperate to impress him. Part of why she'd signed up for the cookery course ... look how that had ended. A laughing stock among her family when she fainted at the sight of raw meat.

With a firm shake of her head, she dragged her brush through her hair and mouthed at herself in the mirror. *This is not a date. Remember. It's like a date but not a date.*

Ignoring the orange dress, she pulled out a plain white cotton shirt and teamed it with a pair of navy Capri pants and her favourite red ballet pumps. This was her and there was no point trying to be something she wasn't. He'd see straight through her and then she'd end up making even more of a fool of herself.

From here on in, she had to get over Sebastian Finlay.

Despite all her mantras and promises to herself, it seemed her body was determined to wangle out of the deal. She couldn't stop her heart skipping about stupidly when she saw Sebastian waiting for her in the lobby. He wore a pale blue shirt and a pair of dark grey trousers, which were stretched obscenely tightly over the plaster cast. She bit back the smile at the sight of his wonky legs, one so much wider than the other. He had made an effort to dress up and look smart and judging by the expression on the face of Nina's favourite receptionist, it had been worth it. She was casting longing looks at Sebastian from her post on the other side of the room. Nina had to admit he did look a little bit luscious.

'Nina, you look ... nice.' He eyed her neat trousers and pristine white shirt, an amused smile playing around his lips as if he were sheltering a secret.

'What?' she asked, full of suspicion.

'Nothing,' he said. 'Shall we go?'

She narrowed her eyes at him and he looked guilelessly back at her and she decided to let it go. Clearly something had amused him.

'You've scrubbed up quite well, although—' she nodded down at his leg '—are you going to be able to get those trousers off later?'

'Are you offering to help?' he asked, that amused smile back again in spades.

'No!' she squeaked and ducked her head. What was he playing at? This was not a date and he was being all smiley and secretive.

'This way.' He turned and headed towards the lift.

Thank goodness she hadn't given into temptation and got all dressed up, dinner in his room didn't warrant the discomfort of the orange dress, even though she looked good in it.

To her surprise the lift sailed past the third floor. She gave him a quizzical look as the lights flicked through, four, five, six before finally settling on seven.

His face hummed with that slightly suppressed smile, as if it might leak out at any second.

'After you,' he said when the lift doors opened. They stepped out into a small square, white corridor which was clearly a service area. But he nodded towards a door six or seven steps to the right.

The door opened to a flat roof, encircled by a low-walled balustrade. She looked back at Sebastian.

'We're not allowed within five feet of the edge. I promised Alex. We're breaking every health and safety rule in the book. This way.' He gestured with one crutch and she turned left and walked around the brick built block housing the stairwell.

'Oh!' She stopped dead. 'Oh,' she said again as she took in the view of Paris and the fairy lights strung around a small oasis on the roof. A blanket had been spread on the floor filled with jewel bright cushions, and in front of it was a blue velvet sofa, each end bookmarked with a table and a tall vase of deep blue iris. Around the blanket were pretty glass votives with tea lights that flickered in the early evening dusk.

'Oh,' she said for a third time, completely unable to string a sentence together. Her brain was too busy trying to compute what was going on. It was rather like swimming against the tide.

'I thought this was easier than going to a restaurant,' said Sebastian with a hesitant smile. 'I wanted to do something special ... to thank you.'

For a moment hope warred against all her good intentions.

'Consider me well and truly thanked,' she said, matter-of-factly. All the thoughts in her head were fighting against each other, as if her brain was trying to do impossible sums and reject the answers because she had no idea whether they were right or wrong. 'This is gorgeous. And totally unexpected. Getting that sofa up here must have taken some doing.' She looked from it to his crutches.

'Admittedly, I can't take the credit for the actual work, Alex and his team helped out but ... it was my idea.'

'It's lovely. Thank you.'

'Have a seat.'

They made their way to the sofa, Sebastian glancing at his watch, and Nina perched on the edge, not wanting to relax in case she let her guard down and her brain came to the wrong conclusion. The skyline around them was breathtaking and after taking in the overall shimmering view of golden lights and shadows, she took her time focusing on individual elements, the dark path of the Seine meandering under the bridges, lit up with the gilded glow of lights, the elegant upward sweep of the Eiffel Tower picked out against the dark sky and the elegant straight lines of the wide boulevards fanning out through the city.

'Would you like something to drink?'

'Yes please.' Nina looked around expectantly but couldn't see any sign of a champagne bucket – which surely the scene cried out for – or glasses or bottles of any description. That reassured her. She'd read this right. This wasn't romance.

Sebastian handed her a menu.

'We're ordering by text. I wasn't sure what you'd like.' The uncharacteristically uncertain smile he gave her confused her again. 'Alex has a waiter on standby.'

'Handy.'

'It's amazing when you know the manager ... and have lots of dirt on him.'

'That's clearly a man thing, as I thought he seemed quite nice.'

Sebastian's face sobered. 'He's a good bloke. And very nice. I don't really have any dirt on him. He's just a good person and a great friend. And if I'm honest probably a better man than me, but I don't care about that anymore.'

She frowned. It seemed as if he were trying to make a point but she hadn't a clue what he was getting at.

'He ... he wants to go out with you again.'

'I know,' said Nina feeling guilty but also hopeful. Her heart started to pitter patter with nerves but she forced herself to ask the question. 'And is that a problem?'

'Yes,' said Sebastian.

The sums in her head suddenly started to add up and she felt that if she took a step forward she'd be on surer ground.

'You sound like Nick.' Her mouth twisted in amusement and exasperation. The same sort of protection and concern.

'Nick. Oh shit. Nick.' Sebastian rubbed his finger along one of his eyebrows as if he were trying to erase it.

It would have been comical if it weren't such a visual indication of Sebastian's agitation. Nina suddenly wanted some straight talking. There was plenty she could read between the lines, but she'd misread Sebastian once before.

'Sebastian. I'm ... I'm going to be blunt. I'm a little confused here.'

He stilled, his finger hovering over his eyebrow, like a clichéd cartoon character frozen with wariness.

'Confused?'

'Yes, Sebastian. Confused. You invited me for dinner. Like a date but not a date.' She gave him a direct piercing look, to show him she was over taking any crap from him. 'This is not like any other dinner date or not dinner date that I've been on. This feels like a date. A romantic date.' She raised both eyebrows and folded her arms. Her rib cage contracted almost painfully as she waited for him to speak.

'Would that ... would it be a problem if it was? I know you've been seeing Alex.' He reached up his hand and smoothed away a stray curl from her face that danced in the light breeze swirling around the rooftop.

The barely-there touch stole her next breath. 'W – we've been out a couple of times … he's lovely but…'

'If it was a date, do you think Nick would mind?' he asked, his eyes suddenly shadowed. She sat up, sharply surprised by the sudden change in direction of his thoughts.

'Nick! You really care what he thinks?' she asked with a quick scowl, watching the white tip of one his teeth grazing at his lip. Seriously? A touch of heartburn seared the top of her stomach along with a punch of anger and frustration. At this moment in time she felt anything but datelike, she wanted to strangle the man. 'Did Nick have anything to do with … well, it was pretty obvious I had a crush on you years ago. I thought maybe you … you were nice to me then.'

Sebastian bit his lip. 'I'm sorry I've been so grumpy. That's why I invited you up here tonight … to say sorry and to thank you.' He rubbed a hand over his face and looked away over the rooftops.

'You're avoiding the question,' said Nina contrarily pushing for an answer even though she was pretty sure she wasn't going to like his response

'At this moment in time, it would probably be—' he gave a mocking smile '—nice to kiss you and to wipe that angry look off your face. But in the cold light of day, yeah, unfortunately what he thinks does matter.'

In a scant second her hopes rose and fell as Nina swallowed down the lump of disappointment and let her silence speak for itself.

He winced. 'You're mad now ... sorry, I'm not great at this stuff. You need to bear with me.'

She held her tongue, prepared to give him one last chance and let him explain. 'You know relationships. You're so much better with people than I am. I'm good at being a boss. Good at being a chef. And pretty average at the other stuff. I say the wrong thing. Especially when I'm upset about something. Whereas you ... people like you. They like you a lot. You spread all this good cheer and happiness around. They talk to you. Open up.'

Nina shrugged, slightly embarrassed. She didn't think that was anything special. Certainly no great achievement.

'When we were younger, you made me feel like some super-hero. And for a while I believed that we ... then Nick warned me off. That last week. Just before I was due to go back to Uni.'

'Warned you off? What, me?' Nina clenched her fist, digging half-moons into her palms.

'Not in a "stay away from my sister or I'll see you sleep with the fishes" warning but more of a "ha! Isn't Nina's teenage crush on you hilarious? She had one like this on her teacher six months ago and one on the postman before that."'

The bite of her fingernails started to sting.

'And you believed him?'

'He also pointed out that if I was serious about being a chef, I wouldn't be around that much.' He rubbed at his eyebrow again. 'It made me realise, crush or not, you deserved someone that would be there for you. Someone waiting at the finishing line for your races, someone who took you out. I was going away, it wouldn't be fair to ask you to wait for me for years. And I figured you'd move on.' Sebastian looked uncertain and took a quick look at the watch on his wrist. 'And when I came back from uni, you barely spoke to me.'

Nina scowled again. 'I barely spoke to you because I was so flipping embarrassed. I'd completely humiliated myself.'

Sebastian shrugged and looked away at the skyline and then did a quick check of his watch again.

'If you look at your watch one more time I'm going to throw your crutches off this roof and leave you up here.'

'Turn around,' said Sebastian, suddenly pushing at her shoulders and turning her to face the opposite view across the city.

Nina panned the view but couldn't ... and then. 'Oh! Oh, how gorgeous.'

Over on the horizon, the Eiffel Tower began to sparkle and glitter like a magical firework. Twinkling and flashing with diamond bright light darting and shooting into the night.

'Wow,' she breathed, entranced. 'I never knew it did that.'

'Every night for the first five minutes of the hour.'

'How on earth did I miss that?' she asked, turning back to him with tears in her eyes.

Sebastian's gaze met hers. 'Sometimes we all miss things that are right in front of us but...' He sighed and looked beyond her. She could see the shadows playing over his face as he studied the light display. He took her hand and squeezed it, but the brief touch didn't detract from the bleak look in his eyes.

'Nina I really ... I like you a lot but...'

'It's fine, Sebastian.' She cut him off, her words quick and sharp, like cauterising a wound. The *but* spoke volumes and if it was of the *I don't fancy you, I don't want to go out with you* or the *you're not the girl for me* variety, she couldn't bear to hear it. 'It was all a long time ago, we've both grown up a lot since then.'

Turning away on the pretext of watching the lights fizz and buzz in the night sky, she blinked back stupid tears that had no place leaking their way out. But her brain insisted on picking and poking at things, like sorting through jigsaw pieces, and it couldn't leave two outstanding facts alone; one, Sebastian was still holding her hand, his thumb gently stroking her knuckles and two, that bleak look in his eyes. Why?

She was about to ask him about the *but*, when a loud voice boomed across the rooftop, the sort of loud that a person used to signal their presence in case they were interrupting.

'Evening all.'

Sebastian pulled his hand away and they both turned to see Alex balancing a tray with a bottle of champagne tucked in an ice bucket and two flutes on a tray.

'Hi ... oh it's you, Nina.' He shook his head, blinking for a second. 'I thought it was going to be Ka...' He beamed at her. 'Sorry, Bas, I was worried that maybe you weren't getting a phone signal up here. You said you'd text for drinks but I didn't hear, so I thought I'd go for broke and bring some champagne up.'

'We just hadn't got around to deciding what to drink,' said Sebastian. 'We were talking.'

Despite his pointed words, Alex beamed. 'And now I realise

it's Nina up here with you, champagne's probably not the thing,' said Alex. 'Sorry I thought …' He winked at Nina. 'Although I did wonder why he didn't ask for something romantic like a couple of Kir Royales. Now I know. How are you Nina?'

'I'm fine.' She dredged up a smile. Alex wasn't to know he'd walked in on something that still needed resolving. And how could she have forgotten about the super svelte Katrin?

'I'll take this back then, unless you fancy some fizz Nina? Seb, what would you like?'

'I'll take a small beer. You can have the champagne if you like, Nina.'

She shook her head, it felt hopelessly inappropriate. 'I'll just have a glass of red wine, please,' she said in a small voice. Clearly it was business as usual as far as Sebastian was concerned.

'And what sort would you like? I can recommend a nice Bordeaux or a lovely fruity Vins de Pay d'Oc. Or there's a—'

'Alex.' Sebastian glared at him.

'I'll just have the house,' said Nina.

'And would you like me to send dinner out?' asked Alex. Nina couldn't decide whether he was oblivious to Sebastian's eagerness to be rid of him or was deliberately outstaying his welcome. Either way, she couldn't shake the feeling of unease at Alex's blithe assumption that it was the gorgeous and immaculate Katrin up here.

'That would be great, thanks.' Sebastian's clipped tone seemed to bounce off Alex who winked at Nina and headed towards the door to the lift, already on his walkie talkie ordering the wine and beer from someone down below.

While he was absent Sebastian turned to Nina and muttered rather like some film spy, out of the side of his mouth, 'And he's got it wrong. Katrin's not on the scene anymore.'

Alex, with his continuing sense of impeccable timing, reappeared, wheeling a trolley bearing silver domed dishes as Nina tried to digest this information and the urgency with which Sebastian had mouthed the words.

'Shall I serve?'

'No, thanks, I can take it from here,' said Sebastian, less than deftly getting to his feet.

'Don't be ridiculous,' said Alex, taking a napkin and flicking it out with great aplomb, before lifting one of the domes. 'Tonight for your pleasure, we have—' he paused for effect '—spare ribs in barbecue sauce with coleslaw and French fries.'

Nina shot a glance at Sebastian – was that a blush on his face – and started to giggle. He lifted his shoulders in one of those well-what-can-you-do sort of gestures.

'I trust it meets with your approval, madam,' said Alex totally unaware of the dimpled smile that Nina gave Sebastian.

'It's a favourite of mine,' she said unable to stop the smile turning into a full-blown grin.

'Excellent taste' said Alex, busy rather incongruously serving several ribs onto a bone china, gilt-edged plate.

Sebastian shared a look of amusement with her and leaned back into the sofa, keeping quiet while Alex kept up a running commentary as he served up two plates.

'Will that be all folks? Someone will be here with your drinks shortly.'

'That's everything, thanks,' said Nina, jumping in before Sebastian could say anything. She had a feeling that any minute now he was going to tell Alex to take a running jump off the roof.

When at last Alex had gone, Nina turned to Sebastian. 'Ribs?'

'You used to love them.'

'And you don't think my tastes might have changed in the last few years? You know, become a touch more sophisticated?'

Sebastian frowned. 'Is this a trick question?'

'Yes,' gurgled Nina, still touched that he'd arranged what had once upon a time been her absolute favourite meal. 'My favourite meal now is linguine with clams...'

'Ah.' Sebastian's disappointment was almost palpable. 'Like you said, it was a long time ago and we've grown up a lot since then.'

'At least that's what I tell everyone...' She gave him a naughty grin, delighted that she'd disconcerted him. Then she softened her expression, 'But some things never really change...' She bit her lip and looked at him, waiting for what felt like a full minute until his gaze met hers. 'I'd forgotten how much I love ribs and coleslaw. Thank you.'

It was almost comical watching him add everything up, the swift head jerk when he ... when he finally got the right answer.

'So...' He frowned, as if still struggling with a difficult equation. 'When I said, I really like you a lot but ... what I was trying to say was ... I don't want to come between you and your family.'

Nina shook her head and smiled at him, lifting her hand to touch his. 'Nothing will come between me and my family ... ever.' She rolled her eyes. 'But ... they might just have to learn to lump it.' With a lift of her heart, she felt his fingers lace through hers.

'And what about Alex?'

She focused on his warm, dry hand laying heavy in hers. It wasn't any sort of declaration but it felt like an anchor. It was enough to start with.

Nina squeezed his hand. 'He's lovely but the last thing I need is another brother.'

'Good, you've got enough of those.' Sebastian's words had her turning her head sharply.

'I've never thought of you as a brother.'

A dull flush ran along Sebastian's cheekbones. 'G – good. That's good. I wouldn't want you to.' He squeezed her hand back before disentangling it and becoming all practical again by picking up one of the serving dishes. 'Now are we going to tuck into this highly sophisticated offering while it's still hot?'

Nina bit back a sigh. Was she ever going to know where she stood with this man?

Chapter 28

Nina gave her favourite receptionist a brilliant smile as she wheeled the chair through the lobby. She and Sebastian were friends again. That was a positive step forward. A huge step forward. It was a very good thing. And friends was better than ... no, it wasn't but it was something.

Sometimes she thought Sebastian might like her and other times, she wondered if all that was on offer was friendship. But she wasn't going to make a fool of herself a second time. She wasn't going to let any of her inner confusion show.

She'd taken the initiative on Sunday, asking if he'd like another wheelchair outing. He'd been busy until today but that was fine because it had given her time to do her research.

'Morning,' she sang, deliberately chirpy as she opened his room door. 'Your chariot awaits.'

'Good morning. Am I pleased to see you!' Sebastian appeared at the bedroom door balancing on his crutches and gave her a brilliant just-for-you sort of smile that made her toes curl. 'It's a gorgeous morning and far too nice to be cooped up with a stack of paint charts.'

'Delighted to be of service,' she said, smiling so hard she

thought her cheeks might pull a muscle. Great to know she was of use. 'You're looking a lot better,' she said, giving in to her inner bitch which wasn't taking disappointment quite so well.

'Thanks. You mean as opposed to my former incarnation of the great unwashed. It's amazing how much better you feel after having a shower. Although I'm getting through industrial quantities of cling film.'

Nina immediately felt a bit mean for her earlier pointed comment. 'With or without Alex's help? There was a marked improvement the second time I saw you.'

'Thank you. Although when someone comments on your personal hygiene, it is rather incumbent to do something about it.' There was a teasing twinkle in his eye.

'I didn't!' she said outraged.

'Hmm, I rather think suggesting I might like help with washing my hair was quite pointed.'

'Well...' She gave him a quick grin. 'You did pong a bit.'

'Hey!'

'Sorry, but ... you were less than fragrant. Now enough of the idle chit-chat. Are you ready?'

'Yup. So where are we going?'

'We're going on a grand gastronomic walking tour.'

'Or wheeling tour, even.'

'Yes, thank goodness most of Paris is quite flat. I've got the route all worked out.'

'So what does this tour entail?'

'Patisserie – traditional and avant-garde.'

Since her visit to Ladurée, Nina had been doing her

research during the evenings on her own at the apartment and making notes of places she wanted to see. Today offered the perfect opportunity and there might have been an ulterior motive.

'OK, any particular reason?'

'Yes,' said Nina firmly. 'I ... I want to see more and learn more.' Actually, she wanted him to see more. Somewhere along the way he'd lost his creative spark. 'And show you a bit more.'

'Me?'

'Yes,' she said in a decisive tone that brooked no argument.

'You weren't impressed by my macarons, were you?'

Her smile faltered. 'Busted.'

'What was wrong with them?'

'Nothing. They were perfect ... just a bit ... you know...'

'Marcel said they were a triumphant trilogy.'

'Where Marcel is concerned, anything freshly baked gets a big tick in his book. He loathes selling bought-in patisserie. I'm surprised he never came to blows with the delivery driver.'

Sebastian frowned.

'Anyone would think you spend all week there.'

Nina's eyes widened fractionally. 'Well, I pop in. You know. Check things. You know. Meet Marguerite and Maddie for coffee. That sort of thing.'

Amusement threaded his voice. 'That sort of thing. That's very sweet of you. Are you minding the place for me? I should have realised you'd be at a loose end and on your own a lot. Sorry I could have been—'

Whatever he could have been, she would never know as she hastily interrupted him, guilt making her babble. 'I've been fine. Busy. Exploring. I'm not there that much. And when I am, I'm … well tidying, preparing.'

Part of her hoped he might be impressed with the hours she'd put in perfecting her patisserie, but she couldn't reveal that without explaining about Marcel selling them in the shop.

The research she'd done had paid off and she had the perfect route worked out which would take them out of the hotel and down to Fauchon, the patisserie opposite L'Église de la Madeleine, then on through Place de la Madeleine to Rue Royale and Ladurée before going through Place de la Concorde, over the Seine and then it was quite a good walk to the next two patisseries which were much more contemporary in style.

'Interesting,' said Sebastian as they peered in the window of Fauchon, with its bright pink and black branding. 'It's like the enfant terrible of the patisserie world.'

It was brash, bright and loud. There were shelves packed with chocolate confectionery in the signature Fauchon packaging, white letters on black with touches of bright pink. As they moved to the back of the shop, the patisserie was displayed in wide shallow chiller cabinets, with exotic labels describing the detailed layered cakes – *sablé breton, crème à la vanille de Madagascar, framboises, eclats de pistaches* and *cremeux caramela beurre salé*. Nina wanted to take notes but satisfied herself by taking lots of pictures, particularly of the long glossy éclairs dotted with slivers of gold leaf, the chocolate so dark it was almost black. To the right there were macarons in every flavour and colour imaginable, stacked neatly in rows, reminding her of little untried yoyos.

From there they went to the rather more sedate Ladurée, which was still Nina's favourite.

'This is like the dowager duchess compared to the brash young prince,' observed Nina, as they peered in the window. 'But I prefer it. I came here a couple of weeks ago.'

'And what did you think?' Sebastian glanced up at her.

'I thought the cheesecake was to die for and so was the plasir sucre,' she grinned. 'And the Saint-Honoré and the Ispahan and the rum baba and the pistachio religieuse.'

'How many cakes did you have?'

'Alex ordered all of them.'

'Alex?' Sebastian's voice rose in quick surprise.

But Nina ignored it. 'And...' She pulled a mournful face. 'I tried all of them.' She was relieved to see Sebastian's eyes dance with amusement. He grinned back. 'I can believe that, quite easily.' He paused before adding, with a naughty twinkle that made the butterflies in her stomach dance, 'I've never known you back down from a challenge.'

Nina ducked her head. Neither had he in the past.

They joined the queue which moved extremely quickly and it wasn't long before they were accommodated at a table.

'So what do you recommend, Miss Every-cake-in-the-shop Hadley?'

'You've got to try the cheesecake, it's divine.' She pointed enthusiastically to the top of the menu. She had a soft spot for that little cake. It had definitely inspired her and the customers at the shop certainly seemed to love her Anglo-French fusion creations. Marcel was positively gleeful every time they sold out.

'Cheesecake?'

At the doubtful look on his face, she nodded. 'Cheesecake with a twist. Updated.'

'They're definitely doing something right,' said Sebastian looking around at the busy tables. 'And it's not cheap.'

'What about the décor?' she asked with a tiny inward shiver of delight at the thought of the magical mermaids adorning the walls of the patisserie.

'It's of its type. I guess it has its appeal. Décor is really important. I spend a lot of money on design concepts.'

'So a really fabulous interior brings in the customers?' she asked leaning back in her chair, trying to be casual.

'Definitely. People want to feel like they're somewhere special, it adds to the ambience.'

'Is that the business man talking? Or a customer?'

'Both. I'm always interested to see what other restaurants and places have on offer, what they're doing well, whether I can learn anything from them.'

'So if somewhere was making money, you might not change it too much?' she asked.

'Not if the profit margins were good and they had a good business model. Which they certainly have here.'

'So you think money can be made from a patisserie,' she pressed.

He raised an eyebrow. 'Patisserie C hasn't made money for years. And patisserie is hard work. I'm not going to change my mind on that. Is Marcel enticing you over to the dark side?'

She lifted her shoulders in a non-committal shrug.

'This place has been here two hundred years. They have a reputation. That's how they can get away with charging twelve euros for a cake.' He shut his menu with a firm slap. 'I will try this famous cheesecake of yours. What are you going to have?'

The queue had doubled since they'd arrived and two women in big sunglasses and glamorous floor length wool coats gave Sebastian second looks, their smiles softening as he hopped on his crutches while Nina pushed the chair to a quieter spot on the pavement. 'Where next for our gastronomic adventure?' asked Sebastian as he settled back into the wheelchair outside the store oblivious to the flagrant interest of the two women.

Nina had to admit, he was rather good-looking and she felt mildly possessive of him. They might see the handsome face but they didn't know that he needed someone to look after him for a change. Successful and driven on the surface, he was a catch, she couldn't deny that, but he needed someone to rescue him from that incessant need to prove himself and to show him how to enjoy himself.

'Nina?' he asked, interrupting her thoughts. She focused back on him.

'Where are you taking me now? I could get used to this, being chauffeured around.'

Nina slapped the map into his chest. 'You can be navigator as you're sitting there doing nothing,' she said smartly, trying to ignore the buzzy sensation that made her feel like she needed to go for a long run or maybe just pull him to his feet and kiss him senseless.

Although she hadn't told Sebastian their destinations, she'd mapped out the route earlier.

'This feels quite familiar,' said Sebastian as they walked along Rue Saint Honoré. 'I'd forgotten how compact Paris is.'

'And I'd forgotten how much easier it is to go at a sedate pace,' teased Nina. 'My shoulders killed after last time.'

They took a slightly circuitous route so that they could pass the Louvre and its famous glass pyramid before dropping down onto Quai Francois Mitterrand to cross the Seine over the Pont Royal, the sunlight skipping across the choppy water busy with boats and barges, before continuing to the Rue du Bac. In the warm sunshine, it was easy to amble along enjoying the atmosphere. A group of tourists on a tour sped past, hopping off the kerb anxious to get by and keep up with the guide who marched along spitting out facts as she went.

La Patisserie du Rêves – the patisserie of dreams – was the complete reverse of Ladurée. It had a pristine minimalism about it, with a few star pieces displayed in the glass bell jars suspended from the ceiling, one large cake with an individual sized one beside it. The cakes were simple but oh so elegant, mirroring the shop itself.

Nina felt it looked more like an art gallery. There was very little on show but Sebastian, having abandoned the wheelchair outside, was prowling around examining each of the cakes on display. She was quite taken with the pretty display of sablés à la rose, little shortbread biscuits with rose icing, as well as the large Paris-Brest, a circle of choux buns filled with praline cream and an inner layer of pure praline, until she saw the price.

'Ninety-four euros!' she said in a scandalised whisper, as Sebastian bent his head to get a closer look.

'It serves twelve,' he said.

'Yes but ... do they ever sell any?'

'Yes,' he tapped the glass. 'In France, the culture is very different. People will buy patisserie to take as a gift when they are invited for dinner or for lunch. This place is highly regarded in Paris. The chef here, Philippe Conticini is very famous, a regular on television and has an international reputation. If you turned up with a dessert from here, your hosts would be delighted, it would be rather flash.'

He dipped his head to peer at the Paris-Brest again. 'This is amazing.'

Nina circled the pastry shop and by the time she came back, Sebastian was still studying the cakes with the enthusiasm of a bug collector peering through a microscope. She smiled to herself at the rather intense expression on his face and waited patiently when after his careful examination of each and every one of the cakes in the central display, he engaged the two white-clad serving staff in a long and involved conversation.

She felt a touch smug as he enthused all the way to the next patisserie.

The cakes in Des Gâteaux et du Pain were even more

extravagantly beautiful than the last shop and confirmed Nina's belief once and for all that she would never be a pastry chef. She'd read up on Claire Damon, the pastry chef, who had opened the patisserie twelve years ago and trained with some of the top French pastry chefs for ten years before that.

Nina looked around and knew that she didn't have the patience or the burning hunger to create perfection like this and ... it didn't bother her. With a sudden burst of insight, she realised that what she was doing was enough for her. It still astounded her that people queued outside Patisserie C for her chocolat caramel suprême on a daily basis and that by four o'clock every afternoon Marcel had sold out of her strawberry and chocolate éclairs.

This icy perfection was for Nina a tad intimidating. She thought back to the warm camaraderie of the patisserie last week when everyone had been there to decorate the front. That was more her style. She didn't need to pretend to be something she wasn't.

Sebastian however was entranced and Nina smiled like a proud mother hen as he prowled around the counters.

'So, what do you think?' she asked, as he got back into the wheelchair and she began pushing him along the street.

'I think my Triumphant Trilogy is a load of bollocks,' he stated. 'This is amazing. It makes me realise I don't spend enough time in the kitchen these days.' He glanced backwards at her. 'Is that a smug look I see on your face?'

'I couldn't possibly comment,' said Nina holding back a smile.

'You remind me of your mother,' he said, still twisting his neck to look up at her.

'No!'

'Well, not that you look like your mother, you don't look like her at all obviously', added Sebastian hastily. 'But it's that knowing, see-I-was-right-all-along smile hovering around your lips, which is so much kinder and easier to take than a full on told-you-so.' He turned back and lifted his leg tapping his cast.

'God, I can't wait to get this bloody thing off. I've suddenly got loads of ideas. I want to get into the kitchen.' He looked back at her again. 'I don't suppose you fancy putting in some extra hours? Learn from the master at work.'

'You mean not get paid,' she teased, lifting an eyebrow.

'Yeah, something like that. Although the others have been paying me. Let's say if you're not completely satisfied you can have your money back.' At this rate he was going to get a serious crick in his neck, looking round trying to talk to her. 'I'd like to do a bit of experimenting. Today's given me plenty of *food for thought*.'

Nina groaned at his emphasis on the words. 'That's terrible.'

He gave her a ridiculous wink before turning his head back to face the direction they were going.

She'd missed this playful side of Sebastian. For so long all she'd seen was the staid, serious side of him. He looked younger and far more light-hearted today than he had for a long time. 'How do you know I wouldn't like hard cash?' she teased back, allowing herself to look down at his dark glossy hair and wonder what his reaction would be if she gave into the compulsion to brush away the hair touching his collar. He was overdue a haircut. Probably not a priority at the moment.

He turned his head to look at her. 'Are you alright?'

'Yes,' she said hastily, realising he'd caught her staring at the back of his neck.

His face softened and he dropped his voice, 'Would you help me tomorrow, after the course has finished, when everyone else has gone?'

She clasped the handles of the chair tighter. There was no reason why the quiet request should set off that odd squirming in her stomach but it did.

'Tomorrow?' she repeated, unable to break her gaze with him, her voice calm even though inside it was shouting 'Tomorrow! No!'

Damn, they had a full schedule planned in the kitchen tomorrow before and after the course, so that she could make up the time she'd lose while Sebastian was there. Both Maddie and Bill had signed up to help from six before the course started and Peter and Jane had offered to stay afterwards to put in a couple of hours.

'Today has really inspired me.' His words warmed her. 'Thanks, Nina. I've suddenly got lots of ideas.' He gave her another one of those serious, intent looks over his shoulder. 'I'd like your help. Your flavour combinations in those éclairs were brilliant.'

'Flattery will get you everywhere,' she said, trying not to let his words affect her.

'I meant it, Nina, you have a real flair.' Was there an

additional warmth in his eyes or was that wishful thinking? She'd been down this road so many times before.

'In fact *you've* made me rethink the final course next week.'

Nina's steps faltered for a minute at the sincerity and ... was that admiration in his voice?

'What do you think of us making a grand piece where everyone can do a bit of everything using the techniques we've practised during the course?'

At first she thought it was rhetorical question, but no, he was looking up at her waiting for an answer as it counted. Unable to help herself, she gave him a smile.

'I ... I think that sounds a great idea.'

'Croquemboche?'

She gasped. 'That would be amazing. Although wouldn't it be a bit ... ambitious?' She'd seen pictures of the profiterole towers. They looked fabulous but she was sure they were difficult to make.

'Yes but...' Sebastian's slow smile did crazy things to her pulse. 'I want this last class to be spectacular. A team effort with everyone working together to choose the flavours, fillings and overall look. I want them to finish on a high and have a real sense of achievement.'

'That's wonderful.' She smiled back at him delighted at his idea. 'They're such lovely people, they'll love it.'

'I hope so and tomorrow will be a nice easy day. We're doing little French style cakes, madeleines and financiers, which I think everyone will enjoy making.'

She bit back another smile but he caught her.

'What?' he asked with laughing suspicion.

'You. You've changed your tune. You sound as if you're almost enjoying teaching the course.'

'Do you know what? I am.' He shook his head as if in surprise.

'And it's nearly all over. You'll be getting your cast off next week. Back on your own two feet.' Nina's words came out in stilted chunks.

'You said you'd come with me. To the hospital. On Tuesday. Is that still OK?' Sebastian sounded equally stilted.

'Tuesday?' She echoed in dismay. 'Next week?'

He nodded, his Adam's apple bobbing.

Tension took hold of her shoulders with a vicious grip. She'd been so busy and focused on the patisserie, she'd been in complete denial about what would happen when Sebastian was back on his feet.

'So will you?' he asked

'Yes, of course.' The life drained out of her voice. 'I'd forgotten I'll be going home so soon.'

Sebastian's face dropped. 'Yes ... I guess you will.' His eyes darted to her face and away. 'It feels like we've ... like the sand in the timer has suddenly run out far quicker than...' He lifted his eyes up to hers, his voice unexpectedly hoarse. 'We've run out of time.'

Nina swallowed hard, keeping her face perfectly still.

'Nina.' He grabbed her hand and pulled her round in front of the wheelchair, pushing himself to his feet, muttering, 'blasted bloody leg.'

Feeling her heart thudding she raised her gaze to his as he lowered his forehead to touch hers. 'Shit, Nina. I don't want you to go.'

Her heart was thumping so hard, it could have outdone the drum beat in a rock anthem.

'Neither do I,' she whispered.

For a moment they held each other's gaze, in a long searching look. Nina wanted to capture the slow sweet smile that began to blossom on Sebastian's face for ever. He lifted a hand and touched her cheek.

'People! Can you move? You're blocking the whole darn pavement.' The angry American tour guide stood in the road, his eager group behind peering with avid curiosity at them.

Flustered, Nina pulled away and with a scowl, Sebastian sat back down in his chair. It took Nina a few pushes to get the wheelchair moving again from a standing start. She felt as if she'd stalled her car at a busy junction.

It rather spoiled the mood and they walked back in silence, both lost in their own thoughts. Sebastian had hunched down in his chair and Nina kept wondering what else he might have said.

He turned to her as they arrived outside the front of his hotel. 'Would you like to—'

'Were you expecting two tons of Molteni oven to be delivered today?' asked Alex, appearing immediately, his hair so tousled it was almost standing on end. 'To your suite?'

'What!' Sebastian's head snapped up. 'What do you mean?'

'I've had a bloody delivery driver, and three men insisting that they were due to deliver an oven to you today. Here.'

'Bloody fools. It's for the restaurant.'

'Well, I knew that but it was rather difficult to convince

them in your absence. And you weren't answering your phone.' Alex's voice took on an accusing tone as he looked at Nina.

Sebastian shrugged. 'I switched it off.'

Alex's eyes narrowed. 'Working?'

'No, Nina took me on a grand tour of patisserie.'

She could have killed him when he added with a cat-got-the-cream smile toying on his face, 'She took me to Ladurée.'

Alex arched an elegant eyebrow, his Scottish accent deepening. 'Oh aye?'

'Yes. Very nice it was.' Sebastian's voice held a definite touch of cockiness.

'And did you buy Nina every cake on the menu?'

Sebastian's lip curled. 'No. Sounds like you were trying to impress her.' The lazy drawl implied that Alex was trying too hard.

Nina wanted to knock their heads together. She was well used to pissing contests, although it was the first time she'd been in the centre of one, metaphorically thank goodness. With a roll of her eyes at their childish behaviour, she decided that the only way to diffuse the situation was to leave them to it.

She was halfway across the hotel lobby before she heard both men call. 'Nina!'

Without turning round, she waved her hand in the air and dived out of the hotel doors, relieved to have a bit of peace and quiet to think about what had happened earlier in the day.

Chapter 29

'No!' said Nina. 'Absolutely not.' She put her coffee cup down with a rattle in the saucer.

'Why not?' asked Maddie, her face flushed as she looked at Bill and Jane on the other side of the table for support. 'It would put Patisserie C on the map.'

'Because ... I feel bad enough that Sebastian has no idea what we've been doing, this feels like it's really trying to force his hand.'

And she didn't want to jeopardise what ... whatever was happening with him. Yesterday's class had been – her heart danced in her chest – the best yet. Sebastian had been, the Sebastian she remembered, light-hearted with everyone, full of banter and careful and attentive to her. Lots of smiles sent her way, touches on her arm, a caress on her cheek when a strand had fallen loose from her ponytail. By the end of the day she'd been fizzing with pent up longing, hoping that they'd have some time together when the class finished. And then he'd got a phone call about that bloody oven again and had to dash off.

'I've got to go, Nina.' He'd touched her hand, stroking her

knuckle before he left. 'I'm tied up in meetings tomorrow, but would you come to dinner on Friday?'

The day had left a magical tingle and she'd hugged the feelings to herself all evening, going over every word and touch of the day and hanging onto those heartfelt whispered words from the day before. *I don't want you to go.*

All of which had made her feel worse about her deception. Her eyes felt gritty and sore after a sleepless night. The combination of guilt and anticipation was not a great bedfellow. And it was exacerbated by being in Sebastian's apartment. At every turn there were reminders of him and the realisation that time was running out both for her and for the patisserie.

Nina suddenly realised that Maddie and Marguerite were looking at her. She'd missed something that had been said.

'Yes, and if they come and do the judging and the patisserie gets placed, there'll be lots of publicity. Sebastian could see the patisserie is worth keeping open,' said Marguerite.

Nina frantically tried to catch up.

'No,' she said firmly. 'It isn't what he wants. We'll have to decline, besides—' she grasped at another line of argument '—there's probably not much chance of us even getting placed.'

'The best newcomer category isn't going to be that big,' said Bill. 'We probably stand a good chance. Especially now we've put up that chandelier. I bet nowhere else has got one like that.'

Nina almost caved in. Bill and Peter had been thwarted in their desire to get the chandelier up at the weekend, realising that cleaning it would take a lot longer, but they had worked with painstaking thoroughness to clean every last bit of crystal over the last few days before finally hoisting the stunning piece into place.

'It's still a no,' said Nina, rubbing her eyes.

Maddie snapped her mouth shut looking like a mutinous turtle, tapping her cup with a knife.

'But what about Marcel,' Marguerite reminded, gently.

'Sebastian will offer him a job,' said Nina, casting a quick glance over at him in his usual place behind the counter. He looked up and caught her eye but his solemn expression didn't change. 'He's already said that.'

'But Marcel loves this place as it is.'

'I know…' said Nina miserably. Marcel almost smiled far more often these days and was positively helpful with customers. 'But he might be happy working here when it's changed.' But she knew in her heart of hearts that the grumpy, idiosyncratic waiter wouldn't adapt that well. He was far too set in his ways and used to running things the way they were.

'Well, it's too late because I've completed the entry and they're coming to judge on Tuesday,' said Maddie, pushing her cup away from her and standing up. With feet planted hip width apart, her sturdy body radiated pugnacious defiance.

Nina sagged in her chair, feeling worn out and exhausted. She didn't want to fight with anyone, least of all Maddie. 'I'm sorry but you'll have to tell them no.'

'But what difference is it going to make?' asked Maddie, throwing her hands up in the air and raising her voice. 'Sebastian is going to be mobile again next week anyway. What were you going to do?' She sneered. 'He's going to see the transformation we've made. It's not just about him. What about all of us? We've invested a bit of ourselves in this place. It's alright for you, pushing off home. I guess you don't care what happens to the building once you've gone.'

'Maddie,' remonstrated Jane in her gentle voice.

'That's not true,' cried Nina jumping to her feet as Maddie's face flushed red with accusation.

'Isn't it? You've gone along with everything. Kept Marcel's hopes up. Let us do all the work. And you're going to walk away. You're on Sebastian's side.'

'There isn't a side. I don't want this place to be closed. But it was always temporary.'

'It doesn't have to be if you were prepared to fight for it. Stick up to Sebastian. You're just a coward. You're so hung up on wanting him to like you. Get over your crush. If he really liked you, he'd have done something about it. You're just useful to have around.'

'That's a really mean thing to say,' said Nina, taking a sharp indrawn breath, shocked by the sudden pain as Maddie's words struck direct hits. A wave of fear flooded over her. What if Maddie was right and she was useful to have around? She'd waited for Sebastian to notice her for years, if he felt the same why hadn't he ever come looking for her? What if this was all convenience? What if when she went back to England, he realised he didn't need her?

'She didn't mean it like that,' said Jane, putting out an arm to touch Nina's.

'Yes I did,' said Maddie, her arms on her hips. 'You're being a selfish baby. This isn't about you. It's about Marcel and

Marguerite. And all of us. We've worked hard and helped you. You could at least give this place a fighting chance.'

Marcel, hearing his name, looked over at them, his face impassive as always but Nina remembered the anguish in them when he'd told her about his wife. The drawn pinched look around his mouth had been rubbed away and although smiles from him were still few and far between, when they happened it was as if a light had been turned back on.

Selfish baby. Nina drew herself up to face Maddie, her fists clenched tightly and her eyes narrowing. The last person that had called her the baby had been Dan and she'd left him with a split lip, although Mum had sent her to bed without any tea that night. And no one called her selfish.

'Fine,' she spat. 'I'll do it. Now if you'll excuse me, I've got cakes to make.' She stormed back to the kitchen, tears stinging her eyes.

The choux pastry was in danger of being beaten to death. It probably wouldn't rise at this rate. Nina still her hand and lifted the beaters out of the mixture.

'Are you OK?' Jane's soft voice penetrated her thoughts.

'Yes,' said Nina in a small voice. 'I hate arguing with people.'

'Me too. I don't think Maddie meant to upset you. She's just one of those people who talks before she thinks.'

'Unfortunately, she was probably right. I have been a coward. I should have told Sebastian what we were doing, but I knew he'd put a stop to it. I let everyone keep going because it was good for Marcel and now I don't know what to do.'

'Do what you think is best. Do what you think is the right thing to do, not what anyone else wants you do. Don't worry about what anyone else thinks. Follow your heart. Listen to me!' Her soft brown eyes twinkled. 'Before I met Peter, I was never this fanciful.'

'You two really love each other. It's lovely to see.' Nina pushed down the spike of envy. Would Sebastian ever feel like that about her? It was pathetic really, loving someone from the sidelines for so long. Now it was almost too difficult to believe he might feel a fraction of the same way.

'Second time around, it's that bit more precious because you know how bad it can be when it goes horribly wrong. You take better care of each other.' Jane gave her a quick hug. 'Don't worry about Maddie. I'm sure she's probably just as upset with herself as you are. Now do you want a hand?'

Nina smiled at her. 'I wouldn't say no, and you are quite a dab hand at caramel now.'

'That's because I enjoy eating it so much. Honestly I'm going to be the size of an elephant before long. It's a good job we're going home soon.'

'You've decided to go back to England?'

'Yes.' Jane gave a rueful laugh. 'It's wonderful living in Paris, but it's not home. And, absence seems to have made our families forget how cross they were that we got married.'

'Did you always intend to go home?' asked Nina, with sudden insight.

'Yes, but don't tell Peter,' she winked. 'It's better that he thinks it was his idea.'

* * *

Nina, with Jane's help, worked solidly until three when Jane and Peter left. Despite feeling absolutely knackered, Nina decided to whip a final batch of cake mixture to make her miniature coffee and walnut cakes. Thank goodness the wholesaler delivered as she'd got through a whole kilo of walnuts this week, not to mention the vast quantities of chocolate. She smiled to herself as she thought of that first trip with Doris. Gosh, hadn't she come a long way since then. Her éclairs could rival any patisserie in looks these days, and the customers seemed to love her flavour variations.

'Nina.' Maddie's voice made her start. Her heart bumped uncomfortably but before she could say a word, Maddie had thrown her arms around her. 'Please, please, please, please forgive meeee. Sorry for being such a bitch and a horrible bossy, mouthy cow. I didn't mean what I said. You've been amazing and no one has worked harder than you and you did keep telling us that Sebastian wouldn't approve and now you're in an impossible situation. And I think he really does like you because he never takes his eyes off you and I think I'm probably a tiny bit jealous. Actually a bit more jealous than that.'

'Oh Maddie,' Nina hugged her back, tears pricking her eyes at the sight of the vulnerability in Maddie's admission. 'I'm sorry too. You're right. I've been a complete coward.'

'No, you have not. Don't you dare say things like that about my friend.'

Nina half-laughed and took in a gasping breath, dashing away a tear.

'I'm sorry, Nina. We can cancel the judges' visit, if you want us to.'

'But I've been thinking about it. It's the right thing to do. We've worked so hard and if I didn't believe in the patisserie, I should have said so before. We have to give it every last chance, to show Sebastian it is viable. Although I should have said something to him before.' She gulped. 'And now it's too late. He's going to be furious.'

'And is that going to matter?' asked Maddie her eyes searching Nina's.

Nina nodded, swallowing. 'I still ... love him. Stupid I know but I want him to like me. Like what I've done. I'm still trying to impress him and this ... he's not going to be impressed.'

'Why ever not? Look at how this place has been transformed. It looks fabulous—'

'That's all down to all of you.'

Maddie ignored her with a quick shrug. 'And it's busy. People love your cakes. Sebastian should be bloody kissing your feet and have the socks impressed off him. You're brilliant. This place is brilliant. It's not as if you've done anything wrong. And as you said, this doesn't really stop him from closing the patisserie if he really wants to. Although he'd be bloody stupid to. People queue for your patisserie. No harm has been done.' She giggled. 'No one has been harmed in the making of this patisserie and all those in her.'

Nina gave a reluctant smile. 'I guess you're right.'

Maddie hugged her again. 'Listen to big sis. If he seriously throws a hissy fit he's mad. When he sees how brilliant it is, he'll come round.'

* * *

Her finger hovered over the screen. With a sigh, she gnawed at her lip and put the phone down. Two seconds later she picked it up again. And then she put it down on the table, pushing it out of reach. Instead she stood up and wandered around the apartment. Tempting as it was, this was her mess. She was not going to phone her mum.

Everything in the room looked so familiar now, she'd stopped seeing things. For a second she looked around trying to see the room with fresh eyes. She'd felt like an intruder when she'd first arrived but now she felt at home and she'd got used to living with Sebastian's things, got used to seeing how he lived. She ran a finger down the spine of one of his collection of recipe books, shelved by theme – Chinese, Thai, Meat, Vegan – in an unruly zigzag height order. It amused her to see the way that his sharp Sabatier knives in the kitchen were closeted in reverential splendour in one drawer, while the cutlery was left in abandoned disarray in the next drawer, forks, spoons and knives not even separated out. Tidiness was related to priorities, tea towels were neatly folded in a cupboard, coffee decanted into separate Alessi containers while the teabags were left in a torn foil packet and paracetamol, throat sweets and anti-histamine tablets in battered boxes were dumped in a jumble in a china bowl on the crockery shelf.

She paused over a picture of Sebastian, stiff in chef whites shaking the hand of a man in a suit, receiving a large framed certificate. The first chef competition he'd won. Just looking at the picture brought back the smell of pork belly, the dish he'd cooked over and over, until he thought it was perfect. Even Nick had got fed up with it towards the end.

With a heavy sigh, she pushed her hair off her face. She didn't need to phone her mother to hear it, she already knew what she needed to do. Sebastian was a perfectionist. He liked order. He liked being prepared. He liked having a plan. She was going to have to come clean and tell him about the patisserie's transformation.

Chapter 30

Every step through the hotel lobby felt like those of a condemned man. But it was the right thing to do. Honesty was the best policy and all that. And she wasn't just going to blurt it out, she'd build up to it. *Soften him up?* suggested a cynical voice in her head.

With a deep breath, she pushed the key card in the slot. It would be alright. He'd be cross but then he'd come around. Of course, he'd be cross and she'd agree with him but she'd done it for good reasons.

'Hi!'

There was no answering call back. The corridor was ominously quiet. She padded down to the door and pushed it open.

'Surprise!'

There was a blur of movement and a kerfuffle of noise. Through it all Nina's eyes zeroed in on Sebastian sitting on the sofa with a resigned expression on his face.

'Nick! Dan! Gail! What are you doing here?'

'We thought we'd come and surprise you,' said Nick, enveloping her in a big hug.

'You've done that, alright,' said Nina squeezing her brother back.

'I hope you don't mind,' said Gail apologetically. 'But these two had decided they were coming—' her face broke into a wide grin '—and there was no way I was missing out. This oaf has been promising me a weekend in Paris for years.'

'Is that any way to talk about your beloved husband?' said Dan scooping her up and nuzzling at her neck.

'Enough, you two.' Nick rolled his eyes. 'I thought Sebastian might fancy some company and I suddenly had a free couple of days, the only ones I'll get now until the autumn, so I just booked a Eurostar ticket ... and the oaf decided to come too. Luckily his saving grace is that he has a lovely wife.'

'Why would I mind?' asked Nina, ignoring her brothers, as she crossed the room to give her sister-in-law a quick hug. 'It's lovely to see you. Shame you had to bring both oafs with you.' Despite her words with a sudden pang, she realised how much she'd missed them all.

'I know,' said Gail, hooking her arm through Nina's, 'but you have to let them out occasionally. And how are you? You look great.' She gave her a quick assessing study and raised an eyebrow but didn't say anything. The look she gave Nina said, *you can tell me all later.* Gail looked at Sebastian and then back at her. Nina pursed her mouth – her sister-in-law didn't miss a trick, but she knew she wouldn't say a word.

Nina risked shooting Sebastian a quick glance. He was laughing at something Nick was saying but he looked up caught her eye and smiled and quickly turned his attention back to whatever Nick was saying.

'So, Nina you're just in time for dinner. We thought we'd go out. Dan's found a place on TripAdvisor.'

Nina laughed. 'Of course he has.'

'And we're staying just around the corner. Can't afford a fancy place like this.' Nick knuckled the top of Sebastian's head.

'Oy,' said Sebastian, pushing Nick's hand away, laughing as he did, his handsome face relaxed and carefree, his eyes crinkled up with amusement.

Nina's heart turned over. He was gorgeous and suddenly she was eighteen again, Nick's little sister and Sebastian as unattainable as ever.

'There's a table booked for half seven. We've just got time to change.' Nick looked at the time on his phone. 'Aw Nina, have you got a phone charger I can borrow, forgot mine and Dan's one of those Apple junkies.'

'Sure.' She rummaged in her bag. 'Here you go but I want it back.'

'Yeah, no probs.' He looked at his phone again. 'Actually guys we'd better get a wiggle on. See you downstairs in half an hour, Bas?'

'Sure.'

Dan and Gail were already at the door, Nick following when he turned around. 'Coming Nina?'

'Actually, I need to go over a couple of things for the course this Wednesday,' said Sebastian smoothly. 'I'd asked Nina here for a quick meeting.'

'Saved you, sis,' said Nick. 'You now get dinner thrown in.'

Nina kept her face as expressionless as possible.

'Bonus.'

'You guys can talk business over dinner,' declared Nick, waiting by the door for Nina to join him. 'See you downstairs, if you can manage with those bad boys.' He mimed using crutches, with a hunchback of Notre Dame lurch contorting his face.

Nina opened her mouth but Sebastian beat her to it.

'If you don't mind, it'll be easier to go through a few things quickly on the laptop.'

There was the briefest moment of silence as Nick stared at Sebastian and then at Nina. Of course, she blushed. Of course she flaming well did. Nick's jaw tensed.

'Anything I need to know?' he asked, his body suddenly predator still and poised, ready to pounce.

Nina swallowed at the unfamiliar and ridiculous sudden turn of Mafia menace in his voice.

'No,' she said rounding on him, with her hands on her hips, 'And even if there was it has nothing to do with you.'

'Nina.' He stepped up to her.

'You have nothing to worry about,' said Sebastian grimly. 'Your sister is safe with me.'

'OK then.' To Nina's relief, Nick finally turned to go, adding with a dismal and far too late attempt at humour, which fooled no one, 'But no sitting on the boss's knee, Nina.'

'Oh, for goodness' sake, how old are you!' snapped Nina, conscious of the two burning spots on her cheeks.

'See you later, sis.'

The minute he left, her eyes met Sebastian's as he stared at her, his jaw clenched so hard she could almost feel his tension from the other side of the room.

'Well, that's that then,' said Sebastian.

She ignored him. If he thought her family's arrival made any difference to anything, he was a bigger idiot than she thought.

'Did you mean it the other day when you said you didn't want me to leave?' she blurted out.

It was Sebastian's turn to look cautious.

'Seriously?' she said and rolled her eyes as she went to sit down beside him on the sofa. Enough was enough. Without giving him chance to respond she leaned in, slid a hand around his neck and meeting his suddenly wary gaze, she kissed him on the lips. For a second he didn't move, but there was no way she was letting him get away again. And then a magical thing happened, he kissed her back. Really kissed her back. Kissed her with a hungry passion that took her breath away and made her feel warm inside and out. Kissed her like he really meant it.

Firecrackers burst in her head. Kissing him was every bit as good and better than she'd ever imagined.

'God, I thought he'd never go,' muttered Sebastian, leaning his forehead against hers. 'I love him dearly but Christ, he's a pain in the arse sometimes.' He pulled back and smiled down at her. The tender 'this is just you and me' look in his eye made her heart stall for a second.

'Welcome to my world,' said Nina, unable to stop her smile filling her whole face. He was utterly gorgeous and quite possibly the best darn kisser on the planet.

'And this is not what I had in mind for tonight.' He groaned and took her hand, linking his fingers through hers and lifting it to his mouth.

Feeling a touch breathless, she widened her eyes. 'What did you have in mind?'

'Kissing.' He drew her to him. 'We seem to be the victims of constant interruptions. I wanted to invite you up here the other day after you took me out in the wheelchair but Alex ... well, he was acting very strangely.'

Nina snorted in an inelegant way. 'You were both being ridiculous.'

'Oh, we were, were we?' Sebastian's voice softened.

'Yes, you were, but I've sorted it out.'

'You have?' Sebastian looked surprised at her firm voice.

'Alex is a good guy. We get on well, but he deserved to hear it from me that...'

'That?' Sebastian raised a teasing eyebrow.

'You know,' she said with a reproving tilt of head.

Sebastian smiled. 'I know...' He kissed her again, a gentle beguiling kiss, which gradually deepened, his lips exploring hers, his tongue make a tentative foray along her lower lip. She felt heat nip at her core and opened her mouth as the kiss got hotter. With one hand she stroked the back of his neck, her fingers rubbing over the short hair at his nape as she pushed her body closer to his. He responded with a low moan and she felt a little smug spike of triumph. She liked that she was affecting him as much as he was turning her inside out.

With a long exhaled sigh, Sebastian pulled away. 'You do realise we're going to have to stop this, otherwise the others are going to take one look at us and know exactly what we've been up to.'

'We could just run away. Or lock the door.'

'Both sound excellent options.' He grimaced. 'Except I wouldn't be able to keep my hands off you if we did that.'

'Who says I want you to?' asked Nina, with an arch smile.

'Are you being a hussy, young woman?' he asked, a teasing hand skimming down her ribs.

'I think I might be. Are you complaining?'

'Jeez Nina, not at all. I just ... you're Nick's little sister ... I was planning to wait, seduce you with a bit more finesse and without this thing on.'

His words sent a flash of heat fireballing its way through her, leaving her ever so slightly turned on and very weak at the knees.

'You were planning?' she asked archly.

He blushed. 'Fantasising ... for a long time.'

Her pulse leapt at the brusque, impatient words.

'Well, my family have well and truly put a spoke in the works.'

'They have.' He gave a heavy sigh and rubbed his forehead. 'We're going to have to...'

'I'm assuming you don't want to go public with them,' said Nina watching his face carefully.

'No, I don't ...'

His words pinched at her heart.

'Nick's just going to have to get over it.'

'Nina!'

'I'm serious. This isn't about him, it's about us.'

'Yes but ... he's my family too. Jeez, your mum, dad, brothers, they're more like family to me than my own family. What if Nick never speaks to me again?'

'Don't be ridiculous. Of course he'll speak to you.'

'OK, what if things don't work out and we break up.'

Nina swallowed. After waiting for him for all this time, she didn't even want to think about it.

'Sorry.' He stroked her cheek as if to soothe away her stricken look. 'I want this to work. I've ... when you kissed me that night in the kitchen, the night before I was due to go back... it was heaven and hell. All my Christmases married with all my worst fears. I wanted to kiss you and carry on kissing you but ... Nick. Your family. They're important to me. And all I could think was, what if you didn't feel the same way as I did? And if you did, it wouldn't be right. I knew I had to give all my focus to my career if I was going to make it. I couldn't bear to hurt you. And then I told myself, someone like you would never want someone like me. And rather handily I had the get out clause that Nick had been warning me off. And what sort of best friend would I be, if I ignored that?'

'Wow. And I thought that having my heart crushed was enough,' said Nina, trying to take in everything he said. 'Part of me is furious that you listened to Nick. And I will be having words with him one day about it. The other part of me is ... kind of heartbroken that you thought like that.'

'Sorry.' He winced. 'Your timing was unfortunate. It gave me the chance to run away and bury myself at uni. And when I came back, you barely spoke to me. So I thought Nick was right, it had been a passing thing.'

Nina scowled again. 'I barely spoke to you because you'd rejected me.'

'I don't recall that kiss being a rejection.' He lifted a finger to her lower lip and gently traced its edge.

Nina raised her eyebrows and frowned. 'I ... you ran off pretty sharpish afterwards.'

'Because it floored me.' His hand slipped along her face sliding underneath her hair, his fingers idly stroking her hairline. Nina didn't dare move in case she was imagining things and this was all a dream or she was getting the wrong end of the stick. 'I've wanted to kiss you again for a long time.'

'But ... why didn't you ever say anything?'

'Nina.' His sharp self-deprecating laugh made her face relax and almost smile. 'You've been giving me a hard time ever since. I thought you hated me. And I put that down to embarrassment that you'd ever kissed me. Or thought you wanted someone like me.'

'Stop saying, someone like you,' she said, irritated by the phrase. 'There's nothing wrong with you. You're driven, a bit grumpy and very focused but look at your friends. Alex, Nick and my Mum always adored you. And if you must know,' she added indignantly, 'I was trying to treat you normally, like one of my brothers, to show that you didn't mean anything, when for the last ten years I've been looking for another sodding man to match up to you.' With that she leaned into him and kissed him hard because she was cross with him for being such a flipping idiot for all this time. It was possibly the least romantic kiss ever.

'Mmpf.' Sebastian muttered beneath her lips as she sat back and glared at him.

He laughed. 'Shall we try that one again?' And he did.

When they final drew apart, each a little flushed and breathless, Nina wasn't sure whose heartbeat was pounding the most.

'I also don't want to say anything to Nick or anyone else because this is new and I don't want to share it with anyone yet. I like it just being us. Learning to be with each other, without anyone watching, commenting ... if we did go public before we're used to being us, don't you think it would be like being under a microscope?'

Nina's heart stuttered in her chest. There was a reason she'd adored him for so long. Despite being grumpy and overbearing, he was also careful and attentive to the things that mattered.

She gave him a gentle smile. 'That sounds a much better reason.'

With a disgruntled scowl, he touched her lips, 'Which means we have to stop this and try and look respectable. Have I got time for a cold shower?'

Lovely as it was to be reunited with her family, dinner was excruciating. There was no other word for it. Inside, she was fizzing with excitement and the rush of remembered kisses. It had been hard tearing herself away from Sebastian.

It was only halfway through dinner that Nina remembered that she was supposed to tell Sebastian about the patisserie. Sneaking a glance to see Sebastian talking animatedly to Dan, the warm glow still resonating through her from his hungry kisses and heartfelt words, gave her hope that he would forgive her. Declaring mea culpa and apologising would help but she suddenly felt a lot more confident.

'So how has it been in gay Paris?' asked Nick who was sitting next to her. 'Enjoyed it?'

'Not that gay to be honest. I've been working too hard.'

'Sebastian always was a slave driver.' Nick put down his knife and fork, having polished off a huge steak. 'But I thought you were only doing a couple of days a week.'

'Well—' Sebastian was still deep in conversation with Dan '—I've been practising my skills. Doing a lot of cooking. Making the most of being here.'

'Good for you. So any idea what you're going to do when you get back?'

'No,' said Nina abruptly.

Nick smirked. 'That means yes but you're not going to tell me.'

She swiped at him with her napkin. 'How do you do that, it's so annoying. I have an idea but ... I just want to think about it a bit longer.'

'That's cool. And,' his mouth quirked, 'you always answer quickly when you don't want us probing too much.'

'I'll have to remember that,' she said wryly.

'So how's Sebastian been? Being out of action can't have been much fun.'

'He's better now,' said Nina with a grimace. 'He was like a bear with a sore head when I arrived.'

'And have you two played nice?' he asked with a sly smile, picking up his wine glass. 'Not been tempted to brain him with a rolling pin.'

Nina took her time answering. 'We've been working. It's all been very professional and the people on the course are all lovely. We've had quite a laugh. There's a girl my age, Maddie, she's become quite a good friend. She lives here, so she's been showing me around.'

If he noticed she'd changed the subject, he didn't comment and she spent the next few minutes telling him all about Maddie, Marguerite, Marcel and the others.

'Excellent, you can give us some suggestions. Want to join us tomorrow?'

'I can't, I'm...' She glanced at Sebastian who was now talking to Gail. 'I'm busy.'

'Busy doing what?'

'Working.'

'Sebastian will give you the day off.'

Nina sucked in a noisy breath. 'You're doing it already.'

'What?'

'Trying to organise my life for me.'

'I was trying to do something nice,' said Nick, looking utterly confused.

'I know you were, but if I had another boss, not Sebastian, would you gaily suggest that he gave me a day off because you were unexpectedly in town? If it were you, how would you feel if I told you I'd arranged it with your boss so that you could take the day off.'

'Point taken, sis. Sorry. Force of habit.'

'Yeah, which I haven't missed at all. Although as it happens I'm not working for Sebastian tomorrow.'

'So you can take the day off.'

'No, I'm busy ... I could meet up with you after lunch.' She was starting early in the kitchen to bake everything for the day and Maddie and Bill were finishing off the last of the blue sky and clouds on the walls. With the increasing number of customers, they'd had to do it in small sections each day to minimise the disruption, although most customers seemed fascinated by the work and often stopped to chat and question Maddie as she hung from her ladder, a second paintbrush in her teeth as she alternated between blue and white paint.

'Busy...'

Nina shot him a look.

'Sorry.' He held up his hands. 'None of my business. So you've enjoyed being on your own, then?'

Nina laughed. 'Do you know what? I haven't really been on my own that much. I swapped you lot for another family. Although they don't all think they know what's best for me. And they don't try and protect me all the time.' She thought of Maddie's straight talking and Jane's gentle habit of talking to her as an equal even though the other woman was in her fifties.

'And what's Sebastian's place like?'

'Very nice,' said Nina, her eyes gleaming.

'I bet he's looking forward to getting back. I presume you'll be home next week. Isn't he due to have the cast taken off next week?'

'Yes, although I'm staying on another couple of days to do the final day of the course. I'm...' Shit! She took a hefty gulp of wine. His cast was coming off the same day as the judges were coming to interview her at the patisserie and make their assessment. At that moment Sebastian looked over the table and she caught his eye and promptly choked on her drink.

Nick slapped her on the back with brotherly vigour as he asked Sebastian, 'I was just asking Nina when the leg's coming out from hiding?'

'Next Tuesday,' replied Sebastian, giving Nina a brief smile. 'Are you alright?'

'Y – yes fine. Wine went down the wrong way.'

'Bet you'll be glad to have it off. That must have hampered any action,' said Nick with a laugh.

Sebastian pursed his lips but Nick was oblivious to his sudden discomfort.

'Been going without for the last few weeks, have you?'

Sebastian flushed.

'Never mind mate,' said Dan joining in. 'The girlfriend will be pleased to have you back in one piece. Get a bit of release.'

Nina didn't dare look at Sebastian.

'Dan!' said Gail, giving her husband a sharp, disapproving nudge in the ribs.

'What?' he asked pretending innocence, grinning like an idiot at her before putting his arm around her and pulling her to him.

'Are you still seeing that girl, Katrina?' asked Nick, leaning to one side as the waiter squeezed between him and Nina to take their empty plates.

'Katrin, and no I'm not.'

'Shame, she looked hot. Don't tell me she dumped you.'

Nina stared down at her lap.

'No, we just agreed to go our separate ways.'

'You dumped her. Why?'

With a shrug, Sebastian picked pushed his cutlery around his plate.

'You met someone else,' said Nick. 'What's her name?'

Sebastian realised the waiter was standing beside him waiting for his plate. With reluctance he let go of his cutlery.

'No one you know.'

Nick turned to Nina. 'Not like him to play his cards close to his chest. You know anything?'

'No,' she said far too quickly which earned a narrow-eyed stare from her brother. 'Like I said, we barely see each other apart from the days I work.'

'Nina, what do you suggest. Eiffel Tower or Notre Dame?'

Nina could have kissed her sister-in-law.

'I'll walk you home,' said Nick as they emerged from the restaurant which meant there was no chance of sneaking back to Sebastian's hotel room. Not that she wanted to sneak around. She slipped a quick glance at him. He was listening to Dan and Gail with a studied interest which suggested that he knew she was looking at him.

Nina wanted to say no to being escorted home but seeing the angle of her brother's chin, she realised it was pretty pointless and besides it was a lovely evening and the walk across the river and down through the maze of streets behind the Musée d'Orsay was preferable to the Metro.

She gave Sebastian a cheerful goodbye, which belied the pang she felt as she realised with her family around she wouldn't see him until Tuesday. It felt as if they always seemed to get so far and then something got in the way. It was unlikely he'd join the others sightseeing, no doubt he'd have his usual ton of work. The arrival of her family had well and truly put a spoke in the works.

'Night, Nina.' Dan gave her hug.

'See you tomorrow,' added Gail as she kissed her on the cheek before snuggling up to her husband. Nina felt a pang of jealousy as Dan gave his wife an affectionate kiss, his hand slipping to cup her bottom.

'Night, Nina,' said Sebastian stiffly.

'Night, Sebastian.' Her heart sank. This felt all wrong. As if there was a huge divide between them, when she should have been able to go over and slide into his arms and trail kisses along his jawline.

Gail and Dan waited for Sebastian, as he organised his crutches without looking at Nina. She waited awkwardly for a minute before he nodded at her and then turned to limp away with the other two.

She and Nick fell into step in silence. They'd walked for five minutes and the silence was starting to feel ominous. As they crossed the Seine, Nina half-heartedly pointed out some landmarks. She knew her brother well enough to know he was building up to something.

'Are you going to tell me what's going on with Sebastian?' he asked in a low voice.

'No,' said Nina. 'I thought I'd made it clear. You're my brother. Not my keeper.'

'So, there is something going on.'

'I didn't say that.'

'But you didn't deny it.'

'Nick, whatever is or isn't going on, is nothing to do with you.'

'Yes, it is.'

'No, it isn't.'

'He's ... my best friend.'

'And that's not going to change, unless you let it.'

'So there is something going on.' He grabbed her arm and turned her to face him.

Nina sighed and shook his hand off. 'For God's sake, just leave it.'

'Are you sleeping with him?'

'Nick!'

At her outraged tone, he had the grace to look a little ashamed which made Nina feel a tiny bit more conciliatory towards him. 'I'm not sleeping with him but even if I were, it has nothing to do with you.'

'Sorry, I was a bit out of line.'

'A bit!'

'It's only because I care. I don't want you to get hurt.'

'And I've been trying to tell you for a long time, I'm a big girl. And why would Sebastian hurt me?'

'Well ... I know you had a crush on him when you were younger. But you're not his type.'

'Thanks a bunch,' said Nina, all her insecurities flooding back. 'And you don't think he could possibly fancy me?'

Nick paused and pulled a variety of different faces as he realised he'd put himself between a rock and hard place. 'I'm just looking out for you.'

'And like I said, I'm a big girl.' Hurt at his earlier words made her tone harsh.

'Hey, I'm sorry. Force of habit.'

'Yeah, well you need to break it,' said Nina with a snap to her words. 'I've really enjoyed being out here, meeting new people and doing my own thing.'

'I gathered. Are you going to tell me what you're up to tomorrow morning?'

Nina bit her lip. Confessing to Nick before Sebastian didn't feel right.

'I'm meeting up with Maddie, one of the friends I've made on the course. But I'll be free after lunch to see you.'

'Fair enough.'

Chapter 31

Everything alright with Nick? He didn't suspect anything?
Nina wasn't sure quite how to phrase her text back to
Sebastian as she sat on the edge of the bed. Despite her
brother's prying, and it really was nothing to do with him,
she hated lying to him. And she wasn't going to lie to Sebastian
either, well, not about this. And she was irritated by his less
than lover-like text.

He asked a few awkward questions, which I refused to answer.

*Sorry to put you in a difficult spot. I wish you could have
come back here with me. I'm missing you. xxx*

OK, that was a bit more like it.

Good. xxx I miss you too.

*How does that happen? How can I miss you now, when we've
been apart for all these years? Wish you were here. xxx*

Nina's heart did a little flip as she stared down at the words
on the screen. With a smile, she quickly ran her fingers over
the screen. *I wish I was there too. Weird that I'm here in your
apartment in your bed. xxx*

I have had a few thoughts about you being in my bed. xxx

Now that really did have her heart racing. She looked at

the second set of pillows on the bed, the ones she'd not touched since she'd been here.

Are we sexting? xxx

Best not, having a cold shower at this time of night with this cast is a bit of a palaver. xxx

She laughed out loud.

Wouldn't want you to suffer unduly on my behalf. Night xxx

Night Nina. Sweet dreams (in my bed) xxx

Night xxx

Nina slept with the phone next to her on the pillow, a smile on her face when she woke at a ridiculous hour. Getting to the bakery at seven had quickly become a habit, and she'd become a dab hand at knocking up enough pastries to start the day off. Marcel had been the one to suggest that she limit the amount she made, to keep things exclusive. From ten o'clock when the patisserie opened there was often a queue waiting and usually by two they'd sold out of everything.

Today she wanted to practise a few finishing touches to make them look that bit better, ready for the judges next week and she need to get herself super organised to be ready to cook up a batch on Tuesday morning before the judges arrived. Oh dear God, another thing she was hiding from Sebastian. She knew it was cowardly, not telling him about the patisserie's transformation, but now that ... they were finally on the same page, she couldn't bear to risk it.

It might be wrong, but she'd waited so long, she wanted to enjoy these magical, spinetingling feelings.

Perfect Parisian weather, she thought as she danced up the steps to meet Nick, Dan and Gail outside the Musée d'Orsay in glorious sunshine. Having passed the museum so many times and not been in, it had been her must see in Paris suggestion.

Although now she was beginning to regret it a little; the place was huge and she'd already put a busy few hours in at the patisserie this morning. How she would have managed without Maddie and Jane's help this morning, she didn't know. If she were to do this full-time, she'd need an assistant.

Spotting her brothers and Gail already in the queue, she looked at her sister-in-law, wondering what she'd have to say about Nina's idea. Would it be possible to persuade the family to make the farm shop café into more of a destination tea shop selling her fancy Anglo-French fusion cakes? At the moment, it was a coffee shop with a few cakes and biscuits, a useful stopping off point for coach tours in the area and for locals who fancied a coffee out, but it could be so much more.

'Hey, Nina,'

'Sebastian!' She hadn't spotted Sebastian in his wheelchair behind the others as she approached and, now she was terribly conscious of him. The chambray shirt he wore made his eyes looked bluer and the warmth in them made her swallow hard as her heart leaped at the mere sight of him.

Her face lit up and then realising that Nick was looking at her, she turned to show she was delighted to see all of them.

'Hi all, how was this morning?' she gabbled ignoring Nick's narrowed eyes.

'Afternoon,' said Nick, stepping in front of Sebastian and giving her a big bear hug and lifting her up.

'Put me down,' she muttered against his chest. 'What have you been doing?'

'Charming,' said Nick as Gail laughed, saying, 'We've been to Galeries Lafayette this morning.'

'Isn't it gorgeous?' enthused Nina. Maddie had taken her there one afternoon last week.

'Pretty swanky,' agreed Dan as Gail nodded, holding up a little string handled bag with the Chanel logo on the side.

Gail linked arms with Nina. 'We've had a fabulous morning.'

Nina shot a quick look down at Sebastian being pushed along in the wheelchair by Dan. This was torture being so close and not being able to touch or say anything.

In the busy crush, when they were queuing to get inside, she brushed her arm against his. Stupid but she was desperate for a connection, to reassure her that she hadn't imagined last night.

She felt his fingers slide up her arm in silent acknowledgment and breathed a small sigh of relief even though neither of them were looking at each other.

The first sight of the light airy space, the curved glass roof and the extravagant golden clock was so utterly glorious it made her chest hurt and even silenced her brothers. The soaring roof arches, perfect symmetry and the sheer artisty and engineering involved made her stop dead. She might be a complete philistine when it came to paintings or sculptures, but it didn't matter because she'd completely and utterly fallen in love with this amazing, gorgeous, huge, wonderful building.

Transfixed, she stood and stared upwards.

'Something else, isn't it?' murmured Sebastian beside her, stretching out his index finger from where his hand lay on top of the wheel to very lightly graze her leg just above the knee.

'Wow, this place is huge,' said Gail looking upwards before ducking her head to look at her guidebook. 'Now, where do we start?'

She and Dan began bickering about what they wanted to see and Nick chipped in deliberately winding them both up.

Ignoring them, Nina was happy to stand and stare, conscious of Sebastian's quiet stillness next to her as her gaze traced the lofty arches, the light spilling in the through thousands of panes of glass.

'Incredible, isn't it?' he said to her in a quiet voice.

She nodded. Both of them seemed in tune with the reverential hush. Despite the large numbers of people wandering about, it was if the vastness of the space made people talk in whispered hurried bits of conversations, too much in awe to risk disturbing the sacred air.

Nina's eyes were drawn back to the golden clock dominating the huge arched glassed wall at one end of the former station and it was easy to imagine a passenger hurrying along the length of the station, one eye on the clock, and the billowing steam of the trains waiting like magic iron dragons waiting to be let free.

'It must have been an amazing sight when it was a station,' said Sebastian, following her gaze.

'You read my mind,' said Nina. 'It's beautiful. I could stand here all day.'

'Me too.' He glanced at her family. 'Although the ants in the pants pair there are desperate to get moving.'

'Philistines,' grumbled Nina with a grin, tuning into their conversation.

'I want to see some Monet,' Gail was saying and Dan was looking at the map as Nick tried to take it from him.

'Maddie said that one of the best things is to go to the fifth floor, if you like impressionists,' chipped in Nina.

'Right then, that's where we'll go,' said Nick, pointing upwards at the sign denoting a flight of stairs.

Sebastian folded his arms and raised his eyebrows

'Sorry mate,' said Nick. 'Forgot. Must be a right ruddy pain.'

'Tell me about it, but it's been six weeks now, so I'm about used to it. I'll take the lift.'

'Race you,' said Nick immediately. 'Ten euros we'll beat you up there.'

'You're on,' said Sebastian and wheeled himself round to head towards the lifts back in the entrance hall.

'Want me to come with you, in case you ... need some help?' asked Nina.

'That would be great,' said Sebastian. 'Right Nick, clock starts ticking now.' And he pushed himself off hard, wheeling quickly towards the lift.

'Bugger,' said Nick. 'Come on, Dan.' The two of them began weaving quickly through the crowd following the signs to the far end of the huge space.

Gail met Nina's eyes and laughed. 'Can't beat em, join em,'

she said setting off after her husband. 'See you up there.'

Sebastian had a good head start and she caught up with him by the lifts. As she arrived and went to press the button to call the lift, he caught her hand and placed a lazy kiss in the palm.

'There's no hurry,' he said with a wicked twinkle that had her hormones dancing about in a very discombobulated way.

'But ... what about the bet?'

Tugging on her hand, he pulled her down until her head was level with his, eyes dancing with merriment. 'It will be the best ten euros I've ever spent,' he said as he kissed her quickly on the lips.

Unfortunately the lift was in big demand, so they were squashed in but Sebastian held her hand the whole way up, gently squeezing her fingers. When the lift stopped, just before the doors opened, he kissed her knuckles.

'God, I can't wait for them to go. Talk about bad timing. And then I've arranged to go to Lyon tomorrow, I won't be back until late on Monday.' He sighed as she pushed the wheelchair out of the lift.

'Don't worry. I've got lots to do.'

He gave her a quick quizzical frown.

'I'm ... seeing Maddie, helping Marguerite with a computer thing.' She pasted a bright smile on her face as inside her stomach lurched. She still hadn't told him about the patisserie.

'You've made good friends with them. I'm glad. It's going to be Tuesday before I see you again.' With a huff, he shook his head. 'Our first proper date, in the fracture clinic at the hospital.' He pulled a face. 'Not exactly...'

'Beat you!' panted Nick appearing with Dan close behind. 'You owe me ten euros mate.' 'And a glass of cold beer,' added Dan, 'Where's the nearest bar?'

'We've only just got here,' said Nina, knowing him well. She watched her sister-in-law arrive serenely behind him, not seeming at all out of breath. 'You can't leave until you've at least seen some paintings.'

Dan grumbled something and Gail cuffed him gently around the head.

Nina followed them all slowly to the gallery, keeping behind Sebastian, her head a mix of conflicting emotions.

Chapter 32

The morning of the judging brought with it another day of blue sky and bright sunshine, creating dappled patches of shade on the pavement along the tree lined boulevard. Nina felt as if she were having a slightly out of body experience as she veered from excited nerves to terrified foreboding. Today was going to be a day of reckoning.

Her family had finally left yesterday evening after a couple of gruelling days of sight-seeing which left her feeling as if she'd walked every inch of Paris. She'd also been cross-examined by Nick who'd overheard Gail say to Dan that there was no way on earth that there wasn't anything going on between her and Sebastian.

Irritated beyond anything, she'd finally snapped and said yes, there was something. Of course he'd then wanted details, which she refused to give him, not that there were any as it was all so new but there was no way she was going to tell him that.

This morning she was doubly irritated when she realised that he'd gone off with her phone charger. Her phone was on the last bars of battery and in danger of dying any minute.

She'd have to buy a new one later today unless Nick had remembered and left it with Sebastian.

Sebastian hadn't come back from Lyon until late last night, so there'd still been no chance to talk to him about the patisserie. But she was seeing him today, meeting him at the hospital. She'd worked out she could just about to get there for his appointment providing the judges didn't stay longer than an hour. Surely an hour was more than long enough for a visit. There wasn't that much to see.

She was meeting Maddie and Bill early to give the patisserie an extra spit and polish, although she was already running late. Thankfully the hospital was right by Notre Dame according to Sebastian, so it would be easy to find without Google Maps.

'You look very chic,' said Maddie as Nina arrived in a billowing navy skirt, with a cute white shirt with bows on the cap sleeves.

'Thank you. Inside I'm a bag of nerves.' She looked around the patisserie with a critical eye.

'Don't worry. You're rocking the Audrey look. If you weren't so nice I'd be well jel. The judges are going to love you.'

Nina pulled a worried face. 'Are you sure you don't want to do the talking?'

'Nope,' said Maddie, with a cheerful grin, her lips smacking together with a decisive snap. 'We must all stick to what we're best suited to. Today I'm armed and dangerous with cleaning products and I'm not afraid to use them.' With an exaggerated swagger, she lifted her can of polish, aimed and fired it at the nearest table, before polishing with great gusto.

'I'll leave you to it.'

'Bonjour, Marcel.'

'Bonjour. You are looking very nice today.'

Nina beamed at him, totally taken by surprise by the unexpected compliment. 'Thank you, Marcel.'

The fully stocked cabinet in front of him was immaculate, the glass without a single finger mark or smear and everything arranged beautifully, although she could still hear the laboured hum of the refrigeration unit below. A frisson of pride sizzled through her at the sight of the rows of patisserie, the line of chocolat caramel suprême, each one gleaming with a single piece of gold leaf, the neat rows of strawberry and cream éclairs, the perfect rounds of coffee and walnut mini cakes, the glistening red glaze of her version of mille-feuille jammy dodgers, plump with raspberries and Chantilly cream.

'Doesn't it look lovely?'

He inclined his head. 'It does.'

'Are we all set?'

Nina whirled around at Bill's voice. 'Yes, I think we are. The new lights in the cabinets look great. Thank you for doing those.'

'My pleasure, pet. I couldn't get rid of the humming noise. Reckon she's got a couple more years in her. I've had fun tinkering trying to fix her. Fact is, I've had more fun this last month, than I have for a long time. Living in Paris isn't so bad after all. Funny old world,' he mused. 'Never thought I'd live aboard. But it's not so bad. And I'm going to try and pick up a bit of electrical work. Peter's recommended me to the caretaker chap at the place they've been renting and he's asked me to put in a few lights and such.'

'Oh, that's good. Maybe Sebastian might need some work doing ... he was complaining he couldn't always get good tradespeople.'

'If you can put in a good word, hen, that would be grand.'

'What time is it?' asked Nina for the fifth time, cursing her brother. Being without her phone was driving her nuts. Why did the whole world have iPhones?

The kitchen was spotless, everything was put away. There was nothing for her to do. She couldn't even rearrange the drawers. She folded the cloth by the sink and put it neatly beside the taps and then she moved it to the other side.

'Time you got a watch,' said Peter. 'It's ten minutes since you last asked.'

'But they should have been here half an hour ago.' She picked up the cloth again, refolding it and gave the clean sink, another wipe. 'I'm supposed to be going to the hospital to meet Sebastian.' If she didn't leave in the next ten minutes, she was going to be late and even then, it was pushing it.

'They'll be here soon, I'm sure. They're visiting everywhere today, and these things always take longer than people think.'

'Well, they should have planned it better,' she said, rubbing at the draining board.

'Don't fret pet,' said Bill.

'Easy for you to say that. Oh God, sorry. I'm so nervous and I promised Sebastian I'd be there. He hates hospitals.' She couldn't even text him to let him know she was running late, her phone had well and truly died.

'And you will.' Bill patted her on the arm and took the cloth out of her hand. 'Now leave that. Go and have a coffee and sit.'

'If I drink any more coffee I'll be peeing pure caffeine.'

Maddie, Marguerite and Jane were on look-out duty on the street and unable to sit down, Nina joined them.

'I bet that's them,' said Maddie. 'Five o'clock. Blue hat. Big bag'

'No,' said Marguerite. 'She's not smart enough.'

'What about six o'clock,' said Jane. 'Older man and woman.'

'He's wearing a cardigan,' said Maddie. 'No way could he be a judge.'

Nina paced up and down outside the dark grey painted windows, touching the smooth paintwork. They'd done such a good job and ... bugger, what time was it?

'There, that has to be them,' whispered Maddie. Nina whipped her head round to see a glamorous brunette woman in heels trotting towards them, accompanied by a slightly older silver fox of a man.

'You think she's been walking around Paris judging patisserie shops since 9 a.m. in those beautiful shoes?' asked Jane in her usual gentle tone. 'They are lovely but impossibly impractical.'

'Hmm you're probably right. With that figure, I doubt she's even so much as sniffed a cake let alone eaten one.' Maddie's gloomy observation almost made Nina smile, except she was starting to get exasperated with the three of them. As if they had any idea what the judges looked like or how many there would be or which direction they would be coming.

'I'm sorry,' she snapped. 'If they're not here in the next two minutes, I have to go.'

'But you can't,' wailed Maddie.

'I have to. I promised Sebastian. You can talk to the judges.'

'But...' Maddie looked at Marguerite.

'My dear, they will want to talk to you about the inspiration behind the patisseries. No Paris patisserie is anything without its wares.'

Nina flapped her hands trying to deny the words but Marguerite's steely blue eyes stared at her.

'I'm going inside,' she said and wheeled round. She didn't dare ask anyone the time. She had to go. Crossing to the rack of coat pegs she unhooked her coat.

Bill and Peter emerged from the kitchen with Marcel.

'It's no good, I'm sorry, I've got to go.' She took her coat down again. 'I have to.'

'Ah, pet.'

'Look you can talk about the patisserie. Tell them what we've done. Can't you?' She looked around the room; they'd achieved so much but it had been a team effort. 'It's a shame we never thought to take any before and after pictures. We could have shown the judges, how we've brought this place back to life.'

Marcel smiled. A proper full on smile. 'Wait here.' He reached behind her to the hook on the rack where he kept his coat and hat, a smart felt trilby that Nina had never seen him wear but he always hung up. He brought a cloth bag out from behind his coat and opened it up to give her what looked like scrapbook, looking a little shy.

'I ... made this ... for you. A memento. It was for when you left ... but if you think...' With an embarrassed shrug, he thrust it into her hands and scuttled back behind his counter busying himself with something. Quite what, she wasn't sure but there was the sound of china chinking and spoons clattering on saucers.

Completely nonplussed and still aware of the clock ticking. Nina set it down on the table. The front cover had a stylised table with two ornate bistro chairs, picked out in blue against the backdrop of the Seine. She opened the first page. On the left-hand side was a close up of the peeling turquoise paint on the window sills, even though it was the shabby exterior, it was still a beautiful photo. Opposite was the same sill, now painted in the dark grey matt with golden aura of sunlight glowing on the painted woodwork.

Each page held pictures illustrating before and after, the horrible pink dado rail, the mysterious secretive glowing eyes of the mermaid, the empty patisserie, the queue outside the door but each of them also told a story.

Nina touched the pages reverentially, the photos were extraordinary.

'These are incredible,' she said. It was all she could say as she fought against the lump in her throat.

She could have predicted the dismissive gallic shrug he gave her as he carried on working at whatever he was doing.

She walked up to him, joining him behind the counter. As she suspected he was polishing already clean teaspoons.

'Thank you,' she said quietly. Leaning forward she gave him a quick kiss on the cheek. 'I'll treasure this. It is beautiful. I'll wait until the judges get here.' Sebastian was probably going to be a while at the hospital. She'd just get there late.

He nodded but didn't say anything.

Knowing that he wanted no further fuss, she retreated and went through to the kitchen, feeling a little choked. It was as if all the emotion locked inside him was able to spill out in his photographs. And she'd never ever seen him with a camera.

She stood for a moment in the quiet stillness of the kitchen, grateful for its coolness, suddenly filled with absolute conviction that she was doing the right thing. She would explain to Sebastian. He might be a businessman but surely no one could fail to be moved by the depth of emotion in these pictures and the passion Marcel had for the patisserie.

'Nina! Nina!' Maddie skidded to halt nearly falling down the stairs. 'They're here.'

'Oh God.'

'You'll be fine pet. One taste of your cooking and they'll be eating out of your hand.' Bill winked and patted her on the back, almost sending her flying.

She trotted up the stairs, the photo book tucked in one hand, smoothing down her skirt with the other, hoping she looked professional.

'Bonjour, welcome to Patisserie C.' As soon as she said it, she immediately wished they'd changed the name. Why hadn't she thought of that? Patisserie C sounded horribly impersonal and nothingy.

'We've heard a lot about it,' said the older of the two judges, once the introductions had been made. With her no-nonsense attitude, smart grey suit and clipboard, she looked more like a government official, while the young man with her, in his beanie hat and heavy framed glasses, looked like he might work for a hip magazine.

Quickly, they explained that they'd take a look around, select some pastries to try and then ask her a few questions.

Bill, Maddie, Marguerite, Peter and Jane were all sitting at one of the window tables, with one of the cake stands in the centre as if they were ordinary customers, tucking into an afternoon tea selection. Nina envied them and wished she was sitting with them, instead of sitting here on her own, tapping her foot incessantly. She tried to force herself to stop and then realised she was now rubbing the table with her thumb in endless circles. She watched as the two of them, heads together, nodded, pointed, made notes and murmured in low flat voices, their faces expressionless.

'They hate it,' whispered Nina to Maddie who walked past on her way to the toilet.

'Don't be ridiculous. They're just not giving anything away.'

'I'm not so sure.'

Maddie rolled her eyes and then put her fingers in her mouth pulled the sides out and went crossed eyed.

Nina snorted and then started to giggle, which immediately relieved her nerves.

'You're mad,' she said.

'And you've only just figured that out now,' said Maddie with a humorous lift of her eyebrows. 'Lord, you're slow on the uptake.' Shaking her head, she disappeared back to join the others.

Nina's smile faded when the judges came to join her.

'Perhaps you can tell us why you decided to set up the patisserie?' The woman's tone, slightly accusatory, made Nina think of a police officer asking her to account for her actions.

Her hands cramped with tension out of sight under the table. For a minute, she froze.

She swallowed. Every word that she'd planned to say had gone. Evaporated.

'Well ... it was ... erm.' She could feel the clammy sheen taking hold on her forehead as her tongue flatly refused to cooperate.

'Perhaps, I can be of assistance,' said Marcel suddenly appearing, bowing with polite formality. 'I have been here for a number of years and have been delighted to see Nina's passion and enthusiasm for restoring Patisserie C to its former glory. Perhaps you would like to see what it used to look like before Nina decided upon the renovations.'

With shaky hands, she slid the book over to them and sat back as Marcel with quiet dignified authority talked them through each page.

By the time he reached the end, Nina had just about relaxed and she was able to speak normally when the woman said they'd now like to try some patisserie.

'What would you like to try?'

'Everything,' said the young man in heavily accented English, and then after a quelling look from his colleague, clamped his mouth shut.

She selected for both of them and Nina was pleased to see that they'd tried the chocolat caramel supreme – it was still her favourite.

It was all going rather well, and the woman was scribbling hasty notes after taking a forkful of the strawberry and cream éclair, the young man had even let out a little moan as he tasted the chocolat caramel suprême, when Nina looked up to see Sebastian standing in the doorway.

He looked furious and for a minute she wasn't even sure he'd noticed the changes, he was staring so hard at her. She tried to give him a tentative smile but it was tricky given the narrow-eyed stare he was beaming her way. She swallowed.

The judge put down her fork. Nina looked back at Sebastian who'd started to limp forward. The cast had gone. Shit his appointment had hardly taken any time at all. She'd honestly thought she'd get there before he left the hospital.

'Well, Mademoiselle Hadley,' said the judge as Nina started to rise.

Her eyes darted to the judge and then back to Sebastian and half in and half out of her seat, she froze unable to move either way. The sudden silence from the table in the window heightened the sudden sense of tension as one by one Maddie, Bill, Jane, Peter and Marguerite's face reflected horrified awareness.

The judges had both stood up now and the woman was holding out her hand to shake Nina's.

As she took the hand, Sebastian drew level.

'Thank you for your hospitality. We will be deliberating today. Thank you for entering your premises in this year's Patisserie Nouveau Award.'

She didn't need to look at him to know that Sebastian had just gone very still.

'The category winners will be announced this evening. Come, Pierre. Au revoir.'

'Au revoir,' said Nina finding her voice, quashing the desperate urge to grab the woman and beg her to stay.

Chapter 33

Sebastian didn't say anything which was actually far, far worse. Standing there with that impassive expression on his face was awful. If he'd been angry or upset, she could have gone on the defensive but if anything he looking slightly defeated. There was an uncertainty about his posture as if he were waiting to take a blow and it hurt Nina more than she could have imagined.

'I'm sorry,' she said. 'I was going to come but...'

He didn't helpfully fill in the silence for her.

'You see the...' The patient expression on his face as he waited for her explanation reinforced the sense of shame rolling over her. She'd let him down ... if only she could explain she'd done for a good reason.

'We ... I ... the patisserie was entered in a competition.' She drew in a breath. There was no explaining this away. 'The judges were coming this morning, except they were late and ... originally there would have been plenty of time to get to the hospital but ... I, well I was going to come but then they turned up and...'

He frowned as he caught sight of the painted wall, his eyes drawn to the mermaid. 'Where did that come from?'

'Ah, well ...'

Pacing he turned a slow circle taking in all the changes. Nina's throat constricted.

'Well, you see ... the painting. The walls. The mermaid. She was always there. It w – was always there. Just hidden behind the panels.'

'And the chandelier?' His raised eyebrow, somehow managed to convey a world of displeasure in the single elegant movement or hang on, had she read him wrong? Was he intrigued? He seemed to be studying the chandelier with the same fascinated curiosity that Peter and Bill had when they first mooted putting it up.

'Upstairs in the storerooms.'

'And the china?' He leaned forward and picked up one of the delicate cups, holding it by the handle between his finger and thumb. 'Looks expensive. And vintage.'

'That was upstairs too,' she said before adding defensively, 'so, it didn't cost anything.'

'Nina.' To her surprise, he looked hurt at her insinuation. 'I was admiring the authenticity of everything. It all looks ... beautiful. And perfect. It's ... well, a perfect patisserie. You've done ... an amazing job.' He looked around before giving her a slow smile. Nina's heart picked up in hope. Did he look proud of her?

'And you have a new patisserie supplier, I see. That's a real improvement.'

'They're all home-made on the premises,' she ventured as he crossed to the cabinet to examine them. Behind the counter, Marcel stood watchful and still distinguished.

'Marcel, may I try one of these? And what would you recommend?'

'All of them, monsieur. However, I think that this is Nina's signature dish.'

Nina pressed her lips together and waited as Marcel handed over a plate and fork with her millionaire's shortbread twist.

'Nina's signature dish?' Sebastian shot a look her way. 'You made these?' His smile broadened. 'Or course you did.' He shook his head as if to say, *what an idiot, I should have known,* and the half smile playing around his lips threw her for a minute before he picked up a fork and took a measured portion, giving a careful once over before putting it in his mouth. For an agonised moment, which had nothing on Paul Hollywood on *Bake Off,* Nina waited, clasping her hands together.

Sebastian's expression didn't change as he chewed and considered. Nina swallowed and then he nodded, still serious. She wanted to shake him.

He cocked his head and turned to her, his mouth curving into a slow smile that gradually lit up his whole face like the sun emerging from a cloud. 'Wow, that is … amazing.' His dazzling smile of approval made goose bumps rise on her arms. 'This is really, really good. I love the balance between the crisp biscuit with the mousse and then that lovely sweetness of the caramel. It's a brilliant idea.'

He looked back at the cabinet, peering now at the contents. Everyone in the patisserie seemed to be holding their collective breath.

'Clever,' he said. 'Very clever. French patisserie meets English teashop.' With a laugh, he pointed. 'Are those Jammy Dodgers and custard creams, by any chance?'

Nina nodded, some of her tension starting to dissipate. 'Anglo-French fusion.'

Sebastian shook his head in surprise. 'It really is a clever idea and the execution looks fantastic. A little rustic—' he shot her a grin '—but they have that "eat me" look about them instead of being too perfect.'

Nina would take that as praise.

'This place looks amazing. You did all this?'

A spark of pride burned bright in her chest. 'Not just me. Everyone. Bill, Maddie, Jane, Peter, Marguerite and Marcel. But yes, we've done most of the work ourselves. Painted the outside, removed the old panelling. Everything was already here, it just needed some TLC.'

'You've certainly given it that.'

He began to walk around, taking a closer look at everything. Nina wasn't sure whether to follow him but in the end decided to stay put, avoiding the what-do-you-think looks of the others who were avidly looking on.

Sebastian who'd studiously ignored them all, finally finished his inspection.

'It looks great in here,' he said out loud so that everyone could hear him before he dropped his voice so that only Nina could hear. 'Your family...' His words faltered. 'They'd be very proud of you.'

A chill crept over Nina as she realised that his stance had suddenly changed, his final words were flat when they should have been more ... and with a horrible inevitability

Nina realised that despite everything, the battle was lost.

'What?' she forced herself to ask.

'You told Nick.'

She closed her eyes in quick acceptance. She had to.

'You told Nick about us.'

She lifted her shoulders in a silent what-was-I-supposed-to-do?

'He's ... not best pleased.'

'Well, that's his problem,' said Nina hit by a wave of fury that made her lock her knees as if she were worried it might bowl her over. For a moment she wavered, unsure as to who she was the most cross with, Nick or Sebastian.

He shook his head. 'No, it's not. And now everything's...'

Nina felt her heart stall.

There was almost a pleading tone to his voice when he said, 'I thought we'd agreed that we wouldn't say anything while he was still in Paris.'

'I had to,' said Nina in a small voice. She'd assumed, wrongfully it appeared, that he'd forgive her.

'Did you?'

Sebastian closed his eyes and her guilt ratcheted up a notch when she saw the defeated look on his face, the droop of his shoulders and the resigned line of his mouth.

'You realise Nick is absolutely furious with me. If duelling were still in vogue I'd be dead before I'd even taken a pace.'

Nina winced. Nick was slow to anger but boy, when he was angry he was explosive.

'He called me in Lyon before he left. Made it clear that I'm no longer welcome at the farm.'

'Well, that's ridiculous because Mum wouldn't have that.'

Sebastian smiled sadly. 'No, she wouldn't but then she wouldn't want her children at odds, would she? Nick says if I ever visit he'll make sure he's not around.'

'Are you saying Nick's fallen out with you just because of us.'

Sebastian nodded. 'He pretty much told me not to contact him again.'

'Oh Sebastian, I'm sorry.' He and Nick had been friends forever. 'He'll come round.'

'I don't think so. But I was prepared to ... to put up with it because I thought, it's OK I'll be with Nina, we can be together, I can rely on her – but I'm not so sure now.' He looked around at the patisserie. 'This is all wonderful but part of me feels you've been ... less than honest, playing patisseries, despite the fact you knew damn well I had plans for this place. So now—' he indicated the others at the front of the room, keeping his voice simmering with emotion '—in front of all your new chums, I look like the bad guy. Shutting down the lovely patisserie.'

'It ... it wasn't like that at all.' But Nina realised, with sudden shaming honesty, it had been a lot like that. She'd assumed Nick would be fine. She'd indulged in a daydream that Sebastian would be begrudgingly thrilled at what had been achieved in the patisserie and blown away by her innovative pastries. 'I thought ... well, I didn't think it would do any harm. You were planning a renovation, so I didn't think it would matter at first ... and then well, things just...'

'So why didn't you ever mention it?'

She opened her mouth but what could she say. There'd been a thousand opportunities to tell him about what she'd been doing.

'Do you know what I think? I think you got carried away, without thinking of the consequences, because ... you've never really had to face any consequences. You've got a big loving family, they're there to rescue you when things go wrong. Nick will still speak to you, you're his sister. Your family will always be there to help sort things out. I don't think you realise it, but you've never really had to fight for anything. When it didn't work out being a chef, it didn't matter. You went back to your family. You went to work in the bank, that didn't work out. You worked in a nursery. You gave that up. Umpteen jobs. Your family's always there to ease the way for you. And whenever you struggle or can't hack it, there's always a "don't worry Nina" or a "Come work in the farm shop." "You want to go to France, don't worry. We'll do the job for you."'

'It's not like that,' said Nina hotly, stung by his comments and the touch of truth in them. 'I just didn't know what I wanted to do.'

'And you do now?'

Nina's shoulders drooped as she pinched her lips, regret and shame washing over her. So much of what he said was true. And what was worse was that most of the time, she'd been trying to find a career, something she was good at, something that would impress him. What a waste of time. He had the career, the success and it didn't make him happy or appreciate the important things in life.

'No answer, Nina? He shook his head, sadness filing his

eyes as if the words hurt him as much as her. 'You've never fought for anything you wanted. Never stuck it out. You're not even prepared to train to be a patisserie chef. Too much like hard work, I'm guessing.'

'Actually...' Nina suddenly found her voice. She was in the wrong here, she knew that, but she'd worked hard to turn the patisserie around. Rising to her feet, she squared up to him. 'I do want to cook ... but not like you. I want to feed people, nurture them. I don't want to do fancy rose-flavoured macarons with flavour so subtle that you need to be a trained wine taster to enjoy them. Those macarons were so clinical.'

'I beg your pardon.' His sudden surprise was almost comical.

'You heard me. I didn't like them.' She bit out the words carefully. Too many people tiptoed around him. He needed to hear some constructive criticism for a change. 'They were cheating, playing it safe with sophisticated flavours designed to impress rather than feed. You're cheating. What happen to the passion you once had? What happened to the Sebastian I used to know who wanted to feed people? Who wanted to give people big, full-flavoured platefuls of food?' She glared at him. 'You've lost your creativity and appetite for cooking. It's all about business. Making money and being successful. You weren't even prepared to consider running this as a patisserie. All you were interested in was the bottom line. When was the last time you did some proper cooking? When was the last time you felt passionate about it?'

Sebastian took a step back as if she'd physically assaulted him and instead of feeling bad about it, she was pleased. He deserved a taste of his own medicine for a change. She wasn't perfect, had never claimed to be, but neither was he.

She enjoyed his shocked expression for a moment until she saw the quick anger building. The firming of his mouth, the slash of his eyebrows drawing together and the quick indrawn breath.

'And what? Since Miss Amateur's taken over, it's a thriving concern? I think you need to grow up, Nina. You're like a little girl playing at patisserie.' He raised a dismissive hand towards the glass counters. 'But what about the rent, the rates, the bills which I happen to be paying?'

'They're—'

'Er, *excusez-moi*?' Nina and Sebastian both whirled round in horror to find the female judge standing there watching them uncertainly. '*Je ... I...*' She lapsed into French and Sebastian answered, almost snatching the proffered clipboard from her.

With an angry scrawl he wrote on the page and handed it back to her, his body language radiating with dismissal. Looking startled, she took it, nodded at them both and strode away with dignified but confused speed.

'What was that about?' asked Nina wishing she'd spent a bit more time practising her French while she'd been here. No doubt Sebastian would think it another wasted opportunity.

'She needed the details of the registered owner of the premises,' he said with a heavy sigh. 'I think we're done here. I'd like the keys back. My team can move in next week.' He held out his hand.

'Fine,' said Nina, snatching up her handbag. 'Here you go.'

She slapped the keys into his hand, wincing as they dug into her palm.

'Thanks. I'll probably close the patisserie with immediate effect. I'm guessing you'll want to go home sooner rather than later.'

'But you can't. What about …?' Nina's eyes darted towards Marcel, whose face held its usual stoic expression as he polished yet another glass. She lowered her voice, almost whispering. 'Don't get rid of him. He has nowhere else to go.'

'Is your opinion of me really that low?' Was it possible for Sebastian's scowl to deepen? With that he moved past her and went to speak to Marcel. A brief even conversation was conducted in rapid French, with Marcel nodding frequently and not saying much, before Sebastian gave him the keys.

'Right, that's sorted. There's no point the patisserie staying open for the rest of the week. It will close tonight.'

The finality of it hit Nina like a full-blown punch. No! It was impossible to imagine not coming back here again after today. Not going into the kitchen. Not singing along to her music as she whipped and whisked. Not carrying through all her baked goods for Marcel to lay carefully in the glass cabinets. Not seeing Marcel's ghost of a smile when he opened up to a queue outside.

'I've agreed with Marcel that as soon as everyone has gone today, he will lock up.'

Nina looked up at him, her vision slightly blurry.

'I'd like to move back into my flat this weekend. You can get the Eurostar home tomorrow and can leave the keys with Valerie.'

'Fine,' said Nina, determined to hold it together. She. Was. Not. Going. To. Cry. Not in front of *him*. 'I will,' she ground out between gritted teeth. Hauling her bag onto her shoulder with every intention of flouncing out, she and Sebastian moved towards the door at the same time in a comedy moment of excruciating ridiculousness.

'After you,' he said.

'No, after you,' she said with exaggerated politeness.

Sebastian turned and limped towards the door, passing the table where Bill, Maddie, Marguerite, Jane and Peter sat in stunned silence.

'Show's over, folks.'

Bill jumped to his feet but Nina rushed over, shaking her head with determined fierceness and holding up a hand. The last thing she wanted was for any of them to get involved and try and take the blame. Sebastian was right, this was wholly her responsibility. She'd been left in charge of the building, in loco parentis as it were, and had had no right to make fabric changes without his express permission. There was absolutely no denying he had every right to be furious. But she knew it wasn't the patisserie at all that had upset him. Nick and Sebastian had been friends since their first day at school, joined at the hip throughout their school years. Their friendship was a bond forged in memories, shared experience and brotherly love. And she'd ruined it. Well, she and her stupid pig-headed brother who she was going to have some serious words with.

'Maybe he'll calm down,' said Jane as they watched him stalk down the street, favouring one leg slightly.

'And maybe he won't,' responded Peter putting an arm around her as if to shield her from any further unpleasantness. 'I feel quite bad now ... I didn't think...'

'Please, please don't worry,' said Nina. 'This is entirely my fault.' Her smile was sad as she looked around at them all. 'I think I fell a little bit in love with the patisserie and all of you and ... it just felt right. But it wasn't. Sebastian is right. This is his building. He should have been consulted.'

'But I don't understand why he's so mad.' Maddie's words tumbled out in indignant haste as she angrily brushed her hair from her face. 'You should have told him that people queue for your famous chocolate crème suprêmes.'

'It wouldn't have made a difference.' Nina felt hollow now that the adrenaline of the fight was starting fade. 'He was right. I went behind his back.' And she'd messed up his friendship with Nick, which was the worst thing and she couldn't bring herself to tell them because she felt ashamed of herself. Sebastian had known her brother better than she had. He'd known exactly how Nick would react.

'But...'

'Maddie!' Nina couldn't bear it any longer. 'I know you mean well and you're on my side, but I was in the wrong. There's no escaping that.' She spoke with quiet sincerity.

Nina gave the kitchen one final visual sweep, she remembered the first day of the course, everyone introducing themselves. Bill waving his big hands. Maddie in her crocs. Marguerite, more competent and skilful than any of them. Peter and Jane gently teasing each other. Who'd have thought they'd become such good friends? As she mounted the steps for one last time, she remembered Sebastian wobbling on the penultimate step, the almost kiss. A sob threated to break and she blinked hard as she turned on the top step and gave the room one last look. With everything stored away and nothing left out waiting for the next day, it looked as bare and barren as the first day she'd walked in. All the laughter, colour and warmth had been erased.

Her mouth crumpling, she turned and walked back into the main patisserie. Marcel was waiting by the coat rack, his coat over his arm and the trilby hat in his hand. Everyone else was waiting by the door and in Peter's arms were a stack of the confectionary boxes containing the rest of the day's stock. The cabinets were now dark and empty, the power switched off. It felt symbolic. The ever-present hum silenced once and for all. The last thing to be turned off.

'Thanks Marcel. For everything. I hope that ... things work out.'

He lifted his shoulders with a defeated shrug and put on his hat, walking slowly to the door. Nina began to follow but she veered left to trail her hand along the underwater scene painting on the wall, pausing at the painted mermaid.

'Goodbye Melody,' she whispered, taking one last look up at the chandelier, its glittering refractions were blurred by welling tears. She sniffed hard, and crossed quickly to the door, where Marcel waited.

Everyone filed out in front of him with Nina the last to step out onto the pavement. It had just begun to rain and the air was filled with that damp, early evening smell, tainted by the fumes of the day and waiting-to-be-collected rubbish.

They watched in silence as Marcel took the bulky bunch of keys and one by one locked the locks at the top, bottom and middle of the door. He turned and faced everyone, his face blank and his body stiff and upright. Peter handed him one of the boxes of patisserie. '*Bon soir,*' he said, pocketing the keys, taking the box and tipping his hat over his face. Before anyone could say anything, he wheeled to the left and walked away with quick, brisk, no-nonsense steps without a backward glance. In silence, they watched him stride away down the street, a shabby solitary figure on the wide rain-spattered boulevard.

Chapter 34

Why had she ever thought she could manage with her case, handbag and a holdall, on the Metro, by herself? The change at Republic had left her stressed and anxiously watching the clock. She was cutting it very fine. She was supposed to check in at least half an hour before departure and it was already twenty to three as she emerged onto the concourse at Gare du Nord.

It looked completely different from when she'd arrived and it took her a minute to find her bearings and realise that she was in a different part of the station, before she began to follow the signs for the Eurostar.

Feeling hot and flustered, she headed towards the escalator, relieved that she was almost there. She could relax on the train and think about what next. Last night had been hideous. She'd barely slept after spending all night cleaning and straightening, doing her absolute best to eradicate all sign of herself from Sebastian's flat, while seeing signs of him at every turn.

It had been hard to fight the temptation to take his clip-frame apart and remove the picture of her winning the cross-country medal. He'd kept it all these years, the sight of it had originally given her so much hope. She'd lost track of how long she'd stood there looking at all the pictures of him. Those dark eyes staring out at her. Her heart feeling as if it really might be breaking, which was ridiculous because hearts didn't break. But they did get bruised.

With a sigh and blinking back tears, she stepped onto the escalator and threw up her head and stared up at the glass ceiling high above before giving in and pulling the photo of her out of the side pocket of her handbag. This morning she'd broken. Taken it out of the frame. Tucked it in her bag. And still her heart felt bruised.

It felt as if she'd touched the sun and nothing would ever feel the same again. Nothing would ever beat the fluttering heartbeat euphoria, when he'd said, 'I've wanted to kiss you again for a long time.' Or 'I don't want you to go.'

Suddenly she knew exactly what Jane had meant.

He was her final jigsaw piece.

As soon as she reached the top of the escalator and the three lanes towards security, she made a sharp turn right and started straight back down the stairs. What was it Sebastian had said? You never fight for anything? You never stick? Well, she was going to fight this time.

She was going to make him see that she'd made a mistake. A ton of them and she'd apologise for every last one of them. She wasn't going home without putting up the fight of her life, even if it meant punching him right on the nose.

'Nina! Nina! Nina!'

She was halfway down the staircase when she looked down

to see Bill and Maddie shouting and waving up at her, both of them looking rather red-faced and breathless.

She paused on the steps incurring the tuts of people trying to come up past her, as she balanced the case and holdall precariously in front of her. Thankfully Bill raced up the stairs to take her case from her to carry it down.

'What are you doing here?' asked Nina once safely at the bottom, giving them both a welcoming hug. 'If you were coming to wave me off, you've had a wasted journey because...' She beamed at them with a bit more confidence than she felt. 'I've decided to stay.'

'No, we were coming to collect you. You have come to the patisserie now.'

'Did we win best newcomer?' asked Nina.

'No.' Maddie shook her head. 'Some fancy place that does organic only did, but—'

Bill shushed her. 'Come on.' They ushered her towards the cab rank and the three of them hopped in.

Maddie could barely keep still in the back of the cab and Bill keep shooting her warning glances.

Nina figured that as soon as she'd been to the patisserie, she could go to Sebastian's hotel and if he wasn't there she'd go to his apartment. She was going to track him down and wasn't leaving until he'd heard her out. Yesterday she'd been too wrapped up in guilt to fight. Today she knew exactly what she needed to say to him, although she hadn't quite worked out the words yet

Maddie kept checking her texts. Suddenly she tapped the taxi driver on the shoulder and gave him instructions in

French. The driver pulled a surprised face but muttered something back.

'*Bon*,' said Maddie sitting back.

They drove for another ten minutes. Nina turned her head. That was odd.

'Maddie,' whispered Nina. 'I think this driver's taking the piss, I'm sure we've been down this street once before.'

'No, I don't think so.'

They drove for another few minutes and then Nina saw the same café again.

She prodded Maddie and hissed. 'We've definitely been down here three times now.'

Maddie's eyes widened in some kind of plea as she looked across at Bill.

'Don't look at me. I wasn't built for subterfuge,' he said leaning backwards into his seat. The taxi driver asked Maddie a question. She shook her head and then suddenly changed her mind as her phone beeped.

Nina folded her arms and swung her gaze from Maddie to Bill and back again. 'Are you going to tell me what's going on?'

'Nothing to do with us. It might be a bit of a leaving party for Marcel.'

Nina frowned. There was no way Marcel would agree to anything like that. He didn't do fuss or limelight. 'Does he know?'

'No.' Maddie shook her head, all innocence all of a sudden.

'He definitely doesn't,' said Bill with new confidence.

'Should be interesting then. Did Marguerite organise it?'

Maddie mimed her lips being zipped. Nina rolled her eyes. 'Bill?'

He copied Maddie.

Nina hissed out a sigh. 'You two are driving me nuts.' She didn't want to say 'this had better be good' but seriously? All she wanted to do was find Sebastian. She wondered if she could get hold of Alex to find out if he'd moved out of the hotel yet.

'We're here,' trilled Maddie, shrill with excitement.

The taxi had brought them to the back entrance of the shop.

'I take it Sebastian doesn't know anything about this?' asked Nina, chewing at her lip. The last thing she wanted to do was go behind his back again.

Bill and Maddie exchanged furtive looks.

'Oh for God's sake. I've got enough explaining to do to him, without a new crime on my conscience.

'Just bear with us, pet. Come on.'

Leaving Maddie to sort the taxi driver out, Bill opened the back door and peered inside.

Nina rolled her eyes. She didn't want to be sneaking around anymore. 'Come on, let's get this over with.'

Bill cocked his head and listened, waiting until Maddie joined him.

There were signs that the kitchen had been in use, water on the stainless-steel benches and crumbs on the floor. Well, it wasn't her problem anymore.

'Wait here, a minute.'

'Bill, we're good to go.' Maddie waved her phone at him

with a sitcom-style, rather too obvious waggle of her head. They were rapidly turning into a comedy duo.

'Oh, yeah. OK. You can go through.'

Intrigued but still a little irritated, Nina did as she was told. The quicker she got through whatever this was, the quicker she could speak to Sebastian.

There was no sign of Marcel in the silent patisserie. No sign of anyone but sitting in the middle of one of the tables was an ice bucket with a bottle of champagne. Curiouser and curiouser. Next to the table on the floor was an A4 sheet of paper with a large black arrow pointing towards the door. A second one with another arrow halved the distance between her and the door. A third arrow pointed under the door. What was going on? And where was everyone? She'd assumed the gang would all be here.

There was no sign of anyone in the street when she stepped out. Another arrow pointed left. After only one step there was another notice. *Look Up.*

At first she looked up to the sky a little unsure where she should be looking. Clouds, blue sky, sunshine. Everything as it should be. Lowering her gaze, she swept the first-floor windows, which had missed out on the smart new grey paint but luckily had never had the turquoise treatment. Nothing of note there.

Was this some kind of riddle? What was she missing? She turned and looked over her shoulder half-expecting some television crew to jump out candid-camera style.

It was only when she turned back she saw it.

'Oh!' she gasped, her hand over her mouth. 'Oh.'

Pale pink letters had been painted onto the dark grey.

Nina's

'Oh,' she said again, taking a step back.

The S was still glistening as if the paint had yet to dry.

A swirly sensation of excitement danced in her stomach, sudden hope leaping about like demented butterflies. No, it couldn't be. There was some other explanation. But surely after yesterday...

Only the registered owner would do this.

Clasping her fingers together she stared up at her name. *Nina's*.

'What do you think?' asked a low voice from behind her.

Whirling round, she gave him a crooked smile. 'I think it beats jewellery.'

'It's supposed to be an apology.'

'It also beats my apology, which was going to be heartfelt and sincere. I am so sorry that I told Nick and that I wasn't honest with you. I had no right to treat this place as if it were mine—'

Sebastian laid a finger on her lips with a solemn smile, leaving a dart of pleasure dancing over the tender skin there. 'I'm upset that Nick is mad with me ... but he's going to have to suck it up. Being with you makes me happier than I've ever been. You're the one that counts.'

'Oh Sebastian, I...' He was so much more vulnerable than he ever let one see.

'Sounds stupid but after the showdown with Nick and then you didn't turn up at the hospital, I ... I thought you didn't care enough. I only came here because I needed something to do to take my mind off things. I came to read the electric meter, never dreaming that I'd find you here or that you'd be busy. To be honest, I was doing that stupid thing where you come up with a million reasons why you might be wrong and I was still trying to persuade myself that you were stuck on the Metro somewhere. Ord that you'd had an accident or been caught up in something. And that Nick had forced you tell him.'

Nina hid a smile. He sounded as bad as her mother.

'And there you were as cool as a cucumber chatting to that couple as if there was nowhere else you needed to be. I flipped.'

'Oh Sebastian, I'm so sorry, I was on my way ...'

'Marcel told me.'

'Marcel?'

Sebastian's face relaxed. 'I had an interesting conversation with Madame Colbert this morning.'

Nina shook her head.

'The lady judge.'

'Oh.'

'She was very impressed with the innovative home-made patisseries and I realised that I'd let my temper get the better of me. I'd been oblivious to quite how much you'd achieved. So I called Marcel, we met up and we had a bit of a chat.'

Nina stiffened, catching her lip between her teeth.

'Everything you've done has been bloody amazing. Your flavours are incredible. And I love the Anglo-French fusion idea. So clever.'

'Well, not really because I'm copying—'

'Yes really. The flavours, the ideas, the interpretation. They're all so original. Seriously, I am so impressed. This morning when I arrived with Marcel there were a few disgruntled customers outside waiting apparently for something called chocolat caramel suprême.'

'We got lucky with that one. It looks good on social media.'

'No, you got lucky because it tastes amazing. And you were right, I realised I've completely lost my passion, that creativity. You've inspired me to do something different.'

Nina gave him a shy smile. 'Well, I've enjoyed experimenting, but I still shouldn't have done it without your permission.'

'Well, I'm prepared to overlook it.' He stopped looking worried. 'Will you stay? Despite everything I said yesterday. I was wrong.'

'No, you were right. In the past I have given up too easily. I realised that I was so busy looking for the wrong thing. I thought I wanted to escape from my family, but I realised I need family around me. People, friends, a form of family. That's where I thrive. That's what I fight for. I was on my way back today when Maddie and Bill found me. I was on my way back to tell you that I wasn't going anywhere without you.'

'Marcel told me that you'd done this for him. And the others too.'

'Well, not just for him, I was being selfish too.'

'He told me about his wife and his sister and his nephews.'

'Perhaps he can just work lunchtimes for you.'

'I don't know what it's got to do with me. What do you think that is?' Sebastian looked up at the sign above the patisserie.

Nina's heart bumped. 'I thought it was ... a gesture, an apology.'

'Well it is that, but I'd like you and Marcel to carry on as you have been, although I'd like to get involved ... you know, managing the practical things like paying the bills.'

'And what about Nick?' She winced, gnawing at her lip.

Sebastian eyes softened. 'He's just going to have to get used to the idea. But when he realises how I feel about you, that we have a business to run together, that we have—' he gave her a hopeful look '—a future together, maybe he'll come around.'

Nina smiled gently up at him. 'I know Nick, once he's calmed down, he'll think it through and once he realises that...' She lifted her shoulders not wanting to presume anything.

Sebastian took both of her hands. 'Once he realises that I love you and I've waited for far too bloody long. When we were teenagers, I liked being the hero, sticking up for you when your brothers ganged up on you but ... that day, the one when you came off the cross-country course, covered in mud and grinning from ear to ear, something went ping and I knew. You were the one. And then...' He sighed. 'Life got in the way. I ballsed it up. I chickened out. But not anymore. I love Nick like a brother, but once he realises...'

Heat suffused through her at his vehement words. 'Yeah, once he realises...' She couldn't quite frame the words that had filled her with silent joy bubbling. It was like standing on the edge of a cliff, one false step and all her hopes could evaporate, but luckily Sebastian came to her rescue.

'Once he realises that I love you.'

'And I've set Mum onto him.'

Sebastian rolled his eyes.

'I know ... but being a spoiled princess sometimes comes in useful.' She gave him a cheerful naughty grin, 'Although it's going to cost you.'

'It is?' Sebastian looked wary.

'A kiss will do for starters.'

'Ah, that I can do,' he said with a slow smile that lit up his face, a dimple puncturing one cheek and his eyes crinkling with amusement.

As he claimed her lips there was a loud cheer and a lot of banging on the window. They ignored the noise and carried on kissing. When they finally looked up at the rowdy rabble, Bill, Maddie, Peter, Jane and even Marguerite were all cheering and beckoning and Marcel was waving the champagne bottle at them.

'I think that's our cue,' said Sebastian putting his arm around her and guiding her back into the patisserie.

'A toast,' said Marcel a few minutes later, with a rare smile. 'To Nina and Nina's!'

'To Nina and Nina's,' chorused everyone.

Epilogue

There was a rousing cheer as Nina smeared the final profit-erole with a dab of dark chocolate and secured it to the top of the pyramid. The croquembouche looked amazing, the plump cream choux buns spiralling round in alternate lines of strawberry cream and plain cream filling topped with dark chocolate and white chocolate interspersed with regularly spaced halves of strawberries which looked like love hearts.

It was the final day of the course, which had been postponed the previous week. And what a week it had been.

Stepping back, she felt Sebastian's arms close around her pulling her back against him, dropping a quick kiss in the crook of her neck, where he'd quickly figured out that it tickled and made her squirm. In the last week he'd learned a lot of things about her, most of which couldn't be mentioned in public.

'Get a room,' shouted Maddie licking white chocolate before sidling up to Nina. 'The man's besotted. Has he left your side this week?'

'Apart from the trip home to the farm, no.' Nina couldn't help but beam. 'I can't believe he did that.'

'And it's all sorted with your brother?'

'Yes, thank goodness. Thankfully Nick was already starting to come round. I think my mother might have had words. But I think Nick genuinely approves now. A bit jealous, if anything.' Nina's voice faltered. 'I would have felt bad for Sebastian if ... he'd lost Nick.'

'But,' Maddie gave her a hefty nudge, 'he was prepared to, that says a lot in my book.'

'But I wasn't.' She watched him gently teasing Marguerite who was flapping a tea towel at him, a fond motherly smile on her face. 'Sebastian needs people, he just doesn't always realise it.'

'And now for some champagne,' demanded Marguerite, commandeering Marcel and collecting the tray of flutes waiting in readiness.

As Marcel expertly filled the glasses, everyone waited, standing around the glorious confection, which really had been a team effort. Between them they'd all come up with the ideas, Nina had suggested the idea of alternate fillings, Maddie had insisted that one of those should be Nina's 'magic' strawberry cream, Bill had wanted white chocolate and Marguerite dark, and Peter and Jane had jointly voted for the strawberry decoration.

Sebastian, standing opposite her, raised his glass. 'I want to make a small toast to you all. It's no secret that I had no intention of keeping the patisserie open, and I don't know how many of you knew that I really didn't want to teach this course,' Maddie gave an outraged gasp and Marguerite tutted.

He shot the older woman a charming smile and winked at Maddie. 'But it has been … an absolute privilege to get to know you all and to see how much the patisserie has come to mean to all of you.' He gave a lopsided grin. 'I don't often admit I'm wrong but … I want to thank you all for helping to show me the magic of this place. And for all the amazing work you've done. Most of all I want to thank Nina, who has worked so hard.' He smiled at her, looking at her with an intensity that made her sight a little blurry, 'And for giving me a piece of myself back.' He paused, swallowing hard and taking a moment before he was able to continue. 'A wise woman said to me that being with the right person is like the last piece of the jigsaw slotting into place.' He tipped his glass towards Jane. 'And she was right.'

Nina's eyes widened and she mouthed 'when' at Jane, who gave her a serene smile and hooked her arm through Peter's drawing him closer.

Sebastian began to walk towards Nina and came to stand in front of her, his voice dropping and Nina heard in it that delicious timbre that made the hairs on the back of her neck rise. Standing with what felt like momentous stillness, he held her gaze. 'Nina, you are the piece of jigsaw that makes me feel complete.'

Everything went out of focus except for Sebastian's dear, familiar face as around them she was aware of an almighty wolf whistle, cheers and glasses chinking. He leaned forward and grazed her lips with his before whispering, 'I love you.'

All she could do was smile helplessly up at him because any second she was going to cry. She placed a hand on his chest and he put his hand over hers and held it there. With the other he lifted his glass. 'To us.' The simple words sounded like a promise.

'To us,' she echoed, still grinning like an idiot. They both took a sip still unable to tear their gazes away.

He touched her mouth with the top his glass. 'I love your smile. And—' cocking his head, sudden amusement on his face, he mock growled '—I want that photo back.'

'I didn't think you noticed it had gone,' she giggled feeling light-hearted and wonderfully happy.

'Of course I did, it's my favourite picture of you,' he said before adding in that familiar smoky voice, 'It's all I've had all these years to keep me going.'

That really did finish her off but luckily a long tender kiss proved the perfect distraction.

Bonus material

Loved gorgeous Scot, Alex? Well keep reading
for an exclusive look at the next book in the series,
The Northern Lights Lodge

Chapter 1

Bath

'I'm afraid there's still nothing. Like I said last week and the week before. You have to understand it's a difficult time, economically people aren't moving around as much.' This was said with a mealy-mouthed, pseudo-sympathetic smile and shark-like small eyes that slid away from meeting Lucy's as if being unemployable was catching.

Difficult time? Hello! Lucy was currently writing the bloody book on it being a difficult time. She wanted to grab the recruitment consultant by the throat and shake her. Instead she shifted in her seat opposite the other woman in the brightly lit office, with its trendy furniture and state of the art Apple Mac screen taking up most of the desk, trying to look serene instead of utterly panic stricken.

The other girl was now dubiously eying Lucy's lacklustre blonde hair, which hung in limp rats tails, unable to hide an expression of horrified curiosity. Lucy swallowed and felt the ever-present tears start to well up. You try styling hair that's been coming out in handfuls for the last three weeks, she thought. She didn't dare wash it more than once a week because seeing the plug hole full of blonde strands seemed even more terrifying than all the other crap going on in her life right now. Things must be bad when your own hair started jumping ship.

Lucy could feel her lip curl. Oh God, any minute she might snarl like a wild animal. It was increasingly tricky to try and behave like a normal human being these days and now at this moment, it was a particular challenge as she looked back across the desk at the girl sitting there in her cherry red, fitted power suit, with her perfect glossy bob and darling plum gel nails. The epitome of success. What someone looked like when they were going places. When their career was on the up rather than going completely down the swanny faster than a canoe going over the Niagara Falls.

With a sigh, Lucy swallowed hard. For the last twenty minutes, she'd fought the temptation to grab Little Miss Professional by the lapels and plead, 'there must be a job somewhere for me'. She'd had to resort to sitting on her hands with her shoulders hunched up by her ears as she listened to the same spiel that she'd heard in the last ten other recruitment consultant offices; the market was down, people weren't recruiting, no one had a career for life these days. They didn't need to bloody tell Lucy that, she'd discovered that inconvenient fact the hard way. *But*, whined the persistent voice in her head, she was looking for a job in hospitality, the whine became shriller and more insistent, *there were always jobs in hospitality*.

'Perhaps if you could ...' The girl tried to give her an

encouraging smile, which didn't disguise her raging curiosity, 'you know ... get some more recent references.'

Lucy shook her head feeling the familiar leaden lump of despair threaten to rise up and choke her. The girl tried to look sympathetic, while taking a surreptitious glance of her watch. No doubt she had an infinitely more placeable candidate for her next appointment whose CV was dripping with recommendations from her last boss and hadn't had her shame shared among all in her professional world.

'There must be something.' Desperation chased the words out with the glee of naughty fairies escaping. 'I don't mind taking a step down. You've seen how much experience I've got.' She heard herself utter the fateful words, which she'd promised herself, no matter how bad things got, she wouldn't say. 'I'll take anything.'

The girl arched her eyebrow as if wanting her to elaborate on *anything*.

'Well, almost anything,' said Lucy, suddenly horribly aware that anything covered an awful lot of situations, vacant or otherwise and this woman's income was derived from placing people.

'W...ellll, there is one thing.' She gave an elegant shrug.

Now Lucy regretted the 'almost anything.' What was she opening herself up to? She didn't know this woman. How could she trust her?

'It's ... erm ... a big step down. A temporary to permanent contract. On a two-month trial. And out of the country.'

'I don't mind out of the country,' Lucy said, sitting upright. A two-month trial was good. And, actually, out of the country would be bloody marvellous. Why the hell hadn't she thought of that before? A complete escape. Escape from the sly sniggers behind her back from her former colleagues, the *that's her, you know the one who* furtive looks, the *we know what you've done* secretive smiles and the occasional *I bet you would* knowing leer, which made her feel positively sick.

The girl stood up and strode several paces to the corner of her office to rummage in a small stack of blue files on the beech console table behind her. Even from here Lucy could tell that they were the barrel scrapings, those jobs that had been consigned to the 'we'll never fill these in a month of Sundays, Mondays, Tuesdays and the rest' category. With a tug, a dog-eared folder was pulled out from near the bottom of the pile. Lucy knew how that poor file felt. Overlooked and cast aside.

'Hmm.'

Lucy waited, sitting on the edge of her seat craning her neck slightly trying read the words as the other girl trailed a glossy nail down the A4 page. 'Hmm. OK. Mmm.'

Lucy clenched her fingers, glad that they were jammed between her thighs and the chair.

With a half-concealed tut, the girl closed the file and looked worriedly at her. 'Well it's something. Anything.' Her expression faltered. 'You're very over-qualified. It's in ...' and proceeded to say something that sounded rather like a sneeze.

'Sorry?'

'Hvolsvöllur,' she repeated. Lucy just knew she'd looked the pronunciation up.

'Right,' Lucy nodded. 'And where exactly is ...' she nodded

at the file, guessing that it was from the sound of the word somewhere in Eastern Europe.

'Iceland.'

'Iceland!'

'Yes,' the other woman carried on hurriedly. 'It's a two-month post for a trial period in a small lodge in Hvolsvöllur, which is only an hour and half's drive out of Reykjavik. An immediate start. Shall I call them, send your details over?' Her words spilled out with sudden, unexpected commission bonus enthusiasm.

Iceland. Not somewhere she'd ever considered going. Wasn't it horribly cold there? And practically dark all the time. Her ideal climate was hot with tepid bathwater temperature seas. An hour's drive out of Reykjavik sounded ominous, the sub text being *in the middle of nowhere.* Lucy gnawed at her lip.

'Of course they might not want you ... you know.' The girl's smile dimmed in silent sympathy. 'I don't want to get your hopes up. But I will tell them what good previous experience you've had. It's just the ... er recent references might be a problem. You've got a bit of a gap.'

'Perhaps you could just say I've been taking a sabbatical.' said Lucy, hurriedly.

The girl nodded, plastering her smile back on. 'Let me go and make the call.' She stood up from her desk looking a little awkward. Lucy suspected she usually made her calls from the phone on the desk but wanted some privacy to try and persuade the client to take someone on with a three-year gap on their CV.

For the last year, she'd been Assistant Manager for the

flagship hotel of a big chain in Manchester having worked her way up through the company during the previous two, until said big chain sacked her for gross misconduct. Lucy gritted her teeth at the memory of the heartless HR storm trooper of a woman Head Office had sent up from leafy Surrey to deliver the killer blow. Of course, they hadn't sacked Chris.

For a minute, self-pity threatened to swamp her. Job application after job application, rejection after rejection. Not one single interview. Every time she got another rejection, the bleakness grew, like a shadow spreading in the setting sun. Her bank account was running on empty, she was rapidly running out of sofas to bunk on and, the end of the road, holing up in Mum and Dad's two up, two down terrace in Portsmouth, was looming large. And there was no way she could do that. Mum would want to know why. The truth would kill Dad. Lucy gnawed at her lip, opening up the bloody ulcerous sore already there. For some reason, she'd taken to chewing the inside of her lip and it had become a horrible habit over the few months that she couldn't seem to shake.

'It ... it is live in?' asked Lucy hurriedly as the girl was about to leave the room.

'Oh Lord yes, no one in their right minds would look at it without accommodation.' Her eyes suddenly widened as she realised she'd probably said far too much. 'I'll be right back.' Rather tellingly she'd scooped up the file to take it with her leaving Lucy alone in the office.

'Are you sure it's the right thing to do?' asked Daisy, shaking her head, an expression of diffidence on her face, as she stared at her laptop screen. 'You're massively over-qualified for this. It's only got forty rooms,' she paused. 'And you hate the snow. You'd only just acclimatised to Manchester. Iceland will be far worse. Although,' she wrinkled her forehead, 'it does look very nice.'

Lucy nodded, nice was an understatement, according to the gallery of photos on this website, it looked gorgeous. The outside with its turfed rooves and hotchpotch of buildings was dwarfed on one side by a snow-covered hillside strewn with the dark shadows of craggy outcrops and on the other a wild rocky coastline where foamy waves crashed onto a narrow shingle beach. The beautifully photographed interior showed stunning views from each of the lodge's windows, several huge fireplaces and cosily arranged nooks with furniture which invited you to curl up and doze in front of a warming hearth. It all looked fabulous. Which begged the question, why hadn't the job of General Manager not been snapped up before? Her teeth caught at that damn sore on the inside of her lip and she winced.

Daisy mistaking her sudden intake of breath, gave her a stern look. 'You don't have to take it. You know you can stay here as long as you like.' Her eyes softened. 'I really don't mind. I love having you.'

Tempting as it would have been to stay in Daisy's cute one man flat in Bath, Lucy had to take this job. 'Dais, I can't sleep on your sofa forever and if I don't go for this job, it probably will be forever.'

The familiar gloom threatened to descend again dragging her down. She swallowed ignoring the panic beating like the wings of a bird inside her heart and glanced at Daisy. How did you admit that you no longer thought you were capable of doing a job? She was so trapped by indecision at every turn, constantly questioning her own judgement.

Should she go for this job? The brief Skype interview seemed a mere formality, a quick check to make sure that she didn't have two heads or anything. They didn't even seem that bothered as to whether she could do the job. Which was just as well as all her stuffing had been well and truly knocked out of her and if she'd had to sell herself she'd have withered on the spot.

Daisy put an arm on hers jolting her from her thoughts. 'Don't take it. Something else will come up.'

Lucy raised a pertinent eyebrow and her best friend had the grace to smile weakly.

'Ok.' Daisy clenched her petite little hands into fists. 'But it's so f-fu flipping unfair. It wasn't your fault.'

'Daisy Jackson! Were you about to swear then?'

A dimple appeared in the other girl's cheek as she smiled like a naughty pixie. 'Might have been. But it makes me so mad. It's so ...' She made a 'grrr' sound.

'You see, another reason I need to get out of here. You're making animal noises too. I'm a bad influence. And it was my fault. No one's fault but my own ... and Chris's for being a grade A shit.'

'It wasn't your fault! Stop saying that,' said Daisy, her voice shrill with indignation. 'You can't blame yourself. It's Chris's fault. Although I still can't believe he did it. Why?'

Lucy's jaw tightened, they'd been over this a thousand times over the course of the last 62 days and numerous glasses of prosecco, wine, gin and vodka. Rumination and alcohol hadn't provided any answers. It was her fault, for being so utterly, utterly stupid. She couldn't believe how badly she'd got it wrong. Four years. A flat together. Working for the same company. She thought she knew Chris. One thing was for sure ... she would never trust another man as long as she lived.

'It doesn't matter 'why' he did it. I need to move on and I need a job.' She gritted her teeth, going to Iceland was a terrible idea but she was all out of options.

Chapter 2

Paris

'Here you go.' Nina slid the coffee cup across the table towards Alex and handed him a plate with a gorgeous looking confection on it. 'On the house. I want your opinion, it's my latest idea. Raspberry Ripple Éclair. It might cheer you up,' she added with a smile that was underpinned with a smattering of sympathy.

Alex felt a touch of regret. Nina was lovely. His plans to get to know her better had been well and truly scuppered by a prior claim. Sadly, she'd been in love with his mate Sebastian for ever and he had to admit as he looked at her now, requited love had put a gorgeous bloom on her cheeks. You couldn't begrudge anyone that shiny happiness. He took a bite of the éclair and groaned.

'Wow, that's good, Nina. Really good.'

'Excellent, now are you going to tell me what's wrong?'

He rolled his eyes, as she pulled up a chair and sat down ignoring the outraged glare from Marcel, the manager of the patisserie. Nina might officially run the place, but Marcel

416

definitely wore the trousers in this business partnership, ruling the roost with silent, stern officiousness.

'Who said anything was wrong? asked Alex, trying to sound blithe.

'I have brothers. I have a Sebastian. I know when the weight of the world is bowing those broad shoulders. You have a distinct droop about you,' she declared with a knowing grin.

He glanced left to right at both shoulders and she gave a peal of laughter.

'I'm just a wee bit pissed off. The new hotel opening is delayed and the manager lined up to take over from me has already rocked up.' Alex was due to take over the running of a brand new, minimalist, uber trendy boutique hotel on the other side of Paris any day now, except during the renovations the builders had discovered bones in the cellars. Human bones. Thankfully they were at least two hundred years old but it had still caused a humungous delay.

'You can take a holiday then,' said Nina.

'You'd have thought so but my boss in his infinite wisdom has decided to give me a temporary posting.'

'You're not leaving Paris, are you?' Her pretty mouth pouted and Alex felt another one of those little pangs of regret. Nice guys did finish last. He'd well and truly missed the boat with her.

'Only for a couple of months. Quentin wants me to go and check out a hotel he's planning to buy. He wants me to assess the viability of the place and put together a report on my recommendations to turn it into one of our boutique hotels.'

'Where are you going?'

'Iceland.'

Nina's mouth dropped open into a little 'o'. 'I thought you meant somewhere else in France. Not another country. Well that doesn't sound so bad. Isn't Iceland supposed to be beautiful with all sorts of amazing natural wonders? Bubbling geysers, hot springs and glaciers? Being Scottish I'd have thought you'd like the idea.'

'No problem with going to Iceland. It's the job Quentin wants me to do, which isn't that great.'

'I thought you said you had to put together a report.'

'Yes but it includes reporting on the current general manager and how the place is being run without telling them who I am. It doesn't sit right with me. The last thing I want to do is be a spy.'

'James Bond,' said Nina, sitting up straighter. 'You've got the Sean Connery accent.' She launched into a dreadful impersonation of his Edinburgh accent. 'Ah Moneypenny.'

'Well, that must mean I'm qualified,' Alex quipped, amused by Nina's enthusiasm, his spirits temporarily lifted.

He was still rattled by the meeting and the conversation with his boss when he'd raised a certain disquiet about not telling the manager why he was there. He had no qualms about being a bar manager for a couple of months, that would be a walk in the park, but not being honest about what he was doing didn't sit right. His boss's response to that had stung. 'Thing is Alex, nice guys finish last. This is business. Pure and simple. I need someone to report back, warts and all. Without any sugarcoating it. It's far easier if the staff don't know who you are. I'm not hearing great things about the management of the place. The recent Trip Advisor reviews have been shockers. With you on the ground, I'll get a much better picture. You've got a good eye and you'll be able to tell me what needs doing to sort the place out. And what the staff are like. Whether I can keep them? Or fire their sorry arses.'

The 'nice guys finish last' bit kept going around in his head. What was wrong with being a nice guy? Besides, he could be tough when a situation needed it. Last week he'd thrown a customer out of the hotel's a la carte restaurant for pinching one of the waitress's bums, faced down a belligerent delivery driver who reversed into the hotel gates leaving a hole a herd of cows could get through and fired the pastry chef he'd caught hurling a frying pan at the young, barely out of school, dishwasher.

'Alex is going to be James Bond,' announced Nina as Sebastian walked in and put his arm around her placing a confident, lazy kiss on her lips, completely ignoring Alex.

'Hi gorgeous, mmm you taste of raspberries and delicious-ness.' He went back for a second longer, lingering kiss, which had Alex rolling his eyes.

At last Sebastian drew back from Nina and turned to face him. Alex's mouth twitched, he'd got the message loud and clear.

'Bond, James Bond?' Sebastian lifted a perfect Roger Moore eyebrow.

'No, Nina's exaggerating my undercover credentials. I've been asked to do some recon work for Quentin Oliver at head office. They're looking at buying a place in Iceland and as I'm between hotels at the moment, I've been asked to go and survey the place. On the ground as it were.' Sebastian would laugh his head off if he mentioned he was going undercover as a barman!

'Sounds like a great idea,' said Sebastian with a sudden grin, which Alex could guess had a lot to do with just how far away Iceland was. Although Alex had backed right away when he realised that Nina had been in love with Sebastian since she was eighteen. For a second he wondered what might have happened, if he'd put up more of a fight for her, if he'd really thought he had a chance. Had he bowed out because it made it easier on Nina?

As he thought about it, he gave Sebastian a broad smile, maybe the best man had won. Nina adored Sebastian and she was good for him. Possibly too good. But Alex had never seen Sebastian so settled and happy.

'I have no problem with going to Iceland. Like Nina said, I'm used to a Northern climate. It's the undercover element of it I'm not so keen on.'

'Why not?' Sebastian shrugged. 'You just need to remember it's business. It's easy to be ruthless when something you really want is at stake.' Was there a knowing look in his eye as he stared at Alex?

And then he flashed Alex a warm, approving smile. 'There's no one else I'd rather have on the team, mate. I know why Quentin Oliver's asked you. Better that it's you. You've got integrity and you don't bullshit anyone. You don't suffer fools that's for sure. If the current manager is an idiot, are you seriously going to have a problem reporting back on that? You hate coasters and people who don't pull their wait. If this guy is any good, he's got nothing to worry about.'

Chapter 3

Iceland

Lucy's thoughts came back to haunt her as she stood outside the firmly closed front doors of The Northern Lights Lodge, in total darkness, her breath huffing out in a great cloud of white as the cold nipped at every last one of her extremities. This was a terrible idea. Why had she listened to a perky recruitment consultant with her eye on her commission? Why hadn't she remained in Bath with Daisy?

She almost laughed out loud, mild hysteria threatening to take hold of her. *Because you were desperate. You knew it was a terrible idea and you were right. You should have trusted your own instinct.*

Blinking furiously, because bloody tears were not going to help, she hammered on the door for the third time, stupidly crossing her fingers, as if that would help, and praying that someone would answer. Why had she let the taxi driver drop her at the bottom of the path? She should have made him wait but no the taxi had roared off, twin brake lights vanishing into the distance leaving her totally alone. On the journey here, she'd only seen two cars. Two! Both going the other way.

Why hadn't she stayed the night in Reykjavik?

With a shiver, she glanced around into the total blackness, the only light from her phone. There was absolutely no sign of life, not human anyway. As she got out of the taxi, after a two-hour drive in the pouring rain — it hadn't stopped raining since the plane landed in Reykjavik four hours ago — there'd been a low growl to her left and the glow of yellow eyes as she swung the torch on her phone in that direction. Did they have wolves in Iceland? The pathetic beam of light caught the flash of a tail as something slunk away but she'd been extra wary as she'd traipsed up the path, picking her way over the stones, her suitcase complaining with each jolt and dip.

Now standing outside the solid wooden porch trying to peer through the glass lights on either side of the double front doors, she could see the place was in complete darkness. Above her she could hear the rustle of the grass on the roof or were there more creatures lurking. There were far too many Lord of the Rings images dancing fancifully in her head. With a last burst of energy, she wrenched down the ornate iron scrolled door handle, with that fruitless bang your head against a wall hope that she'd got it wrong and the door had been open all along, even though she'd tried it umpteen times already. So much for everyone leaving their doors open, which she was sure she'd read somewhere about the country. She banged her fist on the door, before looking at her phone and the rapidly dwindling battery. Sinking to the floor, she slipped off her gloves, which weren't going to cut it in this climate and phoned the only contact number she had. Mr Pedersen, the hotel owner, currently in Finland, was the man who'd officially hired her, but he'd given her the number of one of the hotel employees. For the second time, her call went straight through to voicemail and this time she listened with growing despair to the message in a stream of what she assumed was Icelandic, a volley of harsh syllables and guttural sounds.

Taking a deep breath and hoping she didn't sound too panicky she spoke. 'Hi, this is Lucy Smart from London. It's eleven o'clock and I've arrived, but there doesn't seem to be anyone here.' She'd sent an email with her date of arrival. And had received one back in confirmation from someone called Hekla Gunnesdottir. Her hand shook, her grip was so tight on the phone. *Where the fuck is everyone?* But she didn't say it because she was going to have to work with these people and she was desperate to make a good impression. 'I wonder if you could give me a call back.'

More than a good impression, she needed them to keep her on after the two months. She had to survive at least a year here to make her CV viable again. Besides, she had nowhere else to go.

Half an hour later, her phone battery had died and she was pacing up and down, trying to keep warm, although the rain had now stopped, as her mind feverishly raced through the options. All of which seemed in short supply. One, walk down the road and see if she could find any kind of settlement nearby despite the complete absence of any lights in the near vicinity, two, stay put and hope that someone had listened to her message or three, break in. How much longer should she give it before she started breaking windows?

Scudding clouds streamed across the night sky, periodically revealing pockets of a star laden universe. The number of the pinprick lights was astonishing. No light pollution here. Lucy had never seen so many stars and in one brief break in the clouds had even seen a shooting star in the last few minutes.

Now that her eyes had adjusted to the dark and the cold had numbed her fingers and toes, she decided to circle the building. Maybe she'd find an unlocked door. With a shiver she walked along the front of the building. Did she dare pick up a stone and break a window? Although, in the images of the lodge on the internet there'd been rooms with floor to ceiling windows. She couldn't break one of those.

Rounding the corner praying she'd find a stray door or window that had been left unlocked, she felt her way along the cold damp stone walls and quickly realised the structure of the lodge wasn't in her favour. There didn't seem to be any windows or doors on this side of the building. After a while she could feel the ground level starting to fall away, quite steeply and she stumbled as her ankles felt the sharpness of the sudden decline. She could just make out the shadowy corner of the building. With a sigh, she wilted, watching the icy puff of white breath roll away from her. She could however see a faint glow as if there was a light on around the next corner of the building. Maybe there was someone at that side and she could attract their attention.

Carefully she began to pick her way down the steep slope, slipping and sliding on lose scree. Each crunch and skitter of stone echoed noisily making her jumpy and disorientated. Every now and then she paused and thought she could hear water lapping but the sound bounced around in the darkness and she couldn't quite determine where it was coming from. Cocking her head to one side, she listened carefully and took another few steps forward and then stepped into thin air.

As she stumbled forward, arms flailing like spokes on a spinning bicycle wheel, she registered the glint of water and tensed for the cold as she pitched in face first.

If it weren't for the weight of her clothes and the unexpected shock of falling headfirst into shoulder deep water, the warm, no, piping hot, water, might have been quite pleasant, except for the rush of water up her nose and swallowing a great mouthful. Yeuch. Lucy shoved her head up to the surface spluttering and gagging. That was disgusting. Her head felt even colder in contrast to the cosy cocoon from the neck downwards. The heat flooded Lucy's fingers and ears with sharp pain like pins and needles just as a flashlight came bobbing around the corner and tracked its way across the stony ground to land full on her face.

'No using the hot springs after nine pm,' called a deep voice, brimming with amusement as the light came closer and closer. Lucy muttered to herself, '*Kill me now*,' feeling at a distinct disadvantage under the nearing dancing spotlight. Her sodden parker suddenly seemed to wrap itself around her like a duvet weighted with rocks, her ankle boots loosened almost floating away with each step and her jeans seemed to have a strangle-hold on her legs as she floundered towards the edge.

'Here, there are steps,' said a second singsong voice with a musical up and down inflection, using the torch to guide her along the wooden edge towards a set of steps that rose up out of the water.

Lucy put her shoulders back and waded through the water towards the wooden handrail the other side of whatever she was in, with as much dignity as she could muster given she was close to tears.

Lights suddenly came on illuminating the whole area. She was in the equivalent of a small swimming pool sized hot tub surrounded by wooden decking, with two sets of steps descending into the water. Above her on the side were two figures, wrapped up against the cold night air.

'Are you alright?' asked the taller of the two crossing quickly and holding out a hand to help her, stepping down into the water to grasp her arm and help her counter balance the weight of her ten-tonne coat.

Kind eyes, thought Lucy as she caught a glimpse of concerned blue eyes above a tartan woolen scarf as she let him haul her up the steps.

'Let's get you inside quickly before you start to chill down. That heat isn't going to last long.' Kind voice too. The slight Scottish burr was soft and gentle, a rather wonderful contrast to his firm and decisive hold as he pulled her forward and steered her off the decking.

'Thank you,' she said subtly shaking off his grasp, even though for some contrary reason she didn't want to. Kindness had been in short supply in her world for a while. 'I'm fine,' she added, with more of a sharp bite to her voice. After everything she'd been through this year, she was never taking anything at face value again. Kind was as kind did or whatever the phrase was.

'I'm Alex.' The man's hand still hovered by her side as if ready to catch her. 'And this is Hekla. I'm so sorry there was no one to check you in. We weren't expecting any guests today.'

'No. It is most strange. Did you have a booking?' asked Hekla, in her glorious voice.

'I'm not a guest. I'm ...' Lucy swallowed. No crying. Dripping from head to toe had put her at enough of a disadvantage as it was. 'I'm the new manager, Lucy Smart.' Automatically she lifted a business-like hand and then dropped it quickly as she realised how ridiculous it must look, with water dripping from her sleeves.

'Oh!' The girl's voice echoed with surprise. 'But you are not expected until next week.'

'Everything was confirmed by email,' said Lucy. The last thing she wanted was these people thinking she was a bit slapdash or all over the place.

'But we had a phone call yesterday saying your plans had changed and you would be coming next week.'

'Well that wasn't me,' said Lucy.

'Must be the elves up to mischief,' said Hekla with a straight face, nodding. 'But you're here now and we'd better get you inside, quickly,' she paused and then added with a mischievous twinkle that once upon a time Lucy might have been charmed by, 'It is usually best to wait until daylight before using the hot springs.'

'I've been waiting to get inside for the last half hour,'

muttered Lucy, wincing as her feet splish sploshed on the wooden decking, the water squelching out of her favourite boots and great clouds of steam rising from her sodden clothing. Great, just bloody marvellous. These people were clearly her new colleagues. So much for making a good impression from the start.

Feeling unaccountably tearful, she pinched her lips and took in a half sob half breath and ducked her head as if concentrating on maintaining a secure purchase on the slippery wet planks.

'Hey, let me give you a hand,' Alex's voice lowered, his tone gentle. She jerked her eyeline to meet his. Warmth and compassion lit those kind eyes as he took her elbow. For what seemed far too long they held hers with a serious steady gaze, as if he could see right through her to the constant shadow of misery that resided in her chest. When he gave her a reassuring smile, his eyes never leaving her face, she felt a funny salmon leap in her stomach.

A Q&A with
Julie Caplin

What was your inspiration for the series?

I used to work in public relations specialising in food and drink PR, so I organised a lot of press trips to European cities as well as liaising with food writers, who were always lovely to work with. For *The Little Café in Copenhagen*, I drew on my experiences of organising press trips abroad. They always sounded glamorous and exciting to my friends but in reality they were hard work and occasionally a bit fraught. Trying to round up grown adults on a press trip can be interesting and on one memorable trip I really did lose a journalist before we'd even left Heathrow! On another trip I took food writer Sophie Grigson to Milan, she was the most delightful company and had a real and enthusiastic passion for food. Her catch phrase when she was encouraging us to try new foods was that it was 'good for our food education' and I borrowed this line for Sophie who appears in both *The Little Café in Copenhagen* and *The Little Brooklyn Bakery*. When it came to writing *The Little Paris Patisserie* I wanted to learn more about cooking patisserie and found that Sophie Grigson was running a course in Oxford. Not having met her for a further twenty years, I signed up for the course and discovered that she was just as passionate and enthusiastic in her teaching about food as she was back then.

Have you always wanted to be a writer?

Since the age of eleven, when I announced that I was going to write a book, I've always wanted to be a writer. As I grew up and started working in PR that idea got put to the back of my mind. It resurfaced when I was put on gardening leave between jobs and decided that I would sit down and write that book. It was only a few years later, after I'd written several books, that an old school friend, now in Australia, contacted me and reminded me that as a child I'd always said I'd write a book one day.

Are any of the characters based on you or people you know? If so, which ones?

Very occasionally I might base a character on someone I know. For example Nan in *From Paris With Love This Christmas* (one of the book I've written under my real name, Jules Wake) was partly based on my paternal grandmother, who was what one might call a feisty character. However most of my characters pop fully formed into my head. To me they are like real people and while I'm writing a book, I often have conversations with them in my head.

It's amazing that you have the opportunity to travel so much and use your own experiences in your books, but how do you find time to write? And where do you write when you do?

I'm very lucky that I can write anywhere. Even when I'm travelling my laptop comes with me and I usually write first thing in the morning before taking the rest of the day off. I plan my research trips well in advance of writing a book, so that often I write the book once I'm home. I'm very disciplined when I'm working on a deadline and have a daily word count target which has to be met no matter where I am. Luckily my husband is self-employed, so no matter where in the world we are, you'll find us both tapping away at our laptops!

What has been your favourite place to visit?

Gosh, that's a tricky one. It's often the people I'm with that make a trip. When I went to Copenhagen, I took a couple of friends, now known as travel elves, with me. They were such good company that they really made the trip something special. Likewise when I went to Brooklyn and the Hamptons, it was a family holiday and we stayed in Armgansett with a very special friend, so that trip also holds a very dear place in my heart. When I went to Paris recently I took my husband and we had a wonderful time visiting various patisseries in the city, so that also has special memories.

Have you got any funny travel stories you can share with us?

I'm not sure that this is funny, but I'm rather accident prone and on my last trip to Paris I didn't *mind the gap* between the Metro and the platform. I came home with a rather nasty gash on my leg and now have a less than fetching scar as a permanent reminder of the trip. One story that I have used in *The Little Paris Patisserie* comes from the time I was in New Zealand and working in a rather busy wine bar. I took an order from a gentleman at the bar and had to ask his name. Unfortunately, with the noise in the crowded bar and his very strong Kiwi accent, I couldn't quite hear his name so had to ask three times. This proved to be rather hilarious to my colleagues as this man was actually very famous in New Zealand. It was akin to asking someone like David Walliams what his name was!

Do you have any advice for readers who want to follow in your footsteps and visit these gorgeous places?

I would heartily urge anyone to visit Copenhagen, it is a very small, compact city so it's easy to navigate on foot and you don't need to worry about public transport. Everyone speaks fantastic English and is so friendly and welcoming.

Wherever I'm going, I always buy a local guide book for the city and pick a few places before I go to visit when I'm there but I also make sure I leave some time to take up any tips from other tourists. I'm a bit of a chatterbox, so where ever I go I end up talking to people and it's a great ice breaker to ask other people for their tips and suggestions.

What would you like your readers to take away from your stories?

One of my favourite phrases is 'Walk a mile in another man's shoes'. It's important to remember that there are always two sides to a story and that other people think in different ways. I often explore this in my books. We need to learn our own strengths and weakness as well as recognise that other people have theirs, which won't be the same as ours. Sometimes we need to listen to what's not said in order to really understand each other.

Who are your favourites authors and have they influenced your writing in any way?

I'm a huge romance fan and always want a happy ending. I adore Jill Mansell's stories, particularly her happy-go-lucky characters and easy, sparky dialogue. I'd love to say that has influenced me, but it's still a work in progress! I'm also a big fan of Katie Fforde and I love her settings and the kind-hearted characters in her books. More recently I've become a big fan of Sue Moorcroft and I particularly like the way that her stories have plots that twist and turn to constantly keep the reader on their toes. All of them have influenced me in different ways, so that I focus on character, dialogue and plot and hopefully I produce stories that really engage you, the readers.

If you could run away to a paradise island, what or who would you take with you and why?

Well, obviously, Captain Wentworth from *Persuasion* is purely fictional, but in his absence, I'd take my very own hero, my husband. He's brilliant at looking after me (especially when I fall over, a frequent event!), makes me laugh and is super organised when we're traveling. And I always have to have a book with me. My trusty Kindle goes everywhere … although on my last trip it died, which was an absolute disaster! I was half way through a really good book and had to finish it by using the Kindle app on my phone.

Acknowledgements

Each year, my friends Shane and Jenny O'Neil organise a quiz and raffle in aid of the Alzheimer's Society and this year the first prize in the raffle was the winner's name being used in my next book. Imagine my surprise when the winning ticket belonged to the couple sitting next to me in our quiz team! Huge thanks go to Peter and Jane Ashman for lending me their names. I'd like to think I've done them proud and they agree that the imaginary Peter and Jane are just as lovely as the real ones.

I also owe a special thank you to my lovely friend Alison Head who bought me the most wonderful book on Parisienne patisseries which was absolutely invaluable, especially when I planned my research trip to Paris. I have to thank hero husband, Nick, who patiently escorted me around dozens of patisseries in central Paris without a peep, when I think he really would have quite liked to have had nice cold beer instead.

I met some lovely people while researching this book, most notably the fabulous Sophie Grigson, food writer and broadcaster, who runs a pop up cookery school in Oxford. Thanks to her brilliant Easy Patisserie course, I can now make a mean coffee éclair, whip up a crème pâtissière and knock out delicious madeleines.

Endless gratitude goes to fellow author Donna Ashcroft, my writing buddy, who is so supportive and generous with her time when I'm trying to work through plot problems, character misbehaviour and suffering from that frequent writer's I'm-rubbish-at-this malaise.

And super special thanks go to the two people who really are my rocks, my gorgeous editor, Charlotte Ledger and my wonderful agent, Broo Doherty. Writing might be a solitary profession but getting a book out into the big wide world is a team effort. I couldn't do it without either of these warm-hearted, generous spirited and hugely talented women. Thanks my lovelies.

Last and most certainly not least, I must thank all my readers, especially those that take the time to let me know how much they've enjoyed my books. I tell you, when I'm slaving away at my laptop when the words are that bit too elusive, your kind messages and heart-warming reviews are the things that keep me going. Keep them coming and I do hope you have enjoyed *The Little Paris Patisserie*.

Jules x

HELP US SHARE THE LOVE!

If you love this wonderful book as much as we do then please share your reviews online.

Leaving reviews makes a huge difference and helps our books reach even more readers.

So get reviewing and sharing, we want to hear what you think!

Love, HarperImpulse x

Please leave your reviews online!

amazon.co.uk   kobo   goodreads   L♥ve**reading**   iBooks

And on social!

f/HarperImpulse   🐦@harperimpulse
📷@HarperImpulse

LOVE BOOKS?

So do we! And we love nothing more than chatting about our books with you lovely readers.

If you'd like to find out about our latest titles, as well as exclusive competitions, author interviews, offers and lots more, join us on our Facebook page! Why not leave a note on our wall to tell us what you thought of this book or what you'd like to see us publish more of?

/HarperImpulse

You can also tweet us @harperimpulse and see exclusively behind the scenes on our Instagram page www.instagram.com/harperimpulse

To be the first to know about upcoming books and events, sign up to our newsletter at: http://www.harperimpulseromance.com/